GORDON'S QUEST

BY

DOUGLAS KOVATCH

ISBN: 9798705219483 (paperback)

For my dad.

He likely wouldn't have read this novel, but he sure would've boasted about it to everyone he knew…

BOOK ONE: MOURAIN

From the rich shoreline with its sand of gold
Running through fields as the winds take hold
Freedom rises with each gust
Stoking fires of wanderlust
To where legends are made, their tales unfold

Young lives are found in the open breeze
Their dreams as high as banyan trees
Thoughts race, spirits swell
Home is bid a fond farewell
A traveling life puts the soul at ease

*—Traditional song of the people of Winston, which is located
in the southeast corner of the continent of Hyboria.*

CHAPTER 1

"Excuse me, what town is this?"

A woman mending a hole in a dirty and tattered rag looked up into the bearded face of a man. His bright green eyes were bordered by creased and weathered skin, as if he'd spent many years exposed to the elements. At first glance his hair and beard appeared light brown, an illusion caused by the presence of interspersed gray and white hairs through the darker brown of his youth. He wore thick leather armor, masterly crafted and strong, but heavily pockmarked with abrasions, splits, and worn edges. On his hip was a long sword in a scabbard, and strapped to his back was a leather bag tied with twine. His expression was kind and his words polite, which made her want to answer his question, but his mere presence bewildered her. She hadn't seen a stranger's face in three years. She stared at him without a word.

"Ma'am? Did you hear me? We've traveled for a long time over dangerous country, and I'm not sure where we've ended up. What's this town called?"

The woman swallowed, assessing the possibility that she was imagining the man who stood in front of her. She hesitantly sputtered a response; "M... Mourain."

"Mourain. Excellent. My name is Gordon. My friends and I need to find a place to restock our supplies. Is there a general store or a pub in this town?"

After replaying the words *our* and *friends* in her mind, the woman adjusted her gaze to see several other similarly-dressed, bearded men standing a few yards behind the one addressing her. The sight of the five travelers was startling, causing her to drop her sewing and rise to her feet. She glanced at the doorway of the hut behind her.

Gordon took a small step back and gave her some space. "It's okay. You don't have to be alarmed. We aren't here to hurt anyone." Met with silence, Gordon continued, "Is there someone in charge we can talk to?"

The woman bent down to collect her sewing, then stood and squeaked, "Lord Hammond." She turned and entered the doorway to her hut. Before she fully closed the door, she poked her head into the gap and pointed with her eyes. "Big house. That way." She closed the door with a demonstrative bang.

Gordon looked around the village of Mourain. For the middle of the morning there seemed to be a lot less activity than on a typical day where he was from. There were no goats or sheep in pens, no chickens wandering the streets. The buildings were in disrepair. Some roofs were patched, while other structures were missing a roof entirely. The cloth coverings to windows were torn. Exterior walls were missing stones or were altogether crumbled in some cases. The graveled road had been mostly reclaimed by weeds. There was a general sense of carelessness about the town.

He turned to his men and said, "Let's find this Lord Hammond!"

They hoisted their gear and made their way down the main road. Darting movements and glancing eyes could be seen inside some of the homes they passed, but when they turned their heads to peer into windows, the movement inside stopped and curious onlookers disappeared.

In the center of the village was easily the most significant building they saw. It was a large and ornate stone church, looking completely out of place compared to the decay surrounding it. The architecture of the church was hulking and beautiful, with a complex of round towers topped with spires, enormous stained glass windows with carved stone tracery above them, flying buttresses, and intricately sculpted statues. The way the stone was arranged, raw and muddled near its base and more organized and brick-like as it rose, made the church appear as though it had grown out of the ground like a giant tree. Most of the care and maintenance that could have gone into the surrounding shops and homes was instead done here.

It was obvious that the people of Mourain, like most other towns in southeast Hyboria, took their worship very seriously. The men paused for a moment to quietly inspect the church before moving on.

When they reached the end of the road they came upon a stone wall partially covered in ivy. Where it intersected the main road was a large and heavy iron gate, taller than any of them. "This must be the place," said Gordon. The other men nodded in agreement and fell into formation behind him. He struck the metal with the hilt of his dagger, causing a loud clanging sound to echo into the gardens behind the wall.

After a minute, three soldiers came into view and slowly strode to the gate. The lead one grunted, "Yes?" He was a handsome and muscular man with long wavy light brown hair and piercing blue eyes the color of the midday sky. He was a head taller than the other two, themselves bigger than anyone in Gordon's party. His sleek athletic frame was poured into lavishly-adorned leather armor, crafted to be lightweight but strong. He carried no shield, but the sleeves had metal plating melded with the leather. Above his right shoulder protruded the grip and pommel of what looked to be a massive two-handed sword. The end of its scabbard dragged from below his left hip like a tail.

After introducing himself, Gordon said, "My men and I have traveled from the east to find able-bodied men."

The trio glared from behind the gate, saying nothing.

"Are you Lord Hammond? We'd like to discuss terms with you."

The tall one blinked and responded, "I'm Rugen Sloane, Hammond's son."

"Glad to meet you," said Gordon, smiling.

Rugen scoffed back at him. "How did you get here?"

"No doubt it was a difficult journey, but my men and I are strong," he replied, gesturing to the group behind him. "I'd like to speak to your father about having some of his soldiers join us."

"There are no soldiers here."

Nodding to Rugen and the two guards behind the gate, Gordon said, "You three look more like soldiers than anyone we've seen in weeks."

"Our place is in Mourain. We're charged with defending our people."

"In that case, I'd like to speak with Lord Hammond about other arrangements. Can you take us to him?"

"Just one of you," responded Rugen, scowling, "and leave your weapons."

Gordon handed his sword and shield to the burly red-headed man standing behind him and said, "I'll be back as soon as we're finished."

Rugen fished a large key from his pocket and opened the gate. After Gordon passed through, the gate was quickly closed and locked behind him. The four of them walked toward the house, Rugen in front and the two guards behind, flanking Gordon.

Sloane House was certainly larger than the other huts and shops in Mourain, but it was by no means extravagant. The walls were made of layered stone and mud, devoid of color other than natural browns and tans. The windows were small squares. The roof had the same thatching as the rest of the structures in the village, but it was well kept, clean and fully intact. A thin wisp of smoke rose from the large chimney on the side of the house.

Rugen turned to Gordon and said, "Wait here. I'll bring my father out." He disappeared inside.

Addressing the two guards, Gordon said, "We saw no one on our way through town. How many people live here in Mourain?"

The guards stood with stern expressions, saying nothing and making no movements. Gordon sighed, realizing he'd get no answers from them.

In the doorway appeared a tall and slim man, bearing facial similarity to Rugen but with short graying brown hair and a goatee. He appeared to be about the same age as Gordon. He was wearing a blue tunic with gold trim. With Rugen standing by his side, the two men looked like twins separated by a generation. He beamed, "Good morning, sir. We're quite surprised to see you. We don't get visitors anymore."

Gordon bowed and answered, "I imagine that to be true. My men and I are lucky to have made it. I assume you're the lord of this village?"

The elder Sloane walked to Gordon and shook his hand, grasping his other shoulder as he did. "I am. My name is Hammond Sloane. You've met my son Rugen. We are in charge of this once-great town. Come inside and we'll talk." He addressed the guards, saying, "Thank you. You can return to your duties."

Gordon followed Hammond and Rugen into their home. The main room was mostly empty, just several chairs spaced around a large fireplace. The floor was made of wooden slats, and the walls were bare stone. There were small unlit sconces dotting the room. Hammond offered Gordon a seat.

Gordon thanked Hammond and explained, "My name is Gordon Tully. I'm from a town called Winston. It's a six-day walk to the east, on the coast."

Hammond raised his eyebrows and widened his eyes. "How are things to the east? Here we're burdened by dangerous and relentless beasts."

"The same. Demons running amok. They're all over the roads and wilderness."

"It's been terrible burden for us in Mourain. We don't have many resources. Those who haven't been slaughtered have died of starvation, dehydration, or infection. Our only blessing is that the creatures haven't entered the village."

"That seems to be the general idea—force us to remain confined to our towns and slowly choke us to death."

"Whose idea?" said Rugen, chiming in.

"That's why I started this journey. I hope to find out the who and the why." He looked back at Hammond. "Most of the people we've met refer to what has happened with the arrival of the demons as The Isolation. The talk is they came from the cursed lands of the north, on the other side of the Ovid Graan Mountains. My men and I intend to find whomever is behind this plight and bring them to justice."

"That's a long way from here," said Hammond. "It'd be a difficult journey even if there weren't deadly monsters to contend with." He turned to Rugen, "Son, would you get our guest something to drink?"

Rugen paused long enough for Gordon to appreciate his reluctance, then huffed as he left the room.

"I'm rounding up able-bodied men to help my quest," explained Gordon. "Next I'll recruit sorcerers and clerics from Ravenwood. Then we'll build an army in Lundgren."

"May God watch over your journey," said Hammond, nodding. "But we can't help you." He sat back in his chair. "When the monsters came, a lot of our people were outside hunting, farming, trading with other towns. They were overrun. Some made it back here; others did not. We dispatched soldiers to reclaim our farmland and hunting grounds, but any success they had was later erased. Every few trips the groups would come back one person short or with someone severely wounded, until the people who were left could do little more than protect a humble plot of land just beyond the borders of our village. Even with rationing our resources, the old, the sick, and those who couldn't stand up for their own share died off. At first we held grand funerals respecting the dead, but in a short time deaths were so frequent all we could do was move the bodies as far as we could and leave them on the ground. Burial was out of the question, lest the gravedigger become another victim while he was digging. After the dying slowed, things haven't gotten any better. Food is hard to come by. People spend their days foraging for scraps while dodging monsters. Meanwhile buildings are in disrepair, and families are broken and in mourning. The misery has touched everyone."

Gordon lowered his head and whispered, "The Isolation is a terrible thing. The men behind it need to be destroyed. I mean to do that."

"There are those who say this is a curse from God," said Hammond, "the monster plague is meant to punish us. They don't believe a mortal man is behind it."

Rugen returned carrying cups of water. As he entered he interjected, "Punish us for what? What did we do to deserve watching our family and friends die?"

"I can't speak for Mourain," said Gordon solemnly, "but in my experience there are many people in Hyboria who foster pain and suffering and thus deserve retribution. If what's happening now is a cleansing of the evil in the world, I would ask God to choose his targets with a little more precision and subtlety." He turned to Hammond and added, "But this is no curse from God. This evil came from the minds of deranged men." He gazed at the ceiling and raised his arms in a reaching gesture and cried, "Let me be the hand of God. Let me dole out vengeance on behalf of the people who follow in your image."

Hammond smiled at Gordon. "You are a man of honor. I truly hope you complete your quest. For all of us. But I'm sorry to say I can't help you. The people of Mourain have nothing. We're slowly dying. The loan of our best men would end our hope and seal our fate, if it hasn't been sealed already." He nodded to Rugen and looked back at Gordon. "My son will show you to somewhere you can stay the night, but we can't offer more."

Gordon slowly nodded and said, "God be with you. I appreciate your hospitality."

Rugen led the way through the gate and back down the main road. When they were out of earshot of his father's property he blurted, "I'll join your quest."

Gordon's opened his mouth to respond, but couldn't think what to say.

"There's nothing left for me in Mourain," said Rugen, his face darkening. "My mother and sister were killed by the monsters. It's just me and my father now."

Gordon lowered his eyes.

"What my father said about the people who were slain outside of the town that day, it should come as no surprise that those were our most capable. Mourain died with them. The heart of it anyway."

"I'm sure your father does the best he can."

"That's just it. He doesn't. The death of my mother broke him. He thinks our personal losses give him the right to neglect his obligations as lord. He hoards supplies for us and our guards. We have food on the table while the rest of Mourain starves."

"In that way he's no different than any lord I know," assured Gordon. "It sounds like he's just looking out for his own."

"But his duty is the townspeople. They appealed to me to convince him to share what we have. I tried, but he refused to hear it. The people saw me as weak, which made their jealousy grow. I got into fights nearly every day, first defending my family's honor, and later, when it occurred to me that our honor was gone, to preserve my life. Eventually the lack of food made them unable to muster the strength to fight me, but their hatred is as strong as ever."

Gordon and the men listened intently but said nothing.

"You coming here is my opportunity to do something with my life," said Rugen. "I suspect after you leave, the next visitor will be Death himself."

Gordon put his hand on the younger man's shoulder. "How do we explain your leaving to your father?"

"He'll figure it out. I've lived under his thumb all my life. It's time I start making my own decisions."

"Do you worry what'll happen to Mourain when you're gone?"

"My father has control over his people. He's always had. He's been holding the loss of my mother and sister over their heads for years. The disappearance of his son will be yet another tragedy he'll use to manipulate them."

They stopped in front of what appeared to be an abandoned home. "Gentlemen, you can stay here for the night," said Rugen.

"I'm not going to claim we can't use the help. You're an adult. If your mind is made up, meet us back here just before sunrise tomorrow."

CHAPTER 2

Rugen woke with a start. He gazed out his bedroom window to find the soft, serene yellow-orange of the morning glow. The excitement of what lay ahead had made falling asleep difficult, but he awoke with no weariness. He hurriedly donned his gear and grabbed the bag of extra supplies he had packed the night before. He quietly snuck out of the house and into the dawning day without a glance behind him.

As he slowly made his way toward the inn where he'd left the men the previous evening, the quiet, empty street reminded him of all that had changed. Several years ago, the village was bustling. The scent of freshly baked bread permeated the air, and the clucking of chickens and bleating of goats would swirl with sounds of neighborly chit-chat and fussing babies. This memory, a stark contrast to the near ghost town Mourain had become, made Rugen think about wanting to stay and rebuild. Deep down, however, he knew that was impossible as long as the town was cut off from the rest of Hyboria. He adjusted his bag and pressed onward.

As he approached Gordon and his four companions standing on the street, he saw one was chewing on what looked to be dried salted meat and another was drinking from a water skin.

Gordon greeted Rugen and then introduced his men, gesturing to each, "This is Billy, Casey, and JJ." He paused and patted the back of a white-haired soldier, "And this fine man is Thomas. He's been with me from the beginning."

Rugen looked them over. They were fit and strong, wearing either leather armor vests or light chain mail. Each had a sword sheathed at his hip and a shield on his back. Of all their characteristics, what mostly stood out was the long flaming orange hair and beard of the one identified as JJ. He and Billy seemed to be about Rugen's age. Thomas and Gordon looked to be about the same age as Rugen's father. Casey was somewhere in between.

"Well boys, we'd better get moving before someone figures out I left."

"One day you will return here and be celebrated as a hero," replied Gordon. He turned to the others, "Everyone ready? Let's go to Ravenwood."

As they walked out of the village in silence, Rugen glanced back at his dying hometown with a mixture of nostalgia for what it once was and shame for its current state. After they left the borders of Mourain, Rugen asked, "What's Ravenwood?"

"We were headed there when we stumbled upon you," replied Gordon. "It's where magicians go to learn their craft."

"It must be far away if I've never heard of it."

"It's a distance, yes, but more likely you've never heard of it because the people who live there don't want you to know it exists. Mystical people aren't the type to advertise. They enjoy their privacy, and don't invite people to Ravenwood unless it's to join them."

JJ, who had the mane of red hair, asked, "Do you think they're going to welcome the likes of us?"

"I'm sure we'll get the same warm reception we've gotten everywhere we've been," laughed Gordon, prompting all of them to sneer and chuckle.

Rugen was intrigued. "What kind of magic do they do?"

"They call it divinity and sorcery. Divinity is white magic performed by clerics—healing and blessing and the like. Sorcery is black magic done by, well, sorcerers. That's where they crush foes with just their minds."

"How do you know they won't crush us?"

Gordon half-shrugged. "I don't. But believe me, from what I've seen of the world we need them on our side."

Rugen adjusted his bag and looked around the barren landscape. "What are the monsters like? I've heard stories but have never seen any myself."

With mock-disgust, JJ said, "You never fought one, huh?" He turned to Gordon with a grin on his face. "Boss, we better train this guy before he gets us all killed."

"He's had as much training as any of us," replied Gordon. "From what I gathered his father's guards taught him all manner of lethal swordplay ever since he was old enough to lift a weapon." He reached up and put his hand on Rugen's shoulder, which was even with the rest of their heads. "And have you seen the size of him? He'll be fine. After a couple of days he'll be a monster slayer like the rest of us."

Casey chuckled and said, "To answer your question, as far as we've seen there's a couple different kinds of monster. The most common ones are massive." He raised his arms to demonstrate the size. "They're as fast as rattlesnakes, and have thick arms and big hands. The skin on their hands and forearms is hardened, like steel plating. They can knock your sword away or grab the blade without getting cut. And their fingers end in sharp claws."

"Claws like daggers," added Billy. "They have huge horns growing out from the sides of their heads that curve around to protect their face like a helmet." He made a hand motion to demonstrate. "They stand a little hunched over so when you swing a sword at them your clearest target is either the thick hide on their arms or their horns. You really have to maneuver to get to the vulnerable spots beneath."

Casey continued the description, saying, "Their faces look deformed. Permanent snarls, wide noses, bloodshot eyes, drab gray skin like a corpse. They don't wear any kind of armor, but they don't need it. Their hides are tough, tougher than you would ever expect. I've butchered a lot of animals in my day, and never have I seen skin as resistant to cutting as what they got."

"Don't forget the jaws," said Billy. "Their teeth are thick, round, and pointed." He held out his pinky finger and bent it. "Each tooth is about as long as the last joint of my finger."

"A couple of years ago I was surprised by one of the beasts when I was chopping wood, interrupted Casey. I buried my axe in its chest. You think that would've killed it. Next thing I know it had me on the ground. I managed to get a piece of split wood into its mouth, which distracted it long enough for me to scamper to my feet and use every ounce of strength I had to slice its throat." He nodded his head. "That was a satisfying rush of goo, given the circumstances."

"We call them gmorks," Thomas quietly added.

"Yeah, gmorks," agreed JJ. "They give us a lot of trouble, but don't let these guys scare you. They can be killed just the way anything else can be; pierce the heart, cut the windpipe, or open a big blood vessel. You have to get past the defenses first, which isn't easy. But we manage."

"The other type we've seen we call ursinoxes," said Gordon, with a serious look. "They're rare, thank God. An ursinox is the reason we ended up in your town. We caught sight of one and had to take a big detour. We lost track of where we were and when we tried to get back on course to Ravenwood, we found Mourain."

"What do they look like?" asked Rugen.

"No one I know has ever gotten near an ursinox and lived to describe it," said Billy. "The most we know is they look like bears. Enormous, furry, brown, walk on four legs."

"Except they're bigger than any bear I've ever seen," interjected Casey. "Much bigger. My dad and I used to hunt. We came across a bear or two. These things are different. I don't want to have anything to do with them."

"Which is why we need to get to Ravenwood and find sorcerers and clerics to help us," said Gordon, his voice raised, as if the whole conversation had been held to prove his one point.

The men walked on until the sun was more or less directly overhead, at which point they decided to stop to rest under the shade of a large tree to evaluate their supplies. They could see a reasonable distance along the road in either direction, and the flanking forest gave a sense of shelter and safety. While the roads in southern Hyboria were well-maintained before the monsters arrived, the three years of neglect saw weeds and grasses overtaking the crushed stone. Despite all of this, it is was still clearly a road and was certainly easier to navigate than the ever-thickening forest.

Gordon shuffled through his pack. "I only have enough food for about two more days. You boys have the same?" The men assessed their provisions, nodding. They had various combinations and amounts of hard cheese, dense bread, salted meat, and dried fruit.

"I overpacked," said Rugen, pawing through his stash. "I'm sure I can stretch all of us another day or two."

"I'll say!" whistled JJ as he eyed Rugen's hoard.

"I can make a small animal trap," said Casey. "But that might require us to stay in one place longer than we want."

"Speaking of that, what do we do about sleep?" asked Rugen. "Won't we be completely vulnerable?"

Thomas, who was chewing on a piece of dried meat, quietly said, "Guard rotation."

"Yes, that's benefit of having a lot of people with you," explained Gordon. "When Thomas and I started this crusade, we each had to stand post half the night."

"The guy whose turn it is on guard duty drives himself mad trying not to doze off while the rest of us get broken sleep at best," said Billy as he looked up from inspecting his provisions.

"I sleep," said JJ with mock-annoyance. "I guess I trust you guys more than you trust me."

Casey eyed JJ and frowned. "It's no fun sleeping out here, but most of the noises you hear at night are innocent; the wind, wood popping in the fires, trees creaking. So far we haven't been attacked at night."

"Maybe the gmorks are less active at night. Maybe it's the fires scaring them off. Or maybe we've just been lucky," said Billy, shrugging. "These things are hard enough to kill during the day, I can't imagine fighting one in pitch black after it wakes you up from a dead sleep."

"Yeah, you'd go from dead sleep to just plain dead," chuckled JJ.

"You both said *fires*, plural," said Rugen. "You light more than one?"

"It's an old trick," responded Gordon. "Having several fires makes your enemy think there's more of you. It also expands your perimeter and makes it easier to see what you're doing in the middle of the night."

"And it gives the night guard more motivation to stay awake, having to keep a bunch of fires fed with fuel," added JJ.

"Not to mention more smoke means less bugs," said Billy.

All at once from the trees opposite from where the men were resting a thunderous crash sounded. Their quiet comfort was interrupted by four gmorks bearing down on them. Rugen stood frozen as the other men yelled, grunted, and scrambled, picking up their swords and shields. JJ had just gotten his sword into his hand when the first monster swung its foul claws at his head. He managed to duck the blow, but lost his grip on his weapon in the process. Billy charged the gmork attacking JJ as Gordon, Casey, and Thomas paired up with the other three.

Rugen bent down to where his own sword lay in its scabbard on the ground. He found his hands shaky and fumbling while trying to unsheathe it. He couldn't fathom how to get enough traction on the scabbard to allow it to uncouple from the blade. Desperate and panicked, he picked the whole thing up by the handle and frantically shook it. As he did he saw in his peripheral vision the other men flailing wildly as their weapons clanged against the steely claws of the gmorks.

Calmly retrieving his lost weapon from the dirt, JJ yelled to Rugen, "C'mon boy! What did we bring you for? Get in the fight!" He whooped a battle cry and ran back to the skirmish, excitedly waving his sword above his head.

Rugen took a deep breath and closed his eyes. He put one hand on the hilt of his sword and the other on the scabbard and pulled. It slid out easily. He stared at the sharp shiny edge of the metal glimmering in the sunlight. It mesmerized him for a moment, before he adjusted his gaze to the fight going on to his left. He wondered how to best get involved. If he charged in with abandon like JJ there was a chance he would strike one of the men or they would inadvertently cut him on a backswing. He stood frozen, considering a plan, while Gordon victoriously buried his blade into the chest of the gmork he was fighting.

Casey was in a back and forth fight until a gmork grabbed the edge of his shield and twisted his whole body to the right, so that his left foot left the ground. The beast violently scraped his unprotected shoulder and upper arm with its claws. Already off balance, the force of the blow knocked Casey to the ground with a thud.

That same gmork lost interest in Casey and ran toward Gordon, who was struggling to retrieve his sword from the chest of the demon he had impaled. Gordon gave up his efforts to allow himself the time to brace for the oncoming assault behind his shield.

JJ spun around, swinging his sword behind him, and sliced across the hamstrings of the gmork engaged with Billy. It fell forward, knocking down the farmer as it went. Billy had a look of panic in his eyes until he realized he'd instinctively removed the dagger from its holster on his thigh on the way to the ground. He plunged it into the neck of the wounded gmork in his lap, hearing a satisfying snap as it slid in. The beast grimaced momentarily and then stopped squirming.

JJ turned his attention to Gordon, who was doing his best to defend himself with just his shield. The red-headed warrior whistled to the older man as he tossed his own sword through the air. Gordon caught it by the hilt and in one svelte motion swung at his foe.

After successfully rearming his friend, JJ casually slid Gordon's sword from the chest of the skewered gmork.

Thomas had been in a stalemate with the monster he was fighting until it swiped at his sword, knocking it to the side. It took advantage of the opening by driving its shoulder into Thomas's chest, knocking him to the ground. The gmork straddled over him ready to strike until Rugen's giant blade sliced through its neck, launching its head clean off of its body. Gordon and JJ looked up at the scene as they simultaneously stabbed the final gmork to death.

"Whoa new guy, that was a heck of a swing," said JJ. "I've never seen a flying gmork head before."

"Everyone all right?" asked Gordon.

"Yeah," said Casey, "but I'm going to need someone to bandage up my shoulder."

Thomas coughed and sputtered, "Wind knocked out. Okay…"

"I'm all right," said Billy, "and I'll fix that shoulder. After a lifetime of farm work I've seen worse."

"Casey, I understand your shoulder needs tending," started Gordon, "but we still don't know what draws these beasts. Maybe they're attracted to blood, maybe the scent of their dead, or all the noise we made. Regardless, I'd rather be somewhere other than this spot in case more come." He wiped the debris from his leather armor and said, "Let's clean up as best we can and head down the road, where we can rest and regroup."

Casey, clearly in pain and holding a rag to his shoulder as a bandage, nodded. The rest of the men dragged the bodies of the gmorks into the woods and hastily covered them with sticks, leaves, and dirt. They tried their best to smooth out any signs of a scuffle on the ground, but it was pretty obvious that something significant had happened there, and someone skilled in tracking could easily figure out which way the survivors had moved next.

Chapter 3

After moving on from where they'd scuffled with the gmorks, Gordon and his companions came across the sounds of running water in the forest and decided to make that the place to rest. There was area to the right of the path near the bend of a large stream where the ground cover was light and there was a canopy of trees overhead. It was obvious that it had been used as a resting place in the past, a time when the road was busy with travelers. Gordon said the stream, which had a strong flow and looked plenty deep, was a tributary of the Stock River, the largest river in southeast Hyboria.

JJ and Billy went to the stream to fill their water skins as Casey sat on the ground and inspected his wounded shoulder. There were three separate lacerations about an inch apart, corresponding to the three claws the gmork had swiped across it. The one in the middle was the longest and deepest, and was nearly matched by the upper cut. The third one was more or less a scratch.

Billy returned and poured water over the wounded area. Casey dabbed with the rag and watched as blood oozed out. Both men thought the wounds looked rather clean, considering they were put there by *the filthy claws of an abomination of nature*, as Gordon had put it. Billy pulled a pouch from his bag that contained needles and catgut sutures. The needle he selected was as long as a child's finger and deeply curved, making almost a semi-circle.

Billy strung the catgut on the needle and looked into Casey's eyes, stating plainly, "This is gonna hurt." Then, as gently as he could, he pushed the needle into the corner of the longest laceration. Casey groaned and looked away. Billy worked the needle up and out of the other side of the wound, and then double-knotted the ends of the catgut. He then moved the needle a short distance and made another pass, pulling the skin taut as it came out. He paused and asked, "You okay?"

Casey refused to avert his eyes from a spot on the ground next to him. He muttered through gritted teeth, "Keep going."

Billy repeated the process a dozen more times, making a neatly cross-laced line of sutures. He tied it off and inspected his work.

Sensing Billy was finished, Casey mustered the will to look at his shoulder. He widened his eyes and said, "Wow. It looks great. Where'd you learn to do that?"

"I always had an interest in mending skin and setting bones, and there's a lot of opportunity to practice while living on a farm." He smiled and added, "You're easy. There's no fur blocking my field of view."

Gordon came over and handed Casey a full water skin. "Looks good, Billy. Do you think he'll be able to fight with that shoulder?"

The tip of Billy's tongue was protruding from the side of his mouth as he started working on the other cut. He responded without looking up, "He oughta be fine. It'll be sore for a while, but he'll still be able to defend himself with his shield."

"Hopefully we won't have to worry about fighting or defending ourselves rest of the way to Ravenwood," said Gordon, "and once we get there the clerics can fix the wound like it never happened."

When the shoulder repair was complete, Billy covered the whole area with a medicinal plant tincture he'd brought from home.

"Listen, that last run-in took a lot out of us," said Gordon. "What do you say we stay the night here? I'll appreciate the time to double-check my maps to figure out where we are. The rest of you can find us food, light a fire, and make sure the area looks secure."

The men split up, keeping each other within eyesight or earshot as they worked on the delegated tasks. Over the course of the afternoon and evening, each of them, including Gordon, shared domestic duties. Edible plants and mushrooms were foraged, tinder, kindling, and wood fuel were collected for the cookfire and the decoy fire, small animal traps were set, and fish were caught and dressed.

Rugen thought to himself how nice it was to have some normalcy after the afternoon of fighting.

As the sun set, the men relaxed around the fire digesting their meal of fresh fish, tubers, morels, mulberries, and dandelion leaves. Casey sipped tea Billy had brewed from the bark of a white willow tree known for its analgesic qualities.

"Gordon, are you for sure on the path we need to take tomorrow?" asked JJ.

"Absolutely sure," responded Gordon. "We've been heading in the right direction since leaving Mourain."

At the mention of his village, Rugen's head popped up, "You guys have seen so much of Hyboria. How are things where you're from?"

"Your place seems to have it worse than Dyersville, where Billy and call home," answered JJ. "We woke up one morning to find gmorks outside of town. A few guys went out to investigate what they were. The gmorks attacked. The men fought back," he said, simply.

Billy added, "The town was lucky the monsters arrived when they did, in the middle of the night rather than during the day when more people would've been exposed."

"When they came to Bomont," started Casey, "my father and I were out trapping by the Stock just past dawn. I was kneeling along a riverbank adjusting a trap when he screamed my name, frantic. I ran toward his voice and didn't see anything. Then farther off in the trees I heard a rustle of leaves and branches breaking."

The rest of the men were silent while Casey lowered his head, blinking his eyes slowly. After a long pause he continued, "Three of them were standing over my dad with his blood on their claws. I couldn't do anything. He was already dead." He swallowed. "I wasn't carrying a weapon aside from my folding knife. I quietly snuck away then ran back home as fast as I could." He shook his head sadly, then chuckled. "I guess these things aren't real smart. If they had any sense they would have realized my daddy was yelling for somebody. Somebody they could've gone after next."

"It seems to me they just mindlessly wander the landscape without any sort of plan," Billy said. "If they happen to come across a person, they attack. There's no strategy, no goal, no destination."

Casey took a moment to collect himself and continued, "When I got back to town everyone was telling stories about attacks, deaths, and narrow escapes." He paused and sighed. "My dad was a good man. He didn't deserve to die like that. I wish I could've...I mean I just wish we had a chance to fight them together."

The men sat watching the dancing light of the fire as it projected onto the leaves above. The tree trunks, most of them no more than crooked skinny poles, looked pale white in comparison to the dark orange leaves and the blackness of the forest behind. They crisscrossed in front of the background like rib bones haphazardly sprouting from the dirt. The reflected fire's glow made for a beautiful and quiet light show and gave a false sense of serenity to their situation.

"It's a terrible curse on the whole country," agreed Gordon. "My son Wil was taken last fall. He would've been with us tonight. He'd be about your age," he said, glancing at Rugen. "Thomas and I started preparing shortly after the monsters first infiltrated. We collected and studied every map we found and educated ourselves on the creatures as best we could. Then we trained Wil and some other boys to fight and took them with us to scout the area around Winston. After a few months everyone got careless. Wil and his friend were on a scouting mission by themselves, something they did from time to time. It was supposed to be nothing, a short trip to figure out the way to a new water source. When they didn't come back that afternoon, we sent out a search party." He took a slow breath and carried on. "We had to give up at sunset. We went out again at first light, and did the same the next three or four days. All we found was this."

Lying across his open palm was a dagger. The blade was white and had a streaked texture. It was shorter and thicker than a typical steel dagger but looked sharp and menacing. The grip was wrapped in finely pitted black leather. "I gave this to him on his 18th birthday. It's whale bone." He handed it to Rugen, who inspected it in the firelight.

"I've seen a few bone knives over the years," said Rugen, "it's beautiful."

JJ motioned for it, and after inspecting it closely asked, "Does it hold an edge?"

Gordon frowned. "Whale bone is denser and stronger than the bones of other animals, and this one's been specially treated. It holds an edge fine."

JJ rubbed his fingers over the length of the blade and then handed it back to Gordon, saying, "I didn't mean any offense."

He stared at JJ, displaying the knife. "The grip is wrapped in whale leather. It's not just for show. It's deadly sharp and durable." He made a slow-motion slashing movement, then brought it back to his chest as if he were hugging it. "I plan on burying this in the skull of the man responsible for the scourge, God willing."

"May we all be there to witness that joyous day," added Thomas.

"Some of the others who were training with us lost interest in the cause after the boys died. Only Thomas stayed on, and now we've found all of you. The farther we go, the bigger our army will become until we finally get to taste vengeance against the one who made these vile beings." The men emphatically grunted their agreement.

"How about you, JJ?" asked Rugen. "Did you lose anyone to the monsters?"

"I never met my father. He was passing through Dyersville when he and my mother got together. I was born from one night of drunken debauchery. He was gone before she woke up the next morning. I'm not sure if she even got his name. If she did, she never told me. My mom did what she could to raise me on her own, but she was more interested in herself than anything else. She'd leave me with whoever while she was out looking for a 'new father figure,'" he said, rolling his eyes. "She never found one. Sometimes I'd wake up to find the house empty and her hungover and beaten up in the street. Sometimes she wouldn't come home for a couple days. Eventually she disappeared for good and I was on my own. I was thirteen years old." He looked at the ground. "Through it all I learned to fight, steal, hustle, and survive. So when the monsters arrived my life actually didn't change much. I had already mastered all the skills the rest of the world was being forced to learn. I guess for that I owe my parents everything." He chuckled. "They couldn't have prepared me better for the way things are now."

The men quietly absorbed this as the fire crackled and the leaves swayed in the gentle night breeze.

Billy broke the silence, saying, "JJ and I met when he came to my parents' farm looking for work. He fit right in with our family, kind of like an older brother to me." He paused for a moment, staring into the warming fire. "One day we were working in the fields and a—well, we didn't know what a gmork was at the time— came bearing down on us in a full sprint. We were dumbfounded. I started slowly walking backward and JJ turned to me, wide-eyed, and yelled, 'Get a weapon!' I didn't know what he was talking about. I just froze. He handed me his pitchfork and picked up a hoe. He braced the back of it against the ground and held the business end out in front of him like a lance. The gmork ran right into it. JJ had it raised to catch it under the chin. It fell to the ground on its back grasping the stick end with the blade buried in its neck. I stood like a statue, stunned. The next thing

I know, JJ was standing over the thing repeatedly banging its head with a shovel until it was dead."

"It was the greatest feat of farming of all time," laughed JJ.

"How someone could instantly flip into action without any hesitation amazed me. I'd be dead on the spot if not for him. I've been watching him ever since trying to learn what I can."

"I appreciate that," said JJ. "I always wanted a little brother." He playfully ruffled Billy's hair as he attempted to duck away.

"For as terrible as these things were when they first showed up," started Gordon, "They seem to be stronger now. It's like each new one is an improvement on the last. They might be even more lethal the closer we get to where they're coming from, once we cross the mountains I mean."

"Well, there'll certainly be more of them over there," added Billy. "If they're spreading out from one source like you said. It only makes sense the farther they have to travel the less packed together they are."

"You're exactly right," agreed Gordon, "which is why we need all the help we can get."

Casey finished the last of his pain-dulling tea and winced as he set it next to him on the ground. "Who gets first watch tonight?"

Gordon looked at Rugen. "New guy always gets first watch. He's not used to sleeping outdoors and will probably be up anyway. The rest of us can rest until it's our shift."

"Makes sense to me," said Rugen. "How will I know when to wake the next guy up?"

Gordon pointed to the small decoy fire in the distance. "I left four logs in a row over there. About equal size. At the start of your shift you set one of them on the fire. When it collapses, it's the next guy's turn."

Rugen narrowed his eyebrows. "I'm no scholar like Billy, but four logs...aren't there six of us?"

"Last guy doesn't need a log," Gordon said. "His shift ends when the sun comes up. As for why there's four and not five, Casey's taking the night off to heal. We don't need six guards. The night's not long enough for six."

The men made themselves as comfortable as they could on the grass using their rucksacks as pillows. Rugen set the first log ablaze and stood over it while the other men quieted down. To his surprise, they all seemed to fall asleep rather quickly. Rugen still felt wide-awake. The light of the flame burned shadows into his vision, making it difficult to see into the darkness of the woods, but the closer he was to it the safer he felt.

The forest seemed to come alive with sounds while the other men slept. There were hoots and screeches, random thuds and cracks. Every little sound was a jolt, making him whip his head or eyes in the direction from where it came. The feeling of aloneness built up to an overwhelming crescendo of anxiety and irrational thoughts. A few times he contemplated waking one of the other men but realized he would never live that down. The potential of that embarrassment defused his anxiety until the forest started spooking him again and the cycle repeated. It was mentally exhausting.

After what seemed like an eternity, the log collapsed into the fire, and his first overnight shift had come to an end. Rugen quietly crept over to Billy and shook him awake for his turn and then lay down. He tried to get comfortable, but the grassy floor was a far cry from his soft mattress and pillow at home. After much adjusting and fidgeting, he eventually fell asleep.

CHAPTER 4

Rugen awoke with the sun low in the sky to find Casey gone and Billy tending the fire. The other men were still asleep. He nodded to Billy and quietly got up to go find a place to relieve himself. When he returned to camp a few minutes later, Casey was back with two large rabbit carcasses draped over his uninjured shoulder. He held them by their long back legs, which had been tied together with twine.

Thomas and Billy built a makeshift spit over the cookfire as Casey cleaned and skinned the rabbits. He removed the offal and piled it onto a large leaf, which he carefully folded over several times. He looked at Rugen and said, "Bait." He rubbed the rabbits with salt he had brought with him, stuffed them with sprigs of rosemary and wild onion grass he'd found, and tied them closed.

Rugen found himself staring at Casey, watching his cooking skills with great interest. He asked, "How's your shoulder?"

Casey glanced at his left shoulder and gingerly moved it. "Pretty sore. It hurts a lot if I lift it any higher than this."

While the meat cooked, the men prepped themselves for the day by foraging for roots, leaves, and berries, and cleaning themselves as best they could with water from the nearby stream. They were reluctant to disrobe to do a more thorough cleansing, suspecting if they did, that would be the exact moment a pack of gmorks would show up. They resigned themselves to only rinsing their hands, feet, and faces.

After feasting on Billy's delicious herb-roasted rabbit, they gathered their gear, put out the fires, and cleared the camp, ready to restart the journey to

Ravenwood. Gordon and Rugen were at the front of the group, with the other four a short distance behind.

Shortly after they started walking, Gordon stole a side-eye glance at Rugen, and asked, "How was your first night away from home?"

"Well let me see, being dirty and smelly, sleeping on cold ground, and feeling the constant threat of death," he shrugged, "I wouldn't trade it."

"While I'm not going to disagree with you, those minor annoyances come with a sense of accomplishment and self-worth," said Gordon. "How good do you feel knowing you survived a day and night out in the wilderness away from your comfortable life? Not everyone gets to experience that."

"You're right. Almost makes up for my sore back," chuckled Rugen as he dramatically stretched.

"What about camaraderie? We have that in spades. What about being responsible for the lives of others and relying on them in turn?" Gordon gestured to the men around them and said, "In time these men will become your brothers."

Rugen paused to consider his next response. He realized this wasn't the time to joke around. Gordon seemed to love his life of adventure, and did want anyone making light of it.

Gordon continued, "Personal achievements, emotional growth, seeing new places, a story to tell your grandkids, and not to mention a chance to save Hyboria from destruction—these are all great things, but brotherhood is our true reward. I know of no better place to find that than out here."

"Hey, you don't have to sell me on this journey," said Rugen. "To be honest, it didn't take much to convince me to leave Mourain."

Gordon glanced at Rugen and then looked down. "I'm sorry things at home aren't great."

"When I think of home, I see images of my childhood. My mother. My sister." He was quiet for a few moments and then said, "I didn't leave home yesterday. Home left me years ago."

"The memories of our youth are always rose-colored. Reality can be harsh."

"My personal losses aside," started Rugen, "Mourain was crippled when the monsters arrived, more so than in other places—as you guys pointed out. And my father has been slowly suffocating it ever since."

"I'm sure the way your father sees it, he's been keeping alive the person who matters most to him—his son. I can't fault him for that."

Rugen looked into his eyes. "But you just preached about being responsible for your fellow man, your *brothers*. My father has a responsibility to the people of Mourain. When the lord of a village only protects himself and his son, he's neglecting his brothers—all the people who rely on him. Because of him I became a pariah in the village. People sneered at me, and spit on the ground when they saw me approach. A good leader doesn't provoke that reaction."

"Not everyone likes every decision their leaders make," said Gordon. "A quality of a good leader is the ability to make difficult choices against the judgment of the masses."

Rugen said nothing, prompting Gordon to go on, "By Hammond taking care of himself and you, he was making sure the people of Mourain had a healthy leader for decades to come."

The men continued along the empty, neglected roads. As they did, the landscape around them became less sparse. Mourain was situated on a vast plain dotted with occasional trees. The closer they got to Ravenwood, there as a gradual shift to tightly-packed forest. The thickening of the foliage put the men on higher alert, because reduced visibility meant a higher chance of a surprise attack.

They walked the rest of that day, discussing more about their families, hometowns, and lives before The Isolation. Gordon spoke of the wishes and dreams he'd had for his son Wil. The Tully family always had political aspirations, but no Tully had held office since Gordon's great uncle Denny was mayor of Winston for a brief period several decades prior. He was in the process of grooming Wil for leadership before his death.

The tall, gangly Billy talked about working on his family ranch. For many years they had a large tract of land for their crops and livestock. Billy acted as the resident doctor for the animals as well as the ranchers. It was all going very well until the presence of the monsters forced them to consolidate to a smaller, more defendable plot. Maintaining an expansive farm was too difficult under the constant threat of attack.

JJ talked about all the girls he missed. Some of them were killed while others were stranded in neighboring villages because of The Isolation. The rest he left behind when he joined Gordon. If JJ's boasts were to be believed, he was at least familiar, if not intimate, with every farmer's daughter in Dyersville.

He also spoke a lot about Billy's family, whom he considered his own. Prior to meeting them, he had been left to fend for himself for years. The way he talked and acted, it seemed like he was living his life in reverse. Being left ostensibly alone at a young age, he never had the opportunity to be a carefree kid.

The main topics of Casey's conversation were related to wilderness survival. His father taught him to hunt and trap wild game, and how to locate and identify edible plants. These skills gave him a significant amount of pride. He said if it weren't for the monsters he'd have a house of his own somewhere in the woods surrounding Bomont, living off the land and not being responsible to or for anyone else.

Thomas didn't say much of anything. He was content listening to the conversations of others. Occasionally he'd add a few words of agreement whenever Gordon was talking.

The process of locating a good site in which to make camp that second night was already established from the night prior. It seemed like everyone knew what to do and how to do it. Even Rugen, being the one with the most to learn, was starting to feel more comfortable under the stars. The guard rotation made more sense to him, the sounds of night seemed to be less amplified, and when his guard shift ended, sleep came much easier.

CHAPTER 5

Over the next five days and nights of following the path toward Ravenwood, the men got into a good routine of trapping, fishing, foraging, and building fires. There were no signs of gmorks during that time, but they dutifully kept their senses tuned during the day as well as their guard rotation at night. Casey's shoulder slowly healed, but even with Billy's careful medical treatment it remained sore and stiff.

With it being the beginning of the dry season, they had seen very little rain throughout their march from Mourain. Precipitation would likely get less frequent over the next several months until the wet season swept in. The weather was temperate year-round in this part of Hyboria, but they expected drastically different climates as they headed north and west.

Eventually the stream they were following met up with the Stock River, which was a glorious sight. It was wide and deep, with visible currents and eddies. The air seemed cooler the closer they got to the water, as if the river was generating its own wind. The Stock was the landmark Gordon had been looking for as his final guidepost to Ravenwood.

The road widened and led them to a bridge, which crossed the stream they had been following just as it branched from the larger river. It was comforting seeing something manmade after the mostly monotonous journey through the wild. They set up camp in view of the bridge, assured by Gordon that they would reach their destination by the end of the next day no matter what time they got started.

The unspoken plan the next morning was to relax. After a week on the road, they all wanted to rebuild their mental and physical energy before making the last push to the town of clerics and sorcerers. Being in the presence of the Stock and using its resources did that pretty effectively. Casey trapped a guinea fowl, which he plucked, cleaned, and roasted over the fire after stuffing it with aromatic leaves and grasses. He was truly a gifted outdoor chef, which gave Rugen a homey feeling he didn't expect to have on the road.

They waited until the sun was nearing its highest point overhead before cleaning up camp and getting moving again. They continued along the road for a few hours. As their destination neared, the forest on either side of them thickened, causing a corridor effect. The land behind the prickled brambles and thorny hedgerows that bordered the road was darkened by the canopy above to an eerie and constant state of dusk. Far along the path ahead were more trees broken by what looked to be a large gate in the center.

"What is that?" asked Rugen, pointing forward.

Billy squinted and responded, "Is it the edge of a town? It's hard to tell."

"It's Ravenwood!" Gordon called out.

The words leaving Gordon's mouth were joined by a roar erupting behind them. They turned to see a dark mass barreling down from a great distance away. It was so large it seemed to take up most of the width of the path.

The men stared for an agonizing moment until Casey screamed, "Ursinox! Ruuuuuunnnnn!!"

After a slight hesitation, all six men burst into a sprint toward the gate. It didn't take more than a few seconds before it was clear the ursinox was going to catch them.

"What are we supposed to do?!" asked Billy, frantically panting. He was out of breath more from fear than exertion. "Gordon, what's the plan?"

Gordon had a confused and panicked expression on his face as he exclaimed, "God help me, I don't know!"

"Maybe we can get off the road?" suggested Rugen. "Find obstacles to slow it down?"

"This forest is so thick!" cried Gordon, "We'll get caught up in the picker bushes and it will be right on top of us!"

"Oh no!" yelled Thomas, pointing toward six gmorks standing in their path. The men froze where they stood, breathlessly gasping, not knowing what to do next. They were trapped—a line of gmorks in front of them, the massive force bearing down from behind, and thick brambles hemming them in on either side.

JJ pulled his sword from his hip, turned his shield around to the front, and said, "Our only hope is to burst through. It's victory or death, brothers!" He raised his sword and screamed, "Let's GO!"

The men looked to Gordon for leadership. He eyed them back, exuding an eerie calmness through his piercing green eyes, and said, "Seems like our choice is made for us." He then called out, "Wil, my son, I'm coming home!"

The six warriors rushed toward the waiting gmorks, led by JJ and Gordon. JJ targeted the one farthest to the left by jumping in the air and aggressively swinging his sword across its ugly snarling face. The sword sliced through the left eye socket, bridge of the nose, and upper right cheek, splitting its face in two. The gmork threw its massive arms into the air as a defensive effort, but it was too late. It fell to the dirt in a heap.

Billy followed JJ's lead, jumping to attempt to slice a gmork with his sword, but just as soon as he was in the air he was on the ground, having been slashed by the gmork's claws. His twisted body lay on the ground, immobile.

All sound ceased inside Rugen's head as he stopped and watched Billy's life drain from him.

A nearby scream of pain and anger snapped Rugen back to reality. All at once the squeaks, squeals, and clangs of claw meeting metal sprang into his consciousness. He looked up to see a gmork striding toward him, talons at the ready.

While battling his own monster, JJ saw Billy's broken body and was enraged, fighting harder than ever. He yelled "Brother!!" at the top of his lungs, and ran to the murderous gmork with his weapon cutting the air in front of him.

The next few moments were a blur. Swords, armor, helmets, and shields were slashed; gmorks and men fell to the dirt and bounced back up. The maelstrom swirled until a meteoric force exploded onto the scene, jostling the ground and lifting Casey into the air by his torso, his arms and legs wriggling uselessly. The pleading shriek that left his mouth was cut short and turned into a gurgling wheeze as his ribs were crushed in the ursinox's jaws. His body looked like a child's doll in the mouth of the repulsive beast. The ursinox savagely shook its head left and right, spraying blood in all directions, and then dropped him to the ground.

The men were right. It did look like a bear, except twice as tall and ten times as massive. One of its giant paws was the size of Casey's chest. It had thick, coarse, dark brown fur and curved claws the color of jaundice. The beast's attention briefly shifted to the fighting around it, but then it returned to its kill. It nosed into Casey's armpit and then mouthed where his shoulder wound was. It put a giant paw on his back and with a quick flick of its neck easily ripped his arm from its socket. When the massive head arose, it was gnawing Casey's fleshy upper arm with his hand dangling from its mouth.

Distracted by the gruesome scene, Gordon was suddenly struck in the helmet by a gmork. He fell awkwardly and was lying in the dirt semi-conscious with his weapon next to him. Thomas pushed his shield into the gmork he was fighting, knocking it back, and then spun on his heel and ran his sword through the gmork as it loomed over Gordon.

Rugen continued to fight as he tried to focus on his surroundings. He could barely see JJ with all of the dust that was stirred into the air, but could hear him screaming. Gordon was lying motionless on the ground in the middle of the road, and to the right Thomas was fighting off two gmorks. Behind him were the bodies of Billy and Casey, as well as the ursinox, which was occupied with its loathsome business. All he could think about was getting as far from the carnage as possible.

Rugen blocked a gmork's attack and then used the momentum he gained to drive his pommel into its jaw, feeling a crunch of bone and teeth. The gmork was stunned, allowing Rugen to bring his blade down on its left elbow, all but severing it. He then spun around and swung his sword in a devastating two-handed arc across its neck.

As the gmork fell, Rugen ran to Gordon and whisper-yelled, "C'mon, wake up." He put his hand on his shoulder and shook him. "We need to get out of here. Gordon!"

Thomas was trading blows with two gmorks. In an amazing display of speed and agility for an older man, he pushed his shield into the chest of one as he punctured the abdomen of the other. He alternated sword swings until both gmorks lay incapacitated on the road. He turned around and called out to Gordon.

Gordon looked up and smiled at his old friend. Thomas smiled back, and just as he began walking to the pair, one of the gmorks he'd wounded sprung up and jumped onto his back, driving him to the ground.

Gordon screamed, "Noooo!" as the hellacious beast buried its teeth into the back of Thomas's neck, severing his spine.

Rugen ran to the gmork as it lifted its head from Thomas's wound and flashed its bloody teeth in what looked to Rugen to be a sneer. Disgusted and enraged, Rugen raised his sword above his head, braying a tortured war cry, and swung it down like a sledgehammer, splitting the skull of the gmork. It slumped onto Thomas's limp body.

"Where's JJ?" shouted Gordon.

They spotted his bag, soaked in blood, lying next to the body of a gmork. Rugen sputtered, "I don't know, but we need to get the hell out of here."

The two men managed only a few steps before the giant paw of the ursinox raked across Rugen's back, opening several long and deep wounds. He tumbled to the ground, landing face first, as the beast rushed past him and tackled Gordon.

"Oh God! No!" wailed Gordon desperately.

Rugen, completely helpless to do anything, lay in shocked horror as the ursinox grabbed Gordon's head in its mouth and bit down, crushing his skull. It took all of his strength to fight through the searing pain in his back and clamber to his feet. He picked up his sword and began trudging down the road, all the while expecting to be overrun and ripped to shreds. He didn't look back, knowing full well what was happening to Gordon's body behind him.

For what seemed like an eternity, he half-limped, half-trotted from the scene. The torn skin on his back was spasming with pain. Blood dripped down his legs. He began to feel woozy, as much from the worry that he was about to bleed to death as from the blood loss itself. He kept lurching forward, each step more laborious than the last. Somehow the Ravenwood gate seemed to get farther away with every step. A white haze clouded his vision as his extremities went numb. All fear left him. All sound faded. He plunged into a world of white.

BOOK TWO: RAVENWOOD

The G. Wallace School of Divinity is one of the two schools of magic in the town of Ravenwood, located in the majestic Jamescorte Forest. Along with our sister institution, the Mitchell Wyatt School of Sorcery, we are dedicated to cultivating the minds of the world's brightest children. Our vision includes attention to:

- Supervising the magical education of our students and ushering their maturation into adulthood.
- Fostering partnerships within the community and the world at large through collaboration and technical innovation.
- Furthering the venture of our school founders and maintaining the teachings of Pallous.
- Being a sanctuary of inspiration to students, teachers, and parents, among others.

—Statement of Vision; excerpted from the G. Wallace
School of Divinity School Handbook; Page 5

CHAPTER 1

Twelve-year-old Serra Frye sat in her first-year history class at the G. Wallace School of Divinity. She was taller than most kids in her grade, or even the next grade up, and with the wispiness of her limbs and the great length of her auburn hair, it almost appeared as if she could be carried away like a sail in the wind.

Normally an attentive and enthusiastic student, she was at this moment terribly bored. Her teacher, Professor Strickland, was lecturing on a topic that wasn't as interesting to Serra as the distractions of the others around her. She couldn't help but watch the girl one desk over mindlessly dragging her finger through the air. Tiny sparks were dripping off of her fingertip, which glowed a brilliant blue-white. Serra, mesmerized, was unaware of her professor's approach.

"Girls!"

The whole class jumped in their seats. The radiance her neighbor's finger instantly extinguished as she scrambled to attention.

Professor Strickland, a small but stocky bald-headed man with thick eyebrows shaded an unnatural jet black, was standing in front of the two girls and glaring at them with one fist buried in the flesh above his hip. His form loomed over them, but his eyes scanned the room as he said, "To the students who care enough to pay attention, I'm teaching a lesson about how magic came to be." He lowered his furry eyebrows and continued, "A history lesson, and if you don't know your history…"

"The world is a mystery," the class mechanically droned, making Serra roll her eyes.

"Precisely!" declared Professor Strickland. He spun on his heel and made his way toward his large wooden desk, upon which piles of books and papers were stacked. On the wall behind the desk hung a hand-painted map of Hyboria—one mass of multicolor land situated in a field of wavy blue ocean. Breaking the monotony of blue were a dozen or so fiercely breaching serpentine monsters.

Serra always thought of the shape of the land as a fat bug that had been squashed underfoot. It was more or less round except for jutting fingers squeezing out in all directions. Stretching through the center of the country from the northeast to the southwest was a mountain range called the Ovid Graans, which divided Hyboria into two mostly equal halves referred to simply as the Northern Territory and the Southern Territory. On the map, the north was nebulously represented as brownish tan at the bottom blended to snowy white at the top.

The reason for the lack of any other details on that side of the continent, as taught by Professor Strickland, was because of the outcome of a vicious war between the two halves the prior century. It started with a dispute over control of Lundgren and quickly expanded to involve most of Hyboria. The great city was much smaller at that time, but its location was highly prized because of the natural fortification and mineable resources of the surrounding mountains. The war was long and bloody, with many casualties on both sides, but nearly all of the structural damage was in the north. Northern towns were burned, crop fields salted over, and water supplies fouled by rotting carcasses. More people died of disease and starvation than of direct combat. The scattered northern settlements that remained after the conflict couldn't thrive because of regular raids by roving bandits. Lawlessness reigned, and once the Red Gate was erected, chances of rebuilding were greatly crippled.

By comparison, the south recovered quickly, with Lundgren setting the example for the rest of the territory and becoming the center of defense. In the area below the mountain range on the painted map on Strickland's classroom wall, this was reflected by the abundance of tiny details.

The town of Ravenwood, where the schools of magic were located, sat at the bottom of a green wedge labeled Jamescorte Forest. It started in the angle where the mountains met the coast in the northeast and continued a third of the way down the range, making a triangle with the eastern edge of the continent. There were no official inhabitants in the forest, but there were rumors of savages running amok through the trees.

"Many generations ago, gods walked among us. Two gods in fact: Obsidian, the god of black magic, which is taught in the Mitchell Wyatt School of Sorcery." Professor Strickland paused his lecture at the interruption of a boy, whose hand had been raised. "Yes, Mr. Elliott?"

The hand-raiser cleared his throat and asked with hesitation in his voice, "Obsidian. Isn't that also a rock?"

"Correct. There is a deep black yet shiny volcanic glass that people have named obsidian, presumably after the god himself. It's so shiny it burns spots in your vision when you see it reflecting in the sun, but it's so black it darkens the room when you carry it inside." He frowned and added, "Now, Mr. Elliott, please don't interrupt me again."

Dejected, the boy slumped back into his chair.

"The god of white magic," restarted Professor Strickland, "the god we follow at this school, is Pallous." He eyeballed the students intensely and said, "Before anyone raises his or her hand, I'll tell you his name was corrupted into other words meaning white, such as *pale* or *pallor*. Just another way these glorious beings have influenced our language."

Strickland held his hands behind his back and paced the room as he spoke. "Obsidian and Pallous found themselves among mortals and decided to teach them sorcery and divinity. They tried to, anyway. People weren't very receptive at first. Rather, they were terrified, calling the teachings sacrilege and being fearful of everlasting damnation. Eventually though, the idea of being able to accomplish otherwise difficult tasks just by saying a few words didn't seem so bad. Some brave souls tried it..." He paused dramatically. "And failed miserably."

Serra wondered how anyone could know about the distant day to day lives of contemporaries of the gods, but figured Strickland was making it up.

"They didn't know the thing we'll be teaching you. The practice of magic is not just saying a few words and waving your arms around. It takes years of training under intense tutelage to gain the necessary discipline to perform spells safely. You'll need to learn to clear your mind and focus solely on the tasks you are trying to accomplish. From this focus comes everything else a person needs to foster the desired results." He winked at the students. "You'll find this to be good advice in many facets of life, not just in being a better cleric."

Another student interrupted, this time without a raised hand, "Can you tell us more about black magic and Obsidian?"

Strickland shut his eyes and sighed through his nose at the disruption, but answered the question. "Black magic is dedicated to wielding control over the elements: water, fire, air, and earth. Those who practice it can conjure lightning from thin air, turn water into ice or steam, and make the very ground sweep out from beneath their foes. As you can imagine, without proper training, a person could easily lose control over such powers. The would-be sorcerers of Obsidian's time hurt and killed people either by accident or on purpose, and their cleric counterparts did harm while trying to do good. But not to worry, we will teach you to harness magic to your will. By the time you leave Wallace, you'll be adept at healing, protecting, and enhancing the skills of others."

Professor Strickland planted himself on the corner of his desk. "Eventually the idea of performing magic fell out of favor with our ancestors, to say the least. The truth is any would-be clerics or sorcerers were burned at the stake. Or worse. Some people still hold onto these intolerant beliefs today, so keep aware of your surroundings. This is the main reason we built Ravenwood in a tucked-away location and use powerful spells to discourage unwanted visitors."

"When they decided their time in Hyboria had come to an end, Obsidian and Pallous moved on, never to be seen in the flesh again, but to this day we pray to them and honor them. They each left behind a book of their teachings. Pallous's book of divinity is kept in a safe place here on campus. Obsidian's book of sorcery is located at Wyatt."

Serra raised her hand and was reluctantly recognized. "What language are they written in?"

"If you open either book, you will find the page to your right is written in Hybor, interspersed with incantations we will be teaching you over the next half dozen years. The text on the left is in the language of either Pallous or Obsidian, depending on which book you are referring to, Miss Frye."

Serra, not raising her hand this time, blurted out, "What does their language look like? Does it use our same letters?"

"I don't know. I've never opened either of them," snapped the professor. "Now class, please stop interrupting, and if you must, at least raise your hand!"

Serra looked disappointed, which Strickland interpreted as a response to being reprimanded for not raising her hand, but actually it was because of his admission of never being bothered to open Pallous's book. The book was the only surviving link to the genesis of not only his vocation, but also his culture, religion, and the reason for the existence of the schools and the town. She wondered how he could not be curious about the source of all of that.

Professor Strickland stood as his lesson continued. "It's because of these books that we know magic and can teach it to the next generation. After the gods left and the people who had interacted with them died off, knowledge of magic was not passed on. It wasn't until years later these books were discovered by a small group of historians, who in turn founded our schools in Ravenwood. They interpreted the books and revived magic for all of us."

After he finished speaking, Serra thought to herself how she had to get a look at that book.

CHAPTER 2

One year later, Lane Dobbler was walking through a large manicured lawn that lay in the center of the Wyatt School of Sorcery campus. He had dark straight hair, angular features, and a long pointed nose. All around him were other students filling the quad with frenetic action. Everyone was wearing the school uniform—dark blue robes with orange accents. They carried books and bags and talked about topics such as studying, parties, and the opposite gender. Surrounding them was a perimeter of ivy-covered stone buildings.

At the far edge of the quad, in front of a massive stone arch, was an enormous statue of Obsidian. The base alone was taller than a full-grown man, and the deep black effigy stretched far above that. It represented the god in a battle pose—knees bent, his right hand out in front of him, fingers splayed, as if he had just launched a deathblow at an enemy. His other arm was out to the side and behind, maintaining his balance. His lips were curled into a confident sneer and his eyes bulged. The terrifying sculpture was meant to inspire Wyatt students to greatness.

Dobbler had come to Ravenwood from Beckersted, a small island off the southwest coast of Hyboria, where the Ovid Graans continued under the waterline. While the island was visible from the mainland, it was only accessible via boat due to the swirling currents.

Dobbler's ancestors made shoes and thus were known by the last name Cobbler, but a family disagreement three generations prior caused Lane's great-grandfather to change the first initial of his last name from a C to a D. Both sides of the divide remained on Beckersted despite the subsequent estrangement, but they never reconciled. Awkward moments occurred on an almost daily basis over the course of decades between the two families. To this day they considered themselves to be separate, maintaining a shared passive animosity.

Dobbler was very smart and well-read as a child. Results from a test he took when he was eleven were surreptitiously collected by a person representing the Ravenwood schools, and he was identified as a possible magic school candidate. This same chain of events repeated in locations all over Hyboria with other outstanding children and continued until several years later when the presence of the monsters mostly inhibited travel. After a conversation with Lane's parents, it was decided that sorcery school would be a nice fit for his skill set, and the following year he was accepted at Wyatt.

Dobbler sat with his lab partner in Elements of Sorcery class. Elements referred to naturally occurring phenomena harnessed by sorcerers to be used as weapons, such as fire, ice, or lightning. It was Dobbler's favorite class because it was an opportunity to get hands-on experience with potentially destructive magic. With them being in their second year, destruction was not in the lesson plan. Instead they were learning how to harness the power of fire to ignite a small candle.

Dobbler has been practicing with fire spells for a long time using the Obsidian word *engki*, meaning *little flame*. Several days prior he was secretly conjuring large fireballs (*engkau*) against a stone wall behind the school. His partner, Josh, who was not nearly as adept at sorcery, was struggling to muster even the smallest spark on the candle's wick.

With a look of frustration and confusion on his face, Josh desperately barked, "Engki! Engki!" When the candle didn't respond, he threw his hands in the in the air. "I don't get it. It just won't light. Maybe there's something wrong with the wick."

Dobbler made a small movement with his finger and his partner's candle quickly ignited.

"Show off!" whined Josh.

"Don't you practice at home?"

"A little. It worked yesterday."

Dobbler blew out the flame. "Well, keep trying. Maybe now that the candle knows what it's supposed to do, it'll light easier for you."

Josh tried again, unsuccessfully, and gave his friend a look of disgust. "Why are you such a prodigy with magic?"

Dobbler shrugged his shoulders. "Everyone's got their talents, I guess. Yours is scaring girls away."

"Shut up."

"Uh-oh, here comes Mr. Kerber. You better get that thing lit or, well, you know how he gets."

The Elements teacher, Mr. Kerber, was slowly making his rounds, and their table was next. Josh was staring intently at the candle, repeating the incantation over and over again, but the wick remained unlit.

Mr. Kerber shook his head at the scene in front of him. With fake enthusiasm he said, "How's it going, Josh? Are we in danger of the whole school going up in flames?" He gestured to the walls around them. "Be careful. This room is made of wood."

Josh barely looked up from his efforts. "It was just lit, sir. I blew it out."

Mr. Kerber blinked his eyes slowly. "I'm sure it was. Go ahead and light it again."

Josh stared intently at the candlewick, concentrating with all of this might, and bleated, "ENGKI!" Nothing happened. He refocused and tried again, but the only heat generated was from the flushing of his face.

Mr. Kerber stared at Josh. Dobbler's eyes shifted back and forth between the two of them. The moment of watching the unresponsive candle was stretching into an eternity until Mr. Kerber looked away for a moment and Dobbler made an almost imperceptible motion with his finger. Instantaneously, the top of Josh's candle erupted in an explosion of flame, making Mr. Kerber jump and singeing Josh's eyebrows.

Mr. Kerber couldn't hide his look of suspicion, but said, "Well, I'm impressed, Josh. You surprised me. Bravo." He stepped back, straightened his robe, and made eye contact with Dobbler as he said, "Make sure your friend learns to keep his spells under control before the building actually does catch fire."

CHAPTER 3

"Serra?" Mrs. Carla Reed, the G. Wallace Vice Principal, called down the hallway, smiling as she thought of the girl who had gradually become her favorite student. The vice principal wished all students were more like Serra, with her consistently high marks in both classroom and practical work, her perfect attendance record, and her overall pleasant and agreeable disposition.

Mrs. Reed was small and slight but could be intimidating when she wanted to be. She wore her brown hair short in a bob style and had glasses with large dark frames.

Serra stopped and turned around. Three years had passed since she started at Wallace, and she was a taller version of the spindly-limbed girl she was in her first year. She had auburn and caramel curls pulled into a bun with one fat strand dangling in front of her forehead, as was her custom. Her cheeks and nose were covered in a smattering of light brown freckles, contrasting her heather gray eyes. She was dressed in the standard-issue Wallace cleric robe: slate blue trimmed with straw yellow accents. She cheerfully replied, "Hello, Mrs. Reed. How are you?"

"Wonderful, Serra. Thank you. We need to talk in my office later. I don't have much time now, but just so you are aren't worried about it all day, I'll tell you that I think you would be the perfect candidate for the summer internship with the Divinity Mercy Corps. They're accepting one bright Wallace student to join them in providing care and support to citizens of Lundgren. They do amazing work helping the less fortunate who don't have access to Pallous's words. It's an excellent experience for an aspiring cleric of great promise such as yourself. It'll give you a chance to learn about real world divinity from experts in our field. I think you'll find it to be very rewarding."

Serra nervously twisted her foot. "Um. I don't know what to say."

"Oh dear. I sounded like the advertisement just then, didn't I... I don't mean to overwhelm you." She touched Serra's arm. "You don't have to answer me now. We'll talk about it in my office later, okay?"

"Thanks, Mrs. Reed. I'll stop by after school." Serra hurried off toward Incantations class.

As she entered the classroom, her two best friends, Charlie and Kelly, ran over to her. They were rarely seen apart, shared the same opinion on most topics, had the same likes and dislikes, and wore the same vacant grins most of the time. Charlie was petite with dark brown short-cut spring curls and green eyes. Kelly was larger and rounder with straight dirty blonde hair. When they spoke, one of them always repeated what the other one said. The original thought was usually Charlie's, her being the unofficial leader of the pair, and the echo was Kelly's.

"What were you and Mrs. Reed talking about?" asked Charlie.

"Yeah, we saw her talking to you," echoed Kelly.

Serra shrugged. "I'm not sure. It sounds like she wants me to do some internship over the summer."

"She loves you."

"Yeah, Serra, she loves you."

Charlie looked at Kelly, eyebrows raised. "Who wouldn't love her? I love her." She quickly hugged Serra.

"Everyone loves her," exclaimed Kelly, jumping in for her own brief hug. "Hey Serra, did you do your spell homework?"

"Of course she did. She always does. Did you, Serra?"

Serra took the barrage of questions in stride. "Did you need me to go over it with you?"

Charlie played with one of her curls as she said, "Yeah, I didn't understand it."

"I didn't look at it," admitted Kelly with a look of mock-sadness.

The room was full of potted plants and small trees. Leafy vines climbed the walls and hung from the ceiling. Some of the vines had tiny yellow flowers on them, but their presence made the entire room look green and alive. Serra started walking to their table and said, "C'mon I'll show you." The girls followed.

Charlie set her books on their table, which was made of a thick, heavy, darkly stained wood cut to accentuate the natural curves and angles of the grain. She said, "Spells come so easy to you."

Kelly dropped her bag on the floor and added, "Yeah, Serra, you have a gift for spells."

Serra blushed, saying, "It's not a gift. I spend a lot of time practicing, sometimes failing miserably in the process."

Charlie's eyes lit up as she excitedly blurted, "We were at Wyatt last night! You know Dobbler?"

"Dobbler," repeated Kelly, "he's so cute. Do you know him, Serra?"

Serra stopped what she was doing and stared blankly. She was well aware of Lane Dobbler. He was a sorcery student in her same class year who seemed to have a great talent for black magic. The two schools often had mixers, and once he was pointed out to her by Mrs. Reed as *your counterpart at Mitchell Wyatt*. She considered them the best students in their respective classes and possibly the entire school. Since then she'd been infatuated with the thought of him, so much so she was afraid to start a one-on-one conversation.

Wallace and Wyatt students spent a total of six years in school, broken by short breaks and summer vacation, during which some of them took part in internships. Their entire adolescence of living, eating, and breathing magic made relationships with non-magic users awkward, so Wallace students romantically pursued those from Wyatt and vice versa. It was thought of as incestuous for two clerics or two sorcerers to date, and thus inter-school liaisons were really the only available option to them.

Sorcerer boys were seen by cleric girls as dark, brooding, and mysterious; that is, bad boys. In turn these same boys thought of the cleric girls as warm, loving, and caring. Cleric boys saw sorcerer girls as sultry and willing to experiment, while they, in turn, were seen as moral, stable, and mom-approved. It was all a stereotypical fallacy that served the function of bringing teenaged couples together.

"So do you know him?" Charlie repeated.

Serra, whose mind had wandered off, snapped back to reality. "Yes, I know Dobbler. Well, sort of. I mean I've never talked to him if that's what you're asking."

Charlie beamed a bright smile and said in a singsong voice, "He liiiiiikes yooouuu."

Kelly nodded enthusiastically. "Yeah, he likes you, Serra. He talks about you."

Charlie threw her arms out wide and exclaimed, "Everyone likes you!"

Serra didn't know how to respond. Not only was it surprising to hear that Dobbler knew of her, but for him to openly discuss her with Kelly and Charlie? And not only discuss her, but to say he liked her? She was silent as she contemplated this, not knowing how to react. On one hand, she was ecstatic. In Mrs. Reed's words Dobbler was *a smart and fine young man*. Serra liked that he was kind of a bad boy. On the other hand, he really didn't know anything about the real Serra, so what right did he have to say such things to her friends before having a real conversation with her?

All she was able to muster in response was, "That's good. Thanks for telling me. So do you want me to show you those spells?"

Later that afternoon Serra entered the office of the vice principal. "Hi, Mrs. Reed. You wanted to talk to me about an internship?"

They sat down on opposite sides of the desk and Mrs. Reed rehashed everything she had described earlier in the hallway about Divinity Mercy Corps, all the while effusively singing Serra's praises as a student and as a person. She smiled warmly and ended with, "Think about it. Consider it seriously. It's a great opportunity not offered to many students."

Serra nodded. "Where did you say the Divinity Mercy Corps did most of their work?"

"The city of Lundgren." She paused for a moment. "Wait, don't your parents live there?"

Serra crossed her legs. "Yeah. They just moved to Lundgren this year. It's where my dad's family is from, but they left when he was a teenager. He always talked about moving back to the city. Small town life wasn't for him."

"So you haven't seen them in Lundgren since they moved there?"

"Not yet."

"Well then, this makes this an even better opportunity for you. When you go home for the summer you'll have a job waiting for you."

"Would I be the only one going?"

"The only student, yes. Of course there are a handful of professional clerics as well. Service on the DMC renews annually. There's a group waiting to exchange with the ones currently stationed in Lundgren. It's really a phenomenal experience, and I don't want to have to think about finding another student to ask. You are my first choice. I think it's perfect for you!"

"Thank you, Mrs. Reed. I'll think about it." She paused for a moment and looked down at her hands clasped in her lap. "Um, Mrs. Reed?"

The vice principal cocked her head and responded, "Yes, dear?"

"You know the book we have here on campus? The book about divinity? The one Pallous wrote?"

"Yes?"

"I was thinking I wanted to see it."

Mrs. Reed's posture stiffened. "Whatever for?"

"As part of a project."

"What project?"

Serra had practiced this conversation in her head for a long time. It was something she'd been thinking about since the day in Professor Strickland's freshman history class when she first learned about the book. She had painstakingly worked out a legitimate reason for wanting to see it and was waiting for the perfect person to ask at the perfect time. This was her chance.

But before she related her made-up story about a project a teacher had assigned to her, she stopped herself. It sounded like a good idea right up until the moment it was about to leave her lips. She reconsidered, realizing it would be way too simple for Mrs. Reed to double-check the existence of any such assignment. Getting caught in a lie would nullify her chances of ever getting near the book.

Thinking quickly she said, "Well, not a project exactly. It's this internship. When you told me about it in the hallway it got me thinking. I mean, I'm really interested in going, but I'm nervous I won't be as prepared as I could be. I've always been a better learner by reading than by hearing. I'd be a whole lot more sure of myself around those experts if I got to read the real thing. I mean, even the professionals don't have that opportunity. What do you think? Can I see it? I want to put my best foot forward for our school."

Mrs. Reed was stunned. No one had ever asked her to see Pallous's book. On one hand she was offended on behalf of Wallace. She thought, *Is the curriculum not adequate for such a high achiever as Serra Frye? Are students like her not being challenged enough? Is there something in that book that isn't being taught by our teachers?* She said, "I'm not sure, Serra. Students aren't normally allowed where it's kept. I'll have to discuss the matter with Principal Harmon."

Serra lit up, knowing she had just as good a relationship with the school principal as she did with Mrs. Reed. "Oh please! Please talk to him! That would be great. I just know the two of you will let me."

"Okay dear, I'll get back to you."

CHAPTER 4

"Hey, Weasel!"

It was Chet, a sixth-year who picked on Dobbler every chance he got. The name "Weasel" came from what Chet thought of Lane's appearance: small, skinny, pointy nose, big ears. Dobbler winced every time he heard the name, especially when it was followed by rolling laughter from Chet's friends, who were always nearby, craving his approval. Dobbler knew their names to be Teddy and Johnny, but he never cared to learn who was who.

While most people at the school were larger than Dobbler, Chet was decidedly so. He in fact stood a head taller than everyone around him. He had broad shoulders and meaty hands. Up close he wasn't much to look at, and unfortunately Dobbler was well experienced in up-close looks at Chet from multiple prior altercations. He had beady eyes, whiteheads speckling the tip of his nose, acne scars, and thick black hairs not only between his eyebrows but also extending a third of the way down his nose. He had foul breath that blew in Dobbler's face when he held him in the air by his collar. There was no amount of nose-dodging that could staunch the scent of rotting garbage wafting from his open maw. Dobbler had the noxious odor burned into his olfactory memory, and every now and again when something reminded him of it, he reacted with an exaggerated nausea response.

Dobbler did his best to pretend he didn't hear Chet, but the tightly-packed, morning rush of students was funneling him directly toward the bellowing bully. All he could hope was for Chet to get distracted by something else. He continued on, careful to not make eye contact with him or his cronies.

"I'm talking to you, Weasel!"

Why an upper year like Chet would waste his time picking on a younger, smaller, and magic-restricted student was beyond Dobbler's understanding, but Dobbler never had the desire or opportunity to be a bully himself, so he could only speculate about it.

Restrictions on the use of magic were part of school policy. First years had the highest level of restriction put on them by the administration. Successful completion of each term was rewarded with an easing of that constraint. Only seniors had access to all spells taught at Wyatt. Thus, even if Dobbler knew of enchantments that could level the playing field, he wouldn't be capable of using them.

A large hand grabbed hold of Dobbler and threw him toward the wooden hallway wall. While the feeling of being tossed by Chet was certainly not new to Dobbler, being so easily moved through the air made him wonder how it was possible for people to grow into such disproportionately different sizes. He came to a jarring halt against the wall, pinned by Chet's forearm and hemmed in by the two flanking thugs.

A foul wind of bad breath blew into Dobbler's face as Chet bellowed, "Did you forget your name, Wea-sel?!" He poked Dobbler twice in the forehead with a sausage-sized finger to emphasize the syllables of the nickname.

"Yeah. I mean no... I didn't." Dobbler noticed the other students hugging books and notebooks against their chests as they hurried by, careful not to glance in the direction of the scene playing out against the wall. He figured they were just glad it was someone else Chet was focused on. Considering Chet seemed to spend the vast majority of his time hassling Dobbler, there weren't many free moments to bully other kids. Dobbler thought because of this they ought to express their gratitude every time they saw him. In fact, he should have been the most popular kid at Wyatt for how his unwilling sacrifice made their lives less miserable, but he knew that wasn't how the world worked.

Chet removed his arm from Dobbler's chest, took half a step back, and straightened his ruffled robe. The hulking presence of the three older boys kept the younger and considerably smaller Dobbler lodged where he was standing with no hope of escape. Chet casually said, "I need you to do something for me."

Dobbler was dumbstruck by this request for several reasons. First, he was the type of person who would be happy to do something for a friend, or at least an acquaintance who was nice to him, but Chet was the meanest person he'd ever had the misfortune of meeting. He had no interest in doing him any favors. The second thought that ran through his mind was how the request couldn't result in anything good for anyone besides Chet, and that list included his two associates. Third, he couldn't fathom what he would be able to do that Chet, being older and stronger, couldn't. Again, he took too long to answer.

"You hearin' me, you little punk?!"

"Uhh, yeah. What is it?"

"You're going to sneak into Mrs. Barrett's office and get me a copy of tomorrow's astronomy exam. She keeps them in her desk."

Mrs. Barrett primarily taught sixth-year students. Dobbler had heard her name before and had seen her around campus, but he had never interacted with her. He looked up at Chet and asked, "Why?"

Chet's expression changed to fury. "So I won't have to take you outside and beat you to a pulp! That's why!" He stood glaring down at him for a long moment, and then his face softened slightly. "Look, she knows me. She don't know you. And let's be honest, nobody knows you or cares about you at this school." He made it a point to glance around at the students who were shuffling by and purposely not looking in the direction of their discussion. He flashed a sinister grin. "You'll be able to slip into her office, grab the test, and slip out." He paused, maintaining eye contact, and added, "I need it by the end of classes today."

Before Dobbler had a chance to respond, the three bullies disappeared into the flow of the crowd.

Dobbler sat stunned at his easel in Artistic Expression, which was an elective class available to Wyatt students. Painting was one of Dobbler's favorite hobbies, and under normal circumstances he wouldn't miss an opportunity to get lost in the watercolors swirling on his canvas.

The art room was on the top floor in the southeast corner of the castle-like structure that was Wyatt's main classroom building. Large windows, magically forged, allowed in as much natural light as possible to illuminate the work stations. With the room being so high up, the windows provided an excellent panorama of Ravenwood. The room itself was a pretty typical art room: a stone floor with thousands of old dried drops of paint, mostly concentrated around where the easels and stools typically sat; seemingly hundreds of paint brushes strewn about on countertops, dozens of glass containers of paint or colored water, some of which with dirty brushes sticking out of them; and boxes of props for the still life setups.

Seated next to Dobbler, as usual, was Josh, who lacked most of the abilities necessary to be a good sorcery student. Following Dobbler's lead made for enough improvement to raise his grades to passing. Without this help and guidance, Josh likely would have been tossed out of the school long ago.

While Dobbler initially didn't like that Josh was riding his academic coattails, he really couldn't afford to be choosy when it came to friends. His nerdy demeanor and his tendency to blow the grading curve made him one of the less popular students at Wyatt. Abuse from Chet severely tarnished his image as well, and without Josh he really wouldn't have anyone to hang out with.

Mr. Adamley was demonstrating how to add shading into paintings to give them depth, which normally would have interested Dobbler, but he was lost in his own worries.

Josh noticed Dobbler's zoned-out face and whispered, "Hey, Dobbs? What's wrong with you?"

"You don't want to know."

Josh made an annoyed frown and waited for a response.

Dobbler groaned, "Chet..."

Josh's eyes got wide. Everyone on campus knew, feared, and hated Chet.

"He wants me to steal an exam out of Mrs. Barrett's office so he can memorize it and ace it."

Josh rolled his eyes. "I don't know if having the questions in advance means he would ace it. He's probably just hoping to pass."

"That's not the point. He wants to me to get it to him by the end of the day. He'll be waiting for me outside after school. Either I give him the stolen test or he gives me a beating."

"So what are you going to do?"

Mr. Adamley cleared his throat and projected his voice to the corner of the room where the talkers were seated. "Boys! This is very important! Without shading, your paintings will lack depth and realism. Stop the chattering."

The boys quieted down and tried to pay attention until Josh could no longer stand it. He repeated, "What are you going to do?"

"I guess at lunch I'll sneak into Mrs. Barrett's office and grab that test." Neither boy moved a muscle as they spoke. It was lucky for them they were in the farthest possible position from where from Mr. Adamley was teaching.

"You can't do that!"

"I have to. What else am I supposed to do? Have you met Chet??"

"When's it going to end?" asked Josh, breaking Dobbler's rhythm.

"What do you mean?"

"I mean, when will it end? You do this for him today, and then what? He leaves you alone the rest of the year? Your quota with him is met?"

Dobbler stared blankly, contemplating a future of being Chet's slave.

Josh narrowed his eyes at him. "It's time to stand up for yourself. Tell him no and face the consequences. You'll be out in the open, surrounding by kids. He's not allowed to do magic outside of school, especially spells that would hurt another student. That's an automatic suspension. If he attacks you, someone's bound to step in to stop him. Or if not, at least they'll tell a teacher. Then he'll get in trouble."

"That's the stupidest thing I've ever heard," Dobbler responded. "First off, he doesn't need magic to hurt me. He's twice my size. And no one will step in. He's tortured me in plain view many times before. Kids just ducked their heads and scuttled by. No one's ever reported anything. Why would they start now? If they did they'd be his next target."

"So steal the test then," said Josh, waving him off. "Give it to him. Be his slave. I'm sure it won't be too bad."

Dobbler stared at Mr. Adamley's demonstration as he thought about Josh's point. It made sense, but he had no idea how he could stand up to Chet and his friends.

Josh turned to him. "Look, you've helped me... I can't even begin to count the number of times since we've met. We're friends. It's time for me to return the favor. We'll walk out of school together. You'll tell Chet where he can stick his stolen test. I'll back you up. We face the consequences. What's the worst that can happen?"

CHAPTER 5

Serra was the first student in anyone's memory to be granted access to the book that had no title, the book of divinity, the book of white magic, that written by the god Pallous himself. She realized it was awkward and a little silly to have a book without a title. She decided *The White Book* would be the way she would refer to it from that moment on.

Vice Principal Reed led her down a dark, stony corridor deep beneath the school. There were many intersections and turns along the way, and she seriously doubted she would be able to find her way back should she ever need to. Another complication was several locked doors opened by spells quietly murmured by Mrs. Reed. Serra got the impression that only administrators could open them.

When they got to what Serra hoped was the final door, Mrs. Reed said, "Okay, Serra. You are being offered a great honor. I want you to respect it. That very old book in there is the foundation on which everything this school stands. Do not damage it in any way. I'll cast an illumination spell so you can see to read. You are well aware students are not allowed to perform incantations outside of their assigned homework and exam practice. We take this policy very seriously. Do you understand?"

Serra nodded. "Yes, Mrs. Reed. Thank you."

The vice principal whispered "Vleomba Carla Reed," as she unlatched the door. They walked into the tiny space and she said, "Lumea." A soft glow lit the room, revealing a simple floor plan: four stone walls with a podium in the center. Sitting on the podium was The White Book. The cover was ivory-colored leather with no visible words or markings of any kind. It was large and thick, and the pages were gilded.

"This is a trial run," said Mrs. Reed. "You have a brief period with the book by yourself. If you don't break any rules, you may come back another day for a longer period of time. And then that's it. That's all the time Mr. Harmon and I have granted you."

"Thank you. I'll take perfect care of it and everything else in this room." She glanced around, quickly noticing there was nothing else in the room to be taken care of, and added, "I promise."

On her way out of the room, she said, "I know you will, Serra. That's why you're allowed to be here. Now, I'm going to lock this door, but I'll be back shortly."

Serra grinned excitedly, took a breath, and walked to the podium. Slowly and carefully she opened the book's cover. She was looking forward to seeing the title page, as she and her classmates were never told the actual name of Pallous's book. Her eyes fell upon the dusky beige parchment, finding only a floppy three-petaled flower; the same one featured on the official Wallace school crest. It was a symbol she'd seen several times a day during the last four years in various places around campus.

She always thought the flower on the crest was meant to be a representation of the relationship between magic and nature. The town of Ravenwood was very green, with foliage filling the gaps between man-made structures. It was more accurate to say that the man-made structures filled the gaps between foliage. Also, all classrooms inside Wallace and Wyatt played host to copious amounts of plant-life.

Seeing the pure white, embossed symbol inked in Pallous's hand on his own book's title page shed new light on its meaning. She realized what was on the school crest was not a floppy three-petaled flower like people thought. The symbol was a loosely-scripted capital letter P. The author's initial.

She stared at the P for a moment longer before turning onto two pages of text. The left side was what must have been the language of Pallous. Opposite that was the Hybor translation like Mr. Strickland had described. Having the exposed text in front of her was the most beautiful thing Serra had ever seen. She recognized the handwriting, as it was copied on the school crest.

She skimmed the paragraphs on the left side and recognized a smattering of words from spells she'd been practicing for years. She turned the pages, repeating the process. Although seeing words she'd been taught at Wallace written in Pallous's hand was exciting, what interested her more was when she recognized spell-words sitting in a block of explanatory text. This was what she was hoping to find.

She spent the rest of the allocated time casually leafing through the book, familiarizing herself with the layout and trying to estimate its length. She was so engrossed in the pages, she almost forgot the other thing she wanted to do before Mrs. Reed came back. She lifted her index finger and quietly said, "Syoumb iorjae," making the tip of her finger glow a brilliant blue-white. She stared at the glow as it dripped sparks onto the podium. It was a trifling spell many students did when they were bored, serving no function other than providing a bit of visual entertainment. To Serra though, in this situation, it was a good test of whether or not she was being watched for unauthorized spell casting. If some alarm did trigger in administration, she could easily explain away such a harmless spell on her busying herself until Mrs. Reed returned.

Later, Serra sat eating lunch with Charlie and Kelly.

"You got to see the book?!" exclaimed Charlie. "Pallous's book?"

Kelly was munching on a piece of bread and didn't get a chance to mimic her friend.

"Briefly." Serra looked around the lunchroom to see if anyone was eavesdropping. "She said I can go back for a whole afternoon soon."

Kelly said through a mouthful of bread, "Today?"

Serra looked down at her food. "Not today. Another day."

Charlie asked, "Why do you want to see that old book anyway?"

"Yeah Serra, wh…?"

Serra put her hand on Kelly's hand, stopping her from repeating Charlie's question. She whispered, "Can you guys keep a secret?" Both girls nodded excitedly. Like all teenage girls, they loved secrets more than most things in their lives. Serra stared into Charlie's eyes and then Kelly's and quietly said, "I'm going to copy it."

Kelly loudly started, "You're g…"

Serra stiffly squeezed her hand and raised her eyebrows, again silencing her.

"Why?" whispered Charlie.

Kelly was too afraid to say anything else.

Serra leaned back, returning her hands to her own space, and calmly said, "I think there's more to magic than what they teach us. I don't think divinity is just a bunch of spells. I think the language of the spells is a real language. A full language. I want to learn it."

"How come?"

"I don't know," she shrugged. "I don't have a reason. Just something to do."

"How are you going to copy it?" asked Charlie in a whisper. "You know they don't allow us to do magic unless it's for homework or practicing for exams. I feel like they watch us all the time and know if we're casting when we're not supposed to be."

"It's not like a bell goes off in the principal's office every time someone casts a spell outside of the assigned homework," answered Serra, shaking her head. "They don't watch us all the time. Believe me, I know."

A loud, deep voice said behind her, "Miss Frye, don't you have better things to do than spread conspiracies?" It was Mr. Strickland, who in Serra's opinion didn't like any of the students, most especially her. She couldn't remember anything she had done to warrant him picking on her, but he had taken every opportunity to do so since they met in her freshman year. The fact that she had him again for Classics this year felt like divine punishment.

Serra wondered exactly how much of the conversation he had overheard. All she was able to offer in response was, "Umm."

The short, angry-looking, bald-headed man with jet black furry eyebrows smugly remarked, "Maybe we aren't giving you enough study material? That can be remedied." Then he looked around the lunch room and dramatically projected his voice, saying, "Your attention, please!" It took him saying it a second time for the chatter to die down. He then continued, "Miss Frye just insinuated that the students of G. Wallace aren't given enough schoolwork to do at home. I'm going to try, in a very small way, to help all of you with that problem."

Muffled groans and sighs could be heard across the space.

"Those of you who are fourth-year students of mine should study extra hard tonight. The exam we had scheduled for next week has been changed to tomorrow."

More groans rose up from Serra's classmates, which brought a sinister smile to Mr. Strickland's face. He turned back to Serra and added, "Oh and about that exam, you've already lost five points."

It was at that moment Serra decided she was going to have to be a whole lot more careful with whom she talked to about the book.

The second time Serra followed Mrs. Reed down the twisting and dark corridor, she was a ball of nerves. Her mouth was so dry she could barely speak. The only way she could stop her hands from shaking was to keep them tucked into the straps of her backpack.

Mrs. Reed opened the door to the room that housed the book and cast her illumination spell. She looked sternly at Serra before leaving and said, "The same rules we went over last time still apply. I'll be back this evening to retrieve you."

Serra took a deep breath, pulled an empty notebook from her bag, and placed it on the podium. She opened both books and set them adjacent to one another. She put her left index finger on the first word on the side with Pallous's language and her right on the corresponding spot in her notebook. Full of hope, she quietly said, "Slyraba iorju," causing both fingertips to glow a bright green. She began slowly dragging her fingers at the same speed across the two books. As she did, Pallous's words appeared, with exact fidelity, on the notebook page. She increased the speed of the dragging of her two fingers, and the transcription kept pace. When she finished the left-hand page, she repeated the process on the Hybor-language side.

She stepped back and inspected her work before resuming, copying one page at a time.

Processing through thousands of lines of text nonstop over many hours was exhausting. Her back, neck, and feet were all sore from the effort. She had to alternate which fingers she was using to lessen her skin from chafing. She dared not take a break, figuring she would barely have enough time to finish the copy as it was. She couldn't help but think about Mrs. Reed or someone else opening the door to check on her. She had no idea how she would explain what she was doing standing at the podium with green glowing fingers and a guilty look on her face. The fear of this made her work faster and more determinedly.

When she finally finished, she closed The White Book for the last time and slowly leafed through her pilfered pages, breathing a sigh of relief. The transcription nearly filled the six notebooks she brought. She tucked her things into her backpack and sat against the wall near the door, then closed her eyes and cast an analgesia spell on her various aches.

After a short rest the door opened and Mrs. Reed peered inside, and blurted, "All finished?" before spotting Serra sitting on the floor. She touched her chest and said, "Oh dear. Did I take too long?"

Serra opened her eyes, looked over at Mrs. Reed, and calmly said, "No, your timing was perfect."

CHAPTER 6

Dobbler thought all morning about the whispered conversation he'd had with Josh. His self-preservation instincts told him to get a hold of a copy of Mrs. Barrett's exam and obediently deliver it to Chet, thereby avoiding unwanted violence. But the more he mulled it over, the more he realized Josh was right. Chet would likely make him his indentured servant for the rest of the year and then maybe even beyond. He could see himself slowly becoming complacent in being his errand boy, and then one day when Chet did something that got the attention of real trouble, he'd be so deeply entangled in his gang he wouldn't be able to get out of harm's way.

He had no concept of how to sneak into a teacher's office to steal something out of her desk. For all he knew the desk was locked, or the tests were moved, or this was all a prank set up by Chet to get him into trouble. Also, he wasn't enrolled in any of Mrs. Barrett's classes—no underclassman was. Whoever caught him would know he wasn't stealing the test for himself. He'd have to finger Chet under threat of...he didn't know what...from administration. And then when things blew over with them he'd catch a beating from Chet anyway.

It was the beating that worried him the most. Chet had been manhandling him for as long as he could remember, but never anything more than roughhousing. If he walked out of school today without the stolen exam, what sort of pain would he be facing? Broken nose? Missing teeth? Fractured arm? Or just bruises and scrapes? The thought of it sent chills up his spine.

The way Dobbler looked at it, all outcomes ended badly for him. He decided to go with the option that led to the briefest amount of pain for the least amount of people.

The day flew by. Before he knew it, he was methodically marching down the main hallway toward the school exit. Images of a condemned man being led to his hanging fluttered through his overactive mind.

"Hey," blurted Josh from behind, making Dobbler jump, "we're sticking to the plan, right? You didn't steal the test?"

"No," responded Dobbler, looking nauseated, "I didn't."

"Don't worry about it," assured Josh. "We're going to be fine. He's all bluster. He won't do anything. Besides, I got your back." He slapped Dobbler between the shoulder blades.

The other students must have gotten word of what was going on because most of them lined the hallway. They stared at Dobbler and Josh with blank faces. No one offered any encouragement. The crowd following behind the boys stayed at a good distance, wanting to be spectators and not participants.

Dobbler and Josh passed under the archway of the school and onto the quad where Chet stood waiting, flanked by his two meat-headed friends. There was a gathering of students in a semicircle behind them.

Chet had a sinister look on his naturally angry face. "You got what I asked you for, Weasel?"

Dobbler and Josh stopped where they were addressed, well out of striking distance of the three goons. Dobbler quietly mumbled, "No."

"What did you say?" snarled Chet. "I can't hear you all the way over there."

The fact that Chet was referencing his demand out in the open in front of an audience made Dobbler realize the bully was well aware he hadn't stolen the exam. He took a few small steps into the semicircle, followed by Josh. He mustered all of the confidence he could, which wasn't enough to project his voice barely more than a squeak. "I couldn't get it."

Chet roared in laughter and then taunted, "You couldn't or you wouldn't?!"

Dobbler tried holding his eyes steady on Chet, but he couldn't help but look away.

Chet rubbed his hands together. "You know what that means, right Weasel?" He lurched toward Dobbler with Teddy and Johnny following close behind.

Dobbler flinched, starting to take a step back until Josh called out, "Leave him alone!"

Chet paused looked at Josh. "Who's that? Your bodyguard?" He doubled over in laughter.

Dobbler's sense of protection took over, finally giving him the confidence he was missing earlier. He didn't want Josh or anyone else getting hurt on his accord. "This is between you and me!" he yelled.

Chet launched himself toward Dobbler with a face of rage. It was amazing how fast he moved for someone so enormous. His muscles barely twitched and then all of the sudden he was right on top of him. He used one massive hand to push Dobbler, knocking him off balance and into the dirt.

Dobbler lay on the ground gasping for the breath that had been forced out of him.

Chet laughed again and flashed his beady eyes at Josh. "What are you waiting for? Come over and help your boyfriend to his feet.

Josh looked back at Chet, and then his eyes bounced to his cronies and back again.

Dobbler got up as quickly as he could, noting the soreness in his chest where it had met Chet's meaty paw. He sprang forward and buried two hands into Chet's rib cage, which with their height difference was where his push naturally landed. Chet reflexively flinched.

Seeing Chet's pained expression, Teddy and Johnny moved in. Chet put his hand out and said, "Stay out of this. He's mine." He stomped over to Dobbler, closing the distance in a second, and reared back for a face-crunching punch, which was interrupted by Josh leaping onto his back.

Josh's form was oddly small perched on the back of the bully. The two of them looked like a father and son playing piggyback. Chet appeared to be almost enjoying it, knowing the smaller boy wasn't going to be able to do any real damage. He twisted, shook his body, and half-heartedly swiped at Josh. Chet's goons were laughing at the scene, which broadened Chet's smile and broke the discomfort of the onlookers.

Josh was not laughing. In his desperation to hang on he wrapped his arm around Chet's throat. The crook of his arm landed just above Chet's larynx, cutting off his air supply. The bully's expression changed to a mix of fury and fear, and he bucked around more violently in an attempt to get Josh off his back. This made Josh strengthen his squeeze to avoid falling. Chet's face flushed red and his eyes bulged as he clawed at the offending arm.

Unable to breathe, the bully's movements became more frantic. He was twirling and twisting his shoulders, but nothing loosened Josh's grip. He tried to yell for help, but all that came out was a choked gasp, halfway between a retch and a burp.

Dobbler yelled, "Josh, he can't breathe!"

Josh was so worried about his own safety and so charged with adrenaline that he had no idea he was hurting the brute. He adjusted his grip slightly to allow the movement of air, which prompted Chet to grasp under his arm and wriggle himself free.

He peeled Josh off of his back, "You little bastard!" he shrieked, eyes wide, "Are you trying to kill me?!" He adjusted his grip and threw Josh through the air, screaming, "Ixpao duot!" which accelerated Josh's flight over the heads of the spectators, crashing him into a tree.

The thudding, crunching sound silenced the crowd. They stood motionless for a moment, glancing at one another, and then some of them made their way to the tree and gazed at his slumped body.

His neck was bent at an unnatural angle and his eyes were fixed open and lifeless. Several teachers ran from the building and worked their way through the crowd. They surrounded Josh and looked back at Chet with shocked expressions.

"He was choking me!" Chet spat. "Look at my neck!"

The next few weeks brought a lot of change. Chet was suspended from Wyatt while administration conducted an investigation. During the formal suspension meeting, they quoted the first paragraph on page seventeen of the Wyatt School of Sorcery student handbook:

"The use of magic by students outside of the classroom setting is prohibited. However, it can be performed under the supervision of professors or instructors, assigned as part of homework, or done on the student's own accord for the purpose of exam preparation. Any student suspected of the use of magic

that results in the harm of a person or the destruction of property will be in-definitely suspended until a proper investigation is complete, at which point the standing of said student will be reassessed."

Chet's mother traveled to the school to speak on his behalf. She argued that Josh wasn't even involved in the disagreement between the two boys and attacked her son without provocation. She said Chet truly feared for his life and acted in self-defense, adding that he didn't anticipate or wish for *this terrible outcome* and will never forgive himself for what ended up happening.

Although all of that was technically true, it didn't take into account the context of who Chet was and what his presence, or more accurately, what his permanent absence meant to the other students. No less than twenty-nine students and four teachers registered formal complaints during his suspension; including a combination of physical threats, verbal abuse, extortion, plagiarism, vandalism, and forgery. Each of them said they didn't report any of these earlier because they were afraid of retribution from him if they did.

Even his sidekicks Teddy and Johnny spoke out against him, saying they never agreed with his bullying and got caught up in things because they thought Chet was funny. By the time they realized what a *bad seed* he was—both of them used this string of language—they were afraid to try to separate themselves from *his ruling thumb.* They ended up serving weeklong suspensions and were put on permanent probation until their graduation the following year. They never acted out again and became model, albeit mediocre, students.

Of all the people who shared an opinion about Chet and the events that had taken place that afternoon, two that were conspicuously silent were Josh's parents. When they learned the news, they quietly came to retrieve their son's body. It was wrapped in a black shroud emblazoned with the shield of the Wyatt School of Sorcery. They accepted an apology from the school, but aside from that exchange asked or said nothing about the incident. Their son was dead, and there was nothing they or the school could do to change that fact.

The guilt about his role in the events leading up to the death of Josh ate at Dobbler. The friendship of the two boys, which started awkwardly when Josh needed academic help and Dobbler just needed a peer to talk to, had grown over the years into a strong bond. They understood each other implicitly, and treated each other like brothers. Breaking that bond was by far the most powerful blow Chet could ever throw.

Dobbler became more and more reclusive after the terrible events of that afternoon. He wore a brave face in class and continued to excel academically, but he made little effort to interact socially with the other students. Many of them could have intervened over the years of Chet's bullying, but they had always chosen not to, and that apathy was something Lane would never forgive. He escaped the constant feelings of loss and loneliness through his artwork, and longed to somehow bring some kind of meaning to his friend's death.

Due to the overwhelming mountain of evidence regarding Chet's character, his actions on the quad that day prompted his final expulsion. He and his mother stayed in Ravenwood for another week to appeal the decision. Ultimately, Chet was stripped of his sorcery student status, meaning a permanent block-spell enchantment was placed on him. The spell was designed so that only the caster would be able to undo it; that being Headmaster Clark, who was most certainly not intimidated by Chet.

Eventually, the bully and his mother gave up on appealing and started the long, sad journey back to where they came from.

CHAPTER 7

After copying The White Book, Serra spent the next several months learning the language of Pallous. One of the skills shared by students studying the magical arts is the ability to work with language. Many of the classes at Wallace and Wyatt were dedicated to the mastery of vocabulary, grammar, and syntax, as those are vital to proper spell-casting. Just saying the right words in the right order isn't adequate. The way each word is articulated, emphasized, and timed in relation to the other words, can change the strength, meaning, or target of a spell.

The ancient people Pallous and Obsidian tried to teach were unprepared to grasp this. They were too scared, too dense, or too focused on their own mundane lives to open their minds and learn from the gods. Thus the languages were lost when Pallous and Obsidian left Hyboria. Before leaving they wrote their books, half in their own tongue and half in Hybor, and placed them in a mountain cave where the cold dry air preserved them until they could be later discovered.

Luckily for Serra, Pallous's original translation seemed to be devoid of errors, at least there were none she was able to identify through her studies. It *was* produced by a god, so the fact that it was perfect shouldn't have been much of a surprise. Over time the language started to make intuitive sense to her. The genesis of this was when she spotted single word translations about which she was already aware, such as lumea: illuminate, and aerjou: levitate. Beginning with this simple base, she experimented with more complex spells and found them to have equally complex Hybor equivalents. This allowed her to link up more vocabulary words and grammar.

The first real breakthrough was deciphering pronouns such as *my, his,* or *these,* which allowed Serra to target spells without having to lift her arm to point at things. The more comfortable she became with the translation, the less elegant the divinity taught at Wallace seemed to her. Pointing and grunting a word or two was certainly not the most graceful way to cast spells.

Another part of this was decoding conjunction words like *and, if,* or *when,* which allowed her to couple together typical spell words to make more complete sentences, generating doubly complex and better-targeted spells.

Her teachers seemed to lack the concept that simple but powerful words such as these could be part of a spell. Regardless of all the lecturing they did on the importance of syntax and grammar, the reality of what they taught was rote memorization. While this method was sufficient in certain situations, it didn't allow for flexibility should things change, and there was no emphasis on the development of novel spells. The more she learned, the more she realized Wallace was graduating experts in toddler-speak.

The second breakthrough, and the much more important one, happened the day she learned that *any* sentence said in the language, not just what the school referred to as *enchanted action words,* could become a spell if done with the correct focus and intent. This opened a whole new world of creativity. In a given class at Wallace the students might spend a whole afternoon practicing levitation by pointing to a cup and saying "aerjou" over and over until they got it right. With her newfound knowledge, she could keep her hands in her lap and successfully cast a spell that translated to: *Levitate the cup, move it to the sink, and rinse it under the water.*

The significance of this was immediately clear to her. The only limit to the power of a cleric fully engrossed in the language would be his or her own creativity. As she sat in class each day learning spells one by one, her contempt for being subjected to an inferior method of teaching continued to build. She wondered if it were possible that no other person besides her figured out this better way to learn to be a cleric. Having intimate knowledge of the language while her teachers spat out only a collection of key words gave her a feeling of superiority over them as well as a sense of pity for her classmates.

Then she thought about the ultimate expert in the language, the original teacher, Pallous himself. A professor like Mr. Strickland heaped admiration on him, and yet never bothered to read the god's book for himself. Every time she sat down to study her notebooks with their pilfered information, she wondered why this was. She chalked it up to hubris, which further lessened her opinion of them and the process.

Studying his book made her feel a kinship with Pallous. She fantasized about being alive during his time. He'd be her sage and she'd follow as his disciple. She'd defend his honor as people ignored him or chastised him. She imagined them thinking of Pallous as someone who went from town to town trying to teach people, and them thinking of him as a traveling novelty act. The people of that time hadn't the capacity for the level of respect Pallous deserved.

Even if she couldn't be alive back then, she wished at least there was someone to converse with in the white language. That would make it much easier to engross herself in learning it, but she knew it was impossible. Being exposed for copying the book was a risk she wasn't willing to take.

This concern made her unwilling to open up with anyone associated with Wallace, especially Charlie and Kelly. While she considered them school friends, they were far from trusted confidantes. Their definition of a secret was something that needed to be heard by at least one other person or else it didn't count.

Maybe this idea had rubbed off on Serra, or maybe she needed to boast about her deviousness. Whatever the reason, she felt compelled to reveal the secret she'd learned, and she knew of only one person in Hyboria who could both appreciate and make use of the information: Lane Dobbler.

Serra made her way across campus toward the front gate. The setting was a testament to the beauty of nature. Enormous ancient trees, larger than the buildings surrounding them, filled the landscape. Groundskeepers kept them neatly manicured and well cared for. The massive arboreal monoliths were the pride of the school and many had been there long before Ravenwood was founded.

She passed onto the cramped and winding streets of town. There were very few straight lines or right angles designed into the original blueprint, mostly because the founders decreed that the structures spare the trees. This rule was followed for renovations and expansions throughout the existence of Ravenwood.

Wherever possible, trees and plants were included in all construction plans, which generated a lot of beauty in the eye of artists and naturalists, but made the jobs of the city planners and architects that much more onerous.

As she walked, she could feel her heart beating in her chest. She had heard a lot about Dobbler from her friends Charlie and Kelly, and was told by Vice Principal Reed that his prowess as a sorcerer matched hers as a cleric. Other than that, she didn't know much about him. She'd seen him on several occasions, but her palms got sweaty and she couldn't think of anything to say when he was around. Being so bold as to walk to his dorm room and sit with him was completely out of character for her, but she realized her character was changing.

When she entered the building where Dobbler lived, her pulse was thumping in her ears and she felt a tingling sensation in her stomach. Having not been in a Wyatt building before, it took her time to get her bearings, but eventually she found her way into his hallway and tentatively knocked on his dorm room door.

Almost instantly, Dobbler was standing in his entryway wearing a rumpled shirt and short pants. The vulnerability generated by his attire made him look that much more adorable to Serra. He had high cheekbones and a long, distinguished nose. His hair and eyes were dark, and he wore a small beard on his chin. He reflexively brushed some of his tousled hair out of his face and over his ear when he saw who had come knocking. He hurriedly said, "Um, hang on," and closed the door. Then he reopened it slightly and said, "Just a minute," then closed it again.

Serra felt her face flush with the exchange. She could not have been more uncomfortable standing there. Time dragged on as she heard frantic movement inside. Eventually, the door opened, and Dobbler was wearing a dress shirt and long pants. He said, "Sorry about that."

"It's okay." Serra wringed her hands nervously in front of her.

Dobbler stood holding the door, not knowing what to say. Eventually he got out, "Can I... Um... Can I help you?"

"Hi. You're Dobbler? I'm Serra. From Wallace? Kelly and Charlie's friend."

"Yeah, I remember."

"Can I come in?" All of the sudden her mouth was a desert.

Dobbler continued staring for a moment. Finally, he quickly blurted, "Sure. Yes, of course. Come on in." He backed up to allow her space to get by.

Serra entered and immediately felt a sense of wonder. She was expecting his room to be plain, boring, and boyish, but she was momentarily dumbstruck. There were numerous drawings and paintings on the walls. She took her time, allowing her eyes to drink in the room, and then glanced back at Dobbler. "Did you make these?"

Dobbler, looking embarrassed, answered, "Yeah. I like to paint."

Serra walked to each painting and studied them one by one as an involuntary "I'll say" left her lips. There were beautifully crafted landscape scenes, views of buildings with interwoven trees and vines, portraits of people doing ordinary things. There were no pictures that depicted the use of magic. "They're amazing. You're a real artist."

Dobbler quickly brushed off the compliment and offered her a seat and a drink. She nodded and he poured each of them a glass of water and sat down across from her.

She took a sip. "Ooh. Cold water just sitting there in a pitcher. It must be nice having control over the elements." She nervously sipped again. "I heard about what happened to your friend. It must've been horrible."

Dobbler was quiet for a moment before saying, "It was. Josh was a good guy. My best friend."

"They expelled the guy who did it?"

"Yeah, one day too late." Dobbler wanted to admit that although it was sad and unfair that it took the murder of his best friend, life was much better for him now. He no longer walked the campus feeling paranoid that he would be grabbed and assaulted at any moment. It seemed like the whole school could breathe again without Chet around. He said, "Everything changed that day."

"Speaking of everything changing," said Serra, "I wanted to ask you about the black magic book. The one at your school?"

Dobbler raised his eyebrows. "You mean Obsidian's book? What about it?"

Serra shifted in her chair. "Have you ever seen it? I mean, do they let you guys?"

"No. Supposedly it's in a basement somewhere under some magical protection ward. They don't let students down there."

"You should find a way."

Dobbler looked confused. "What do you mean? I always assumed the book was so old it would fall to dust if you touched it and that's why they didn't let us near it."

"I thought the same thing about The White Book." She felt another wave of nervousness sour her stomach. "But that wasn't true in my case and I'm betting it's not in yours."

"You saw the book of divinity?" asked Dobbler excitedly.

"Saw it. Touched it…" Serra grinned. "And copied it."

Dobbler gawked at her. "Why did you do that?"

"Mostly out of boredom… And I was curious to handle a book made by a god. So I convinced my vice principal to give me a private moment with it, and when she did I used a duplication spell to bring home a copy. For the past few months I've been studying the language. I'm pretty much fluent now, but that's not the point. I learned anything can be a spell if I want it to be. It's really simplified my life." She stammered for a moment. "Well, it's complicated my life too because I have to watch what I say and how I say it." She took a deep breath and looked right at Dobbler. "No one knows about this but me." She smiled. "And now you."

Dobbler leaned back in his chair. "So you think I should do the same thing with Obsidian's book."

Serra nodded.

"Why? They teach us every spell we'll ever need at Wyatt."

"Not every spell. That's impossible without learning the language."

"Why tell me all of this? What's in it for you?"

"I don't know," shrugged Serra. "I had to tell somebody, and it can't be anyone at my school. Everybody knows you're the best student at Wyatt. Plus Charlie and Kelly said you were nice."

Dobbler blushed, remembering the conversation he'd had with the two girls about Serra.

"Do yourself a favor and get a hold of that book," she said.

"I'll think about it. I feel the same way you do about being bored in class, but I don't know if breaking rules is the way to make my life more exciting."

"Believe me, it'll be the best thing you'll ever do."

CHAPTER 8

There were frantic whispers all around Ravenwood.

"A man has been found."

"At the gate."

"He's lying there not moving."

"They think he's dead."

Serra rushed through the front gate to find a gathering of clerics and sorcerers just outside the boundary of the town.

"Well who is he then?"

"He's not one of us. Look at how he's dressed, and look at the size of him."

"Who put him here? The monsters have never gotten this close before."

"Is he dead? He looks dead."

Serra looked through the crowd at a man lying in a heap. By the marks in the gravel road behind him it looked like he'd crawled to where he was. Through the throng of people she wasn't able to make out every detail, but she noticed in the waning sunlight reflecting off of his leather armor that it was coated in a layer of blood. He looked so sad and pathetic, and a drive inside of her called out to do something to help him.

At first, she hesitated because no one else seemed to be moving to do anything. It was as if there were an invisible ten-foot barrier around the man. Serra couldn't tolerate all of the people standing there with arms crossed or in pockets, watching him bleed to death. It was made worse by the fact that most of the observers had advanced healing skills they were neglecting to use.

During the past two years since copying the book, Serra had immersed herself in the language as she gradually built a relationship with Dobbler. He had followed her lead by making himself a copy of what was uninspiredly referred to as *The Black Book*. While the structure of the languages was very different, they found being together made the learning process easier. Having a secret they felt comfortable in sharing only with each other brought them closer together while at the same time distanced them from everyone else.

She hadn't hung out with her friends much, always telling them she needed to study. She had developed a growing distaste for what was being taught at Wallace and by extension all of the people teaching it and learning it. While she remained cordial, she no longer felt stewardship toward them or the school. Watching them do nothing in this emergency situation solidified that feeling.

"Let me through!" Serra pushed her way between a group of the gawkers and kneeled next to the injured man. In the dimming light, she could see deep wounds down and across his back glistening with blood. All other exposed skin looked ashen. Serra held her hands over him and whispered, "Eofa sylmea. Olmba raehoum." His wounds slowly began to mend. When they were completely closed, she put her hands on the back of his head. His long hair was matted and dusty. She said, "Aerja ulrab." The man started gasping for air and slowly moving his limbs. She bent down to his ear and whispered, "It's okay. You'll be okay now."

"What are you doing?!" scolded a familiar voice behind her. "Get away from him! You don't know anything about that…person! He could be diseased or cursed!" She turned her head to see Mr. Strickland's hate-filled eyes fixed on her.

Serra twisted her body as she waved her hand in a sweeping arc at the throng behind her, screaming "Umbral valeesy!" An unseen force compelled them two steps back. Some of them struggled to keep their balance. She settled in a crouch and focused her attention back to the man lying in the dirt. "Can you get up? You need to get up now." She put her hand on his shoulder, encouraging him to stand.

He stumbled to his feet but was somewhat hunched over. Serra picked up his massive sword and handed it to him. He held it with both hands in front of him. She touched his muscular arms and repeated, "Aerja ulrab." He sprang to his full height, which was more than a head taller than any of the onlookers. He looked at Serra, confused.

"Okay, we need to go," she said while lightly tugging his arm.

He lurched forward, following her through the stunned crowd and past the gate.

Serra hurriedly led the stranger down the main street until she pointed out a small alleyway, into which they turned and ducked. They stopped for a moment to catch their breath. They were both physically fit, him especially so, but he was recovering from traumatic wounds and extensive blood loss and she was full of nervous energy.

Once she was mentally settled, she cast another spell and then looked him in the eyes and said, "We're going to walk through this alley to the next street over. Stay calm and don't make a fuss. No one will notice you. Put your sword away. It will get us spotted. What's your name?"

He hadn't the mental capacity to do anything other than follow her directions. She helped him sheath his sword in the scabbard on his magically repaired back. He nodded thanks and replied, "Rugen."

Serra scanned the alley in both directions and said, "Okay. I'm Serra. We'll talk more when we get to where we're going. For now, keep quiet and follow me."

The pair walked at an unhurried pace onto the street beyond the alley, Rugen following her close behind. There were robed townspeople jogging every which way, mostly toward the main gate, but no one seemed to be looking in the direction of Rugen and Serra. They proceeded onward through the town, always moving casually and in shadows wherever possible.

Rugen tried scanning the architecture of Ravenwood as they moved, but in the low light, all he was able to appreciate was lush plant life. It was as if the buildings were squeezed into the spaces between the trees, shrubs, and vines.

After many turns, the alley opened into a wide dirt road lined on the side opposite them with brambles. Rugen saw a small, cracked, wooden door buried in thorny vines up ahead. On closer inspection the door was attached to a tiny and dilapidated hut. It didn't look like a place anyone would enter willingly, or even notice among the swirling plant life surrounding it. Just the sight of it made him think of slugs and spider webs. Serra was heading directly for it, so he followed her.

She took his hand in hers and quietly murmured a lengthy statement ending with, "Vleombari Serra Frye," then opened the door and went through. She had to duck to pass under the header.

Rugen crouched down and squeezed through the cramped door, a subtle flash of blue-white light popped into his vision. Inside the hut was nothing he would have expected. It was a nicely appointed room with a bed, chairs, desk, fireplace, and rug. Rugen couldn't fathom how any of this fit into the space he had perceived from the outside. "What is this place?"

Serra put her arms out, showing the space. "My room."

"I don't understand."

"I'll have to explain it to you later. The spells I cast on you were temporary, only meant to give you enough strength to get off the ground. When they wear off, you'll fall unconscious again. You should get into bed now." She pointed to a well-adorned and plush bed to his right.

Rugen blinked several times as his eyelids started getting heavier. He asked, "The cuts on my back will open up again?"

Serra walked to the bed and pulled back the covers. "No, those I fixed permanently. Lie down. I'll talk to you when you wake up."

Rugen did as he was told and almost immediately felt an overwhelming wave of exhaustion. He tried to comprehend all that had happened but his brain involuntarily shut down.

CHAPTER 9

There was a knock on the door of Serra's room at G. Wallace. When nobody answered, several people, led by Strickland, burst through. They saw no one. They checked the bathroom, bureau, and under the bed, but all were empty. Strickland had fury in his eyes as he growled, "She must be using a hiding spell."

In the other manifestation of Serra's room, Rugen spent most of the next three days asleep. He would wake up briefly, accepting small amounts of broth or water. Otherwise he slept, dreaming of the journey, the battles with the gmorks, and the ursinox attack. Serra kept almost a constant vigil as she nursed him back to health, only leaving briefly for supplies.

Taking care of him gave her a renewed sense of purpose. She used to be only interested in becoming the best student. Then it was to learn Pallous's language. Having mastered both things, she decided to devote all of her energy to care for this wounded stranger. Beat up as he was, it must have been a terrible ordeal journeying through the wilderness. There was a reason he'd come to Ravenwood, and a reason she was the one who found him. She looked forward to finding out what those were.

When Rugen finally awoke, he looked around with squinting eyes. Light was streaming in from the two windows that were on the far wall, illuminating and nourishing potted plants that were all over the room. Under the windows was a couch with a pillow and a neatly folded blanket. Next to that was a table with bread, a pitcher, and some other wrapped items, presumably food. Across from the bed on which he lay was a desk with a pile of books and notebooks on it. He saw two doors, one next to the desk and the other opposite the windows, and a tall bureau. Bleary-eyed, he asked, "Where am I?"

Serra offered him a bowl of broth. "In my room. I'm taking care of you."

He took the bowl and sipped. "What about the people who were looking for us?"

"Well they haven't found us in three days, so I'm guessing we're safe."

"They don't know where you…" Rugen's face changed to a look of shocked surprise as he interrupted himself. "Wait…three days?"

"There's a lot to explain. Drink your soup. Would you like some bread with it?"

Rugen nodded as he sipped the broth again.

Serra walked to her table and unwrapped the bread. "My name is Serra. I'm a cleric. Well, not technically. I'm in my final year of cleric school. In fact, graduation is next week. Although I think I may have blown that by assaulting Mr. Strickland…" She said, trailing off. After a moment she asked, "Do you know much about magic?"

Rugen shook his head.

"After I found you I cast a spell that made people not notice us. That's how we were able to walk the streets without being seen."

"We were invisible?"

"Not exactly. We do call it an invisibility spell, but in the brightness of the day it's nearly useless. Even in the dark people will notice you if you yell and wave your arms. It still requires stealth and shadows to be effective, but it got us here safely."

"What I remember is you walking me into a creepy hovel which somehow turned into this place. I must have been really out of it." Rugen dipped his bread into the broth and took a bite.

"No. You're exactly right on all accounts. In reality, we're on school grounds right now in my room." She paused for a minute as she thought through the best way to make him understand. "It's hard to explain. If someone were to walk down the hall and knock on my door, we wouldn't hear it. If they came in, they wouldn't find us. We're in my room, but not in their reality of my room. To get to where we are now, they'd have to go through the same hovel door we used and say the same spell I said, but few people notice that old hut, and nobody knows the exact words of the spell."

Rugen gestured to the room's front door. "What if we open that and walk out right now?"

"We would exit through the same creepy door you saw. I wouldn't recommend it in the middle of the day. I've been coming and going after sunset when the light is low."

"This is all really strange."

"If by *strange* you mean *great*, then yeah. And lucky. Lucky for you to be rescued by the only person here who seemed to care—and knew enough to help you and keep you hidden.

"Why is that? Why didn't they care?"

Serra turned the chair at her desk to face Rugen and said, "Since the monsters came we've not had any visitors, and even before that surprise visitors weren't common. In fact I'd never heard of one. Finding a bloodied and half-dead man lying face down at our front gate couldn't have meant anything good in their eyes."

"And in your eyes?"

She paused and took a breath. "Well, I didn't think it could possibly be good either, but nothing is good right now in the world, right?" She smiled. "I've been doing all of the talking. What's your story?"

"I'm from a small village called Mourain. A guy named Gordon, a great soldier and a great man, showed up on my doorstep… I guess it was a couple of weeks ago now." He shook his head in disbelief as he calculated the length of time. "He told me about his plan to rid Hyboria of the monsters. I joined his team and we traveled and fought together. Even though I wasn't with them for long, I couldn't help but think of him as my mentor. He had that effect on people. He wanted to come here requesting some of you to join him, but we were ambushed… They slaughtered us. Everyone's dead." The words caught in Rugen's throat. "I thought I was dead too."

"So what are you going to do now?"

"Appeal to…" He gestured to the general area around them. "Whoever's in charge here. For help for my trip back to Mourain. I can't go by myself with what's out there. When I get home I'll just resume my old miserable life. The quest is over." He looked at the floor. "Gordon is dead."

"Not going to happen. What's the other option?" asked Serra, with eyebrows raised.

"What do you mean?" Rugen held the bowl up to his mouth and drank the rest of his broth.

Serra took the bowl from him, refilled it, and handed it back. "You *have* to continue the quest...to honor your friend's memory. You said he was on his way here to find clerics and sorcerers. You found a cleric, and I know a sorcerer who will help. Maybe we can rid the world of these things."

"You and me and one other person against the road? Against the beasts who are out there? Have you seen them?"

"No, but I've seen the damage they cause. I took care of some of the people they wounded while in Lundgren a few summers ago. I saw the looks in their eyes. I heard the stories." They both sat in silence for a moment. "Lundgren is probably where Gordon was taking you next. They have a school there. A warrior school."

"Why do you trust me? Why would you help me?"

"There's nothing for me here anymore. Long before I met you, I knew I was finished with this place. I found something that makes me more powerful than any cleric here. I've had to hide what I know because, from what I've seen, the school will consider me a threat. The more I'm around Ravenwood, the more at risk I am. Let me talk to a sorcerer I know. The three of us can go to Lundgren and raise an army."

CHAPTER 10

Under the cover of night, Serra walked the empty streets of Ravenwood. It had been five days since she'd rescued Rugen. She was waiting for classes to end at Wyatt before talking to Dobbler about coming with them. She hadn't wanted to disturb the last bit of his formal education, but with his graduation being a couple days away, she figured it was time.

Wallace's ceremony was the day after Wyatt's, but she hadn't felt in tune with her school for a long time. With her actions outside of the front gate, she assumed the feeling was more than mutual. She planned on being far away from Wallace that morning. She decided that leaving without collecting one silly piece of parchment wasn't going to make her any less of a cleric.

She slipped into the sorcery school dormitory with full knowledge that her invisibility spell wouldn't work because of the close quarters inside, but she figured the students there either wouldn't know her or care about her. Luckily, the halls were pretty empty, and she only came across a small handful of students who were too interested in their own conversations to pay her any mind. Just like at Wallace, while the presence of the sister school's students in the dormitories at night wasn't technically allowed, it was mostly ignored, especially near the end of the term.

She made it to Dobbler's room without attracting attention.

Dobbler opened his door part of the way, peered through the space, and grinned at her. "How's it going, Miss Fugitive?"

"You know about that?"

"It's going around." He smiled, and then poked his head into the hallway, scanning both directions. "Trust me, I know what it's like to feel like an outcast."

Seeing Dobbler check the hallways gave Serra a wave of paranoia, so she hurried into his room. She walked directly to the pitcher of water sitting perfectly cool on his table and poured herself a cup. Even the world's most powerful cleric couldn't control the elements as well as a fledgling sorcerer.

The two of them sat and Dobbler started the conversation by saying, "So I've heard lots of stories about what you did. What's your side?"

Knowing how a juicy bit of gossip gets passed around and twisted to fit the storyteller's whim, Serra wasn't surprised to be questioned by Dobbler, but she was eager to find out what he knew. "What are people saying?"

"I've heard theories. He's your boyfriend. He's your brother. You two are responsible for the monsters and we need to find you and burn you at the stake. You know, stuff like that."

"And what do you believe?"

"I don't have to believe anything now that you're in my room ready to tell me what really happened. Why are you helping him?"

"Basic kindness? A distaste for watching a person lying in the dirt bleeding to death when you have the power to help him. I mean, all those teachers and students were standing around doing nothing." She shook her head. "I feel like I don't fit in with those people anymore. I've been done with Wallace for a long time. We're leaving tomorrow night."

"Whoa. Whoa." Dobbler put his hands up in a stopping gesture. "I didn't expect all of this; done with Wallace?"

"It's been a long time coming. This current situation is just the catalyst."

So you are throwing your career away? For him? It makes no sense."

"I'm not throwing my career away. I know more about white magic than anyone here. Someday I'm going to revolutionize the teaching of divinity."

Dobbler nodded as he said, "I can see that working out well. Parents tripping over each other trying to get their kids into a school run by a drop-out."

"You don't have to be a jerk about it!" snapped Serra as she jumped to her feet. "I thought you were my friend."

Dobbler joined her in standing and, in a calming voice, said, "All right, all right, I was teasing you. Please, sit down and tell me more about this guy. Is he going to bring an end to us like I keep hearing?"

They both sat. "No. Quite the opposite. He's going to save us. All of us. I'm taking him to Lundgren so he can raise an army to wipe out these monsters."

Dobbler blinked. "No offense to the guy, but his resume before meeting you wasn't very stellar. Lying beaten and bloodied, half dead in the street. How is he going to be able to raise an army by himself?"

"Not by himself. He has a cleric…" She looked into her water cup. "And hopefully a sorcerer."

Dobbler was silent for a moment, staring at her. "So that's why you're here? To ask me to come with you to find certain doom on the road to Lundgren. No thanks."

"You're right about one thing, Lane," started Serra. "There is doom out there on the roads, and if it's just him and me it will be certain. But it won't be if you're with us."

Dobbler frowned. When Serra Frye used his first name, it opened his heart, and whatever she wanted from him was hers.

"Look, there's nothing for me in Ravenwood. Mentally I checked out after I realized I knew more than my professors. After I found the book I started wondering why I was here, and then you fell into my lap." She stared into his eyes intently, emphasizing the word *you*. "It's almost like it's part of a grand plan. Like Pallous is guiding me. I believe in Rugen. That's his name, by the way. He needs me, and I need his quest."

Dobbler said nothing as he stared at the floor, a flurry of thoughts were rushing through his head. "The men he was traveling with were all killed by the horrible things out there. Massacred right in front of him." Serra looked away and said, almost to herself, "I couldn't imagine." She reached over to hold both his hands in hers. "You and me? We can prevent that. The three of us will make a good team. I *have* to leave Ravenwood. The sooner the better. I don't trust any other sorcerers. If you don't come with us, it's just me and him on the road alone, and our fate will be sealed."

Dobbler always liked Serra; initially from afar, and since Josh's death their relationship had been gradually blossoming. He fantasized about someday pledging himself to her. A request for him to take part in their probable death wasn't what he envisioned for a relationship, but it was all that was being offered to him. If he didn't agree to go, he feared he might never see her again. Either she'd die on the road or she'd always think of him as the "jerk" who let her down. There was no decision to be made. He looked her in the eyes and responded, "What do I need to bring?"

CHAPTER 11

The next afternoon, Serra was in her room reorganizing and repacking all the provisions she had collected for the journey to Lundgren. It was her fourth time going through everything. She was a little panicked due to a combination of what was facing her on the road, seeing her parents for the first time since the monsters prevented travel, and the fact that she'd spent a week living with an enormous man who didn't quite meet her standards of hygiene.

Due to the limited availability of dorms, only seniors were allowed the option of a single room. Freshmen were housed in large barracks, and the students in the middle years lived in groups of two or three. Serra never had the same roommate for more than a year, and some of them managed only a semester. The break-up was usually mutually requested and more to do with Serra's obsessiveness than any other reason, although she wouldn't admit to that.

Rugen couldn't help but be obtrusive, especially considering he wasn't allowed to leave the room. No matter how hard he tried, there was no way he could make Serra fully comfortable with the arrangement.

Rugen sat on the chair sharpening his dagger with a stone tool. It was the second day in a row he had worked on it, and Serra suspected he had done the same earlier in the week with his sword across her desk while she was out talking to Dobbler. She came back to find her personal items displaced and a mess of stone dust, which infuriated her.

Seeing that he was sharpening the dagger again was more than she could handle without saying something. "Do you have to do that in here? I hate having the little piles of dust everywhere. Even with magic I can never find it all."

"Would you rather I do it outside?" he taunted. "Maybe I could introduce myself to one of your professors while I'm out there."

Serra sighed. "Why do you need to sharpen the dagger anyway? You just did it yesterday and haven't stabbed anyone since then… To my knowledge."

He put down the dagger and stone, reached under the bed, slid out several pieces of carved wood, and lay them next to him on the bed.

Serra stood and walked over to him. "You had asked me for blocks of wood. With everything going on I forgot. What are they?"

Rugen inspected the carvings, saying, "I don't know. They aren't very good. I wanted something to commemorate the guys who got me here. I figure when we got back on the road I'll find a good place to lay them to rest."

Serra sat next to the carvings and picked one up. It was a crudely shaped man holding a pitchfork. "This is amazing." She looked at Rugen, who continued to stare at the line up, and said, "Now I feel bad complaining about the mess."

"I'm sorry about that. I tried to clean up, but I'm not a very good housekeeper."

She looked at the pitchfork man and asked, "Who is this one for?"

"That's Billy. He was a farmer." He paused and their eyes met briefly, and then he looked back at the carving, drawing her gaze there. "He was a doctor too. In one of our tussles with the gmorks, Casey's shoulder was cut pretty good and Billy sewed him up." He picked up another carving and handed it to Serra. She could clearly see a man squatting over a fire with a rabbit on a spit. "This is Casey. He was a trapper and outdoorsman. He kept us fed while we were on the road."

Serra admired the delicate lines and curves on Casey's carving. She would have expected a dagger to be an inelegant implement. It was obvious Rugen put a lot of effort into these. "They're beautiful. I'm really impressed. I'm sure your friends would appreciate them." She set down the carvings and picked up third. It was the bust of a man with what appeared to be fire instead of hair. "Who is this one?"

He smiled. "That's JJ. He had red hair and a fiery personality to go with it. I was trying to be creative."

"You certainly were!" remarked Serra with her hand on her chest. "These are all so wonderful." She set down JJ's figurine and picked up the last two. One was another bust, and the other was the image of a delicately crafted knife. The bust was similar to JJ's but with normal hair, and it seemed like Rugen hadn't yet carved a line for the mouth. "And these?"

"The dagger is for Gordon."

"Oh," said Serra. She set down the last bust and looked over the dagger more intently. She knew how much Rugen valued his mentor.

"He told me a story about giving a bone dagger to his son Wil on his eighteenth birthday. A few years later Wil was killed by gmorks while out scouting. When Gordon led a search party, all they found was the dagger. Gordon kept it as a remembrance of his son until the day he died." He took a breath. "He promised he'd honor Wil's memory by using the dagger on the man who was ultimately responsible for his death. It's lost now, and so is his promise."

Tears were in Serra's eyes. She leaned over and half-hugged Rugen with one arm. "I'm so sorry about what happened to you and your friends. It's just dreadful."

Rugen rubbed away his own tears and wiped his nose with his sleeve. He wasn't able to speak, so the two of them just sat as he let the sadness envelope him.

After he collected himself, Serra asked about the final carving, the man without a mouth.

Rugen wiped his face again and said, "That's Thomas. He was Gordon's closest friend. I don't know if he said ten words to us the whole time we were out there."

Serra laughed. "The guy didn't talk so you made him with no mouth?"

Rugen shrugged and half-chuckled.

"I thought maybe it you hadn't yet finished it," she said, shaking her head. "It works." She rested her hand on top of his and said, "I appreciate you for showing me these. They're a beautiful tribute to your lost friends."

Rugen, feeling a little vulnerable, changed the subject, "So what's the plan now?"

"Tomorrow is my friend's graduation. While that's going on, I plan on sneaking into my school to find someone I need to say goodbye to. I know she's worried about me."

"Isn't that a risk?"

"Most of the students will be at Wyatt. The schools are pretty tightly knit, and with the graduations being on consecutive days, people go to both ceremonies. Also, the graduating Wyatt students like to put on a show. I mean, they can conjure lightning and fire and make things explode just by saying a few words, so it's pretty exciting. Most of the teachers go too. As you can imagine, the presence of the monsters on the roads the last couple of years prevents out-of-town family from being able to attend, so teachers go to both graduations to fill out the audience and support the kids.

"So who is it you need to see?"

"My vice principal. She'll probably be in her office going over the last bits of the plan for Wallace's graduation the next day."

"And then what?"

"And then when it starts getting dark, Dobbler will meet us here. Well, by here I mean out at the hovel door. I'll cast an invisibility spell on the three of us and we'll get on the road."

The next morning, Serra awoke on the couch to the sounds of Rugen doing push-ups on the floor next to her. She whined, "Can't you do that while I'm not here trying to sleep?"

In mid-pushup Rugen replied, "I will," and continued on.

Serra huffed and shook her head disapprovingly. Then she rubbed her eyes and stumbled into the bathroom. A few minutes later she emerged in her school uniform, having brushed her teeth and hair.

Rugen was seated at the table eating sesame cake and drinking water. He looked up at Serra and said, "I've been meaning to ask you, how does the bathroom, um… work? The running water?"

"Magic. Kind of like the door thing. There's a permanent portal at the bottom of the toilet. Anything you put in there gets automatically transported somewhere far away. I've never asked where specifically. I'm assuming it's deep in the woods."

"Hmph," responded Rugen. Then he thought about it for a moment and asked, "Do things ever come back the other way?"

"I'm pretty sure it's a one-way portal, or else the… unpleasant odors would waft back in." She laughed. "But if something did want to come back the other way, it'd be a pretty nasty trip."

"Why doesn't the rest of Hyboria have those toilet portals? Couldn't clerics install them anywhere they want?"

"Lundgren's had them for years. Pretty much have to with all the people who live there. Or else the town would be overrun with filth."

"And the running water? I'm assuming that uses portals as well?"

Serra grinned pridefully. "C'mon, I'll show you." She waved for him to follow her into the bathroom and then she turned the valve on and off as she explained, "It's a whole system. I don't pretend to understand it, but I imagine there're thousands of tiny portals installed in our local river. They transport water to all of the faucets all over Ravenwood." She flipped the valve open and closed a few more times. "And all the drains follow portals back to the river, somewhere downstream."

Rugen made a face of disgust. "That's great unless you live downstream." He paused, staring at Serra.

She stared back at him with a vacant look on her face.

"Mourain, where I'm from, is downstream."

She wasn't sure what to say. Visions of soapy sink water riding the flow of the river popped into her head. Whoever designed it must have accounted for other towns or the environment at large, but really she had no idea what happened downriver. The thought never occurred to her. "Well, it's a long way from Ravenwood to the next settlement. Maybe it just cleans itself before it gets there? I don't know." She felt uncomfortable and knew nothing she could say would change that. "Look, I gotta run. I'll bring back more food."

She spoke the words of the invisibility spell as she exited through the hovel door at the edge of the woods. The bright sun of the mid-morning would all but nullify the spell, but with the Wyatt graduation in full swing, she was hoping the streets would be relatively empty. The other thing she had going for her was that the founding sorcerers and clerics who designed Ravenwood had built in lots of hidden alleys and shortcuts. After six years, Serra was well versed in these. Even so, she couldn't help feeling nervous that the wrong person would identify her.

She made it through the streets to Wallace without coming across anyone who gave her a second look. As she slipped into the school she heard voices off to her right, so she ran to the left toward the back stairwell. Her feet were soundless as she moved. With all of the practice she had since finding Rugen, she was getting good at sneaking. Convinced there was no one approaching at the top of the stairs, she crept up, her eyes and ears on full alert.

When she reached the second floor, she saw closed doors and heard no movement. Vice Principal Reed's office was at the end of the hall around a bend. She walked confidently in that direction, but just as she was about to turn the corner, Mr. Strickland appeared.

For a second he looked startled, but he quickly regained his wits and screamed, "Hrousy emfoi!"

Serra jolted back against the wall. She felt a buzzing vibration starting at the center of her chest and emanating out through her face and extremities. She screamed an involuntary grunt of surprise and fear.

"Miss Frye!" Strickland bellowed. "I've been looking for you!"

Serra couldn't remember a time when he was nice to her, going back to when she met him in her first year history class. Her eyes darted in all directions. She felt completely helpless. Strickland's incantation prevented her from defending herself magically, and she was sure if she tried to run he could stop her with any number of spells.

With fury twisting his face, Strickland growled, "You had gotten away! Why would you come back here?" He paused for a moment, waiting for a response that never came, and then his expression changed to a smug smile. "Well guess what? You and I are the only ones in this building. You can scream all you want and no one will ever hear you."

Serra started to yell for help, but it was cut short by another spell cast by Strickland. Now she found she was unable to speak.

"On second thought, I'd rather you not scream."

He slowly started toward her, prompting her to back up, keeping her distance. He taunted, "You've always been so conceited. Such a know-it-all. From your first day here. Always better than everyone."

Serra continued to scan around for something, anything she could use to free herself from the situation. She couldn't believe she let him get the jump on her. For as much as she thought about herself and her abilities, the fact that he so quickly rendered her helpless was completely demoralizing.

Strickland saw the frantic look on her face and his smile widened. He stopped moving toward her and said, "There's nowhere to go. Except maybe that stairway behind you." She glanced backward. "Be careful if you make a run for it, though. I wouldn't want you to lose your balance and tumble down the stairs. What an unfortunate accident that would be." His eyes grew colder.

"I'll let you in on a little secret. You're nothing special. I've met a lot of pompous little snobs like you. Too many to count in fact. The only difference between you and them is they were too smart to find themselves alone in a building with me."

He gestured behind him. "I have a transport spell on my office door, just like the one I'm sure you used to keep me from finding you and your new friend. You know it's against school rules for students to use spells like that." He put his hand on his hip and shook his head in mock-disapproval. "Never mind. It no longer matters." He glanced over her shoulder and said, "Eorju jousyl."

Serra instinctively stepped back, bumping into a barrier that wasn't there before. She whipped around and pawed at the air with her hands. She felt a strong invisible resistance between her and the stairs that seemed to be flush with the walls, ceiling, and floor. She threw her body against it and felt no give.

Strickland laughed as Serra flailed at the invisible wall. "C'mon, let's go see where the spell on my office door goes. I have to tell you, though, you're not going to like it very much."

He turned and started in that direction, confident that Serra had no other option but to follow him. He called over his shoulder, "And in case you're wondering what will become of me when I'm finished with you. Reprimands and such? I'll be fine. Everyone will blame that bloody stranger you ran off with. And who am I to correct their story?"

Horrible thoughts ran through Serra's head about where Strickland was taking her and what he was planning to do. She was terrified, but did her best to maintain a brave face.

Strickland noticed the mental struggle written on her face and laughed. "Come along, Miss Frye."

She put her head down again and stared at the floor as a lump formed in her throat. She felt so stupid. She always told herself how clever she was, how much better of a cleric she was than everyone else. And here she was cowering, unable to use her abilities, unable to even speak, trapped in a hallway, facing a torturous death by a sadistic man.

As Strickland rounded the corner, a loud bong shocked her out of her misery. She jumped back and, with panic in her eyes, saw his body slump to the floor. Vice Principal Reed was standing over him, holding a large metal trophy over her head with a look of fury.

Serra stared at the scene, stunned for a few seconds. A wave of emotions enveloped her: fear, shame, doubt, surprise, relief, and when she saw Strickland's form lying helpless on the hall floor, a twinge of amusement and pity crept in. The fact that a man of such immense magical power and evil intention could be felled by a simple metal trophy was an irony she hoped would eat at him the rest of his life.

When Mrs. Reed was sure he was unconscious, she turned to Serra and gasped, "My dear! I had no idea Mr. Strickland was capable of, well, whatever that was. Are you okay?"

CHAPTER 12

Serra sat in Mrs. Reed's office, still shaken. Her voice and ability to do magic were restored, but she had yet to say anything. She wanted to let the vice principal speak first. She wasn't sure how much trouble she was in.

"I was around the corner listening to most of what he said," started Mrs. Reed. "I'm sorry if my delay in acting caused you more grief, but I wanted to make sure I knew what he was planning before he had the opportunity to deny it later. I suppose he's been lying to me for quite some time. Don't worry about him now. I cast the same spell he used on you so he can't do any magic, plus I added some binding spells to his arms and legs. He's not going anywhere, and he'll be very uncomfortable when he wakes up. Wallace guards will be here to collect him shortly."

Serra sighed deeply and said, "I'm sorry about this past week."

The two of them had always had a close connection. In fact, there was no student on campus Mrs. Reed thought more of than Serra. And Mrs. Reed was among a short list people at the school Serra fully respected and trusted. Giving Serra the benefit of the doubt wasn't difficult for the vice principal, but she wanted to hear the reasoning behind her actions with the strange man bleeding at the front gate. She responded, "Yes, about that. Explain yourself."

Serra told the story of rescuing Rugen, nursing him, housing him, and about the pending journey to Lundgren. She was crying as she finally let everything out.

"But why didn't you trust us, bring this man to me?"

"When I rescued him I kind of panicked. There were a bunch of sorcerers and clerics there, but no one was doing anything. The only person I recognized was Mr. Strickland, and he was being his awful mean self."

"I see," said Mrs. Reed as she tented her fingers. "So you and this warrior are going to save us, you say?"

"Not just us. There's a sorcery graduate coming along. Lane Dobbler."

"He's a graduate as of today. Had this been yesterday I would've been obligated to contact his school. What you're suggesting would constitute a serious violation of the Wyatt code of etiquette."

Serra looked at the floor, feeling betrayed.

"But, by now he's an official graduate and thus technically no longer the school's responsibility. When do you plan on leaving?"

Serra met her eyes and answered, "Tonight."

"Graduation is tomorrow!"

"I assumed I wouldn't be graduating after what I did. That and I've been missing all my classes recently."

Mrs. Reed stared quietly at Serra and then sighed. She said, "A few missed classes won't prevent you from graduating, and I'd guess where you're headed you don't need to have a diploma." She thought for a moment longer and then added, "To be honest, there's going to be a lot of smoothing over to do with professors and administrators before you should reappear. It might be best for us to let things cool down for a while."

Mrs. Reed suddenly stood and thrust out her open hand with a flourish, startling Serra.

Serra tentatively joined her and accepted the handshake with a confused look on her face.

With as much formality as she could muster, Vice Principal Reed said, "By the powers vested in me, you are a graduate of G. Wallace School of Divinity."

Serra was still a little confused, but ventured a thank-you.

They broke the handshake as Mrs. Reed came out from behind her desk. She put her arms around Serra's shoulder and said, "Congratulations, my dear. After you save the world, come back to me and pick up your diploma."

The two women left the office, pausing briefly to look at the unconscious body of Mr. Strickland. "You'd better get out of here before the guards come up and I have to explain your presence to them. They've been unsuccessfully searching for you, you know."

Serra hugged Mrs. Reed for a long time, and Mrs. Reed hugged her back, relishing the embrace.

"I know, dear. Now scoot before we're too late."

She ran down the hall and stairs, and kept on running until she got back to the hovel door and into her room.

It took a while to settle down from the day's events. Once she did, she managed to catch a nap on her sofa as Rugen slept in her bed. After waking up, she and Rugen spent the rest of the late afternoon going over the evening's plan. She had him visualize every turn, back alley, and landmark until he had it memorized, just in case they got split up. There wasn't much else to do while they waited for the sun to set and Dobbler to arrive.

Serra looked out the window and saw that the sky was in the process of turning from light blue to shades of pink and orange. She was wearing an ivory-colored form-fitting top and matching slacks. They had intricately patterned panels ornately sewn on by thick brown string. She pulled on a flowing ivory-colored robe with wide sleeve cuffs and a bright yellow sunburst emanating from the hem near her feet. It was an extravagance she'd purchased for herself to wear to graduation. She turned to Rugen and said, "It's time. Are you ready?"

He looked her up and down.

"Well?" she said.

He nodded distractedly, and the two of them gathered their travel supplies and headed through the door.

When they got outside, Dobbler was waiting for them in the shadows. He was a little shorter than Serra and wore a long dark coat with a high collar. Underneath was a leather vest serving as light armor. There was a dagger tucked into a sleeve at his belt, and his boots stretched to just below his knees. "It's a nice night to go get ourselves killed," he said, flatly.

"Good to see you dressed for it," said Serra, smiling.

Dobbler glanced at Rugen staring at her. "You too, but is it possible your brightly colored ensemble might get us noticed?"

Serra looked at herself and calmly said, "Syouj rhalrb," prompting the robe to darken into a drab, unobtrusive hue. "I can make it blend in or stand out. Whatever's appropriate."

Rugen had on full leather armor and helmet. His longsword and bag were strapped to his back, covering the long gashes in his vest left by the ursinox. He waved to Dobbler as Serra said, "This is the guy I told you about."

As the men shook hands, a voice came from behind some trees calling Rugen's name.

The three of them turned to see a hooded figure emerge from the dark. He was wearing the robe of a Wyatt professor, but his form was distorted, and it was hard to tell in the low light why that was. Rugen answered back in his most authoritative voice, "Who is that?"

The figure slowly approached until he could be better seen, and when he dropped his hood, red hair reflected in the waning light.

"JJ!" yelled Rugen with a wide grin.

As JJ's form came into view, the group made out that the distortion in his image was the shield strapped across his back and the sword at his hip. He wore a bushy ponytail and had a thick but close-cropped red beard. He wasn't much taller than Serra, who was tall for a woman, and he was massively muscled and athletic. He reached out for a forearm handshake. "How are you, Brother?"

Rugen, who was a giant by comparison, grasped his arm and pulled him in for a hug. "I didn't know you were... Where have you been?"

"I found my way into town through the woods. Since then I've been hiding out. No one else made it?"

"No," Rugen said simply. They both looked at the ground, unable to make eye contact with one another. Rugen continued, "It was horrible. I didn't see what happened, but I assumed the gmork got you."

"Not a chance," responded JJ. He motioned to the two magic users. "You found a new band of brothers I see."

"Hey!" said Serra, brushing back her cape and putting her hands on her hips to accentuate her form. "I'm no brother."

"Yes, I noticed that," said JJ, flashing his most charming smile. "Brother is a figure of speech between Rugen and me. I meant no offense, m'lady." He bowed playfully.

"She's not your lady," said Dobbler, feeling a visceral need to defend his friend. He pointed at Rugen, "I'm not his brother either. I'm here for Serra."

JJ laughed. "You're sweet on her?"

Dobbler snorted and glared at him.

"Calm down, everyone," said Rugen. "JJ's a spectacular fighter and a trusted friend. We'd be lucky to have him join us on the road." He looked at JJ. "You're planning on coming with us, right?

JJ shrugged. "What else am I gonna do?"

CHAPTER 13

The four travelers followed the road out of Ravenwood and continued along the Divine River. They didn't need magical illumination because of the light of the full moon. The fewer things to garner attention, the better Serra's invisibility spell worked.

"Who knows the way to Lundgren?" asked Rugen.

"I do," answered Serra. "I was there for a summer internship a few years ago."

"How far away is it?"

"I can't remember exactly. At least a four or five day walk. We'll make camp for the night after we clear some distance from Ravenwood."

"Good. How do you want to figure out the order for overnight security detail?" asked Rugen.

Serra and Dobbler looked at each other.

"Gordon said new guy gets first watch, but technically we're all new on this trip."

"When you're traveling with a cleric, there's no need for someone to stay awake and stand guard," answered Serra. "We know lots of ways to keep us safe from intruders."

"Right. I should have guessed. I suppose we don't need to collect wood for a fire either."

"I got that covered," said Dobbler.

JJ slapped Rugen on the back and said, "Boy, Gordon wasn't kidding when he said after we got to Ravenwood there'd be no more roughing it."

The group sat around the sorcerer's equivalent of a campfire. It was a flame eerily floating in mid-air a few inches off of the ground, shifting around and popping like a real fire, but without visible fuel underneath.

Dobbler hadn't used any kindling or tinder to light it. All he did was say, "Indagio," and the fire burst into existence. He smiled at Rugen, who was staring at the fire, lost in thought, and nonchalantly said, "Nice, huh?"

"How's it work?" asked Rugen.

"Just like any other spell. It runs on aughra. The actual fire you see is just for show. The visible flame, the sound it makes, and the heat it gives off are all separate components of the same spell. I could turn on or off any one of them without affecting the others, but I like having them all on, so I just say the default word that controls all of it."

"What do you mean? The heat isn't coming from the flame?"

"No, it's all separate. Oh and you'll like this. The heat doesn't get stronger the closer you get. Go ahead, put your hand in."

Rugen laughed and made no attempt to move.

"No, seriously." He got up and leaned into the flame, waving his hand around in it. It's just as hot in the center as it is out where the aura ends." He took a few steps back and felt for the edge of the spell. "It definitely gets colder right at this spot." He waved his hand in the air, pointing out where the heat from the spell ended. "Of course I could stretch out the aura as much or as little as I want, but that doesn't change the intensity of the heat. There's a limit to how far out it will go, but I never tested it because the bigger you make it, the more aughra you use, plus we don't want others to stumble through it and wonder where the heat is coming from."

Everyone was watching Dobbler now, fascinated.

"Go ahead and put your hand in the flame. In fact, you could lie down with your head completely engulfed in it and not notice anything but the light and the sound."

All three of them tentatively put their hands near the flame. Rugen jumped slightly as it popped and sizzled. JJ marveled, "You're right. I don't feel anything different regardless of where my hand is."

"It's more practical than a real fire. You can have it anywhere you want—in the desert where there's nothing to burn or in a forest where there's a lot to mistakenly burn. You could be floating on a raft in the middle of a lake and have the flame sitting right next to you. You could turn off the sight and sound parts and just have the heat, in case you don't want the light to be seen. It won't ignite anything or interact with the world in any physical way." He wafted the air toward his nose. "Because it doesn't need wood or other fuel it doesn't produce smoke or make your clothes smell. And it can be lit or extinguished with a word." He did this several times to prove his point. "It's very convenient. The only downside is you can't cook over it. There are spells you can use to cook food, but I found natural fire and smoky charcoal to be better for that."

Rugen was amazed. He put his hand in the fire again. "It must be fueled by something. What was that word you said?"

"Aughra. It's the life force of all living things. It's the reason there's so many trees and other plants all around Ravenwood. Living things give off invisible…" He paused as he thought about how to explain it. "Have you ever looked at a sunbeam coming in through a window and seen dust floating through the air? I always thought of aughra as kinda like that. Except it's not dust, and you can't see it. Sorcerers and clerics function best when there's a lot of life around them. Aughra comes off of us too, but plants produce a lot more. All of us wear something that's been enchanted to encourage it to flow toward us. It's called an attractor. It's usually a necklace, amulet, ring, or bracelet. That's one way we make sure we have the power to do spells even when there aren't a lot of living things nearby." He pulled a necklace from his robe with an ornate medallion the size of a large coin hanging from it.

Rugen pointed to the medallion and asked, "What about those things? Don't they need that aughra stuff to work too?"

"No. Magically-enchanted items don't need aughra to function and don't use the aughra they draw."

This was all new to Rugen, and he wasn't ashamed of sounding curious. "So what about us not needing a guard tonight?"

"You know that situation with my room?" started Serra. "Where you were sitting in plain view on my bed but anyone who walked through the door would find the room empty? What we're doing now is kind of like that. After the sun went down, I cast a similar spell for this area. It's called an *exclusion field*."

Rugen cautiously nodded.

"Where we are right now is how this exact spot was when I cast the spell. Time hasn't moved for us since then. Any number of things could be happening in this spot in reality right now. Monsters could be having a picnic right here."

She gestured to the area where the four of them were gathered, prompting them to look over their shoulders into the night. "Another group could pass through us, or it could be pouring rain." She waved toward the dark expanse. "Time is frozen for us, but it's pressing on out there as it always has. We just aren't a part of it. If I terminate the spell or we walk out of the area I designated, we'll be back on the world's time, but as long as you stay here, it will be as it is indefinitely. Nothing can see us, hear us, or find us by any means."

"Sounds powerful," responded Rugen. "Why not just continue the spell all the way to Lundgren? That way we'd never run into a gmork."

Serra shook her head. "Exclusion fields don't work like that. We can't leave the designated area without walking back into reality. I suppose you could cast the spell, walk ahead a bit, then cast the spell again, but that would be pretty tedious over miles and miles."

"And more dangerous," added Dobbler. "Every time we exit a field there's potential to be surprised by something hidden beyond the edge. Doing that hundreds of times every day increases your chances of being caught off-guard."

Serra thought about this for a second and then said to Dobbler, "Yeah, that makes sense." She looked at Rugen and asked, "Do you get it?"

Rugen stared into the fire. "Not really. But I'm good." He debated for a moment before commenting, "I didn't realize there were limits to what magic could do."

Serra and Dobbler looked at each other with eyebrows raised. Dobbler responded, "Oh, absolutely we have limits. There's no way to turn one living thing into another. So put any thoughts of turning a gmork into a mouse or a newt or something out of your mind."

"Magic helps us control things that are already there," added Serra. She gestured over their heads. "We couldn't whip up a hut out here out of nothing."

"We find new and amazing uses all of the time. It really just depends on how creative you can be," beamed Serra.

The group got quiet as they all contemplated recent events. Rugen struggled to wrap his brain around it all: leaving his father behind, sleeping out in the open, fighting demons, making new friends, losing them, and now discovering a world of magic and mystery. It was all too much to grasp. Eventually the swirling thoughts exhausted his mind and he drifted off to sleep.

CHAPTER 14

Rugen awoke to find it was still dark. Serra and Dobbler were already awake and chatting around the campfire spell as they drank from water skins. JJ was sleeping in the same spot as when Rugen had drifted off. In a gravelly and sleepy voice, Rugen said. "What's going on? Why are you guys up in the middle of the night?"

"It's morning. We were just about to wake you two," responded Serra.

"But it's still dark."

"No, it's not," said Dobbler. "Remember the spell Serra was talking about last night?" He looked to her and nodded. Serra undid the incantation and the light came up, blinding Rugen for a second and waking JJ, who moaned in protest.

Rugen put his hand to his face and said, "Hey!" as he scrambled to a seated position and rubbed his eyes. "How did you know there wasn't a pack of gmorks waiting to jump us?"

"We just checked a minute ago. Like I said last night, the spell only covers a certain area. By walking in any direction you can poke your head out from the aura and see what's going on in the real world."

"I'm sorry, it might take me a while to get used to this illusion zone," said Rugen.

"Exclusion field," corrected Serra.

"Right. Say you dropped the field, and there were gmorks waiting there. Couldn't you just cast a new field?" asked Rugen.

Serra shrugged. "Yeah. But then we'd have gmorks in our exclusion field with us."

Rugen thought for a moment and then asked, "What if you cast the spell over there?" he pointed to a distant spot, "and then we all ran into the field?"

"Then we'd be excluded from the exclusion field."

JJ shook his head quickly, like he was clearing cobwebs out of it. "So what are you guys drinking?"

Dobbler took a sip, looking satisfied. "Water from the Divine. Tastes like home."

"Is that the name of the river in the woods I heard us walking next to last night?"

"Yeah, it flows down out of the mountains into Ravenwood. We'll keep following it for a while until the road breaks off toward Lundgren," said Serra.

"How's it taste?" asked JJ, nodding at the water skin she was holding.

"See for yourself. I already filled all of them," she answered as she handed him a skin.

Once everyone was prepped and packed to go, Rugen reached into his bag and pulled out the palm-sized woodcarving of the bust with fire instead of hair and handed it to JJ.

JJ looked at it quizzically and asked, "What's this?"

"I was locked in a room for about a week unable to leave. All of you were dead. Last I saw, the ursinox was..." He stopped himself and looked at the ground, unable to meet JJ's eyes for a moment. "I figured there'd be no way to retrieve anything from the site, so I carved these as a memorial to each of you." He dug around the bag and pulled out two more wooden effigies and gave them to JJ.

A lump caught in JJ's throat as he was handed the man with the pitchfork. His eyes started getting red as he quietly said, "Is this for Billy?"

Rugen nodded and showed him the others. "I made one for everyone."

JJ studied them for a while and then looked up at Rugen. "Well, let's have a little funeral service and bury these things. The souls of our brothers will finally be at rest."

"They teach us how to pray at occasions like this in divinity school," said Serra, gently.

They walked across the open grass that shouldered the road and into the thinly wooded area where the river was flowing. There sat a large boulder behind a plot of dirt in the shape of a wide crescent.

The four of them gathered in the grass near the boulder, where Rugen showed Dobbler the carvings and explained who each one represented.

Dobbler kneeled in front of the boulder and said, "Oktuo qincke," causing the index finger on his right hand to glow red. He dragged his finger across the surface of the boulder, which crumbled wherever his finger touched with a scraping and crushing sound, causing flotsam to fall to the dirt below. When he was finished, the dark brown earth had a fine coating of dust.

He stood and took a moment to inspect his work. There on the face of the boulder were etched in block letters the names Billy, Casey, Gordon, and Thomas. Satisfied, he walked back to join the semicircle with the others. Everyone stood still and quiet with their heads bowed until Serra began speaking.

"We are gathered here today to say goodbye to friends of JJ and Rugen." She recited their names slowly, with a short pause after each one, "Whose lives were taken before their time. These men were pure of heart. They took on your greatest mission—ridding the world of the abominations that plague us and protecting the people you created in your image. Please welcome the souls of these great men to your side. Allow them to watch over us in our travels and help us extinguish the evil that took them from this world. We hope to continue their work, not just in place of them, but for them and for their great memory."

After Serra stopped talking, everyone was quiet for a long time. There was no sound except the river lazily flowing past. The wind was light but cool, and the sky peeking through the canopy of trees was bright blue without a single cloud.

It was Rugen's turn to speak. He held the carving of the dagger in his right hand, referring to it as he spoke. "Gordon, you fostered a brotherhood of men. Your leadership inspired us, and I'm sorry we didn't get to spend more time together. My only hope is that through our actions we can make you proud. I vow to do my best to live up to the standard of righteousness you set. I'll do everything in my power to avenge your death and the death of your son."

Rugen slowly walked to the plot in front of the boulder and got onto his knees. He found a large flat rock close by and used it to scrape away a furrow of dirt. He placed the carving into the hole, pushed dirt onto it, and softly patted the ground. He whispered goodbye to the man who so quickly became his mentor. He walked back to the others, who were standing quietly with their heads bowed.

After some time for reflection, he reached into his bag and located the carving he had made for Thomas. It was the bust of a man with no mouth. "Thomas, I have to admit I didn't know you well, other than to say you were Gordon's dear friend. You died defending him and defending me. You were kind, quiet, and gentle, and if not for the terror we all are facing, I'm sure you would have lived out your years in peace, enjoying the harmony of nature. May God rest your soul." He walked to the plot again and buried the bust underneath the etching of his name. When he got back in line, he nodded to JJ.

JJ hastily started, "Billy," and then stopped himself. He breathed heavily, looking very uncomfortable, as if he'd rather be any place else doing anything else at that moment. He swallowed and continued, "Billy, you saved my life. When I met you I was nobody… headed nowhere." He paused as he breathed out his emotions. "I was left first by one parent and then another. You and your family pulled me from what would have been a pathetic life, and at my worst despair. You became my brother—maybe not of blood but my real brother in every other way." He rubbed the carving with his fingers and then wiped his nose. "I'm sorry." His eyes began to well up. "I'm sorry I couldn't repay you for the chance at life you gave me. I'll think of you always. And I'll never give up the fight." He wiped his face on his sleeve as he walked to the plot. After burying the carving, he placed his hand on Dobbler's etching of Billy's name. He kneeled there touching it for a long time before eventually trudging back to the others.

Rugen waited for everyone to get into their self-imposed formation before grasping Casey's carving; the one of the man with the rabbit on a spit. He said, "Casey loved the outdoors. He knew more about surviving on plants and animals than I ever will. He was born for a different time, a more primitive time, with none of the comforts the rest of us couldn't imagine living without." He gazed down at the carving in his left hand. "You were an inspiration to all of us who knew you, and not only because you cooked a tasty rabbit." He smiled. "After we destroy these creatures, we'll go back to Bomont where they'll celebrate you as a hero."

Rugen finished the last burial, and then everyone walked down to the river and collected smoothed stones. They took their time arranging them on the plot.

While they were covering the dirt with stones, it occurred to Rugen that for as haphazardly as the ceremony was thrown together, it couldn't have been a more fitting memorial for these honorable men, whom he had barely known but would never forget.

As they started to head back to the road, Rugen reached into his bag and pulled out the carving he did for JJ and said, "What do we do with this one?"

JJ took it from him and looked at it. "As good of a job you did making this, I'd rather we just get rid of it. I don't want it to be so convenient for you to just pull it out and bury it if I get killed. My death shouldn't be already so prepared for. I'm going to pitch it in the river. If the gmorks get me, you're just going to have to carve another one. And next time, could you make me look more handsome?!"

CHAPTER 15

Serra led the group of travelers on a northwest path toward the city of Lundgren. She was in front with Dobbler discussing strategy for using magic in battles, something of which they had zero experience and little training. Rugen and JJ didn't want to try to understand, so they lagged behind engrossed in their own conversation.

"Thanks for honoring the memories of the guys," said JJ. "I didn't realize how much it needed to be done until we were doing it."

"I wish we'd known them longer," responded Rugen. He thought about it further and added, "I mean, in another time, another life, before The Isolation."

"No doubt."

"Gordon was becoming a father figure to me. I know we only had a few days together, but I guess stress can do that—bind people together in a short period of time."

JJ looked at the ground as he walked. "I knew Billy for a long time. I'd never lost anyone that close to me before."

"I lost my mother and sister. It just about drains the life out of you. It still hurts, and killing the gmorks did nothing to lessen the grief."

JJ nodded initially but then half-shrugged. "I think of it this way: Every time we kill a gmork it's one less around to kill someone later. One less to devastate a mother, a spouse, or a son. One less to destroy a family. If we can stop another person's anguish in the future, I'm prepared to do whatever it takes."

Rugen said nothing. He was deep in thought, mulling what the monsters were, where they came from, and what their purpose was. JJ was right. They had to look forward; get to Lundgren, build an army, and find the source and eliminate it.

A large hawk with a snake dangling from its talons flew overhead, screeching as it passed. The four travelers watched it fly as they continued along the monotonous journey. Aside from occasional commotions like these, silence ruled the day. The only sounds were their own footfalls and chatter, gentle winds, and the quiet babbling of the river behind the trees.

After the hawk had flown out of sight, JJ asked Rugen what he thought of Ravenwood.

"Not much. I spent the whole time stuck in a room. It was kind of like being in prison. I didn't see any of it except when I was shuffled in and shuffled out. How about you?"

"Oh I pretty much saw it all, best I could from the shadows anyway. Beautiful place. Green everywhere. The houses and trees are kind of merged together. It's hard to see where one ends and the other begins."

"How did you get through the gate without anyone seeing you?"

"I hid outside for a while, and then saw you stumble up to it and fall. You were soaked with blood. It was awful. I was about to come out of my hiding place to help you, but then you were spotted by the townspeople. They didn't seem to know what to do with you until she showed up." He gestured to Serra. "Once she was there everyone got out of the way. She peeled you off the ground and walked you inside. As soon as she put her arm around you, I knew you'd be okay."

Rugen glanced at the auburn-haired cleric ahead of them.

"After that it was pure chaos … people in robes running everywhere. I took advantage of the disorganization to sneak through the gate and find a hiding place."

Rugen shook his head in disbelief. "And then what?"

"With all of those trees and shrubs, there were a lot of ways to avoid being seen. I had left my sword and shield outside so I could sneak around easier. I figured they wouldn't be very effective against a town full of magicians anyway. Eventually I came across these two girls … Charlie and Kelly were their names."

Upon hearing her friends' names, Serra turned around and echoed, "Charlie and Kelly?"

"Yeah," responded JJ. "They were great. They told me about your hidden door. I kept an eye on it and saw you coming and going, always around sunset. Between the three of us we decided you'd be making your move at night sometime around graduation."

"Did they say anything about turning me in?" asked Serra.

"No, no, not at all. I got the sense they admire you and would protect you without question. They found me that robe to use as a disguise."

Just then they heard a commotion up ahead. Everyone stopped to try to determine the exact direction of the sound. There was a rise to the left of the path where the trees thinned. Grunts, growls, and the striking of weapons against claws were heard.

"You guys stay here. I'll go check it out," said JJ. "Wait for my signal." He ran toward the rise and then ducked low as he approached the summit. After some cautious inspection he turned back and waved the rest of them in.

Rugen, Serra, and Dobbler slowly crept toward JJ's position near the top of the hill. Over the other side was an easy slope down to a flattened area, which is from where the noises originated. A man and a woman were grappling with two gmorks. The woman was small but lightning fast. She was dressed in light clothing and boots, and was fighting with a long, thin wooden staff. It looked like a spear without the blade on the end. The man also wore no armor. He was using two short swords, each about half the length of the one JJ was using. He also made very fast movements, and the gmorks didn't seem to be able to keep up with the agility of either of them.

Serra whispered, "Should we help?"

"Not a good idea," responded JJ. "If we go running down there, it might confuse things and someone will get hurt." He paused and watched some more. "They seem to be doing okay. If that changes, we can rush in."

As the fight progressed, the woman was able to duck the comparatively slow attacks of the gmork as well as strike back fairly readily, but her hits didn't seem to be more than an annoyance to the creature. The man's luck wasn't much better. The monster was able to block his sword attacks with the stone-hard skin on its hands and forearms. It seemed like a stalemate all around. The outcome would be determined by who would tire first and make a mistake.

Serra said, "I agree we shouldn't rush in, but maybe I can do something from back here. I can't sit and watch the gmorks kill them."

"I agree with JJ," whispered Rugen, "let's wait a little longer and see what happens."

The gmorks were trying to position themselves so they could work their way to an open swipe from behind, but every time they got near the man or woman's back, one of them made an elegant escape move. As the fight raged on, both the man and woman seemed to be slowing down while the gmorks stayed relentless.

Serra noted a desperate and worried look on the woman's face. She frowned and said, "I'm not waiting any longer. I'm helping." She stared intently at the woman and whispered, "Ulrab emfoi ah earha."

At once the woman appeared to have a burst of energy and her swings seemed to have more impact. She lined up a head shot that stunned the gmork, giving her a good look at its abdomen, which she jabbed with the end of her staff. When the gmork doubled over she bludgeoned it in the back of the head, making it slump to the ground.

While this was going on, Serra cast the same enchantment on the man, giving him his own second wind. His sword strikes sped up, which allowed him to get cleaner swings against the gmork, but the creature was too strong for the man to do any real harm.

The woman, who by this time had downed her opponent, yelled something to the man as she ran toward him. As he ducked she jumped into the air and caught the beast full on in the face with her staff. It took a dazed step backward, allowing room for the man to spring up and slip the point of his sword between its ribs. It dropped to the ground, where the man unceremoniously cut its throat. Then he sauntered over to the unconscious one and did the same.

"I don't know what got into me," said the woman. "All the sudden I felt stronger and faster."

The man nodded, looking at his crud-covered sword and said, "Me too."

Serra stood up from her hiding spot near the top of the hill and yelled, "I can explain that!"

The strangers looked shocked. They quickly turned and got into fighting stances—knees bent, legs spread, torsos leaning forward, the man with one sword out in front of his body and the other behind his back, ready to swing. The woman with her staff at her hip with the tip up and level with her chest. They stood there stoic and silent, breathing heavily.

Serra kept her eyes on the pair as she whispered to the others, barely moving her mouth, "Stay here." She started down the hill toward the combatants, calling out, "I'm Serra Frye. I'm a cleric."

They made no movement.

"The reason you were faster and able to swing harder was because of a spell I cast." She was approaching very slowly, trying to look as nonthreatening as possible. "A physical enchantment." She stopped walking when she was still a good distance from them. "What're your names?"

The man and woman glanced at each other. The woman squeezed her eyebrows together briefly and then both of them relaxed their stances and stood comfortably. The woman said, "I'm Claire Grady." She paused for a moment, nodded her head sideways at the man, and said, "This is my twin brother Alex."

Serra relaxed and started toward them again, "Are you from Lundgren?"

"Yeah," responded Claire. "You're from Ravenwood I assume?"

"Yep. But we're heading to Lundgren."

Alex looked confused, "We?"

"My team and I. Would you like to meet them?" She turned around and yelled back toward the hill, "Guys?"

Rugen, JJ, and Dobbler stood, looking a little uncomfortable with Serra's decision to reveal their presence.

The siblings glanced at the group but said nothing.

"We're heading to Lundgren," repeated Serra. "Maybe we can all go together?"

After a long pause, Claire said flatly, "We aren't going to Lundgren."

Everyone was quiet, waiting for Serra's next move, until Rugen called out, "C'mon Serra, it's time to go."

Serra turned to walk back up the hill toward the others until Alex said, "Wait." He made a face at Claire, and then said, "What my sister meant to say was we weren't going back there until we finish what we came out here for."

"What's that?" asked Serra, now stopped and listening.

"We're trying to find a castle…well, the ruins of a castle," said Alex. "Word is it was destroyed by monsters, but supposedly there's a lot of loot there—weapons, armor, treasure. We're here to recover it." He approached Serra, extending his hand. "Apparently we need help."

The rest of the team came down from the hill and there were greetings and introductions all around. Having spent his entire life in Mourain, Rugen had never seen anyone with bronze skin like that belonging to the siblings. Claire's thick dark hair was fashioned in a wide braid sweeping across the front of her scalp, behind her left ear, and down the back of her neck. Alex's hair was short cropped with a part shaved into it. As siblings they had similar facial features, but the most obvious difference was their eyes. Claire's were so dark it was difficult to tell her irises from her pupils. Alex had citrine-colored eyes like the outermost edges of candlelight. They were striking next to his light brown complexion.

JJ gestured to the bodies of the gmorks and said, "We'd better get out of here before more of these things come investigate their dead friends."

CHAPTER 16

Alex and Claire led the others in the direction of where they thought the castle ruins were. As they progressed, the elevation rose so that the tops of mountains could be seen in the distance. Alex said, "Those are the Ovid Graan Mountains, where Lundgren is."

"It looks so far off," said Serra. "How long have you two been walking?"

"Five days," said Claire.

"How many monsters have you seen?" asked Rugen.

Alex lowered his head. "Too many. We used to have escorts with us—soldiers. Yesterday one was terribly injured and the rest of them took him home. We hired them with the promise of gold from the castle. I guess they lost faith us in that after five days of fruitless wandering and being beaten to a pulp, so they went home."

"But you stayed?" questioned Serra.

"It was my idea to find the castle," said Alex. "I can't just give up on it."

"How did you expect to survive on your own?" asked JJ.

Claire shrugged her shoulders. "We had a pretty good scheme worked out. I'm fast enough to occupy the beasts without them being able to hit me back. While I distracted them, Alex or a soldier would cut them down. It was working great while we had all of those hands, but not so much when it's just Alex and me."

"Where'd you learn to fight like that?" asked Serra.

Claire gestured to Alex and said, "Our father was a great soldier. I mean, he still is, but his fighting days are over. Now he fights with his words and quill. He taught Alex and me to use weapons when we were old enough to hold them.

We were both shoo-ins for warrior school, where our father is a legend, but they didn't accept girls."

"Figures." grumbled Serra, shaking her head in annoyance.

"That's until Dad twisted the arms of some pretty high-up people," said Alex, continuing the story. "Claire became the first female student there and the first female graduate."

Claire smiled. "It wasn't easy. I was teased and ridiculed on pretty much a daily basis. Warrior students aren't generally the most empathetic lot. I don't know if I could have done it without Alex looking out for me."

Alex made a face. "Don't let her fool you. She would've been fine."

"When did you graduate?" asked Serra.

"Three years ago," answered Claire. "And ever since Alex and I have been doing private security for my father's company."

"As bodyguards?" asked JJ.

"Short answer yes," responded Alex, "but we handle all aspects of the business."

"What's the business?" asked Dobbler.

"Our father imports construction materials from sites in the Ovid Graan Mountains."

"So what is this castle we're heading to and why do you want to risk your life to find it?" asked JJ.

"It's Castle Igayim," replied Alex. "It was owned by a rich guy from Lundgren named Patrick Igayim. Supposedly, he had a collection of magical weapons and riches, but word is his castle was abandoned. It's so remote no one's tried to get to it."

"Do people leave Lundgren often?" asked Rugen. "Back where I'm from we're pretty much stuck in the village."

"Things are good in Lundgren now. We have the mountains protecting us and we train hundreds of new soldiers every year. Despite the monsters, it's pretty much business as usual."

"What kind of weapons and riches are we talking about?" asked JJ.

"I'm not sure what's still there and what isn't," responded Alex. "But I'm most interested in one thing I heard Mr. Igayim had in his collection. It's a magical item called the Naga. It's full body armor that has blades melded into it; along the forearms, knees, boots. It turns the person wearing it into a walking weapon."

"How'd you hear about it?" asked Rugen.

"Rumors. Supposedly it was crafted by some martial arts specialist long ago and made magical by a wizard."

"You mean a sorcerer," corrected Dobbler.

Alex shrugged his shoulders, "I dunno. I guess. The magic makes it all but impervious to cutting or piercing. It swells or shrinks to fit the person wearing it. The blades are perfectly positioned to allow freedom of movement in all directions. They somehow change to fit the person's body size as well. It was passed down through the best hand-to-hand fighters for decades. It doesn't get old or worn out. And the blades never need to be sharpened either."

"Is there anything there for the rest of us?" asked JJ.

"We'll see. The castle can't be far now."

They continued along the road throughout the afternoon, stopping periodically to drink from the Divine River. Because it was the main water source for Ravenwood, clerics had long ago enchanted it to always be potable. South of Ravenwood, the same flow of water was referred to as the Stock. It wound its way to the south and east through a handful of towns until it reached the delta along the coast. The magical enchantment ended in the vicinity of Ravenwood.

Up ahead in a clearing they saw what looked to be a scattered pile of rubble. As they approached, they realized the rubble had squared off borders. JJ pointed and said, "Is that it?"

The shape of castle ruins came into focus. The exterior walls were mostly destroyed. The stones that composed them were in rubble, and mostly hidden by the overgrown grass. There was a fallen spire lying on an angle from the edge of the building.

The group spread out and walked the perimeter of the ruins in both directions, stepping over debris as they went. There were black burn marks on the faces of the stone. Some of the interior walls were standing while others had tumbled down just like the exterior ones. There were partial stairways, and the exposed wood was charred and broken.

Claire looked aghast. "What do you think happened here?"

Dobbler pointed at all the burn damage and said, "Well, there definitely was a fire. Maybe it was sorcerers trying to fight off whatever was attacking."

"There were definitely sorcerers stationed here," agreed Alex. "Igayim liked having them around."

Claire gestured to the fallen walls and looked at Dobbler. "What knocked all of that down? More sorcery?"

"Maybe. But it would have to be strong magic. Those stones are heavy, especially when they've been mortared in place."

Rugen, who had come around from what they decided was the back of the ruins, said, "I know something that helped in the destruction. Look over here." Everyone followed him to a half-destroyed wall.

There was a set of four large claw marks gouged into the rock. The entirety of the longest mark would have spanned from a man's neck to his pelvis, but it was on a diagonal, not straight up and down. Rugen put his fingers into the gouge at its deepest point, turned to Serra, and asked, "Is this what my back looked like when you found me?"

"Hey, over here!" called Alex. He had wandered off and was standing over a small but sturdy-looking chest. The wood it was made of was a partially split and frayed but not broken. The metal plates covering all of the edges of the box were slightly rusted and mottled but were otherwise intact. The others came over as Alex picked it up, hefted it a few times, and said, "I found it just sitting here under some boards. It's really heavy."

"Heavy is good," said Claire, eyes wide. "Let's open it."

Serra and Dobbler both tried casting several spells on the lock, but it wouldn't budge.

Alex struggled to maneuver the box in his hands. It was about the size of a watermelon. He handed it to Rugen and said, "Here, hold this." He took a closer inspection of the front, alternatively pulling on the latch and peering into the keyhole. He looked at Rugen and said, "Brace it against your body. Let's pry it open." They each grabbed an edge and pulled. Alex twisted and turned his body, using Rugen's much larger mass as an anchor. Rugen in turn had to take little steps backward and forward to maintain his balance. The men strained, using all of their effort, but the box remained closed.

"Boys! Boys!" reprimanded Serra. "What are you hoping to accomplish there?"

JJ held up a couple of skinny metal pieces he'd pulled out of his bag. He walked over and said, "Set it down. I'll get it open."

The group watched JJ try to pick the lock for a long while. One by one they wandered off as the light was getting low in the sky. Alex, Rugen, and Claire left to collect water and forage for food. Everyone carried dried food in their packs, but it was always better to find something fresh to eat. Serra and Dobbler did some mild cleanup of the castle site, prepping it for an overnight stay. By the time the three foragers had returned, JJ had given up on the lock-picking for the night. Serra set up an exclusion field encompassing the castle grounds while Dobbler cast four campfire spells, stretching their auras to cover the whole area of the ruins.

They all sat together sharing food and conversation until they fell asleep.

CHAPTER 17

By the time Rugen woke up, Serra had already ended the exclusion field spell, so his eyes were able to adjust to the sunlight gradually. When he looked around, he saw JJ working on the chest again with his face as red as his hair. Alex was wandering the site nudging debris with his feet or inspecting underneath things with his hands. No one else was in view.

"Where are the girls and Dobbler?" asked Rugen.

JJ pushed the chest from where it had been sitting in his lap and let it crash to the ground. The force of the landing made his picking tools fling out of the stubborn lock and land a few feet away. He stood up, a picture of frustration, and said, "How the hell am I supposed to know?!"

Rugen got up and wandered into the woods where the river was. He looked upstream and downstream and saw no one. After relieving himself in the shrubs, he walked to the water and knelt in the dirt. He put his hands in and splashed them around a few times, then buried his face in the water up to his ears, drinking in the purity. When he lifted his head he saw a golden sheen in the area where his face had entered the water. There were wisps of bright color flowing from that small patch of river, and then as quickly as the color came it dissipated.

He stood and turned around, heading back to camp. As he neared the edge of the forest, he heard a woman's voice behind him. "Rugen?" He turned to see Serra and Claire standing at the bank wearing undershirts and shorts. Serra's normally auburn hair was much darker, pulled back and dripping water down her neck. She brushed hair out of her face with her hand, tucking it behind her ear. Claire's dark brown hair was plastered close to her scalp by the weight of the wetness, making her deep brown eyes look even larger and prettier. Serra smiled at him and Claire giggled.

Rugen blushed. "Where'd you come from?"

"The river, of course," answered Serra. "Can't you tell we're soaked?"

Claire burst out laughing, making Rugen feel uncomfortable looking at them in their state of undress.

"I was just over there. I didn't see anyone."

"You really don't get this magic stuff, huh?" laughed Serra. "I set up an exclusion field. We didn't want a bunch of men watching us bathe in the river." She pointed her thumb back to the water. "I made another field for Dobbler. He's still in there." She turned back to Rugen. "Do you want one too? The water is very cleansing, and the old enchantment makes sure it stays pristine enough to drink even while you're standing in it."

"Is that the golden glow I saw after I stuck my face in there?"

"That's your filth getting destroyed by the spell. It glows bright gold."

"Serra!" Claire chuckled, "His filth? That's pretty rude!"

"Hey, I lived with him for a week. I know all about his filth."

Rugen was trying his best to maintain eye contact and not be distracted as he talked to the women. "Yeah, sure. Let me go get JJ, and then you can set up one of those spells for us."

From the campsite, they heard someone yell, "Hey guys, look at this!"

Rugen, Serra, and Claire ran back to where the others were and found Alex repeatedly tapping his foot on a patch of grass. Each tap made a hollow, empty sound.

Alex looked up at everyone gathered around and said, "I just came back from the river, and as I walked on this spot, my footsteps got louder." He demonstrated again by stomping his feet on the spot. "See? I think there's something underneath."

He got onto his hands and knees and tapped with his fingertips, and then his knuckles, loudening the resonating knock. He got a determined look on his face and started tugging on the grass. It wasn't attached to anything but the greenery around it and came up easily. Underneath was a patch of wood. He took a deep breath and kept clearing the area, revealing slats lined up next to each other making a large square contained in a frame of stone.

He frantically felt around the edges of the square and found a depression into which his fingers smoothly slipped. He lifted the wooden square out of the frame and peered into a deep empty space. Just below the brim of the stone was the top of a ladder. Alex was beaming. He stepped onto the ladder and disappeared into the hole.

"Need some light down there?" asked Serra. She quickly cast an illumination spell, making a yellow glow emanate from the hole.

"I found it!" yelled Alex, "And there's other stuff down here too!"

Everyone gathered around the hole and looked in. Alex was standing in what amounted to a stone room. In his right hand he held a black mass of leather and metal, and in his left was a gauntlet with carved markings on it. Hanging from his mouth on a string was a small key.

Claire turned to Serra and said, "We should go get Dobbler."

Serra had forgotten all about Dobbler in his exclusion field. She said, "Right! We'll be right back." She and Claire threw on traveling clothes and ran off.

"I hope that key does what I think it's going to do," said JJ, who had spent quite a bit of the evening trying to get the chest open.

Alex climbed a few steps up the ladder and handed the gauntlet to Rugen and the key to JJ. Then he retrieved the bundle of leather and metal and brought it to the surface.

"What'd you say that thing was called?" asked Rugen.

"The Naga." As Alex said the word, the leather sprang to life. It billowed out to humanoid shape while a gaping hole opened in the back. He gently set it down and excitedly pulled off the leather armor he was wearing, leaving him standing in an undershirt and shorts. He picked it up by the hips and stepped inside. The leather conformed to the shape of his foot and leg as he did. He looked at the others with a delirious smile on his face, and then climbed in the rest of the way. With all four limbs in position, the leather shrunk to cling to his shape and the gap down the back self-sealed. He pulled the mask over his head, which effortlessly sealed too.

Alex proudly stood, wearing a form-fitting black leather suit that covered every inch of his body with no visible seams. There were blades running the length of his forearms and lower legs, and studs of metal on his hands and feet. The rest of the suit was covered in plates and edges, providing extra defense and even more opportunity for offense by way of shoulder checks and head butts.

Rugen said, "Is it heavy? Cumbersome?"

Alex, whose face couldn't be seen behind the mask aside from his wide, thrilled eyes, said, "Not at all." He tested out the flexibility of the suit by punching and kicking the air, and then by jumping and twisting around. "It feels like I'm wearing nothing."

"How do you pee?" asked JJ.

"Not my top priority right now."

Rugen inspected the blades more closely, lightly rubbing his finger along them. The edges of the metal were rounded off. It looked like it would take a large effort to grind them into shape. He said, "They're really dull. Aren't they supposed to never need sharpening?"

Alex looked at them and replied, "I saw that. It's okay for now. I'm sure I'll figure it out."

As Alex continued to practice attack moves, Rugen looked at the gauntlet he was holding. It was made of dozens of small metal pieces with no obvious bonding between them. He articulated the wrist and finger joints, and the metal pieces easily slid over each other. It was very light. He imagined if it were made of iron or steel it would be much heavier. It was obviously a different sort of metal about which he had no knowledge. It was decorated with strange carved symbols he'd never seen before.

JJ slid the small key into the lock on the chest and flipped open the lid. The inside was loaded with gold coins. He grabbed a handful and held it up to Rugen and said, "Trade you for that gauntlet."

Just then the women and Dobbler arrived back in camp. Dobbler was fully dressed in his light armor and high-collared coat. He looked at the open chest in front of JJ and remarked, "Wow, that's a lot of gold coins." He then looked at the half-metal/half-leather creature Alex had become and said, "And that is some costume! Who are you supposed to be?"

JJ gave the chest to Rugen, retrieved the gauntlet, and slid it onto his left arm. It seemed to conform to him the way Alex's new armor did. He swung his arm around and then put it up in a defensive posture, miming an imaginary sword behind it and said, "Anyone want a beat-up old shield? Because this thing is mine."

Alex mumbled to himself, "Mask." After saying this, the seal along the neck of the Naga parted and Alex pulled the mask over his head, allowing it to dangle in front of him.

"How'd you know the command to take off the mask?" asked Dobbler.

"I don't know," shrugged Alex. "I just guessed. Maybe it doesn't matter what you say. Maybe the Naga somehow reads your intent." He gestured to Dobbler and Serra. "You guys are the magicians. You tell me."

Rugen set the chest on the ground and squatted to get a closer inspection of the coins. They were broad and bulky. He held one up, "They say 'City of Lundgren' on them."

"Oh good," said Serra, "they'll make our stay there a lot easier."

Rugen nudged the chest with his boot. "Who gets to carry this thing all the way to Lundgren?"

"Anyone have a coin purse I can borrow?" asked Serra.

"I do," responded Claire. "It's empty now. I gave all our money to the escorts who deserted us."

"You gave them everything?!" snapped Alex.

"The reason they came with us was that they expected we'd find riches at the castle," retorted Claire. "And they left with one of their guys badly hurt, probably dying. I thought they deserved something extra for their trouble." She retrieved the purse and gave it to Serra.

Rugen noticed the purse looked too small to hold all the coins. He pointed this out to Serra and she replied, "Here, sit down with me and hold this open." Serra handed it to Rugen and they sat on the grass next to the chest. Serra picked up a handful of coins and said, "Ealevy vloum," as she dropped them into the bag.

"They feel so light," said Rugen.

"And they'll continue to be practically weightless until you handle them. As soon as you grab a coin and hold it in your hand, its weight will return to normal. That way they won't be a burden on anyone who carries them." She repeated the process until the purse was full and the chest was empty. Despite the obvious size difference, the purse had space for plenty more coins.

The rest of the morning was spent eating, gathering food and water for the road, and doing one last inspection of the ruins of Castle Igayim in the hopes of another hidden cache. They started the trip toward Lundgren in the afternoon.

CHAPTER 18

The six travelers watched the sun slowly set fire to the clouds as it dipped behind the mountains along the western edge of the Plains of Miramar. The closer they got to Lundgren, the wider and more established the road became. So far, the absence of gmorks allowed them to enjoy their surroundings, which were teeming with life. They saw families of deer, colorful singing birds, flittering dragonflies, buzzing bees, and wide-bodied hawks. The squirrels always seemed to be busy doing one thing or another, while the rabbits were content just sitting and nibbling on grass. Rugen hoped that the fact the animals were engaging in their natural behaviors without alarm was evidence that gmorks were nowhere nearby.

"What are those gold coins worth?" asked Dobbler.

"A lot," answered Claire. "Each one is equivalent to twenty silver, a silver is sixty peltzers, and a peltzer will get us room and board for the night. They have smaller denominations too. You can figure that out as we go."

"And how many were in the chest?"

Serra smiled, "Two hundred fifty-five by my count. All gold."

"Will anyone have anything to say about us taking it from the castle?" asked Rugen.

"Not at all," responded Alex. "Mr. Igayim is long dead. His castle was destroyed. According to the law of Lundgren, anything left behind is free to the finder.

"But it's not like we can stop at an inn with a gold coin and ask for eleven hundred and ninety-nine pelts in change," added Claire. "We'll have to deposit these and withdraw walking-around money. Non-citizens can't have bank accounts, so the money will have to go into either my account or Alex's."

"Your personal account?" asked Dobbler.

"Well, yeah," said Alex, "You guys can't do business in the bank like a Lundgren citizen can. There's no such thing as a group account, and each citizen is only allowed one account to their name, so it would have to be deposited into mine or Claire's."

"What happens after this is finished and we go our separate ways?" asked Dobbler.

"We're a team," said Alex. "We all contributed to finding the money, and by the end of our journey together I think we'll have each proved our worth many times over. Let's share in the spoils it brings us in Lundgren and split what's left in the bank six ways."

JJ slapped Alex on the back and said, "When I'm done with my spoils, there may be nothing left for the bankers to watch over!"

Ignoring JJ's comment, Serra said to Claire, "There are a lot of people in Lundgren, right?"

Claire nodded. "It's a huge city."

"How do they know who's a citizen and who isn't?"

Claire tugged on her collar, revealing a thin medallion hanging around her neck. It featured a large embossed capital letter L above a six-digit number. "The L signifies Lundgren and the number is unique to me."

Alex smiled at his sister. "Whenever we leave the city we have to check in with the guards at the gate. They write down our name, ID number, and the date."

"What if someone stole it and tried to pass themselves off as you?" asked Dobbler.

"I suppose they could try, but the guard do document your physical description when you check out at the gate," answered Claire.

The road ahead sloped up a gentle hill. At the summit stood a group of gmorks. Rugen was the first to notice them and casually said, "I hate to interrupt the conversation, but we have a bit of work to do. I count four of them."

Alex pulled the hood of the Naga over his head, saying, "Good, I want to test this thing out." He gestured to Dobbler and Serra, "Hold your magic unless things go sour. Okay?" They nodded as Alex donned his mask and it sealed around his neck.

The four warriors took off running toward the gmorks as they came down the hill. Claire was out in front until her brother yelled for her to slow down. He wanted clear space in front of him to test out his new weapon.

Rugen held his longsword like a battering ram. As the gmork got close to the point, it dodged out of the way and took a swipe at Rugen's head. He ducked just in time to avoid the sting of claws across his cheek.

JJ engaged the beast closest to him by his usual method, jumping high and swinging hard. The gmork blocked his sword with its hardened hands, grabbing a hold of the middle of the blade.

Alex jumped, curling himself into a ball. As he sprung open, four lacerations appeared on the gmork's chest, arms and legs. They weren't very deep, but they were bleeding, and the gmork staggered back. Alex looked at the four main blades of the suit; those being the ones along his lower arms and legs, and found they had extended to be sharp as razors. He smiled under his facemask thinking about how amazing the Naga was.

JJ's gmork wrenched the sword out of his hand by the blade and flung it through the air. It looked at him with what almost seemed like a sinister smile, and then moved to envelope him. JJ raised his gauntlet in a defensive posture, and as the gmork took a swipe it was knocked back by a hazy red glow that emanated from the gauntlet.

Claire stopped behind the others and waited for the free gmork to come to her. It slowed to a strut as it approached. When it got within reach of her staff, she staggered it with a quick succession of strikes.

Alex twisted backward and slashed across the neck of Claire's gmork as she nudged it toward him with her assault. It fell to the ground, and without any delay Claire ran to the bleeding gmork that Alex had slashed and whipped it across the face with her staff.

Rugen and his gmork were in a stalemate, mostly because of Rugen's attention being split between fighting it and watching the new weapons on display.

Alex dropped his elbow onto the chest of the gmork that he and Claire fell, and as he did the arm blade lengthened, burying itself in the gmork's heart.

JJ, fueled by confidence behind his new gauntlet, backhanded the gmork he was fighting. As the gauntlet struck its meaty shoulder, red light exploded out of it. The gmork staggered backward and fell at the edge of the road. JJ pulled his dagger from its holster on his thigh and ran toward the dazed creature. He held his gauntlet arm across its throat and jammed the dagger into its eye socket up to its hilt. The eye popped and the gmork stopped moving. Thick dark blood oozed from the wound as he slid out the blade.

Just then the sound of cracking branches broke the silence behind Serra and Dobbler. They whipped around to see another gmork amble out of the woods. It paused for a moment and then hurdled toward them. Serra stared, frozen, until Dobbler grabbed her hand and yelled, "Serra, C'mon!"

Serra was pulled along with him toward their companions. Neither of them had combat experience, so the fact that they could have held their ground and fought with magic didn't occur to them at that moment.

"There's one behind us!" Dobbler called to the others.

Rugen finally outmaneuvered his gmork and sliced downward on a plane between its neck and shoulder. It slumped to the ground as he slid out his sword. He turned, face and chest spattered with blood, and yelled, "I'll get the last one! Go help Serra and Dobbler."

Now that Dobbler saw Alex, Claire, and JJ running toward them, he stopped to face the pursuing gmork. The sorcerer put his hands out in front of him, fingers splayed. His face was contorted as he screamed, "Dengkit tungko duot!" Bolts of blue-white electricity forked from his fingers, knocking the gmork's legs from under it. It flopped forward and landed hard on its face.

With the monster stunned and outnumbered, it was quickly extinguished. The last one, weakened by the multiple cuts Alex's Naga left on it and dazed by the beating inflicted by Claire, was easily bested by Rugen.

The six combatants gathered together and looked themselves over. Short of minor abrasions and bruises they were generally unharmed. "I think it's safe to assume there'll be more of these things as we get closer to Lundgren," said Dobbler.

"You're probably right," said Alex as he unsealed his mask and pulled it over his head, "but we'll handle it." He watched in wonder as his blades slowly molded back into their blunted resting state.

"And what about after we pass through Lundgren?" added Serra.

"That's why we're going to get help from RHS," said Claire.

"What's RHS?" asked Rugen.

BOOK THREE: LUNDGREN

"The mountains are our home. We defend them so they can protect us. We cultivate them so they can feed us. They provide the air we breathe and the water we drink.

We are the mountains. The mountains are us. They are beautiful. They are majestic. And contained within them is great power. The more we can harness it, the more powerful we become.

We live in the mountains and we bask in their glory. But if they were to crumble; if the winds wore them away or the earth opened and swallowed them, we would survive. For we are more than the mountains. The people of Lundgren would rise from the dust left behind. The people would rise, and the people would flourish."

—The last few lines of a speech given at the coronation of Bastian Morla,
The First duke of Lundgren, as they appear on a bronze plaque
hanging outside the administrative building named for him,
located in the center circle of Lundgren.

Chapter 1

Riser Helm School, founded over a century before The Isolation by the eponymous hero of the Marion War, was dedicated to the training of citizens of Lundgren in hand-to-hand combat, battle strategy, and leadership. Just like at G. Wallace School of Divinity and Mitchell Wyatt School of Sorcery, Serra's and Dobbler's respective schools, children enrolled at RHS at the age of twelve and went through a six-year curriculum. The students' time ended with them becoming soldiers in the Lundgren Army.

Throughout its long history, RHS was an all-male school, as women were deemed not strong enough to handle the stresses of the curriculum. A policy to allow female applicants to the school was never considered, not even by the girls themselves, or their families. That was until the day Claire Grady became the first female accepted into RHS, and six years later, the first to graduate.

Freshman year was spent mostly in the classroom getting lectured on topics such as battle mathematics, history of war, including past heroes and leaders of Lundgren, wilderness survival, battle communication, war songs/poetry, and public speaking. Physical training also started on day one, but that wasn't the primary focus of the first-year curriculum.

By the middle of the year, the freshman class would be split into three groups. The highest achieving students were identified for possible promotion into the Elite Program. These students, known as *pre-elites*, were grouped together and separated from the other students for the second half of the year. This early segregation was not only meant to increase the level of competition among the highest-achieving candidates, but also to inspire those not flagged as pre-elites to work harder in the hopes of being selected to join that program.

Program appointments were announced at the end of first year, and the decisions about who was accepted into the elite track and who wasn't were non-negotiable and final. There were no late promotions. Once second year commenced, movement from the regular track to the elite program was something that just didn't happen.

On the other side of the spectrum was an equivalent percentage of students designated as candidates for the Apprentice Program. As with pre-elites, pre-apprentice students followed the same freshman curriculum as everyone else, but unless they picked up their pace before the end of first year, their remaining time at RHS was very different. Apprentice students, sometimes pejoratively referred to as "wash-outs," went on to become blacksmiths, carpenters, masons, coopers, armorers, or other jobs that were vital to any functioning society.

While there was an inherent sense of pride and self-worth among the people who did these jobs, the wish of most students starting at RHS was to become a soldier, and finding themselves placed in the Apprentice Program was a blow to their ego, and even more so to that of their parents.

Grunt was a title of affection given to all soldiers who completed the main program at RHS. *Grunt-in-training* was the proper name for students on their way to becoming grunts, but for the sake of simplicity, the *in-training* part was usually dropped during conversations. Most RHS students were grunts. The difference between elite training and grunt training was of similar magnitude to the difference between that of grunts and apprentices. Grunt did much less class work as weapons training, strength and endurance building, and sparring. Each grunt was responsible for becoming proficient in every known implement of close-range and short-range fighting, including bare-hand combat.

Elites were just as responsible for all of the physical training and weapon mastering as grunts were, but they had a lot more classroom time on top of it. There were courses in battle strategy, triage, critical decision-making, delegation, and leadership. Part of the leadership curriculum course was to supervise the physical training of younger students at RHS. Elites were observed and evaluated on their ability to teach and lead, and it was through this experience they developed the confidence to oversee soldiers of all ages and experience levels by the time they graduated.

The sixth and final year of elite training was an off-campus internship in a real world setting. Senior elites served in the field under working elites, now called officers, supervising grunt infantry. Back at RHS, their absence allowed a small percentage of rising sixth-year grunts to enter into a condensed version of the elite program. This group was dubbed *sub-elites*. Upon graduation, they had opportunities open to them that weren't available to the rest of the grunts, including: infantry squad leader, RHS professor, RHS physical trainer, or a career in civilian relations or diplomacy.

A handful of graduating students each year didn't get conscripted into the military. Usually, these students were the children of parents who had made large monetary donations to the school over the years or had a position of political influence that allowed them to dictate where their child's next stop would be. The general idea was for the school to be the main feeder into the Lundgren Army, which was effectively the Hyborian Army, so deviation from this process was only done with significant cause.

Demotions did occur from the elite program to the grunt program, or from grunt to apprentice, although they were infrequent and only during the second year. A student who may otherwise have been demoted during the third year was more likely expelled altogether. The term used to describe an unfortunate person in this situation was *late washout*. Becoming one of those was terribly embarrassing for the student and his family.

One infamous late washout was Brian Gruhl.

CHAPTER 2

Brian Gruhl was born in Lundgren to a well-to-do family. He had an older brother named Anthony who preceded him at Riser Helm School by three years. Both boys were handsome with short-cropped and tightly curled blond hair, strong chins, and athletic frames. Anthony was quickly noticed by both his fellow students and the RHS teachers because of his respectable demeanor and strong work ethic. He was at the top of his class every year, and earned his way into the elite program, where he did nothing but excel.

The boys' father, Michael Gruhl, held Anthony in the highest regard, much like everyone who came into contact with him. Michael was an RHS washout in his day, but became the owner of a successful blacksmith shop. His hope was to make, by any means necessary, both of his sons into famous leaders of men. He encouraged fierce competition between them, and always belittled Brian for not being more like Anthony. He did this with the best intentions, unable to imagine Brian not wanting to be more like his brother.

Brian always considered himself inherently smarter than his older brother, and the fact that he couldn't keep up physically or socially didn't much matter to him. This supposed mental superiority wasn't based on anything anyone could measure, but it was a fact in Brian's own mind. He wasn't Anthony and didn't want to be, so his father's plan to turn him into his brother made Brian resent both of them. After years of pressure and forced expectations, Brian made it his mission to do everything in his power to be his own person.

By the time Brian was twelve years old and started at RHS, Anthony was a well known student and their father was a well-respected parent, and no one let Brian forget those things. As much as it irritated him, living in his brother's shadow did have its privileges in the classroom. He was given a lot more leeway than the other students. Failures were downplayed or ignored, and successes were over-celebrated. Just like his brother, Brian was made a pre-elite and then an elite, despite the fact he'd earned none of it.

He struggled socially. As the other elite students realized he wasn't living up to the standard set by Anthony, they began challenging him, both on the sparring floor and in the hallways. Defeating Anthony's brother in a sparring match became a badge of honor for them. The more they beat him, the stronger they felt, and the lower his self-esteem sank. What started as a slow downward spiral picked up speed until soon he was routed and embarrassed on a daily basis.

The first time RHS instructors made Michael aware of Brian's inadequacies, he was dumbfounded. Prior to this he had been drunk on admiration of both of his sons. In response, he put more pressure on Brian at home, which only drove the boy deeper into despair and made him rebel against his family even more.

By the end of his second year, Brian was struggling academically, athletically, and socially. Most of his good will was exhausted, and it was only the hollow promises Michael made to RHS administration that kept him from being let go all together. They asked Brian to give up his spot in the elite program and join the grunts, which only served to further his growing distaste for everyone and everything in his life.

The other consequence of his demotion was that his father pressured him even more, fostering more antipathy and ill will between the two of them. Michael's attempts at motivation and redirection turned into outright abuse, and many nights during the summer between second and third year, Brian went to bed crying, bandaged, or with a black eye. He turned to his mother for help, but being under her husband's thumb, she chose to keep her distance from the whole situation. To her, siding with Brian meant going against her husband, which she would never do. Anthony was Michael's hope for the greatness he wasn't able to achieve for himself. She had prayed from the day Anthony was born that he would make the dreams Michael once had for himself come true.

Anthony was no help to his younger brother. Any encouragement he gave to Brian was met with obstinance and defiance, and the path of least resistance for Anthony was to bury himself in the world of being an elite—not only *an* elite, but *the* elite. He didn't have the time to repair Brian's academic and social ineptitude. So Brian had no one he could count on for support. In everyone's eyes he was just a counterfeit version of his brother.

Unsurprisingly, the Grunt Program wasn't a fit for Brian either. He was ridiculed on a daily basis by his peers because of his demotion from elite status. He was frequently and soundly bested on the sparring ground and emotionally abused around campus. The teachers either ignored or encouraged the other students in their mockery of him, thinking it might inspire the boy to improve. After a few months of failures as a grunt, RHS administration called Michael back to the school to discuss a further demotion. No other student would've been offered admittance into the Apprentice Program as an option this late in his tenure. In fact, for a different student, outright release would have been recommended as soon as he wore out his welcome in the Elite Program, but out of respect for Anthony, Brian was treated with kid gloves.

Michael rejected the school's offer for RHS apprenticeship. He was well aware of school policy on washouts and could not bear the thought of further special treatment given to a Gruhl. He pulled Brian from school, saying he would take him under his wing at the blacksmith shop. The day Brian was collected from school for the last time, any hope of absolution from Michael perished.

Michael resented Brian for many reasons: He was mortified that the family name, which had been built through his blacksmithing business, and bolstered by Anthony's wild success at RHS, was being besmirched. Brian's failure also made Michael relive his own bad memories of being a washout, and eliminated the possibility of him living vicariously through his younger son. Michael also resented the way Brian so easily brought his deep-seated anger to the surface. Most of all was the simple fact that Brian wasn't and would never be Anthony.

Brian resented… Well, Brian resented everyone: his father, his mother, his brother, and the students, teachers, and administrators at RHS. He even resented the workers in his father's blacksmith shop for bearing witness to his failures.

Brian found no offer of camaraderie from them. They worked hard their whole lives and were proud of their careers. They saw Brian as a petulant child who squandered every opportunity handed to him, and they hated the thought that working in their shop was considered to be a punishment for failure.

Throughout what would have been his third year at RHS, Anthony's sixth and final year there, Brian's anger and resentment grew. His father assigned him the most demeaning jobs at the shop, never allowing him to do the actual work of a blacksmith. Whenever Brian questioned having to do these tasks, his father cited his lack of training, but deep down Michael wanted to continue to punish him. Brian was charged with cleaning the latrine, which was typically filthy after being used all day by a half-dozen soot-covered blacksmiths, scrubbing the floor, which invariably filled his hands and knees with metal splinters, cleaning out the forge, which gave his skin and clothing a perpetual black sheen, and carrying around heavy and cumbersome pieces of metal, which wrenched his back and other joints. Worse than these daily duties was the constant barrage of insults he endured from the other employees.

At home, his father continued his regular physical abuse and his mother maintained her refusal to help. His older brother Anthony remained as actively oblivious as possible. He was secretly embarrassed to share a last name with Brian and thus buried himself in all things RHS. And through it all, Brian's rage continued to fester by the day.

Brian's catharsis came on the night before Anthony's graduation. Anthony was to be the star attraction, having won every award and accommodation offered at the school. Brian lay in bed, wide-eyed with anticipation, waiting for the rest of his family to fall asleep. Once he was sure he was the only one awake, he climbed out of bed and squatted down to reach under his mattress. It was a moment many months in the making, and this night was perfect for it. The light of the full moon was illuminating the inside of their house with a blue-gray glow.

He crept into Anthony's room and snuck up on his sleeping form, watching him breathe slowly and peacefully, all the while despising his existence. In his hand Brian held a makeshift knife he had secretly crafted in his father's blacksmith shop. In actuality it could hardly be described as a knife. Blades were designed to be an extension of the wielder's hand: ergonomically balanced, beautifully curved, honed and polished, and in some cases adorned with gemstones or precious metals. Brian's knife was crude. He had salvaged a piece of scrap metal he was sure wouldn't be missed and hastily shaped it into a ragged shard. It wasn't pretty, but it was as sharp as anything that came out of the shop, and that's all that mattered.

Without a word, a second thought, or any doubt in his hate-filled mind, Brian lifted the knife to Anthony's throat and smoothly slid it, making sure to cut fast and deep, just like he learned at RHS. Anthony woke for a few seconds, gasping for air with a look of terrified confusion on his face, but he made no noise other than choked gurgles.

While his brother's life sputtered away, Brian couldn't help but think about the irony of the situation. All of those times Anthony was in the sparring circle facing off against another student, he was invincible. He was the biggest, strongest, and fastest; even his trainers could barely lay a finger on him.

But now, as Brian stood by and watched the blood from his brother's grotesque wound slow to a trickle, he felt almost a sense of pity. Not because of any brotherly love or even basic human kindness, but because of how pathetic his once-proud brother's body looked in its lifeless state.

With no further emotion, Brian slunk out of his brother's room to seek out his parents. The sight of them tranquilly lying in bed gave him pause. Even the most horribly abusive people look innocent and kind while sleeping. The briefest wave of sentiment came over him; just a momentary lapse of determination where Brian nearly reconsidered his plan, but this was quickly extinguished when he realized he had already gone too far. There was no undoing what happened in the room next door. He knew he needed to finish the job.

It made the most sense for him to deal with his father before his mother. If he did the opposite and his father awoke to the struggle, he didn't know if he could handle him. He wasn't nearly as physically strong as Michael, and was still subject to his authority and intimidation.

He paused and contemplated the quietest death he could give him so as not to wake his mother. He decided that doing it the same way as with his brother was his only option. He'd slice his neck quickly and hope his thrashing and choking wouldn't wake her up.

There was very little commotion as the life flowed out of Michael, and what there was didn't stir his mother in the least. This was a pleasant surprise to Brian. He was shocked at how easy all of this was.

He inched to her side of the bed where she peacefully slept. This woman, who was supposed to shield him from his father's constant abuse but instead turned a blind eye; who was supposed to love him unconditionally but instead ignored him like trash in the street; she would die just the same as her husband and her golden son.

On her bedside table sat a tiny bottle topped with a rubber dropper. He grasped it and held it to catch the moonlight filtering through the window. It had a square bottom, and its sides tapered as they rose to the top. The hand-printed script on the label read "Kampff Elixir." Below that in smaller lettering was "1–2 drops for a good night sleep." It was mostly empty, but coating the bottom was a small amount of blue-tinged transparent fluid. He didn't know how many drops she had swallowed, but it was enough that she hadn't woken up while her husband was dying next to her. He shrugged. Her decision, her loss.

He set the bottle back on the nightstand and lifted his blood-soaked shank, advancing it toward her neck.

Then he stopped. His father had been his main target because of the years of mistreatment, and now he was dead. Part of the reason he killed Anthony was because he wanted to ruin something everyone cherished, but mostly it was that he didn't want to face him in the morning. He wouldn't have been able to handle his older brother's emotional or physical wrath. His mother's crime was inattention, so would be her punishment. She did nothing for him so he'd do nothing to her. Tomorrow she'd wake out of her drug-induced slumber to find her husband and adored son dead, and her forgotten son gone forever.

CHAPTER 3

Brian changed out of his bloody clothes, cleaned his face and hands, and packed as many supplies as he could. He hadn't put a lot of thought into what to do or where to go after he'd freed himself from his family. By the light of the moon he was able to see well enough outside, so he wandered off into the night. He left Lundgren and walked along a path that led through the mountains, and didn't come across anyone all night long.

As the sky changed from black, to burnt orange, to a gray, hazy day, Brian came across a man he later learned was named Marvin Stiles. Marvin had white scraggly hair, a patchy beard, and sleepy eyes, which gave him the appearance of having a general disinterest. He knew nothing of Riser Helm School or the Gruhl family and didn't care to ask. He referred to himself as a traveling merchant, which Brian later realized was one of his many cover stories. There was no scam Marvin was unwilling to try on some unsuspecting traveler.

Marvin preferred to work with younger people because they were more gullible and malleable, and the marks he preyed upon usually thought of kids as innately trustworthy, a fact he had no qualms about exploiting. The two of them were a good match. Brian was only fourteen years old and needed someone to mentor him and provide for his needs. In trade, Marvin needed the honest face of a young man to help lure victims into his schemes. His previous consort was strangled to death by a person Marvin only referred to as "an unsatisfied customer." Marvin went on to say he *assumed* the strangling resulted in death, as death seemed to be the way things were headed, but he had fled the scene before the final outcome was determined.

They traveled together through the Hyborian north for several years. Brian did whatever he could to in all ways distance himself from his old life in Lundgren. He told no one else his real name, choosing rather to come up with a new alias to use in each of Marvin's scams. By the time Brian reached adulthood, they had joined a group of other misanthropes who had a bunker hideout far in the north with access to a precious metal mine. Neither one of them knew anything about mining, but they did know a lot about people and how best to manipulate them to do their bidding.

Eventually, by gaining the confidence of some of the miners and forcing attrition of others, they took control of the bunker and gradually expanded it deep into the mountain. In doing so, they generated a large stockpile of monetary assets, which they traded for supplies by way of a network leading back to Lundgren.

Marvin had a basic working knowledge of science and magic, and over the years Brian gleaned everything he could from him. Between the two of them they had just enough expertise to exercise their own sick pleasure in animal experimentation. There were hundreds of failures, which in some cases meant drawn out, painful, and torturous deaths of their experimental subjects. The result was a line of creatures specifically designed for sport fighting. Marvin's idea was for the combatants to be strong enough to keep the matches exciting but not so strong that they were lethal.

As more time passed, Brian got bored with the battles as they were and pushed to create more aggressive and violent creatures. Marvin agreed, but when one of the creatures killed and partially ate a lab assistant, he demanded they stop. Brian dutifully vocalized his agreement but then got to work on how best to continue his experimentation behind Marvin's back.

He worked in secret, slowly breeding and refining more and more dangerous creatures. It was a monotonous and arduous practice, full of failures and accidents. About the time his frustration of having to hide his projects from Marvin had built to a crescendo, Brian crossed paths with a disgraced sorcerer named Deckard who shared his views on animal experimentation. The two of them kept the sorcerer's identity a secret to Marvin, which was made easier by the ever-expanding size of the operation, the high level of turnover, and the fact that as Marvin and Brian grew apart ideologically. Marvin found it best to stay out of Brian's business, both figuratively and literally.

Together, Brian and Deckard relentlessly corrupted animals great and small. With each breakthrough, Brian flirted with the idea of telling Marvin, but then reconsidered. This constant rumination about whether Marvin would be accepting of one project or another acted to swell the growing contempt in his mind. Just as he felt superior to his brother Anthony all those years ago, Brian considered himself more capable and clever than Marvin, and thus the alpha in their relationship. The fact that he had to hide his work made him feel like a subordinate. Regardless, deep down he thought Marvin would eventually agree with his point of view when he finally had something really spectacular to show him.

One day, several years later, Brian had just that sort of accomplishment, and decided it was time to present to Marvin. He slowly led a large humanoid creature with great horns, a wide mouth full of sharp teeth, and clawed hands into the main floor of their laboratory. It was wearing a sturdy metal collar, onto which a thick chain leash was attached.

Marvin was struck speechless. Brian admitted it was slow, dimwitted, and clumsy, but explained by bringing it to Marvin's attention, they could work on improving it together.

Instead, Marvin berated Brian and insisted he destroy the creature immediately. Brian appealed to him, saying over time with an army of such beasts they could take control of Hyboria. The argument quickly devolved, and when Marvin realized Brian wasn't going to back down, he asked him to leave the bunker and never return.

Brian was prepared for the possibility that Marvin wouldn't accept the prototype. He stretched his neck slightly to peer over Marvin's shoulder, making eye contact with Deckard. Before Marvin could move to protect himself, two large lab assistants seized him by the upper arms and forcibly led him to a room that was empty aside from chains bolted to the stone floor. Marvin tried to remember what the room looked like the last time he saw it. He had no recollection of there being what amounted to a jail cell in the lab.

The assistants holding him were joined by two others with metal cuffs in their hands, and the four of them forcibly pinned Marvin to the floor. As he was struggling against the younger and larger men, he realized he had never seen any of them before that moment. After two decades of working at and living in the bunker, the fact that four assistants might be employed there without his knowledge made the experience even more unsettling. He quickly determined they wouldn't respond to any notion of his authority, and their presence made him wonder what else Brian was up to about which he was unaware. Eventually they subdued him and locked the chains in place. He was restrained on his back with cuffs on his wrists, ankles, and, most uncomfortably, his neck. They pulled the slack so tight he was completely unable to move.

Brian calmly strolled into the room, having returned the hideous monster to its cage. He explained to Marvin that this would normally be the time to offer him one more chance, but that he wasn't going to extend that pleasure. Marvin had become useless to him, and it was time for them to part company. He was proceeding forward with his plan to build an army, and all Marvin would do was get in the way of that. The last contribution Marvin would have to Brian's research would be as a test subject for another one of his creations. He then left the room and closed the door.

Marvin heard the sliding of wood over stone and turned his head to see a newly revealed gap along the baseboard. Something was moving in the darkness, but there wasn't enough light to make anything out. Whatever it was, it was small. It moved quickly and erratically in the shadow of the hole.

When it came into full view, it was all orange legs and brown segmented body. It was a giant centipede the length of his forearm, with dozens of pointed, striped legs skittering everywhere. Soon more of them appeared in the gap, crawling over each other to get out. The creepy-crawly feeling they inspired was intensified greatly by Marvin being immobilized on the floor with them at eye-level. They were fast, almost supernaturally fast, and their tiny claws made scratching sounds as they scampered along the cold stone floor. They explored the room, bumping the walls and rearing up along the baseboards, but they generally avoided his bodily form.

Marvin pulled all his chains at once, but they held fast. He had a brief calming thought that this was just a scare tactic to get him to agree to Brian's plans. He would endure a few bites, sure, but in no time he and his partner would be talking this out like civilized people. He'd come across centipedes before, much smaller ones of course, and knew from experience that these giant ones likely packed an excruciating sting. He would have a few welts when Brian's men carried him out of the room.

He saw a group of the leggy critters gathering near his left foot, closer and closer until one of them brushed up against him. He tried jerking his leg sideways but the chain held him back. He called out. He didn't want to sound frantic, but knew making a little fuss would stroke Brian's ego. He figured Brian was just trying to prove a point—that he was in charge—and with the situation he was in, a courtesy show of deference was well-warranted.

The next thing he knew his leg was on fire, and not just his skin. It felt like someone was driving a white-hot poker deep into the flesh of his shin. He screamed and tried to pull away, but the chain held fast. The pain was blinding.

When his vision cleared, he looked, eyes bulging, at the window in the door. Brian's face was centered in the glass. His expression was a mixture of childlike curiosity and excitement. Marvin was about to beg to him to stop the torture when his thoughts were disconnected by more bites. The massive centipedes were all around him digging their infernal pincers into his flesh. The pain was unbearable. It consumed his existence until the moment he lost consciousness. He never got to enjoy the relief of the consolation of impending death. The only thing he experienced was searing and excruciating pain until the moment he experienced nothing at all.

When Marvin finally stopped writhing, Brian turned from the window, looked at Deckard, who was now officially promoted to second-in-command, and said, "Let's get back to work."

CHAPTER 4

Rugen, Serra, JJ, Dobbler, Alex, and Claire paraded westward along the Plains of Miramar toward Lundgren. It took them three full days of uneventful travel to get from the ruins of Igayim Castle to the foothills of the Ovid Graan Mountains. This was two days less than Alex and Claire's trip in the opposite direction, mainly because they knew where they were going. As they traveled, the road became wider and less cluttered. There were fewer instances where plants had reclaimed the gravelly space. As the road emerged from the thick trees, the mountains in the distance could be seen in their full looming glory. The first unfettered view of the mountains made them seem like they weren't far away, but after an entire day walking, it didn't look like they got any closer.

They were lucky to find no more wandering bands of gmorks during this leg of the journey, partly because of Serra constantly maintaining an invisibility spell, which, of course, didn't make the group invisible as much as it made them less noticeable. Along the way they came across springs every so often, where they'd quench their thirst and fill their water skins, but it was nothing like the fresh and clean taste of the magically protected water of the Divine. For the most part, they ate the preserved foods they had brought with them, but they did manage to locate a few things to forage. While none of them had the wilderness skills of their departed friend Casey, Rugen and JJ were able to use techniques they'd learned during their short time together. Alex and Claire also had some knowledge from their outdoor survival classes at Riser Helm School, and Serra and Dobbler made things a little easier through the use of magic.

As they approached the Ovid Graan foothills, they were excited at the prospect of finally getting a glimpse of Lundgren, but the view of the city was obscured by the mountains rimming the valley in which Lundgren sat. The Ovid Graan Mountains could be described as the spine of Hyboria. They ran between the northeast and southwest coasts through the center of the mostly circular landmass, splitting the area into two almost equal halves. At their extent in the far northeast corner, where there were no known inhabitants, the mountains ended in sheer cliffs that towered over the crashing waves below. In the far southwest, the mountains continued into the ocean as a series of progressively smaller islands tailing off the end of the range.

Historically, the inhabitants of the two halves didn't do much intermingling because of how difficult it was to traverse the mountain terrain. When a war between the two regions broke out a century earlier, much of the population in the north was eradicated or scattered and their infrastructure was destroyed, so there was no longer reason or opportunity for southerners to visit the north.

Alex and Claire led the rest of the travelers to the base of a long stairway which led to a small, wooden shed, where a tall, slim man with a long spear stood guard. The back end of his spear was on the ground, and the blade was above his head.

"There's the guard station," said Claire. "Let me and Alex do the talking." She waved and nodded to the guard, who turned his head toward the building and barked, prompting a second guard to amble out. This one had a large belly, a thick blond beard, and a sword hanging from his hip.

The group slowly approached the stairs. When they neared the bottom step, the guard with the belly yelled, "Stop right there! Are you citizens of Lundgren?"

Alex was still wearing the Naga, but with the mask removed and hanging in front of his chest. He called back, "I am." He gestured to Claire, who smiled. "And my sister. Everyone else is a guest of ours."

"Show me your identification."

JJ rolled his eyes at the formality of it all, which the heavyset guard noticed, prompting him to glare back. The tall one continued to stand perfectly still and at attention.

Alex struggled to peel the Lundgren identification necklace from the inside of his suit, and ended up having to pull his arms free of the leather. For as confident as he was in his full regalia of armor, he looked meek and uncomfortable in his goose-pimpled light brown skin, standing half-naked and holding a bundle of balled-up leather in front of him. Everything about the Naga was elegant aside from the awkward process of taking it off.

The guard, laughing at Alex's embarrassment, said, "I can see you have the medallions. The two of you can come up and get signed in. The rest of you lot, stay put."

When the siblings reached the top of the stairway, the portly guard squinted while reading the number off of Alex's chest. He found the listing in his logbook corresponding to their departure from Lundgren the prior week and wrote something in the empty column next to his name and identification number. As Alex wiggled back into his armor, Claired removed her necklace and handed it to the guard.

"Everything checks out. Welcome back to Lundgren. Now, what's the story with the rest of your group?"

Claire shot a look down the stairs to her new friends. "They're visiting," she responded. "We have business at RHS."

The portly guard hefted his belt, making the sword and scabbard jiggle around. "RHS, eh? I suppose Lord Volguus is expecting you?" He gave a courtesy look at his book. "I have no note here about non-citizens entering Lundgren to visit RHS." He looked around Claire's hip to inspect the group at the bottom of the stairs.

Alex, who again felt rather silly with his mask dangling in front of his chest, spoke up. "Lord Volguus doesn't know we're coming. But I promise you this is important business." He opened his mouth to say more, but the guard interrupted him by waving his hand dismissively.

"Yeah yeah, I'm sure it is. I don't need to hear it. Your guests will have to check in with the duke. We don't get visitors too often, and when we do, that's the policy. Can't be too careful nowadays."

Alex and Claire nodded.

"They need to leave their weapons with me. The duke doesn't allow armed visitors."

Alex looked at Claire, who met his eyes and half-shrugged. "We'll tell them."

"They also need to be handcuffed, and walked under supervision. Policy."

The guard with the long spear hadn't moved or said anything since the siblings had reached the top of the stairs. He seemed to be impersonating a statue.

"Ohh … kay," responded Claire.

Leaving the two guards behind, they decended the stairs. As they went Alex whispered, "They're gonna love this."

"So what's the verdict?" asked Rugen.

"We can all go in," said Alex, "but you have to leave your weapons at the gate." He started to say more but caught himself.

"And?" prompted Serra.

Alex half-mumbled, "And they want you handcuffed for the walk to the administrative offices."

"What?! They want to put me in chains?" snapped JJ, looking appalled.

Rugen glanced at the guards and whispered, "I didn't come all this way to be paraded through the city like a common prisoner."

"Even if that fat slob could get a hold of me," started JJ, definitely not whispering, "which he couldn't, he wouldn't be able to apply the chains with his bulbous belly getting in the way."

Dobbler and Rugen chuckled, but Claire cringed, knowing JJ's voice was loud enough to carry up to the platform. She looked up and saw the larger guard turn and head back to the shack, leaving only the stick figure.

"It's the only way we're getting in, which means it's the only way we're building an army, which means it's the only way we're crossing the mountains," said Claire, counting on her fingers.

"Are there any other paths into the city?" asked Rugen.

"Not anymore," responded Alex. "When the roads were safer, people would come and go all the time. Back then there was a much larger passage."

"It has to still be there," whispered JJ. "Forget these guys. Let's just sneak in that way."

"No. They walled it off with boulders," said Alex. "Then workers covered the road heading to the gate with dirt and planted thorn bushes and brambles. Besides, even if you could sneak into the city, you wouldn't able to accomplish much of anything without the proper authorizations."

"Chained together and driven at sword-point," said Rugen, shaking his head. "We'll be a spectacle."

"We'll be a spectacle either way," Dobbler pointed out. "And don't worry about being chained. Chains are just jewelry to Serra and me."

Serra added, "And we don't need weapons."

"Okay. Let's do it," said Rugen. "Alex, Claire, I think one of you should carry the gold in case they decide to search the rest of us. You've already been cleared."

"I'll take it," said Claire.

Rugen handed her the nearly weightless coin purse, which she dropped into her bag.

After taking a deep breath, Rugen led the group up the stairs in single file. The stone staircase wasn't wide enough for more than that.

Alex and Claire passed through the checkpoint while the other four were processed one by one. The lead guard took their names and scribbled a short description of them to be referenced later for identification. For Rugen he wrote, "Dopey looking giant, big sword." Serra was "Lanky waif, pretty eyes." JJ was "Flaming hair, thinks he's funny. Isn't." Finally, Dobbler's descriptive words were "Small, rat-faced. Shady looking."

After finishing, he said, "All right, gentleman." He looked Serra up and down, who in return smiled kindly, and added, "And lady." She nodded. "If you don't mind surrendering your weapons..." He took Rugen's longsword in its scabbard, JJ's sword and gauntlet, and all of the various daggers they were carrying. "You can come back here to retrieve them after you meet with the duke."

From behind the guards appeared a man with a white beard wearing an eggplant-colored robe adorned with small patches of green fabric cut into the jagged shapes of chestnut leaves. Without a word of greeting he put his hands onto Dobbler and Serra's shoulders and said, "Hrousy emfoi."

Serra and Dobbler looked at each other, expressionless.

The old cleric turned to the guards and said, "These two won't give you any trouble now."

"What was that?" asked Rugen.

"It prevents sorcerers and clerics from performing spells," answered Serra without any emotion.

"You guys can't rescue us with magic?" asked JJ, almost laughing.

Dobbler shrugged.

The lead guard clapped his hands together and loudly said, "All right boys, link these fine folks up and bring 'em to the duke!"

Chapter 5

Behind the guard station was a path leading to a second stairway that hugged the slope of the foothill up and off to the left. Alex and Claire walked alongside their chained teammates, whose wrist cuffs were shackled to metal bindings encircling their waists, allowing them only a foot of slack to move their arms. The group was escorted by two younger soldiers who had been beckoned to the guard station during the check-in process, one leading the procession and the other at the rear.

As they approached the second stairway, Alex and Claire increased their pace so they could get ahead and be the first up the steps. To their left was the upward slope of the hill and to the right was a rolling drop. There was no handrail. Alex had told them that the distance from the base of the foothill to the top of the stairway was spanned by the rise of about eleven hundred steps, and the rounded peak of the hill extended well above that.

The blowing wind, irregular and slippery stone stairs, lack of a handrail, and the fact that they were chained together made for a slow climb. They had to carefully fix their eyes on the footing, trying not to be the one responsible for taking a misstep that might knock everyone over the ledge. Rugen glanced up quickly to see the siblings, who had reached the next landing, looking back at him and smiling, which puzzled him until he arrived there.

Another guard station was situated at the top. It looked out over Lundgren, the largest city in all of Hyboria, in the valley below.

The siblings had gazed upon this sight many times before, but were excited to see it through the eyes of first timers. The two Lundgren soldiers, who spent their days at that guard station, were indifferent to the view and just wanted to finish transporting the group so they could get back to their regular duties.

The scope of the space in front of them was surreal. It was a wide valley surrounded by a ring of mountains, the peaks of which towered far above the spot where they stood. The foothill was dwarfed by the summits along the ring, and those in turn were dwarfed by the proper mountains in the distance. From their vantage point, they could see bare rock above the tree line and the snow-capped peaks. For the amount of effort it took to get just to the second guard station, they couldn't imagine climbing one of those intimidating mammoths. It was dizzying to think that the plan was to eventually be on the other side of them.

Sprawled across the valley floor was the wheel-shaped network of the city of Lundgren. At the hub, a cluster of large buildings was surrounded by ever-expanding concentric circles of alternating roads and canals. These circles were split into segments by eight long streets—spokes that emanated from the center all the way to the base of the bordering ring of mountains. A river ran from a gap between two mountains in the distance, cutting through the otherwise perfect web of throughways. The river fed the network of canals before exiting the city. It followed the curve of the land off to the right before disappearing into the distance.

Dotted throughout the cityscape were countless squares of brick and stone buildings lining the annular streets and spoked avenues. The monotony of the block buildings was periodically broken by the columns, spires, and domes of more substantial structures.

"It looks like a giant spider web," remarked Rugen.

"Spider webs are for catching and killing," quipped JJ.

Straining his eyes, Rugen spied countless tiny people walking in all directions—in and out of buildings, across bridges, and up and down streets. There were more people than he had ever seen in his entire life.

"Welcome to Lundgren!" exclaimed Alex while holding out his hand to present his city to his new friends. Claire was beaming right along with him.

After a while of staring, one of the escorts grumbled, "All right, let's go. We have places to be." He scanned the path ahead, which wound down the other side of the foothill and into the valley where Lundgren sat. He asked Alex and Claire to go on ahead of the rest of the group.

The guards watched the siblings walk along the path, waiting until they were well into it before restarting the train. Serra tried several times to engage them in conversation. Initially her questions were answered by grunts and shrugs, until finally one of them said, "Look, Miss, we're not here to be tour guides. Save your questions for the duke."

Realizing that trying to appeal to the soldiers would be a fruitless endeavor, they continued the march in silence, gazing at the tops of the massive mountains looming above as they went. The view of the cityscape, so incredible from the upper platform, was now completely obstructed by trees along the path.

Finally the slope leveled out, indicating that they were at street level. Around a bend they found the city gate, which opened to a grand avenue stretching all the way to the hub.

The gate doors were colossal—three times the height of a man, and twenty people could comfortably walk abreast between the massive marble pillars that held them. They consisted of vertical bars that were metallic yellow in color, giving the impression they were made of solid gold. Each bar was about an inch wide and elegantly twisted in a decorative fashion as they rose from the base. Across the top was an arch that spelled out "LUNDGREN" in the same golden metal.

Ever since they first arrived at the guard station, Rugen couldn't help but wonder how Lundgren citizens would react to seeing four bound strangers being marched at sword-point. He imagined a lot of pointing, staring, ridicule, and laughter. He was surprised to find the opposite. People were all around but were seemingly oblivious to the parade. A large number of them walked en masse in every direction. Others leaned on buildings, rested on benches reading books, played music, or ate and drank at outdoor cafes.

The promenade along which they were being led ended at the distant circle of buildings in the center hub. The farther along the road they went, they did start to garner some attention, indicated by the confused looks and curious whispers. Lundgrenians were subject to bizarre occurrences and peculiarity on a regular basis, but a group of chained people being led by soldiers was a novelty.

It wasn't difficult to determine that the group was made up of travelers. Rugen and JJ were wearing leather battle armor crusted in days of dirt and grime. Dobbler's high-collared coat and Serra's cleric robe weren't common Lundgren fashion. All four of them, as well as their unchained companions, had the haggard look and fetid smell of time on the road.

Serra broke the discomfort and embarrassment of her teammates by politely smiling at and greeting some of the gawking citizens. At first they didn't know how to react, but eventually they answered with greetings of their own. Nobody had the courage to further interact with the prisoners when they saw the scowl on the faces of their soldier escorts.

JJ looked at the Grady siblings and asked, "What do you know about the duke?"

Alex responded with a shrug, "Never met him."

"He's responsible for all major decisions in Lundgren," said Claire.

"Has the same guy always been in charge?" asked Rugen, relishing anything that distracted him from thoughts about their current predicament.

"Every so often they appoint someone new to take over," started Alex, "sometimes for a longer term and sometimes shorter. It's always one of the high-up administrators or tenured professors from RHS."

"They stay in the position as long as they're doing a good job and there's no one better to take over," added Claire. "The current guy has been duke for several years. Our dad thinks they'll keep him."

"Do they ever pick a woman?" asked Serra.

Claire shook her head. "No, there aren't any female professors or administrators at RHS. Remember there weren't even any female students before me."

"Are there female students now?"

Claire paused for a moment. "A few. It's not really catching on, which isn't surprising because the training is brutal." She patted Alex on the back. "I couldn't have completed it without my brother's help."

Alex put his arm around her shoulders. "Are you kidding me? I'm the one who needed help."

"Enough with the family memories," growled the rear guard.

Dobbler followed his rude statement with, "Let's stay focused, guys. We're in chains here and possibly being led to our execution."

While they marched onward to the administrative building, Rugen began to fixate on Dobbler's comment. The duke had the responsibility of thousands of people living in the city. Maybe the slaughter of four foreigners would be a fun distraction for him. He asked, to no one in particular, "What if the duke does decide to execute us on sight?"

"I wouldn't worry about it," responded JJ, making Rugen feel a little relieved. Then he continued, "I mean, whether he wants to kill us or not we can't do anything about it, right? He has complete control. We're chained, weaponless, and if it comes to that we'd be completely outnumbered and surrounded. There'd be nothing we could do to stop him, so why worry?"

CHAPTER 6

The travelers stood in front of a large and ornately crafted stone building. It had five floors, judging by the windows, and was topped with a large dome. Rugen momentarily wondered how a dome could be made out of stone, but that thought was quickly replaced by the worry of what awaited them underneath it.

Their escorts consulted with the armed guard at the building's door for a minute before leading the travelers inside. They were met by a flow of cool air as they passed over the threshold. For the building to be cooler inside than outside, it was either a marvel of engineering or Ravenwood magic. They were ushered up five flights of stairs and finally into the antechamber of the office of the Duke of Lundgren, where they were told to sit and wait.

After a moment the office door opened and the escort gestured them to proceed inside. The non-citizens were asked to stand in a line in front of the duke's desk, while Alex and Claire were allowed to sit. An unattractive man with a long forehead and bulbous nose was seated and glaring at them. His thin and wispy hair revealed nearly the entirety of his scalp underneath. "And what can I do for you?" he barked.

"Hello, Your Grace," Alex jumped in, "I'm Alex Grady." He pointed to Claire. "This is my sister Claire. We're citizens of Lundgren and recent graduates of Riser Helm School."

The duke scanned the four travelers in front of him. "And them? I'm told they're not citizens?"

Rugen opened his mouth to speak, but before he could get a word out, the duke silenced him with a raised hand. He stared at Rugen for a long moment before shifting his gaze back to Alex.

"No, Your Grace. They aren't citizens," said Alex, nervously fidgeting in his seat.

"Why are they here?"

"They're on a quest to rid Hyboria of the horrible monsters that have plagued us for too long." He swallowed and added, "We all are."

The duke glanced around the room. "The six of you and... who else?"

"No one else. Right now it's just us. That's why we're in Lundgren. To recruit soldiers to join us."

The duke looked Alex's armor up and down and growled, "What are you wearing, boy?"

The Naga definitely fit the part on the battlefield, but a skintight black leather one-piece complete with built-in boots and imbued with blunted metal blades wasn't proper attire for a meeting with the leader of Lundgren. The fact that a deformed flop of mask dangled from the front of his neck made it all the worse. He half-raised his arms and said, "It's a weapon I found. It's incredibly powerful."

"It looks ridiculous."

Alex's face flushed. He didn't know how to respond to this while trying to remain deferential, so he lowered his arms in silence.

The duke turned to address Rugen. "You tried to talk out of turn. That must make you the leader of this…" He gestured to the rest them standing uncomfortably, "group." He blinked his eyes slowly and dramatically. "What do you have to say?"

"Thank you, sir."

The duke's eyes widened as he corrected Rugen. "I am to be addressed as *Your Grace!*"

"Yes, Your Grace. Excuse me." Rugen swallowed hard and continued, "A man named Gordon started all of this. He traveled from the town of Winston, and along the way collected men to join him. I fought alongside him before he was struck down. All but two of us were killed that day." He glanced at JJ. "We were rescued by these magicians in Ravenwood." He gestured to Serra and Dobbler. "And as you can see now we are six. We need new recruits in Lundgren, because the road from here only gets more treacherous." He paused before hurriedly adding, "Your Grace."

"I understand you've had losses," responded the duke, waving his hand dismissively, "In that you're no different than the rest of us. We've all had losses. You come here wanting; asking for my help, but what do you offer Lundgren in return?"

Thinking what he had said was rather explanatory, Rugen was befuddled by the duke's response. He muttered, "Your Grace." Then cleared his throat and said, "Well, we can offer you what everyone wants. Freedom from oppression. The ability to live our lives in peace without monsters segregating us and killing us every chance they get. We'd like to reopen the trade routes between the towns and exact vengeance for those who were killed."

The duke leaned forward and stared at Rugen. "The people of Lundgren are as free as we want to be. We move through the mountains at will. We farm our own food and raise our own livestock. We have clean water and reliable waste removal. We have masons, carpenters, glaziers, tailors, and landscapers. We have art, music, literature, and theater. Most of all we have peace among our own people and security from intruders. We are completely self-sufficient here. We didn't have the need for outside support before, and we don't need it now."

"Lundgren is truly a magnificent city," complimented Rugen, "but what about the people beyond the reach of your security? The presence of the monsters is slowly suffocating them."

The duke slammed his hand on the desk and exclaimed, "The people of Hyboria should rise up and fight for themselves."

"That's what we're trying to do!" snapped JJ, unable to quash his frustration any longer.

The duke looked momentarily surprised by this outburst, but then his face turned red, making his guards take a step forward until the duke halted them with one slight shake of his head. He swallowed his rage and responded, "This meeting has ended, as has your time in Lundgren." He stood and calmly said, "Farewell, and good luck with your rebellion."

As the guards started moving again, Serra calmly said, "Your Grace, help us help you clean up your mess."

A guard grabbed hold of Rugen's arm as the duke fired his gaze at her, bellowing, "What did you say, girl?!"

"I know about Brian Gruhl," responded Serra quietly. "He's from Lundgren. It's an RHS washout who caused all of this trouble. I think the reason you haven't sent an army his way is that you don't want your citizens or the rest of Hyboria to know the truth."

"And where did you get this ridiculous idea?"

"My father was an RHS student with Brian. He told me he was bullied by a lot of students, including my father. After he murdered his family, things got really tense at school. People wondered if he would go after the students who picked on him. Eventually, my dad washed out and his family moved away. People forgot about Brian, but my dad never did. He felt guilty about his role in twisting Brian's mind. He believes the monsters are Brian's revenge on everyone, especially Lundgren."

"That's preposterous!" yelled the duke, springing to his feet. "Guards, remove them!"

The guards followed the order until a calm voice said, "She's right."

Everyone turned to look at the office door where a tall, trim, well-dressed man stood. He had short gray-white hair and a thin line of beard that ran from his bottom lip to beneath his chin. He had a stern but friendly expression on his face. He signaled to the guards. "Unchain them."

The guards quickly worked to remove all of the bindings from the four travelers, who in turn stretched their stiff arms and rubbed their sore wrists.

The man stepped into the office and put his hand out to Serra. "My name is Alonzo. I'm the Duke of Lundgren." Serra shook his hand and then turned to look at who she thought was the duke.

"Eddie is my assistant. I asked him to stand in for me. I needed to figure out who you were before agreeing to meet with you." He nodded to Eddie, who walked out of the room. Then he said to his guests, "Have a seat and tell me about your quest and how I could be of help."

CHAPTER 7

Thankful to be out of the shackles, resting in a chair, and drinking a glass of water, Rugen spoke to Duke Alonso about how miserable life had become in the towns since The Isolation. He talked about Gordon's mission, being rescued by Serra, meeting Dobbler in Ravenwood, finding Alex and Claire on the Plains of Miramar, and the battles with the monsters.

When he was finished, the duke asked, "And now you are looking to hire some soldiers?"

Rugen nodded. "It's been suggested that the road gets harder from here—more difficult terrain and more monsters."

"We're hoping to talk to Lord Volguus at RHS," added Alex. "Maybe there are some graduating students the Lundgren Army could spare?"

Alonzo nodded as he thought about this. Finally he said, "Maybe…maybe." He raised his eyebrows. "Yes. I think that would be possible. I could mention something to him."

Rugen and Alex looked at each other and then Alex said, "Thank you, Your Grace. We'd really appreciate it."

"Your Grace, what Serra said earlier," started Claire, "is it true that the army never went after the guy who started all this?"

Duke Alonzo blinked hard. "Just like everywhere else, when the monsters came it caused chaos. We had people outside of the city limits when it started. Many of them fled to safety, but others were maimed or killed. For a long time the only thing we cared about was the security of our own citizens. It never occurred to us that a person, much less one of our own, could be causing such destruction and terror, because we were too busy trying to protect our borders. Then one day a note...well, I guess you'd call it a manifesto, appeared at the front gate. It was several pages of mostly blustering nonsense and vague threats. It didn't take us long to figure out who it was from."

The duke had the quiet confidence that made the other people in the room know when it was time for them to talk and time for them say nothing and listen. "I was at RHS when the murders occurred. Brian was always angry and awkward, and alarmingly lacking in empathy and social skills. His older brother Anthony was the complete opposite; a role model for everyone. How the same parents could spawn such totally different boys is beyond my understanding." He stopped and sighed. "I was in the same class year as Anthony. He was well respected. And I don't just mean the other students. Administrators, professors… Everyone who met him was left with a sense of awe and respect, including me."

Alonso paused before continuing, "Did you know that the spineless little ingrate cut Anthony's throat while he slept? And then he did the same to his father! His mother was devastated. I've never seen someone so bereft. It wasn't long after that his mother killed herself. She drank an entire bottle of Kampff Elixir and never woke up."

The duke shook his head in disgust and then went on, "When we received the letter, we scrambled to put more security around the city. We figured an invasion of monsters was coming from the north. Really it makes sense that Brian would have fled there—it's full of the worst Hyboria has to offer. My top priority was keeping Lundgren citizens safe. After that initial flurry of creatures, things calmed down. Life returned to normal inside the city, and we've spent the last few years slowly expanding, searching for suitable space among the mountains to find and develop resources. Every now and again we'll have a scuffle with a small group of beasts. We try never to overreach our capabilities, but Lundgren has doubled in area since then." He looked at his hands in his lap. "We were so focused on ourselves we never thought about how the rest of Hyboria was fairing."

He sighed, then continued, "With that being said, I don't feel comfortable dispatching our commanders and elite fighters to go find Brian. For as great as Lundgren is, I'm not blind to the fact that our citizens can be unruly. The population keeps expanding, and we need a lot of resources to keep peace on the streets."

"I do think we could help though," he said, clapping his hands, "by providing a small fighting force, led by the six of you, to ferret Brian out and bring him to justice." He looked to Alex. "You said you're familiar with Lord Volguus?"

Alex nodded. "My sister and I both graduated from Riser Helm."

Alonzo's eyes got wide as he looked at Claire. "You're Claire Grady?"

Claire blushed and nodded.

Alonzo stood, walked to Claire, and shook her hand. "The first female RHS graduate. Hopefully the first of many. You made a lot of people proud that day." He addressed the entire group. "Go. Get settled in. I'll tell Lord Volguus our plan in a day or two. You can meet with him later in the week." He wrote the name and address of an inn on a piece of paper and handed it to Rugen. "I suggest you stay here. I'll leave a message for you at the front desk when I hear something."

The guards were no longer posted at the door when the group left Duke Alonzo's office, which made the feeling of freedom palpable. Even though the shackles had been applied for less than two hours, being out of them felt like the beginning of a new day. The four newly-authorized guests of Lundgren followed their citizen sponsors through the halls of the administrative building and down the stairs.

"Now what?" asked Rugen.

"I don't care what we do," answered Dobbler, "As long as it's away from this building."

"I'd like to go see my parents," suggested Serra.

Alex gestured to Claire and said, "Us too."

Claire patted her bag and added, "And I don't want to carry all this gold anymore."

"Let's go to the bank," said Alex. "We'll exchange the gold coins for a pile of pelts to split, then we'll take you to the inn Volguus suggested."

Rugen looked confused. "Why are there inns? There can't be much business from tourists since The Isolation."

"There's certainly less than what used to be before the monsters," responded Alex, "but when the soldiers who patrol the mountains are on leave and come back to the city, some of them need a place to stay."

"I bet the inns offer other activities that bring in a lot of revenue to keep them afloat," said JJ, winking.

Claire frowned. "If you're referring to food and drink, then yes, every inn is attached to a pub."

Leaving through the back of the building, they found themselves in the courtyard of the Administrative Hub. They stopped at the fringe and looked at the neatly trimmed grass and manicured trees. People were strolling about or chatting on benches. Children were chasing each other and play-fighting with sticks on the lawn as their mothers looked on. There were a total of eight buildings there, each separated by the beginning of one of the long spoke avenues.

Alex pointed them out as he talked. "Remember the avenues we saw from the top of the hill? This is where they start."

"Or end, depending on your perspective," clarified Dobbler.

JJ scoffed, "Such a nerd."

The group looked around, mentally counting the avenues as Alex went on. "To keep it simple they named them for their directions. We came in on the South spoke. That's the North, East, and West. In between are Northeast, Northwest, and so on. It makes navigating the city a lot easier."

"Which one do we take to get to the bank?" asked Serra.

"None of them," answered Alex, pointing to a building across the courtyard. "It's right there."

CHAPTER 8

Rugen, Serra, JJ, and Dobbler sat on the ground outside the bank building, which was a monstrosity of stone on the opposite side of the Administrative Hub from where they just left. Alex and Claire were inside depositing the gold coins and getting smaller denominations. It was a long wait, but sitting was a nice break from all the walking they had been doing, and it was a glorious mid-summer day under the shade of an elm.

Rugen looked at Serra and said, "So I don't understand. Your father's from here but doesn't live here?"

"No." She shook her head. "He and my mom do live here."

"Why didn't you tell the guards you were a citizen then?"

"I'm not a citizen." She glanced at him, realizing more explanation was in order. "My father's family originated here but they moved to Florin when he was a teenager. Later he met my mom, got married, had me, and I grew up there until I moved to Ravenwood for cleric school. After that my parents came to Lundgren. Later the monsters came, and here we are." She said all this on one breath, then exhaled dramatically and finished with, "Now you know my whole story."

The siblings exited the bank and made their way to the group, who stood up to greet them. They handed out a small fabric bag to each of their friends, keeping one to share between the two of them. The bags were made of purple velvet, tied at the top with a golden-colored length of braided string. Sewn along the side was a stylized capital L. Rugen opened his and spilled the contents into his hand. It was a pile of brown-tinged coins with the same scripted L on one face and a carved picture of a mountain on the reverse. In tiny lettering below the L it read "One Peltzer" and below the mountain, "City of Lundgren."

"So what are these worth?" asked Rugen.

"A night at an inn will cost one or two pelts," started Claire, "depending on how nice the room is. That's also about the cost of dinner at a fine restaurant for a small group, again depending on how many guests and how fancy the restaurant. Sixty of them make a silver coin. People don't generally walk around with silver unless they're planning on making a big purchase, like handcrafted weapons or armor from a blacksmith, for example. The whole lot of us could get kitted out in the best gear for four or five silver coins."

"You mean if we didn't already have stuff waiting for us at the front gate," JJ interjected. "Speaking of which, when can we get that back?"

"That won't be a problem," responded Alex. "I'll go with you tomorrow to get it."

"The most valuable coin, as you saw, is gold," continued Claire. "Those are for major investments, like buying a house or starting a business. Your little velvet bag doesn't have any of those… or silver for that matter. There are smaller denominations too, but you'll figure those out as you go."

Rugen poured the pelts back into the little bag he was given, tied it, and tucked it away. "How many gold coins did you say we had?"

"Two hundred fifty five, pretty much all of which are still in the bank even with all the pelts we withdrew."

"At twelve hundred per gold coin, we're loaded," smiled Serra.

"What did the bank say about you guys bringing in such a large amount?" asked Rugen.

"Like I said the rule around here is finders-keepers," Alex responded. "They didn't question it at all. And Mr. Igayim has long since left this world. He's not going to complain."

"We're sharing the money evenly, right?" asked Dobbler.

Alex and Claire looked at each other and Alex answered. "Yes, but there's way more than we could ever spend in a… Well, however long it takes to build an army. What you have in those bags should be plenty for a good while."

"Don't underestimate how much money young people can spend on their first visit to the big city," said JJ, grinning.

"What if we need more?" asked Dobbler.

"Only citizens can do business in Lundgren banks," responded Claire, "and since you guys aren't citizens, you'll need me or Alex to withdraw the money."

"And then what about after we leave the city?"

"I don't know how useful Lundgren coins will be on the road," answered Claire.

"I think what the wizard wants to know is if you're going to steal his cut of the money," JJ said.

"No. Far from it," assured Alex. "We wouldn't've gotten the treasure chest without you. All of you. We split it equally. We'll spend some of it while we're here, and after the quest we'll come back. If any of you want to apply for citizenship, you can get your own account. Or if you want to leave the city with one sixth of whatever's left, it's yours."

"We already agreed to trust them with our lives by coming here," added JJ, addressing Dobbler. "Trusting them to give us a bunch of money we didn't have or know we wanted before we met them is pretty trivial, right?"

Dobbler nodded then said, "Fine, but just so you know, I'm not a wizard. There are no wizards. I'm a sorcerer."

JJ laughed, shaking his head.

"Speaking of which," Claire said to Serra, marveling, "that spell you used to remove the weight of the coins? That was incredible. The whole bag of them felt like nothing, but as I pulled them out, their weight sprang back to normal."

"I'm loaded with tricks," smiled Serra.

"Speaking of tricks, don't you two need that old man to reverse the spell block thing he did at the guard shack?" asked Rugen.

Dobbler held out his hand, whispered something, and a tiny flame ignited in his palm. He held it there as it changed colors from orange to green to blue. At the same time, Serra was laughing as she waved her fingers around. The tips were glowing with purple light.

"You think we'd let a guy like that do anything to us?" laughed Dobbler.

Claire slid her coin bag into her pocket, saying, "Now that we're all settled on the money, let's get you guys to the Stanley."

"The what?" asked Rugen.

"The best inn Lundgren has to offer," joked Claire.

The group made their way to the Stanley Lodge. Before Rugen, JJ, and Dobbler checked in, Serra and the Grady twins shared their addresses, and Serra invited everyone to her parents' house for brunch the next morning. She knew her mother loved entertaining and was sure she wouldn't mind having her new friends over.

The base fee at the Stanley was one half pelt per night. All of the rooms were singles, so the three travelers each had their own space. After The Isolation, most inns converted their rooms to single occupancy, as the roads to Lundgren were no longer safe for families. Most of the customers were soldiers returning from the front, and to them a private place away from others was a welcome change of pace.

Rugen found his room to be no larger than Serra's dorm at Wallace, which was fine by him. It had a small bed off of which his feet dangled, a single window with a view of the stone wall of the building next door, and a simple wooden table and chair. His primary task was to get cleaned up from the long arduous journey. Fortunately, Ravenwood's magical plumbing innovations were standard in Lundgren and the front desk of the Stanley stocked a considerable supply of soaps and other toiletries available for nominal fees. It also offered laundry service and loaner clothes, the latter because the staff was used to soldiers who were traveling light and needed something to wear while their own clothes were being cleaned.

After washing up and eating dinner, Rugen knocked on JJ's door. When there was no answer, he knocked again, but halfway through he stopped, realizing that the likely reason JJ wasn't answering was because he had fallen asleep. He walked down to Dobbler's room and found him reading a book borrowed from the tiny library next to the front desk. They spoke for an hour about their personal histories—Rugen's growing up in Mourain, swordfight training, and his ongoing but waning contempt for his father; Dobbler's growing up on Beckersted Island, sorcery school, and life in Ravenwood. One topic Dobbler definitely had no comment on was Serra Frye.

CHAPTER 9

Rugen awoke with an urgent feeling that something was missing or needed to be done. This stemmed from the experience of the last few days of waking up on the cold ground with the threat of attack looming. He quickly realized he was in a warm bed surrounded by four walls, which made the anxiety wane and a sense of peace wash over him.

He readied himself in the bathroom and opened his door to find his freshly cleaned leather armor and undergarments lying in a neat pile at his feet. He couldn't help but wonder what additional luxuries a one-pelt-per-night kind of place would offer beyond those provided by the Stanley, but then he remembered each additional frill he'd taken advantage of came with a small fee.

A note sitting on top of his possessions read, "Please inquire about leather repair." He was confused for a moment until he picked up his armor and saw the gashes the ursinox had ripped down the back. Looking at them rekindled a wave of nausea as he recalled the battle that slaughtered his friends. He told himself he'd rather replace the armor than repair it. Some memories were better forgotten.

As he dressed in his torn armor, he thought about how he wanted to spend money on new clothes. That would have to be after Serra's brunch. He found Dobbler's door ajar and knocked lightly on it, eliciting a grunting yet welcoming response.

As Rugen entered, Dobbler stood up from his bed and set the book he was reading on the table. He scoffed, "You think Sleepy's ready to go?"

"For as early as he turned in last night, he oughta be. Let's go get him."

They went to JJ's door and knocked. Having received no answer Dobbler joked, "Maybe you're not doing it right," and knocked out a rhythmic pattern.

A low groan rumbled through the door. "Wwwwwhhhhhhhhmmmmm..."

Rugen and Dobbler looked at each other, confused. Dobbler said, "This is his room, right?"

Rugen rechecked the number above the closed door and shrugged. He loudly called, "JJ?"

After a long moment they heard a thump on the floor and more moaning, followed by a deep, dry, and broken voice. "Yeah, hang on." There was silence for a while and then, "Can you come back later?"

Dobbler chuckled and then the two men turned to walk away.

JJ grunted through the door, "I'll meet you downstairs!"

They waited in the lobby for JJ for a long while. When he finally arrived, his eyes were bloodshot and his long red ponytail was mussed.

He grumbled, "Morning," but didn't wait for a response from the other two before walking out the front door and onto the street.

Rugen and Dobbler obediently followed him.

All awkwardness was forgotten as their senses were overcome by seeing Lundgren for the first time in the light of day as free men. The houses, storefronts, and other buildings were brimming with life. People shuffled in and out, swarming the cobblestone streets. The sound of clomping boots, chattering voices, and rolling carts roared in their ears. The din was a far cry from the quietness of the road. Smells of bread baking, meat grilling, and sauces simmering rounded out the assault on the senses.

As Alex had demonstrated when they left the administrative building, the city was designed to be easily navigated. The spoked avenues were named for the eight cardinal directions. The annular streets were named for war heroes of the past, starting at the center with Apone, Bishop, Drake, and so on. There was no street name starting with C, or many other letters for that matter, but the letters that were represented progressed in alphabetical order, simplifying navigation.

For example, the address for Serra's parents' house was 73 North-Northeast Hudson Street, and the Stanley was on 237 South-Southwest Frost. Rugen, JJ, and Dobbler could have made the trip by taking Southwest Avenue down to Hudson Street and rounding its lengthy circumference, but JJ's sluggish start meant they would have to take a much shorter route. They turned right onto Southwest Avenue toward the city center, cutting through the Administrative Hub, and then followed North Avenue up to Hudson. Dobbler had studied and memorized the map in his room the night before and seemed to know every turn and shortcut.

When they arrived at the address Serra had provided, they found her parents' home to be smaller than what they were used to seeing in Lundgren. It was made of round stones, reminiscent of large river stones, mortared together into an A-frame. There was a chimney on top with a wisp of smoke breathing out of it. Three steps led to the front door, which was flanked by windows with boxes underneath brimming with vibrant greenery spilling over the sides and an array of proud white and yellow flowers.

Rugen climbed the steps and knocked on the door.

Serra's father answered with a scowl on his face. He shook Rugen's hand and said, "So you're the guy who made my daughter miss her graduation. Six years of work and then you came along."

Serra appeared, looking embarrassed. "Daddy! We talked about this!"

Rugen didn't know how to respond. Technically that was exactly what happened, but prior to entering Ravenwood he was unaware of who Serra was, what Wallace was, or the date of Wallace's graduation. All he managed in response was, "Yes, sir, sorry about that."

Mrs. Frye lightly slapped her husband on the arm. "Oh Ed, stop trying to scare the boy."

The scowl on Mr. Frye's face fell to a more neutral expression. "I'm glad you brought her here, but in a perfect world you would've shown up on her doorstep a week later." He looked at his wife. "Well, Grace, at least because of him we don't have to feel guilty about missing our daughter's graduation!"

"Daddy, I told you my vice principal said I officially graduated and can retrieve my diploma whenever I get back there."

"*Vice* principal, huh? What about the principal? What'd he say?"

"You must be Serra's friend," Grace Frye said to Dobbler, changing the subject.

"Yes ma'am, I'm Lane Dobbler. Peop…" He cleared his throat. "People call me Dobbler."

JJ gave a sturdy forearm handshake to Mr. Frye, "And I'm Rugen's friend

JJ, and I had nothing to do with his plan to ruin your daughter's education." He turned to Mrs. Frye and said, "Something smells glorious in here."

"That would be the sausages," she responded. "Let's sit down and talk over brunch."

The house had a courtyard behind it overlooking a canal. It was a perfect morning to eat outdoors—sunny but temperate with a light breeze. They sat and enjoyed eggs, sausage, fresh fruit, bread rolls, homemade butter, jam, and chocolates. Mrs. Frye had gone out to the market that morning to shop for it all. Serra's parents hadn't suspected their daughter to show up on their doorstep the prior night and certainly had no idea she'd be inviting new friends to their home for a meal, but as Serra expected, it was an imposition they were pleased to accept.

The conversation ranged over a wide variety of topics. There were discussions about where everyone was from and what life was like in those various places. The mood got somber at the mention of family and friends who were lost, particularly the fresh losses along the trip to Ravenwood. The most delicate topic of conversation was about the near future, when they were planning to leave Lundgren to find the source of the monsters.

Mr. Frye, pointing at Rugen with the sausage slice he had skewered at the end of his fork, said, "You four are going to take on Brian's army?"

Mrs. Frye, who seemed always to be trying to lessen the impact of her husband's words, put her hand on his non-sausage eating arm as she addressed her daughter. "Serra honey, didn't you say you had others with you? A brother and sister you met on the road?"

JJ looked up from the toast he was buttering. "Yeah, where are those two? You invited them here."

"I have their address," assured Serra. "We'll stop there later." She looked at her parents. "Alex and Claire will be taking us to RHS to recruit our own army after Duke Alonzo talks to Lord Volguus."

In answer to Mr. Frye's question, Dobbler said, "Serra learned a lot at Wallace. She can defend herself." He coughed lightly. "Actually, we're counting on her to defend all of us. She's the key to this whole plan."

Mr. Frye furrowed his brow briefly at Dobbler and asked, "Who's Lord Volguus?"

"We're not sure exactly," answered Dobbler, "But the duke and our friend Alex both talked about him. He must be a big-wig at RHS."

"With all due respect to my lovely daughter, it sounds to me like your friend Alex, and not her, is the key to this whole plan. Without him you don't have a connection to Volguus or RHS." He looked around the table. "Where is he by the way? You don't think he gave you a made-up address and they already emptied that account Serra told us about. Or maybe there never even was an account. Did you go into the bank with them? Maybe they just walked in, made a little change, and walked out with all the rest."

"Oh Ed, stop it," scolded Mrs. Frye, with her hand on her husband's arm again. "Those kids just got back home after a long trip through the wilderness, just like our Serra did. I'm sure their parents wanted them close by today. Stop being such a bear with everyone!"

CHAPTER 10

"Do you think he's right?" asked Rugen.

"Who? My dad?" Serra looked embarrassed.

"Yeah, do you think Alex and Claire gave us a handful of pelts and kept all the gold for themselves?"

The four travelers sat at Serra's parents' table drinking Aslan tea, a fragrant brew cultivated from the high plateaus of the Ovid Graans. Serra's parents had gone inside to clean the dishes and silverware from brunch and to give them some privacy.

"They wouldn't do that," said Dobbler. "They're friends of ours."

"We might think they're our friends," said Rugen. "But we don't really know them."

"We don't really know any of us," said JJ with a half-sneer. "The person I've known the longest in this group is Rugen, and we met three weeks ago."

"Yeah, but it wouldn't be fair," complained Dobbler, "them keeping the money."

Serra said, "I'm sure it's not true. They're back home with their parents after a long dangerous trip. Like my mom said, they probably want them to lay low for a while."

JJ went on, ignoring Serra and eyeballing Dobbler. "Fair? You didn't have any of that gold before you met them and you don't have it now. Sounds fair to me."

Dobbler was uncomfortably slouched until he noticed Serra's sympathetic eyes on him, at which point he sat up and said, "I think Serra and Mrs. Frye are right."

JJ chuckled as he set his mug on the table. "It doesn't matter what you, Mrs. Frye, or any of us think. Alex and Claire got us past the guard station, gave us money, and told us what we needed to know. If that's all we get out of meeting them, it's a win."

"Why don't we stop talking about it and just go over there?" suggested Rugen.

They gathered their things and thanked Serra's parents for the meal before leaving for the Grady's house. Along the way Rugen took some time to appreciate the architecture, which was like nothing he'd ever seen. The prevailing construction was stacked and mortared stone on the first floor topped by a buttressed wooden upper floor, or multiple wooden floors, depending on the grandeur. The forest town of Ravenwood had large buildings as well, but elaborate landscaping camouflaged their dimensions. Lundgren had no foliage aside from what was sequestered into the occasional park square or apartment window box.

They found the address they were looking for without any trouble. The number was painted onto a small wooden plaque above a door set among many other plaques and doors down the length of one long stone wall. Serra said that each was a private residence. They knocked on Alex and Claire's door several times but no one answered.

"Okay, now I'm worried," said Rugen as he scanned the wall of homes searching for something to confirm that this was indeed the Grady's property. There was nothing he could see besides the house number they had written down.

"Maybe they're out on an errand?" Serra offered.

"Yeah, spending the wizard's cut of the money," laughed JJ, gesturing to Dobbler, who rolled his eyes.

"I'm sure they'll be back," assured Rugen. He looked at the leather armor he was wearing. "In the meantime, we have peltzers. Let's spend some of them on walking-around clothes."

"I saw some places selling clothes on the way here," said Serra.

The four of them turned around and retraced their steps until they found a block of shops. As the men stood there deciding which one to go into, Serra excused herself and started home.

Rugen pointed to a store at random and JJ shrugged in agreement. Inside were racks of folded and hanging clothes. There were so many they could barely turn around without bumping into something.

After a few minutes of searching through the various garments, JJ found Dobbler holding an armful of shirts and pants as he shuffled through a section of dress jackets.

"You gonna bring all of that when we leave for the mountains next week?" asked JJ. "I don't think gmorks care what you're wearing on your body while they're gnawing on your head."

Dobbler was annoyed at JJ for ribbing him about everything, but he had to admit the red-headed warrior was right. He wouldn't be able to store extra clothes once they left Lundgren. He selected a few inexpensive things he wouldn't later mind donating to the loaner bin at the Stanley and left the rest of the merchandise where he'd found it. As he was paying the clerk, he realized this was likely how the loaner pile existed in the first place. Soldiers who didn't have homes in Lundgren also didn't require many personal possessions on the front. They probably shopped in the same places and later made the same donations.

The next three days were spent exploring the city, gathering information about the Ovid Graans and unsuccessfully searching for Alex and Claire. They did manage to collect their possessions from the guard station above the entrance gate. They had a hard time getting the guards to hand them over until they produced written permission acquired from Duke Alonzo's office.

JJ was terribly excited to get his gauntlet back. It had instantly become his most prized possession. The boys spent a lot of time testing its magical capabilities by throwing stones at JJ while he defended himself with it. As long as JJ held his left arm up in a defensive posture, any fast moving object that would otherwise strike him was knocked away by the hazy red field that extended from the top of his head to the bottom of his feet. It was something they tested over and over, mainly because it was so much fun.

They also got a kick out of the other special ability of the gauntlet. It amplified the pushing force of the wearer. Countless times the larger and more massive Rugen was thrown back by JJ's gauntlet arm. No matter how braced Rugen was, he couldn't resist the pushback force. The use of this power against inanimate objects such as trees and boulders, however, seemed to have no effect. The enchantment only worked during hand-to-hand combat. How it worked was a puzzle, but that didn't take away from how impressed they were. Bullying an opponent off balance gave an overwhelming advantage in a fight.

Periodically throughout the days, the group tried knocking on the Grady's front door or peering in their window. There was never any answer and the residence appeared to be abandoned. As disappointing as this was, the twins weren't the only ones not responding to knocks on their door. Every evening JJ would become suspiciously absent whenever Rugen or Dobbler would stop by. It didn't take much to figure out he wasn't in there sleeping. They wondered what sort of trouble he was getting into during the Lundgren night. They were also curious as to why he wasn't inviting them to join him.

Rugen started each morning with a jog along the most outer of Lundgren's ringed streets, Wierzbowski Way, which hugged the base of the mountains surrounding the city, passing just inside the main gate. It was a perfect design for city-dwellers looking for a pleasure walk or jog. The full circumference of the circle was nearly ten miles.

As Rugen jogged, he thought about how much work over how many decades had gone into the construction of the city and wondered from where all of the materials for all the buildings and roads had come. He answered his own question by looking up at the mountains, which were pretty much an infinite supply of stone and lumber.

One day, after finishing his loop around Lundgren, Rugen jogged back to the Stanley and found a burgundy-colored envelope waiting for him at the front desk. He picked it up and saw his full name written in calligraphy. On the envelope's reverse was a gold wax seal embossed with a scripted letter L. He was impressed, especially considering he didn't remember telling the duke his last name. He carried the envelope back to his room and opened it. It read:

Dear Mr. Sloane,

I took the liberty of researching your family, as well as those of your companions. As you probably know, the office of the Duke of Lundgren has extensive information resources. Your father is a well-regarded leader, and I'm sure the townspeople of Mourain have great respect for him. From what I read, he sounds like the sort of man I wish I knew personally. You come from good stock, and I'm sure your mother and the rest of your family are very proud of you.

Rugen narrowed his eyes as he thought to himself, *Mother? I guess Lundgren's extensive information resources haven't been updated for a while.* The letter continued:

I met with Lord Volguus and explained your situation. He'd be happy to talk to you next week about the role Riser Helm can play. Go to his office at the start of the school day on Monday morning with the rest of your group.

In good health, Duke Alonzo.

Rugen folded the letter back into the envelope. He went upstairs and stopped outside of JJ's room, staring at the door for a long while as he debated whether or not to knock. He then shook his head and started to skulk away, only to stop himself after two steps. He muttered, "This is stupid." He went back to the door and resumed standing motionless. He imagined the angry reaction that would come from his knocking, which frustrated him. He quietly said to himself, "The world doesn't revolve around your schedule, you red-headed oaf," as he put his knuckles to the door. He hesitated a moment longer before finally knocking.

"Go away," groaned JJ's voice.

Rugen sighed angrily through his nostrils and then said, deeply and authoritatively, "It's Rugen. Open up."

More groaning and then an exasperated, "Just give me a minute."

"C'mon, JJ, what's going on with you?"

"I said hold on," snapped JJ, sounding more awake.

Rugen stood still, waiting for what felt like forever. When he couldn't take it anymore he pounded on the doorframe, making booms that echoed all over the inn.

JJ whisked the door open in a huff. There he stood, half-dressed as a foul smell wafted out of the room.

Rugen stepped back from the odor. "It smells like hell in there."

"I'm a man. I stink." He was completely disheveled. His rust-colored hair was puffed in every direction, his eyes were blood-shot, and his undergarments were ruffled and stained. "What do you want from me?"

"I want to know what you've been doing late at night."

"Who are you, my mom?"

The two men stared at each other, neither wanting to back down, until JJ said, "I'm just out having a little fun. I was on the road a long time... saw a lot of death. I need to let off some steam."

"That's fine. But we still have a job to do."

"What job?"

Rugen made an exasperated sigh. "The quest. The Isolation. Why we're here?"

"The Isolation isn't going anywhere. It can wait a few more days." Under his breath, he added, "Or weeks."

"Weeks?! We're supposed to go to RHS on Monday morning."

"Look, you weren't on the road as long as I was. We're settled here. I'm staying for a while. You should too."

"I agreed to go on this journey because I believed in Gordon!" shouted Rugen from the doorway.

JJ pulled his hair back, trying unsuccessfully to tame it. "You agreed to go on this journey because you had nothing better to do. You saw a way out of your boring life and you took it."

This statement, meant to be intentionally inflammatory, had even more impact because of the fact that it was true. Rugen, like everyone else, wasn't fond of hearing the truth during an argument. He responded with, "So the plan is to hang around this city the rest of your life slowly going to fat?"

JJ ignored him.

"You'll be letting Gordon down."

No response.

Frustrated at the lack of effect his words were having, Rugen added, "And you're letting Billy down."

The mention of JJ's adoptive brother set him off. He quickly stood and shouted, "You didn't even know Billy! Don't talk about Billy!" He stormed to the door to slam it, but Rugen blocked it with his shoulder and then burst into the room, grabbing JJ by the neck.

The two of them tumbled to the ground, scuffling like brothers. Headlocks, arm bars, and other wrestling holds were traded until Dobbler appeared and calmly said, "Either of you boys want to go find breakfast?"

Rugen and JJ stopped grappling and pushed each other away. Rugen stood and looked at Dobbler, embarrassed about the childish scuffle, and blurted, "He's quitting."

JJ smoothed out his rumpled nightshirt as he climbed to his feet, yelling, "I never said I was quitting! I just want to enjoy myself in Lundgren while we're here. This is our last chance to live it up for a while, maybe ever."

Rugen snapped back, "How many people will be slaughtered by gmorks or die of starvation while you get drunk and … who knows what?"

"People have been dying for years. Me enjoying myself isn't going to change that."

Dobbler picked Duke Alonso's crumpled letter from the floor, quickly scanned it, and said, "Guys, this is out of our hands now. Talking to Duke Alonzo has set the wheels in motion. We're his guests in Lundgren and he expects … no, *orders* us to be at Riser Helm School on Monday morning. What do you think he'll do if instead of that we're sleeping in after a night of debauchery? Make apologies to Lord Volguus on our behalf and tell him we'll need to reschedule when it's more convenient for us?" He shook his head. "Our plans have been set for us."

Rugen and JJ stared at Dobbler, unsure how to respond.

Dobbler continued, "Also, Alex and Claire are gone, probably for good. I don't know how much money they put in the sack they gave you, JJ, but I'm willing to bet you've used pretty much all of it, and bartenders don't accept good will or kind words as payment."

After a moment of silence, JJ acquiesced, "Okay. So what do we need to do next?"

"Didn't you hear me earlier? Next we find breakfast."

"Sounds good," said Rugen.

JJ looked put a sly smile on his face and said, "I need one of you to pay. I ran out of money last night."

CHAPTER 11

Rugen, JJ, and Dobbler went to breakfast at a restaurant called Short Round Willie's, which they happened upon by wandering in the general direction of Serra's parents' house. The scene was raucous with loud voices, laughter, and the banging of plates, knives, and forks. The fact that people were suffering in the world outside of Lundgren's mountains was lost on the diners. Lundgren was the world to them, and everywhere else was to be ignored and forgotten.

There were long tables covered with plates, mugs, bread bowls, various silverware, and cloth napkins. Running the length of the tables were matching long benches, mostly crowded with customers. Waitresses were carrying multiple frothy mugs of beer all around the restaurant. One of them called out to Rugen, JJ, and Dobbler as she hurried past, "Don't just stand there gawking, boys! Sit! Wherever you find space."

Rugen nodded in her direction, but she had already turned her attention elsewhere. The three men looked at each other and proceeded to squeeze through the tight gaps between the patrons seated on the long benches. Rugen and JJ sat next to each other opposite Dobbler.

"Can I trust you two boys to behave yourselves?" the sorcerer taunted.

"We're good," answered JJ for both of them. Then he turned to Rugen and added in a mock-serious tone, "But just so you know, if I wasn't so hungover, they'd be scraping you off that floor right now."

Rugen waved away the joke and said, "Do you see a menu anywhere?"

A waitress with long brown hair pulled into a ponytail, a partially open green shirt, and a white linen apron appeared at the table and asked, "You boys eating and drinking?"

They all nodded. Rugen was about to ask for a menu when she scampered away. He turned to the other two and said, "She disappeared again."

JJ shrugged and glanced around the room. Seated next to him was an obese man who was infringing on his bench space. He edged a little closer to Rugen and inadvertently knocked knees with him, making them both uncomfortable. Rolling around on the floor with each other in full physical contact was acceptable, but their mannish sensibilities didn't allow for gentle bodily contact that could be misconstrued as intimate.

"Popular place, huh?" said Rugen, scanning for the waitress who had spoken to them.

On the far wall hung a large tapestry depicting what Rugen assumed was the ring of mountains around Lundgren, but in place of the cityscape was an enormous snarling lion. It was unclear if the lion was meant to be as large as the absent city or if its size was a function of forced perspective. It was hunched in an attack posture, as if it were about to leap off of the weave and into the restaurant. Its eyes were wide and glowing, the skin on its nose was scrunched up, revealing long menacing teeth, and the fur of its mane was a circular explosion around its head. The mountains behind and above looked more jagged and ominous than they did in real life, and the lion's sweeping tail could have doubled as a path between mountain peaks.

JJ followed Dobbler's gaze to the tapestry and said, "Nice cat."

The waitress returned carrying three plates of food on a large round serving tray and three mugs of beer hooked on her other hand. On the plates were fried eggs, sausage, potato hash, and grilled tomatoes. The mugs were enormous, and as she set them down froth spilled over the sides. "Bread will be right out," she hurriedly added.

"Thanks, but we didn't order this," said Rugen.

The waitress looked annoyed and confused. "I asked if you wanted food and drink. You nodded."

"Yeah, but…"

"This is what we serve. If you don't want it, you can leave."

"No, no, it's fine. I…" Rugen stuttered. Some of the other patrons stopped talking with each other to glance at him.

JJ put his hand on Rugen's arm and said to the waitress, "Thank you. This is perfect." She shook her head and walked off.

"I didn't mean..."

"Just relax," said JJ, digging into an egg.

The bread appeared, and the three friends ate and talked about a number of topics, including how they were going to handle the meeting with RHS administration, Dobbler's obvious crush on Serra—which he denied—and theories on where Alex and Claire were hiding.

"Oh they're long gone," said JJ as he bit onto a forkful of potatoes.

"Gone where?" asked Rugen.

"The mountains? I dunno. Does it matter?"

"Why would they leave Lundgren and head into the mountains?"

"They know we're looking for them."

Dobbler put his fork down. "I'll give you three reasons why they're still here. One, Lundgren money is all but useless anywhere but Lundgren."

Rugen interrupted. "I'm sure someone out there would be glad to have the coins in trade for any number of things."

"True, but my point is the money is much more useful in the city than outside."

JJ didn't seem impressed as he mindlessly took another bite.

"Two, they're citizens. Why would they have to be the ones to leave? No matter what the duke led you to believe, we don't belong here. They probably figure after we run out of money we'll have no choice but to move on."

"And the third?" asked Rugen.

"They're rich! If they don't like how long it takes for us to sulk out of the city with our tails between our legs, they could hire any number of thugs to usher us along." He looked at the other people at the long table, who weren't paying attention, and quietly said, "We have no rights here. We could get murdered in the street and nobody would care."

JJ swallowed his food and said, "I'd like to see them try."

The rest of the weekend was spent hanging out with Serra, periodically checking the Grady house, and sharing nervous thoughts about the pending meeting at RHS.

JJ recommitted to the mission, staying away from the late night Lundgren scene. Admittedly he didn't have much of a choice as he was out of money, but he did mirror Rugen's workout schedule of long jogs, calisthenics, and weapons training. They didn't have wooden or blunted weapons to spar with each other but found it to be fully within the Lundgren warring culture to brandish deadly weapons in the public parks. They practiced routines on the lawns fighting imaginary enemies, along the way critiquing each other's technical skills for lethality and, in JJ's case, panache.

Dobbler and Serra didn't find the need to practice their magic, so at the Rugen's urging they completed a few sessions of basic combat coaching at a self-defense school dedicated to the training of novices. Regardless of how Wallace and Wyatt had taught them to devalue the use of the body as a physical weapon, they found the training to be rather fun and relaxing.

Also, it was refreshing to have the opportunity to spend time together without curious eyes watching their social interactions or commenting on every longing look or playful banter between the two of them. It took a lot of mental effort to keep their feelings for each other from coloring how they functioned day to day around the others. Time alone, especially in what amounted to a group-sanctioned endeavor, was a welcome relief.

When Monday morning arrived, the men woke up early and readied themselves for the day. They didn't know what to expect at Riser Helm School, but they wanted Lord Volguus to know they were worthy of his respect. Rugen's armor had been repaired over the weekend by the staff at the Stanley, and he was impressed by the job they did. Nothing would ever make the gashes disappear, but they now looked like four misplaced seams down his back-plate. The Stanley didn't have a replacement plate to offer, and if they did, Rugen was sure he wouldn't be able to afford it. He didn't know how long they would need to stay at the inn, and with JJ's money gone, they were pooling their resources and living off of two shrinking handfuls of coins.

They walked out of the building and onto the street in full battle regalia, which garnered the same lack of interest from the citizens of Lundgren as they were accustomed. The plan was to meet Serra at her house, and then all four of them would walk to RHS.

The auburn-haired cleric was waiting on her parents' front stoop. At their arrival she nodded and stood to greet them. After an exchange of salutations she said, "I bet you guys were too nervous to eat anything."

They indicated that indeed they hadn't eaten, but whether that had anything to do with nerves was left unsaid.

Serra picked up a platter of crusty dense bread smeared with butter and jam. She held it out and said, "My mom made these just in case."

Each of them happily took one. Serra set down the empty plate and rapped on the door twice, yelling, "Thanks, Mom!"

The four of them ate as they navigated the busy morning streets to RHS, quietly contemplating how they would convince the director of a warrior school in a foreign city, one which highly valued citizenship, to allow them, non-citizens, to abscond with students and then march them into possible death. If only they were with Alex and Claire, who were not only citizens but also graduates of RHS. Considering how they were abandoned by the Grady twins, it wouldn't be surprising to arrive at the school to discover Lord Volguus planned to immediately detain them for questioning before exiling them from the city.

Up ahead the cityscape of crowded buildings opened onto a colossal stone wall. It was so large that on first inspection it was difficult to picture that it followed a wide curve. The landscaping in front of it directed their eyes to the center where a large gate stood. Carved above that, in arching lettering, was "RISER HELM SCHOOL." Patterned across the face of the wall were statues depicting men; some in armor, others bare-chested, and still others in formal attire. Some of them were brandishing weapons and others held books. They were presumably famous graduates of RHS or people who were otherwise affiliated with the school.

The four travelers stopped and stared for a minute, taking in the enormous scale of the building. When seen from the bird's eye view at the guard station on their way into the city, RHS looked tiny. Recalling that image and comparing it to the imposing up-close size made it all the more dramatic. Countless students rapidly filed through the gate arch, getting ready to start another day of training.

They continued to scan the scope of the building and the bustling of the arriving students in silence, until Rugen's eyes caught movement next to the front gate. He focused in and saw a woman casually waving. He squinted and asked, "Is that Claire?"

Chapter 12

After all the incoming RHS students cleared the entryway, hurrying to their classes, Rugen, JJ, Serra, and Dobbler were left opposite a visibly uncomfortable pair of Gradys.

Nobody knew what to say until JJ blurted, "Where've you two been?"

Claire cleared her throat before answering. "Our parents wouldn't let us leave the house." Her voice cracked near the end of the sentence.

Alex glanced at his sister and then back at the others, who looked confused and annoyed. He said, "There's a little more to it than that. A day or two before you found us fighting those gmorks near Castle Igayim, we had a group of guards with us."

"Guards our father had hired to protect us," Claire chimed in.

"We remember," said Serra.

"Right. We'd been out in the wild for longer than anyone expected, and when one of them got injured, they demanded we go back to Lundgren. Claire and I knew we were close to the castle ruins and we didn't want to give up the search. Words were exchanged." He shared eye contact with Claire and said, "Well, they ended up leaving us out there."

Claire continued, "So imagine you are the parents who let your son and daughter go hunting for treasure with guards you paid for, and the guards return without them."

"You're getting ahead of the story," said Alex. "Along the way back to Lundgren the injured guy died. He wasn't able to defend himself and a gmork got him. The other soldiers showed up on our parents' doorstep wanting reparations for his loss."

"What'd your parents say?" asked Serra.

"Our dad reminded them they knew the risk they were taking and that they were adequately compensated for it before leaving Lundgren," answered Alex.

"So basically he told them to get lost," said JJ.

"No, he gave them extra money anyway."

"He what?" asked Dobbler.

Alex nodded. "As he put it, Claire and I didn't live up to his standards as leaders. He said good leaders never would have allowed hired guards to exercise such will over them. The reason he gave them more money was to buy back the respect for the Grady name we'd obviously lost."

"As we were returning to the house, we were high on success. We had met you guys; found all that money, the Naga, your magic gauntlet, and taken up a new mission." Alex looked each of them in the eyes, smiling. "But our father had stewed for a few days since the guards knocked on his door. He sobered us up pretty quick."

"So he grounded you?" asked JJ with a sly smile on his face.

"We stayed home out of respect," Alex snapped back.

Claire looked at her feet. "We had let him down once for allowing the guards to leave us. We weren't going to let him down again by disobeying his wish for us to stay home and keep a low profile."

"He asked us to stay home because he was worried about us," continued Alex. "Worry changes your perspective on things."

Rugen nodded, thinking about how he left his own father back in Mourain and wondering how that made him feel.

"So what you're trying to say is our success," started JJ, "and by that I mean our very lives, are depending on a couple of grown adults who are subject to a grounding by their daddy?"

Alex frowned.

"That explains why you didn't come to us," pointed out Serra, ignoring JJ's comment, "But it doesn't explain why we couldn't find you."

"We were home," shrugged Claire. "Well, most of the time. I guess you missed us."

"We went every day, multiple times," said Dobbler, arms folded in annoyance. "The house was deserted,"

"Our house?" asked Alex.

"Yeah."

"161 East-Northeast Gorman Street?"

Dobbler was nodding until it hit him. "Wait, what? East-Northeast? I thought it was North-Northeast."

"So we were knocking on the wrong door the whole time?" asked Serra.

"We were wondering why you weren't stopping by," said Claire. "Between you guys and our father, we thought our whole world was mad at us."

"Now I feel stupid," continued Serra. "We thought you lied to us and ran off."

"Where would we go?" asked Claire. "We live here."

"That's what I said!" exploded JJ. He lightly tapped Dobbler on the back of the head. "This wise old wizard thought you pocketed his cut of the loot."

"I keep telling you," grumbled Dobbler, "the word is *sorcerer*."

"There's another thing I don't understand," said Rugen. "Your father was upset because the guards left you alone in the wilderness. He worries about you. That's what you said."

Alex nodded.

"The next step in our journey—building an army and marching through the mountains to find the source of the gmorks and ursinoxes and extinguish it. Isn't that extremely unsafe? How is it your father let you out of his sight again?"

"Duke Alonzo talked to him."

Claire nodded in agreement with her brother. "He stopped by our house and sat at our dinner table. He told us all about your family in Mourain, Serra's father having been at RHS when the massacre happened, and about Dobbler and JJ. He said it was time for Lundgren to open its eyes to the part it played in the creation of these monsters."

"He said he saw," started Alex, stiffening up for an impersonation of Duke Alonso, "strength in our hearts, passion in our souls, and an undying determination that would carry us to the finish and finally rid the world of evil."

Everyone stood in silent contemplation until Claire added, "Our dad ate it up."

JJ looked at the facade of the Riser Helm School building and said, "Well then, we'd better get inside to start ridding the world of evil."

They crossed the threshold into the school's anteroom where they were met by a guard. He was in formal attire complete with chain mail armor, floor-length cape, and short sword in a decorative scabbard on his hip. All of it matched the school colors: green and silver. Linked into the left chest of his chain mail was an oval metal plate; a smaller version of the RHS coat of arms they had seen bolted to the wall of the building on their way in.

He politely greeted them and asked how he could be of service. As he spoke he rested his hand on the bejeweled hilt of his sword. Alex answered, saying that he and Claire were former RHS students and they were guests of Lord Volguus. The guard acknowledged their credentials and asked them to wait while he made *the chancellor* aware of their arrival.

The room was enormous. Rugen commented that the space inside could comfortably hold the entire population of Mourain. The ceilings were high and vaulted, and in the center hung a large chandelier with seemingly hundreds of individual points of light glowing throughout intricately crafted whorls of metal. It had to be Ravenwood magic keeping it illuminated. If the lights were conventional candles, someone would have to work around the clock keeping them lit, replacing them, and scraping up drips of wax.

Hanging at the end of the room, over the door through which the guard had passed, was a sign that read "HALL OF HISTORY." Along the walls were displays including paintings, weapons, armor, carvings, flags, and other items. The six visitors wandered to various parts of the room, studying the exhibits up close. From afar they blended into swaths of color, but the near view revealed great detail. Some of the displays had placards speaking to their significance, while others stood on their own without explanation.

In the center of the space was a hulking bronze statue of a barrel-chested and bearded man with one hand on his hip. His helmet was tucked into the space between his arm and body. His other foot was perched on a large stone onto which was engraved "CAPT. RISER J. HELM, FOUNDER." His eyes seemed exceptionally large, and even cast in bronze were menacing.

One of the flags, the navy blue one representing the City of Lundgren, was easily identifiable, despite how faded, tattered, and stained it was. Rugen read that this particular flag was flown during the war between the north and south, as the logo of a scripted letter L and mountains were slightly different than the current iteration displayed along the streets and avenues.

The weapons and armor showed signs of heavy usage—including scuffs, fractures, and chips— but overall they were well cared for, as evidenced by the lack of dust and the polished sheen. It was obvious that the scars were left intentionally. Seeing them sparked a strong curiosity for the stories that defined their significance. The imperfections brought to mind the sewn rips along the back panel of Rugen's own leather armor, and the destruction those represented.

Other objects on display were medals and trophies recognizing the best RHS students from each year. They ranged in size and grandeur, and like everything else in the hall were well cared-for. Each of them had a name and year engraved on them. At first Rugen wondered why the winner himself didn't get to keep his own trinket, but when he looked closer he realized the most recent awards on display were dated several decades prior. He could think of two reasons for this: either the school stopped giving out medals and trophies that long ago or the only ones hanging in the Hall of History belonged to former students who had since died. Given how much the school cherished its history, he figured it had to be the latter. His imagination wandered to a scene of a grieving family ceremoniously presenting a medal or trophy to the school after it had been in the possession of its winner throughout his lifetime.

Everyone looked over the exhibits in introspective silence or with brief and muted conversation. To the RHS students, the museum likely represented simply an expanse of space between the front gate and their eventual destination in the school, and held no more significance aside from something that had the potential to make them late for lecture or training. To people like Rugen, JJ, Serra, and Dobbler, who had never before seen it, or to Alex and Claire, who were seeing it as nostalgic alumni for the first time, it inspired awe.

Eventually the guard returned and reported that Chancellor Volguus was ready for them. They gathered their things and marched up several flights of stairs and into the hallways of RHS, along which were classrooms to the left and right. Peering inside they saw groups of students seated at desks listening to lectures or watching teacher demonstrations.

"Before we get to the administrative wing, I wanted to show you this," Alex said, gesturing to an archway at the end of a short passage. The six of them walked onto a balcony overlooking an immense outdoor space. They reflexively squinted at the bright morning sun and fluttering wind against their faces. Above them was a pristine blue sky with wisps of clouds, and below that was a wide flat plot of land bustling with activity. Half of the plot was made of packed dirt and stone pebbles while the other half was impeccably-manicured lawn. The grass appeared lush and green, and there were several men on their hands and knees trimming it and bagging the clippings into cloth sacks. For as large an area as it was, the task of maintaining the landscaping must have been a full-time job.

Many dozens of students occupied the space, engrossed in various training exercises. Most of them were in small groups, but some were training by themselves. The activities included assaulting fake soldiers made of hay-filled burlap bags, archery practice, and sparring, both hand-to-hand and with wooden practice swords. Activity filled the arena, and even from this high vantage point it was hard to take it all in.

Alex sighed, "This is called *The Stage*. Brings back memories, huh Claire?"

Claire smiled, not averting her eyes from the view. "Some good, some not so much."

They continued to watch while a group of students practiced a routine with fighting staffs. They were in a square formation of four rows and four columns. Facing them at the front of the square was their instructor, who was calling out cadence like a coxswain on a rowboat. They responded with synchronized thrusting and parrying moves to the slow, methodical beat, every so often grunting in time with the rhythm.

"A lot of those instructors don't look much older than we are," said Rugen.

"They aren't," responded Alex. "Those are students in the elite program. One of their duties is to teach and train younger students. They get evaluated on their instruction techniques by the older guys you see."

"You were right about it being a boy's club," said Serra. "I don't see any girls down there at all."

"Yeah, me neither," said Claire as she scanned the action. "Last I heard there were a few enrolled, but they must be inside right now."

"They are," a voice said from behind them, "and they're enrolled here because of you."

Claire turned to see the chancellor of Riser Helm School, Lord Peter Volguus, standing behind them, smiling widely. She startled a bit and then caught herself, exclaiming, "Lord Volguus, good to see you!" She wrapped her arms around him, knocking him slightly off balance.

"I always enjoy when my students return, especially the most famous one we've had in recent memory." He addressed the others, saying, "Our Claire has been an inspiration to many people, male and female, students and teachers alike."

Alex greeted the chancellor with a forearm handshake, followed by everyone else expressing their gratitude for hosting them.

After the pleasantries, Lord Volguus said, "Duke Alonzo told me why you're here. Let's go to my office and talk."

CHAPTER 13

The Office of the Chancellor overlooked The Stage via a viewing platform. Exposure to the elements was usually not an issue, as the Lundgren climate was temperate. Even in winter, snows didn't often reach the southern face of the Ovid Graans, and the ring of mountains surrounding Lundgren kept the nastiest weather at bay.

Lord Volguus's office was decorated like a smaller version of the Hall of History. There were flags, plaques, medals, and weapons, all of which bore his name or had some personal connection to him. It was a large space, mostly square but with an alcove to the right of the entrance door. In this alcove was where the chancellor's ornately carved desk and chair sat.

Just after everyone entered the office, a group of maintenance workers appeared behind them carrying a large round tabletop and its center pedestal as well as matching seats. On the bottom side of the tabletop was a circle of dowels that fit snugly into corresponding holes in a flange on the pedestal. The men made short work of assembling the table and placing the chairs around it. After they left, a final one entered carrying a tray of small glasses and a pitcher of ice water. He set the seven glasses onto coasters, filled them, and left the room.

"They take good care of me around here," the chancellor remarked. He gestured to the chairs and said, "Please, sit down."

The seven men and women sat around the table. A few of them took nervous sips of water, waiting for Lord Volguus to speak.

"I heard Duke Alonzo made you squirm with his 'Duke Eddie' routine."

Everyone looked around the table at each other, unsure how to respond, until he continued, "I figured because of that I ought to be extra welcoming."

An audible sigh of relief was heard and then everyone started chuckling, except JJ who seemed nonplussed by all of it. Volguus continued, "Alonzo told me you are planning to go after Brian Gruhl."

"Yes sir," said Rugen.

"I knew him when he was enrolled here. I knew his brother Anthony as well." Lord Volguus lowered his gaze to the glass in front of him. "People always talk about how smart Brian was, like he was some kind of misunderstood genius deserving our reverence. I never saw him like that. As far as I'm concerned Brian was a smear on this institution's good name long before he murdered his family. If he were really a genius he would've figured out a way to excel at RHS like his brother did. They say he got swallowed by Anthony's shadow and had no choice but to be a rebel. That's a load of garbage as far as I'm concerned."

He gestured to the memorabilia all over his office. "I've always said, if you find yourself in someone's shadow, be the light."

Alex and Claire nodded admiringly.

"My opinion is there's nothing redeemable inside Brian. He needs to be held accountable for what he's done; for his brother, his father, his mother, and for the countless other people he's killed and terrorized with these creatures he created."

Volguus stood, walked to the large open window, glanced at the students training below, and said, "His actions left us in chaos. Many people around Lundgren, in the mountains or on the roads, were caught off-guard when the monsters came. A lot were killed. We needed to quickly organize a defense plan to keep people safe. Since then we've been so busy trying to survive we didn't realize we were thriving. The overarching thought that we needed to be Lundgren-centric blinded us from the plight of the rest of the world. We lost sight of what we were meant to be, the center of defense for all of Hyboria." He sat back in his chair. "You six are exactly the motivation Alonzo and I needed."

"I think I speak for all of us," started Rugen, "in thanking you for being so welcoming. To be honest we didn't know what to expect before coming here."

Volguus reached over the table and shook Rugen's hand. "How could I be anything but welcoming? You will be undoing the damage of not only our school's biggest embarrassment, but the years of neglect perpetrated by the past leaders of Lundgren. I'm glad to help."

"How?" asked JJ, never a stranger to bluntness.

"Well, Duke Alonzo and I were talking. We can't take working soldiers from their posts around Lundgren or in the mountains. They need to remain in place to keep the city safe. I can't allow any RHS instructors to leave, because they're needed to train the next generation. We want to help," he looked around the table, "but we can't cut the legs out from Lundgren to do so. Alex and Claire can tell you how well-trained our students are, especially those in their final year. We will grant you a portion of our graduating class to accompany you on this mission."

Alex nodded. "Elites?"

"Sadly, no. We can't offer anyone from the elite program. They already have their post-graduation assignments, and that's where they'll go." Volguus looked at Alex. "I don't think you'd want elites anyway. They're trained to be leaders. Leading this quest is your task. I'm happy to loan a large contingent of grunts and sub-elites to the cause. You'll find them to be ferocious and loyal."

"You bless us, Lord Volguus," said Claire. "We are forever in your debt."

"It's the least I can do. They'll be adequately armed and supplied, and I'll make sure of that as well.

"This is exactly what we were hoping for," said Rugen, to which Volguus noded magnanimously. Rugen gave him a sincere look and said, "But now what?"

"What do you mean?" asked Serra.

"I feel like everything we've been doing has been leading up to this point. Everything we've done, everyone we've met, all of it has been with the goal in mind of getting to Lundgren and building an army. I took over leadership duties when Gordon was killed, and now I feel a sense of completion. I know that's wrong, but maybe it's because I don't know what we're supposed to do next. At the start, all I had in mind was to get away from watching Mourain slowly decline into oblivion. I had no concept of what I was getting into. Since then I've been following other's people's plans. Gordon said we should find clerics and sorcerers in Ravenwood. Serra said get to Lundgren to build an army. Now we're supposed to head to the north and kill Brian. When people say it like that it sounds so simple, like its already done and we're just playing out the story." He slid his chair back and rested his hands on his thighs. "Now that we've made it here, I haven't the foggiest idea of what to do next."

"Well," started the chancellor, "we have soldiers in the mountains and a communications network between them. We'll send word ahead, and they'll help you all the way to the Red Gate." He cocked his head to Rugen. "So there's your next step. After that," he paused, "you're on your own."

After a moment of silence, Alex cleared his throat and said, "Sir, RHS has meant so much to the Grady family." He reached into his bag. "Please accept this as a donation to the school from the six of us." He handed Lord Volguus a stack of ten gold coins.

Although Alex and Claire hadn't discussed this with the rest of the group, Rugen thought it was a nice gesture, and the right thing to do.

Lord Volguus examined the coins in his hand for a long moment and then met Alex's eyes. "This is quite generous. I can't thank you enough." He set the coins on the table, nodding in gratitude. "It will do a lot to help teach our students."

"Our pleasure, sir. It's a drop in the bucket compared to what you've done for us."

Volguus slid out his chair and stood, prompting the others to follow, then raised his glass, widened his eyes, and projected his voice as if he were speaking to a large crowd, "Ladies, gentlemen, it's time for Brian Gruhl to pay for what he's done!"

BOOK FOUR: THE NORTH

Learn the sounds, learn the smells,
Learn the marks of our forest dwells.
Paths we take, paths gone by,
Some paths lead to the open sky.
Trust no one your mind can't hear,
Travel not away from near.
Tread you light, your heartbeat thrums,
In the dark of night when the stranger comes.
Don't call out, keep words confined,
Or else reveal my form behind.
Brave soul yours have no despair,
Eternal quiet my trap ensnares.

—Traditional Ione prayer; translated with a conscious effort to
approximate the rhyming quality and
themes of the original work.

CHAPTER 1

In a massive and nearly impenetrable forest known as Elsinore lived an elusive and primitive race of people. The western border of the wedge-shaped forest was demarcated by the foothills of the Roussi Mountains, where cool water flowed into the valley, causing welling updrafts to crisp the air. The eastern edge met the crashing waves of the coast, and in the south the land merged with the open plains.

The inhabitants of the forest were the Ione people (pronounced eye-OWN-ee). They shared the same ancestors as the rest of the people of Hyboria—referred to as Proto-Hyborians by university scholars. They were nomadic people who wandered the plains, foothills, and coastlines of Hyboria, sustaining themselves as hunter-gatherers for thousands of years. Most of the Proto-Hyborians eventually developed agriculture and settled into ever-expanding groups, but at least one small contingent, who generations later became the Iones, moved into the forest and cut off contact with the rest of the burgeoning civilization.

Elsinore Forest was a dangerous and unforgiving place, and as a result the Iones had the region to themselves for centuries. They thrived in their self-imposed isolation and independence, developing a unique language, culture, and religion. They led simple, primitive lives under the watchful eye of their supreme deity, Graehym. It was their belief that he created the Ione people in his own image and protected and provided for them.

What originally drove the Ione's ancestors into the forest was subject to much speculation by historians. Either the people leading the migration had the personality types that longed for solitude, or they were being persecuted, or they found themselves there by happenstance and decided to make the best of it. Whatever the reason, they went in, found a niche, and never left.

Over thousands of years, life in the deep forest gradually changed their bodies. Hunting and gathering was more difficult among the trees and thickets than it was in the open plains and coastlines. Farming never took hold aside from small-scale and fleeting endeavors that narrowly fit only the broadest definition of agriculture. As a result, proper nourishment was harder to come by for the Ione people. Gradually, the limited food access caused the proliferation of shorter and slighter body types. Lumbering brutes couldn't compete.

The Iones took advantage of their diminutive body frames by becoming experts in stealth. Agility, flexibility, and small feet allowed them to move through the dense forest silently despite the presence of dry twigs and leaves on the forest floor. This skill came as handy on the hunt as it did while scouting for intruders in their territory. Invasion into Elsinore was an infrequent occurrence, but when it happened it was usually dealt with quickly and nonviolently.

The Ione's skin was much paler than that of their Hyborian counterparts living at equivalent latitudes. The general rule is that pigmentation increases in sunnier climates due to the interplay between the production and expression of various body chemicals, although none of the mechanisms behind this were known at the time. The Hyborians only knew what they observed. Hyboria featured a rainbow of skin colors, from darker shades of tan and brown in the south to lighter in the north, but no known population had complexions milkier than the forest dwellers.

Living under the thick canopy also gradually changed their vision. The sun seemed to rise later and set earlier in the forest. Even in the middle of a cloudless day in summer, only a modest amount of light filtered down to the forest floor. As of result, visual acuity in low light became progressively sharper in the population over time. Generally speaking, surviving the hardships of the forest caused a gradual improvement in all of the Ione people's senses.

As their frames gradually shrunk, the use of bulky or heavy weapons for hunting or combat became impractical. Short, light weapons were much more handy and useful, but even more so was the avoidance of close-quarter fighting altogether. The Iones negated the disadvantage of their small size by using their keen eyesight and nimble fingers to become a culture of stealthful, sharp-shooting archers.

Male children started their informal schooling in archery using hand-me-down bows around the age of three. As they grew stronger, their parents commissioned custom-made ones. Anatomical measurements were taken and handed off to a master bowyer, which in Elsinore wasn't difficult to find because of the popularity of the weapon. The presentation of the new bow was done during an annual ceremony, usually corresponding to the anniversary of the boy's birth. The expectation was that each boy was responsible for the proper care and maintenance of his own bow, although, especially in the early years of life, parents would assist with this.

For many reasons, Ione longbows were the best in Hyboria and the Ione archers were the best at using them. Having full and exclusive access to Elsinore Forest for centuries, the Iones collected and tested different materials in an effort to determine which made the deadliest and longest-lasting weapons. The bows were highly individualized, not only due to the anatomical measurements, but also because of subtle personal adornments, which made each one unique.

Full-sized bows required a substantial amount of force to pull. Without the years of training that began in childhood using sequentially larger and stiffer bows, even the strongest Hyborian would find it difficult to handle the draw weight of an Ione longbow.

The ancient people who were to become the Iones of Elsinore Forest shared the same Proto-Hyborian language as their counterparts on the plains, but over time their language gradually evolved to be very different. This wasn't just in vocabulary, but in some of the grammar as well. While it was a totally normal and inevitable process of the languages of all cultures, for the Ione people the evolution went a step further. It's unclear how, but the language took on magical qualities like those of Pallous and Obsidian. The Iones couldn't cast spells to control the elements or heal wounds, but their power was no less fascinating or useful. They had an innate ability to speak to each other over long distances without projecting their voices, a process called *shuesa*.

Two criteria needed to be in place for shuesa to be successful. First, the speaker (*shuesar*) and the listener (*shuesal*) needed to have at least an acquaintance-level relationship. Strangers who spotted each other across a forest clearing would be unable to engage the ability.

Second was line of sight. Partial obstructions like leaves, branches, or fog wouldn't interfere with the cerebral connection, but anything that completely blocked eye contact, such as boulders, hills, or tree trunks, made shuesa impossible.

That said, the Iones didn't need to maintain eye contact during the entire message. Once initiated, the shuesar could be heard by the shuesal for about five to ten seconds after contact was broken regardless of where the eyes deviated. That length of time would be significantly shortened if the speaker paused or the listener's attention wavered.

With those stipulations met, multiple Iones could effortlessly engage in a quiet conversation, regardless of the distance, ambient sound, or physical activity. Even surrounded by blowing wind, pouring rain, or clanging weapons across a large distance, they could communicate as if they were seated next to one another on a calm afternoon.

The Ione population was spread across a complicated network of small groups called squatas. Most squatas consisted of fewer than twenty people. Some contained more, some less, but no single squata had a significant population. There were no cities or towns in Elsinore Forest, and the squatas had no formal names aside from the family name of the patriarch or matriarch, which could change over generations as groups diverged or converged.

When describing the Ione people, the word population lost some of its meaning. While all Iones descended from the same group of Proto-Hyborians, lived for generations in the same region, shared similar customs and ideology, and generally looked and acted the same, they didn't function as a cohesive society. There were many proprietary rules governing the inhabitants within a squata, but they had no centralized government, no cross-culture laws, and no jurisdictional construct.

There was little attempt to share information between squatas aside from the ones which neighbored each other, but because they led simple lives that perfectly fit their environment, technological progress was generally unnecessary and unwanted, so a lack of information exchange didn't impede them. While neighboring squatas helped each other whenever they had the opportunity, there were no rules compelling an Ione from one squata to do anything on behalf of another.

The Iones were a peaceful, quiet, and solitude-respecting people with rich internal loyalties and family values. Skirmishes did occur on occasion, sometimes resulting in bloodshed, but for the most part Iones were generally peaceful to their own kind.

They were not nearly as peaceful to those outside the borders of Elsinore. The Iones considered anyone intruding on their land to be a threat that needed to be extricated one way or another. They referred to outsiders, people from the Hyborian villages on the plains or along the rivers and coasts, as Damones (pronounced duh-moans). The Damones spoke a different language (Hybor), worshipped a different God, had darker skin, and were generally physically larger and stronger. Size and strength, however, was nullified in the thick forest by Ione stealth and quickness. In the domain of the Iones, the Damones were clumsy and awkward and couldn't navigate without hacking down branches and uprooting plants. All the Iones needed do to locate them was to follow their wake of destruction.

Nonviolent eviction was the most effective means and the one most often employed. Most of the Damones forced out of Elsinore were thankful to be allowed to leave with their lives, and tended not to return. The Ione scouts would enter the Damone camp in the middle of the night and remove or destroy survival equipment. This was usually enough to deter them from staying in the woods, but occasionally a group of infiltrators would proceed farther into the territory despite the subtle warning that their presence was unwelcome. For this, the Iones used other, more drastic tactics to compel Damones to leave.

Regardless of the time of year, visibility was poor under the thick forest canopy, and trying to walk through the forest in the dark without spraining an ankle or sustaining some other physical injury was impossible. Being able to navigate the forest at night and seeing better than any Damone explorer gave the Iones a great advantage. There were many hours when scouts were able to sneak around and scheme while the Damones could do nothing but sit anxiously and wait.

If they were dealing with a small group of Damones relatively close to the border, the backup plan to stealing or destroying equipment was to use poison-tipped darts and blowguns under the cover of night. A single dart was usually enough to incapacitate a Damone. The Iones preferred to strike just before sunrise as that was the part of the night in which their targets felt safest and were most likely to have their guard down. Once unconscious, the Damones were moved to outside of Ione territory. Because of the size difference, this was usually a massive undertaking requiring the recruitment of several squatas-worth of able-bodied men.

If a Damone party was too big, too deep into the forest, or didn't respond to gentle encouragement, more aggressive means were employed. The Iones recruited large numbers of archers, usually at a three-to-one ratio to the number of invaders, and would launch a barrage of arrows at the camp at dawn. The initial intention, to put it simply, was to miss. Waking up to arrows flying overhead was usually enough to get the Damones to flee. However, on many occasions over the centuries, the mere suggestion of danger wasn't enough. In those unfortunate cases the Iones adjusted the aim of their arrows with the intent of killing. Causing non-lethal injury to groups like these was inadequate because it resulted in a long, drawn out, and usually unsuccessful escape from Elsinore. Allowing survivors to limp out of the forest was also undesirable, as that could encourage vengeful visitors later.

All things considered, the best strategy for the Ione people was to foster disbelief about their existence in the minds of the Damones. Everyone was much better served by avoiding face-to-face confrontations, and the thickness, wildness, and darkness of the Elsinore Forest was usually enough of a deterrent to ensure that.

The only exception to the rule of general intolerance of Damones was in regard to the inhabitants of Ravenwood, who had been a part of Elsinore Forest for many generations without any significant Ione interference. The Iones referred to the arboreal town by its Damone name, "Ravenwood," although in their accent it came out "RAH-feen-woot." They respected the townspeople enough to not refer to them as Damones. Instead they called them Ravens (rah-FEENS).

There were several reasons the Iones were so tolerant of the Ravens. First, the groups seemed to share their prejudice against outsiders, although in the case of Ravenwood it was far less stringent. It confused the Iones spies when the people there periodically accepted new Damones into their town, but the new recruits almost always assimilated into Raven culture, following the same principles and practices the Iones had come to rely upon over the generations.

The Iones never entered Ravenwood, and the Ravens shared the same territorial respect. No contracts were ever offered and no handshakes were ever shared between them, and yet neither group set foot onto each other's land.

The Iones also tolerated the Ravens because they seemed to have the same respect for the plants and trees around them. The Iones were truly one with nature, and their way of life caused very little change to the forest around them. They constructed nothing like the stone buildings, paved thoroughfares, or massive statues that were present in Ravenwood, but the Ravens did all that with as little impact on the surrounding flora as possible. The builders of Ravenwood chose to work around the old trees rather than cut them down.

The final, and arguably the most important, reason the Iones tolerated the occupancy of the Ravens in Elsinore was because the Ravens were feared by the Damones. The average Damone farmer, servant, or laborer had a distrust of magic and those who purveyed it. Most suspected that the Ravens pranced through the woods cavorting with demons and performing evil rituals, which was enough to keep them out of Elsinore and away from the Iones. Anything the Iones could do to perpetuate that misconception was in their best interest, as it led to overall less interactions with outsiders.

CHAPTER 2

Throughout the centuries since the Iones first moved into Elsinore Forest, visitors were uncommon. That was until the time referred to by the Damones as The Isolation, when misery fell onto Hyboria. This event was a little less dramatic for the Ione people, as they were used to being isolated. Their first clue that something had changed was a slight increase in the frequency and distress of Damone intruders.

The Damones fleeing from the influx of monsters were offered no sanctuary in the woods. The Iones still discouraged them by the usual methods: scare tactics, incapacitation and expulsion, or for the more persistent Damones, arrow assault. The rapid influx of Damones caused the Ione scouts to increase patrols along the southern edge of their territory. After the initial flurry of activity, the Damones stopped arriving altogether, and that's when the monsters started wandering in.

Some unknown Ione warrior dubbed the monsters *sunamors*, which loosely translated to *gray savages*. The moniker spread throughout the squatas situated along the southern border of Elsinore. The little information that was known about them was also shared, but much of it rumor and misinformation. The sunamors were described as being twice as tall and ten times as heavy as an adult Ione male, but that was a gross exaggeration.

Hyperbole aside, it was true that they were large, ungainly oafs who made a loud ruckus as they crashed among the trees, snapping every branch and crunching every dry leaf along the way, so the Iones didn't have to try very hard to locate them. Their removal, however, presented a problem.

The sunamors couldn't be reasoned with, appealed to, bartered with, or communicated with. While these were not generally part of Ione strategy for ridding their land of invaders, a few desperate attempts were found to be fruitless. They carried no supplies to be destroyed or stolen, and trying to threaten them with warning shots only served to alert them of the presence of the archers. Hand-to-hand combat was completely out of the question because of the disparity in size and strength, and poison-tipped darts couldn't pierce their hides. The only way the Iones could protect their squatas was to do what they did best, hide in the shadows and coordinate long-range attacks through the use of shuesa communication.

The sunamors were no different than other animals in their inability to survive a direct center-chest arrow strike fired at peak draw weight, but the beasts had an uncanny ability to deflect arrows with their armor-plated upper extremities. They had enormous horns that curved down around their faces, protecting them like helmets, and their natural stooped posture closed the neck as a target.

Stealth, teamwork, and an accurate first arrow were the most important factors in quickly neutralizing one of these infiltrating beasts. The benefits of an incapacitating first shot could not be overstated. If the opening volley missed, or if the sunamor detected the archers before they could get into position, the Iones had an arduous task ahead of them.

Communicating via shuesa was a major advantage, allowing the Iones to simultaneously fire arrows from multiple directions. The more the better, as even accurate shots could get hung up in a mass of bone and muscle before they hit something vital. Only in dire emergencies would a solo archer attempt to take on a sunamor.

Tenacity and persistence served the Iones to the point where they figured out the most efficient and safest ways to protect themselves. Eventually fighting them off became routine, that is until the day a gigantic creature, one that looked like a freakishly overgrown bear, was spotted lumbering through the forest. It exploded onto an Ione scout, killing him before he barely had time to scream. It then consumed most of his body, leaving only part of his mangled torso to be later found by his wife. After that, the creature wandered into a small squata, terrorizing several children who were playing together at the base of a tree.

This monster, which the Iones came to refer to as a *brevell*, gradually forged a path of misery and death from one squata to another. For as enormous as it was, it had a preternatural ability to glide between the trees faster than people could get away. Attempts were made to confront it, but nothing the Iones did had any significant impact. Poison darts harmlessly disappeared into its fur and arrows didn't fare much better. Someone came up with the idea of painting the arrowheads with poison. It was an exciting moment when the first poison-tipped arrow lodged itself in the brevell's shoulder, but the poison had no noticeable effect.

The invasion of the brevell was a seminal moment for the Iones. While its presence meant terrible tragedy for the people in southwest Elsinore, those who lived in the east and the north had no idea the creature even existed. They continued their way of life as it had always been. This was especially true for those in the north who, because of geography, had no experience with any sort of intruder. It was impossible for them to even conceptualize the significance of The Isolation. Their very existence depended on their own self-imposed isolation that had been cultivated over centuries.

On and on the beast lurched through southwest Elsinore. There were countless failed attempts to stop it, slow it down, or drive it away. The archers who made themselves responsible for those efforts seemed to have no influence on the brevell's path through the woods. All they could do was keep an eye on where it was and try to guess where it was next headed so they could warn the squatas in harm's way. Most people were evacuated before the brevell got to them, all but the ones who were either too infirm or too stubborn to leave. Many Iones met their end in the creature's jaws, and it was their unwitting sacrifice that in part saved hundreds of others by slowing the beast's progress. After several harrowing weeks, and purely by chance, the monster mercifully wandered out of the woods and did not return.

Once the calamity came to an end, the displaced Iones reclaimed their homes, buried the remains of their dead, and tried to regroup and reclaim their quiet existence. A large number of survivors came together to discuss the invasion by the brevell and the continuing presence of the sunamors. It was the largest gathering of Iones in one place by anyone's memory, and resulted in two unprecedented decisions.

First, a group of nine of the most able hunters were dispatched to leave Elsinore in the hopes of discovering why the world outside had changed so drastically and to see if they could do something about it. Second, and just as much out of character for the Iones, representatives from the affected area would travel the length and breadth of the forest to educate the rest of the inhabitants of Elsinore about the sunamors and the brevell. For a population defined by its absence of unity and its respect for privacy among squatas, this was a major shift in dogma.

CHAPTER 3

Nine Ione hunters, now self-appointed crusaders, traveled southward along a path through the woods of Elsinore. They moved in single file, not for any reason other than the space didn't comfortably allow for side-by-side walking. It was better described as a game trail; a thin clearing in the underbrush worn down by years of foot traffic. All around them were ferns, shrubs, and wildflowers, each vying for a tiny fraction of the sunlight that found its way to the forest floor. The underbrush also contained an endless array of brambles, which the Iones loved for their sweet berries but hated for their equal number of sharp thorns.

Above their heads was the ever-present, sun-obscuring canopy. Many times the Iones would find a small gap in the curtain of leaves due to a recently fallen tree. It was a beautiful sight in the relative darkness to see streams of sunlight pouring through and illuminating the interior of the forest with a golden glow. The open space would be eventually obscured by the stretching limbs of surrounding trees, but for the short time it lasted the Iones felt Graehym was looking down on them, casting a blessing.

The crusaders wore their traditional travel gear of animal skins and furs adorned with patterned beadwork. Much of it was purely decorative, but some displays identified their respective squata, and a few pieces symbolized prayers to Graehym to protect the wearer from harm. On their feet were flexible yet protective shoes made from woven strips of birch tree bark treated with a waterproof resin. The weave was thicker at the sole but easily flexed for walking or running, and the inside was lined with animal fur. A longbow and quiver of arrows were slung over their shoulders, as was a rucksack.

At the front of the line was Blain, who had spent the last several years traversing the forest as a scout. He had assumed the leadership role without having discussed it with the others. Behind him were Dutch, Dillon, Andy, Mac, Phil, Hawkins, Jesse, and Poncho.

"Once we leave the forest, what's the plan?" asked Dillon, who at that point in the journey was walking closest to Blain.

"Just keep your eyes open and follow me," answered Blain.

"Who put you in charge?" called Poncho from the rear of the procession.

Blain stopped the line and turned to face the rest of the troop. "Is there a problem?"

"I just want to know what qualifies you to be our leader."

It was the middle of the day, but the sun was mostly shrouded by foliage. The forest was alive with sound—songbirds chirping, squirrels skittering up the sides of trees, a solitary woodpecker tapping in the distance.

Blain scanned the body language of the rest of the men. They avoided his gaze, attempting to minimize their involvement in the confrontation. He met Poncho's eyes and said, "You seem to be the only one who has a problem here."

Poncho approached and responded with an accusatory tone, "You wear no family mark." He pointed to a series of beads in an identifying pattern on his own chest. "I'm from the Ahnodo squata." He gestured to the absence of such identifying features on Blain's clothing. "Which squata are you from?"

Blain made no change in his neutral expression. "What do you say we keep walking before we lose the light? If you don't like how I'm doing things, you and I can discuss it later in private."

The two men continued to stare at one another until Poncho responded, "Lead the way, Sauti."

The word *sauti* held a dual meaning in the Ione language. It was a term of great respect for a squata patriarch (the feminine version being *sauta*). The other usage was pejorative, a way to disrespect a person who acts like a leader but wields no actual power.

Blain chuckled at the ribbing, and then turned to continue to lead their journey along the game trail. Everyone followed, relieved that the confrontation had fizzled before anything serious had happened.

Later that day, at the edge of Elsinore Forest, the nine Iones were gathered in a clearing, sitting in a circle on logs and large stones. It was dark where they were because of the canopy above, but out on the open plains it was twilight. They were waiting for night to fall on Hyboria, at which point they planned to emerge from the forest and continue south. As the men rested and talked, they dined on some of the provisions they had brought with them.

Much of the conversation revolved around their home squata and what life was like there. Even though they came from different places in Elsinore, they found a lot of similarities in their upbringings and shared a lot of the same beliefs and dreams. All the men spoke freely except Blain, who quietly listened. Aside from Poncho, the men held him in an authoritative role and were reluctant to treat him as casually as they treated each other. Blain was older than the rest of them and carried himself in a way that commanded respect.

During a lull in conversation, Poncho said, with a gregarious smile, "Now that we heard from everyone else, how about we learn the origins of our great leader?"

The other men, who before this moment were laughing and relaxed, tensed up and froze. Some of them even stopped chewing the food in their mouths.

The silence drew out for an uncomfortably long time until Blain flatly answered, "I have nothing to say."

Poncho frowned at this, but he was not about to give up. After a moment he said, "I'm the type of man who needs a little more than a stern facial expression before I recognize someone as leader. It's not unreasonable to ask you to share as everyone else has."

Blain cleared his throat and dropped his gaze to the ground. "You press. You push. I suppose a man can't be anonymous and a leader at the same time." He lifted his head and said, "What's I'm about to tell you I've told no one before."

The men silently stared at Blain.

"I grew up in a squata far in the north of Elsinore. There were ten of us. My parents, me, my older sister, and another family—their father, whose name was Clayber, his wife, three daughters, and his mother, who was the sauti of the squata. Clayber is the only one you need to know about for this story."

"We all got along and everything was fine until the day Clayber's wife died. She was bitten by a rattle-tail snake. I was only five, but I remember it well. It was dreadful to watch. She rotted from the inside out and died after four days of excruciating pain."

"Things were never the same after that. My mother took more of a role in the lives of Clayber's daughters. Everyone worked a little harder, and eventually things settled down."

"A few years later, when I was eight, Clayber and my father went out on a hunt, and only Clayber came back. He was scraped and bruised, and his eyes were wild and frantic. He said they were surprised by a pack of wolves and were surrounded and attacked. He said the wolves took my father away." Blain paused and took a deep breath. "Clayber fell to his knees at my mother's feet, sobbing. He told her he tried, but there was nothing he could do. He said it was only by Graehym's grace that he escaped with his own life."

"We all went to where Clayber said the wolf attack occurred. I was terrified. Leaves were kicked up and it was obvious there had been a struggle. We searched that entire day, but found no sign of my father. It took a long time for me to accept the fact he was gone."

"Over the next couple of years Clayber began to take more of an interest in me. He taught me how to hunt and fish. He treated me as his own son, and a boy needs a father, right?" The men nodded, but no one said anything.

"One day my sister started showing signs of being pregnant. She was only thirteen." Blain looked away after saying this and then squeezed his eyes shut. "I was completely confused. The only person I knew who could have been the father was Clayber, but that didn't make sense. I asked my mother about it, and she confirmed my suspicions, saying we needed to start building the next generation to continue the squata, and who better to father a child than Clayber. I respected my mother, and she seemed content, so I swallowed my disgust."

"After the baby was born, a boy, Clayber didn't have much to do with me. That was fine as far as I was concerned. By this point I was eleven and thought it was time to be my own man. I kept to myself, pretending I was the patriarch of my own squata."

"One night a few years later, with my sister pregnant a second time, I caught my mother…" He swallowed. "…lying down with Clayber." Blain looked distant as this image washed over him. After a minute he continued. "I was repulsed by… well, everything."

Some of the men grunted in pained empathy.

"I ran away, grabbed what I could and went south. The people closest to me had betrayed everything I knew to be right, and running away was all I could think of to betray them in return. I lived on my own for a long time, taking what I needed from the forest, and when that failed me, I took from other squatas, either by begging or stealing. For years I wandered the woods alone."

"One day I came upon the southern edge of Elsinore. I knew the forest had to have an end, but it was strange to see it staring me in the face. I walked to where the trees stopped growing and peered out onto an enormous field. I looked hard for Damones, foolishly imagining they'd be waiting there with weapons, ready to hack me to pieces, but there was nothing but naked land before me stretching for miles. I stared for a long time, thinking I saw movement in the distance, but it was just a trick of my eyes. I cautiously paced the tree line, stalling." He took a long blink and a deep breath and said, "And then I left Elsinore."

"What do you mean you left Elsinore?!" spat Poncho.

"You have to remember I had nothing holding me back. I belonged to no one. Everything I believed in was gone. I just...left."

There was a growing murmur among the men as they uncomfortably muttered questions to themselves and each other. Finally, Mac spoke up, asking, "What did it look like? The world outside the trees?" His question emerged with the tone of curiosity rather than judgment.

"It was different than what I was used to seeing. I'll put it that way. Eventually I came upon a small group of Damones. I did my best to hide from them and observe what they were doing. I listened to them talking to each other. Of course I had no idea what they were saying because I didn't speak the language, but from their actions I was able to figure out a word or two. They didn't realize I was there, so I kept watching until they went away."

"I repeated this every day, hiding, watching, listening. I was really good at blending in and being quiet. If I really concentrated I could focus on what they were saying. After a while the language started making sense to me. I'd practice it as I was falling asleep at night."

"You learned their language?" asked Jesse.

"At that point, no. But I knew enough Hybor to get by working as a laborer in a little coastal village. A place called Winston." He paused for a moment and then said, as an aside, "You men understand that Damones live together in massive groups of unrelated people, right? They call where they live a village; or a town." He used the Hybor words for these names, saying them with an accent that would sound funny to a native Hybor speaker.

The men responded with a mixture of nods and shrugs.

"As I was saying, you don't need to be fluent in the language to be able to load and unload boats. Gradually I got better at speaking and understanding their language. The people I was around just saw me as a smaller, lighter-skinned, not-so-smart fellow Damone."

"So they thought they were better than you?" asked Dillon.

"It's natural to think of people who struggle to speak your language as less intelligent," answered Blain. "I didn't blame them. I just worked harder to learn to communicate. Actually, I was surprised at how accommodating and welcoming they were, after all we'd been warned about them. Regardless, I didn't let on who I really was and never got too close to anyone."

"After about ten years of moving from town to town, completely immersed in their culture and language, I decided it was time to go back. I don't know what drove my decision. Nostalgia for the happy parts of my childhood before everything fell apart? Wanting to atone for disrespecting my family by leaving? Whatever it was, I left all the possessions of my Damone life and came back to Elsinore."

"I had no idea how to make clothes and couldn't be seen in my Damone disguise, so I had to scrounge what I could from unattended squatas. I promised myself that this would be my final offense to the Ione people. I was fully committed to joining as one of us again."

"What did you say to the first Ione you saw?" asked Dutch. "That must have been strange."

"I avoided interactions for a long time. After all of those years I needed time to reacquaint myself with our language and customs."

Dutch nodded.

"Eventually I came upon a group of scouts tracking what I later learned was a sunamor. I joined them in killing it and my identity as an Ione was reestablished. I spoke with them briefly and then we went our separate ways. I decided protecting Elsinore from this new threat would be a way to repay for my misdeeds. So far I've been involved in the killing of six of those beasts."

He paused, allowing the other men to digest the story, before addressing Poncho. "You asked me why I make a good leader for a quest that involves leaving Elsinore for the world of the Damones. After hearing my story, do you still question my qualifications?"

Everyone was silent. None of them had ever heard of an Ione leaving the forest before. In a different context the story would make them want to reject Blain, but given their proposed task, it seemed there was no Ione in existence better suited to lead them. The silence was broken by Phil, who had a puzzled look on his face. He said, "I haven't known a pack of wolves to hunt and kill someone, especially two full-grown and fully armed Ione men."

Hawkins nodded in agreement. "In my experience it's a rare day if you even see wolves, and if you do, you get a brief flash as they're running away."

"Right," added Phil. "They don't come near us unless it's to steal food when we're not looking."

Blain nodded. "That's one of the many reasons I think Clayber invented the wolf story. I believe after his wife died he wanted my mother to himself and concocted a plan to get away with killing my father."

"That's unforgivable," said Phil, shaking his head.

"Maybe after our mission with the Damones we'll all go back with you and help you get revenge on Clayber." said Jesse, half-joking.

"Believe me I've thought about that countless times. Thoughts of killing him kept me up at night, but I can't imagine the years have been easy on him. My mother probably knows his actions with her and my sister are why I left. She's probably been taking out her misery on him ever since."

Poncho stared at Blain for a long time before standing and walking to where he was seated. He extended his fist. Blain stood and the two men shared the traditional greeting of Ione warriors: bumping fists followed by an open-hand slide starting from the backs of the wrists down to the fingertips. When they were finished, Poncho said, "You have my greatest respect, sauti."

Chapter 4

Rugen led a party of Hyborian soldiers up a hill toward their first stopping point since embarking on Graan Boulevard, the road that wound through the mountains from the city of Lundgren to the gateway to the Northern Territory. They had been walking since leaving the city that morning. During the days leading up to their departure, the group settled debts, finalized plans with Lord Volguus and Duke Alonzo, said goodbye to families, and tied up any other loose ends they had in Lundgren.

Their first destination was the Lundgren Army barracks most proximal to the city. There was a series of barracks along the way, sequentially named B-1, B-2, B-3, and so on. Each was separated by about a day's walk. The plan was to traverse the entirety of the meandering road, spending a night at each barracks, until they reached the Red Gate. While on the road they would have the full support of the Lundgren Army, including supplies, lodging, and good will. Once they passed through the gate, they would be on their own.

Leading the procession were Rugen, JJ, Claire, Alex, Serra, and Dobbler, followed by a mixture of eight sub-elite and nineteen grunt RHS graduates, as supplied by Lord Volguus. These non-round numbers represented the fraction of that year's graduating class he was willing to part with. As discussed, no elite graduates were made available.

Graan Boulevard was a well-traveled supply route. As the warriors proceeded, they passed Lundgren Army soldiers returning to the city as well as workers laboriously pushing cartloads of fruits, vegetables, grains, and butchered meat up and down the serpentine hills. Carts were also heading from the city, supplying the soldiers with clean uniforms, new weapons, and fresh linens.

The view from the road was of the majestic Ovid Graan Mountains, which served as the backbone of Hyboria. The range spanned hundreds of miles between the northeast and southwest edges of the continent. Popular belief held that the range made a fairly straight line, but Lundgren Army surveyors and cartographers determined it to have an overall slight northerly curve, allocating a larger area of flat land to the southeastern portion of the continent. This interesting nuance of geography led some Lundgrenians to refer to the Ovid Graans as the "Crescent Range."

As the warriors reached the top of the hill, they saw a clearing ahead. To the right was a large stone building with a navy blue Lundgren flag waving at the top of a wooden post. Below that was a smaller black flag with "B-1" in white text. "That must be the barracks," said Rugen. Everyone looked up and spotted the building, which was an oasis for their sore legs and empty stomachs.

A man in a Lundgren Army uniform stepped out from the doorway and nodded to the approaching soldiers. When they got close enough, he said, "You must be Gordon's Army." He offered his hand and Rugen shook it.

"I'm Rugen, and yes," he smiled, "I suppose we are, although I didn't know we were called that."

The welcoming soldier brushed it off, slightly embarrassed. "One of the men made it up at Duke Alonzo's briefing, and it stuck."

"It would make Gordon proud," said Rugen.

"I'm Sergeant Ziskey. I run this barracks. I sent most of my men on assignment so you'd have a place to spend the night. Alonzo asked me to put you up, feed you, and provide whatever else you might need."

"We really appreciate it."

Ziskey held out his hand, presenting the building entrance. As Gordon's Army processed inside, they saw an expansive room full of long wooden tables and benches. The walls were decorated with banners the colors of the Lundgren flag in long stripes. Along the back wall were empty racks for hanging weapons, coats, and bags. There were several doors around the perimeter of the room, presumably to the kitchen, stairwell, and storage closets. The scent of cooking food excited the air.

Ziskey pointed to one of the doors and said, "Go through there. Up the stairs you'll find bedrooms and bathrooms. There's lots of space. Each bedroom holds eight people. It's up to you to figure out the sleeping arrangements. The cook will ring the bell when he's ready." Rugen nodded, and then Ziskey added, "Our quarters, the staff and I, are down here. The second floor is yours."

The travelers paraded upstairs, intent on making use of the facilities and sorting out who would be in which room. A short while later, a loud bell rang and everyone returned for a hot meal of roasted meat, root vegetables, and thick bread with butter. This was followed by pastries for dessert. Sergeant Ziskey commented several times about how well they ate in the Ovid Graan Mountains. It seemed to be a source of pride for him.

Once finished, Rugen stood and addressed the room. "Gentleman!" He looked down at Serra and Claire, who were seated at his table, and in a regular speaking voice said, "And ladies." All of the RHS graduates quieted down from their own conversations to listen to him. "We decided to organize the army in small groups."

"Squads," called out JJ.

Rugen briefly frowned at him, to which JJ smiled and nodded. Rugen continued, "Right. Squads. Each squad will be headed up by one of us." He gestured to his table. "The reason we're doing this is to simplify battle strategies and establish camaraderie."

The newly designated squad leaders: Serra, Dobbler, JJ, Alex, and Claire, were nodding along as Rugen spoke. "Once assigned, your primary responsibility will be to the members of your squad. You watch their backs and they watch yours. As for who gets assigned where, each squad will have two sub-elites and four grunts, except for the one led by Serra and Dobbler. They won't be on the front line and won't need sub-elites."

Some of the heads in the audience nodded. The RHS graduates had a general familiarity with who everyone was from the previous few days of interactions and from conversing during the long walk that morning. "So that's four grunts each to four squads. The magicians will be joined by the other three, as bodyguards. That accounts for all nineteen."

There was whispering and snickering at one of the tables. Rugen looked in the direction where the sound came from and asked, "Does someone have something to say?" Nobody moved or responded. Rugen pointed and said, "You there. You need me to clarify something?"

A young man sat up straighter and said, "Nothing, sir. We were just wondering who was going to be on which team."

"What's your name?" he asked. "Did you have a preference?"

"Curtis, and um..." He stopped talking when two guys sitting next to him, sub-elites named Emilio and Duncan, burst out laughing. Curtis's face turned red in embarrassment.

"I think what he's trying to say," started Claire, looking annoyed, "is he doesn't want to be on the girl's team."

"No," Curtis stammered, "all I said was whoever was assigned to her team would have to, you know, be extra careful to make sure she stays safe."

"And they'll have to put up with me crying all the time or being moody if I break a nail, right?" taunted Claire.

Curtis's head and shoulders dropped.

"Do you know who this is?" Rugen said loudly as he pointed toward Claire. "She..."

Claire interrupted him. "Rugen, I've dealt with boys like him all my life." She stressed the word *boys* as an insult. "They don't listen until I demonstrate what I can do." She jumped to her feet, scowling.

Rugen smiled. He looked at Sergeant Ziskey and said, "I'm assuming you have training weapons here?"

Ziskey nodded and said, "Of course we do. What would you like?"

"I'll use my own staff," responded Claire. Really there wasn't a significant difference between a fighting staff meant for practice and a fighting staff meant for combat. She gestured to Curtis. "He'll need a helmet. A good one."

Ziskey raised his eyebrows at Curtis, asking what else he would need. Emilio and Duncan started pushing him, partially playfully and partially to get him out of his chair. He brushed them off, stood, and said, "I'll take a wooden sword and shield."

The entire barracks population, visitors and staff alike, gathered behind the B-1 building along the fence that encompassed an outdoor training yard. Within the fence were Curtis and Claire. Curtis had taken Claire's advice and worn a helmet, which was made of hardened leather lined with padding. He was hefting a wooden sword and small shield, trying to get used to their weight. Claire leaned in a casual manner on her staff, seeming almost disinterested.

Ziskey nodded to both of them and said, "You've both done this before. Let's try to remember we're on the same team." At that Claire lifted her weapon and started walking to the middle of the yard. Seeing her move, Curtis did the same. When they got within striking distance, they tapped weapons and settled into battle stances. Claire's body language changed from indifference to steely focus. Ziskey yelled the starting command, making them circle each other.

Just like the combatants, the crowd also came alive at Ziskey's word. They were clapping and cheering, encouraging the sparring fighters. Curtis took a tentative swing, weak enough for a child to deflect. Claire blocked it and immediately slapped his shield with the other end of her staff. They circled some more and Curtis swung again, with a little more enthusiasm this time. She tapped his sword away and said, "Harder. You're not going to break me."

Curtis swung, and again Claire knocked it away. The contest went on like this for a while, with Curtis swinging and Claire either dodging or blocking but not fighting back. The crowd around the fence started getting bored and restless. Their gazes wandered away from the yard.

Emilio yelled, "C'mon!" Curtis looked over, took a step back, and then took a lunging swing. Claire ducked the painfully telegraphed assault, and as she popped up she struck his shield hard, knocking him off balance. In a flash she was on him—twisting, sliding, and peppering him with shots. He backed up several steps almost to the fence. Seeing this she ceased her attack and sauntered to the starting point in the middle of the yard.

Curtis joined her and Ziskey gave the command to restart. Claire initiated contact this time. Before Curtis's brain was able to register her lightning fast movement, she struck the bottom of his wooden shield, knocking it upward and briefly obstructing his vision. She used the momentum of a quick spin to hammer the shield into his face, splitting his lip.

Curtis was stunned for a second, but quickly came back at her with his sword. He saw a wide open target in her shoulder, but by the time the wooden blade got there she was gone. She had spun again, winding up nearly behind him and knocking his shield out of his hand.

Everyone laughed as Curtis wiped his mouth and picked up his shield from the dirt. Duncan yelled, "You better watch yourself, Curt. She bites." Laughter roared with this.

Curtis's face was red with embarrassment, his bottom lip was bloody and swollen, but no part of him was bruised more than his ego. He was inspired to stop holding back and start taking the fight seriously. He used every technique he'd learned in his six years at RHS. He was fast, but Claire was faster. Each time he thought he'd outmaneuvered her, she'd duck, dodge, spin, or slide away.

When Claire decided she had sufficiently proven she could protect herself from physical harm, she went on the offensive again. A series of well-placed strikes knocked Curtis off balance and dislodged his sword from his hand. As he was falling backward, she swung a vicious blow over the top of his shield at the side of his helmet. Curtis saw the leading edge of the staff coming and knew he was powerless to stop it. He reflexively squeezed his eyes shut, awaiting oblivion, but the strike never came. Claire stopped it just inches from his temple. Curtis fell to the dirt, embarrassed but relieved.

The crowd was silent as Claire stood over Curtis, open hand extended. He looked up at her with wide eyes and a shocked expression.

"Help you up?" she asked.

Curtis grabbed her hand and pulled himself to his feet. He didn't know what to say.

"We're on the same team, right?" said Claire.

He nodded and the onlookers cheered.

Rugen decided that since they had access to practice weapons, open space, and nothing better to do, it was a good idea for everyone to pair off for some sparring. Rugen was never one for missing an opportunity for training. Serra and Dobbler practiced some of the techniques they had learned at the self-defense school; that is until Serra needed to tend to some minor lacerations and abrasions on the combatants. Rugen had them practice until sunset, when they all went back inside to wash up and have an evening snack.

Serra and Claire roomed together while everyone else sorted into bunks according to their assigned squads. There weren't many arguments about the squad assignments, as the groupings followed predetermined social lines. One major exception to this was Curtis, who didn't join JJ's group with his two friends from earlier. Instead, he opted for Claire's team.

CHAPTER 5

Gordon's Army woke with the sun the next morning and sat down to an elaborate breakfast, complete with Ziskey again pointing out how well Lundgren's Army was fed. They packed their gear, thanked the staff for the hospitality, and got back onto Graan Boulevard to make their way toward B-2. Ziskey's staff gave them plenty of snacks and water for the road.

The views from the mountain pass were endlessly impressive and varying. There were undulating swells of rolling grass broken up by jagged, rocky slopes. In the distance were snow-capped peaks, some so high they breached the blanket of clouds above. Where there weren't walls of rock looming over the road, there were fertile valleys full of endless rows of vegetable crops, fruit trees, grapevines, or wide grassy pastures dotted with grazing livestock. The valleys were alive with the constant movement of workers tending to everything.

It was a beautiful late summer day in the mountains, perfect for a casual hike. Everyone commented on how much cooler it felt compared to the lower elevation in Lundgren.

After walking most of the day, they arrived at B-2, where just like at B-1 they got cleaned up, ate, trained, slept, and moved on. This series of activities was repeated at B-3, B-4, and B-5. Along the way they learned a card game called Mogwai, which was a favorite of Lundgren Army regulars and quickly became an obsession of Gordon's Army. Many scuffles broke out over disagreements about the game.

Each barracks had mass quantities of fresh food, all expertly prepared and excellent, as well as the equivalent of a Sergeant Ziskey excitedly touting how wonderful everything was. Duke Alonzo must have ordered the barracks leaders to put their best foot forward for Gordon's Army, which Rugen assumed might be related to the stack of gold coins Alex had gifted.

By the time they arrived at B-6, the routine changed somewhat. It was clear even from far away that the building was considerably larger than the previous five. They were greeted at the door by a small group of people, most notably a scientist named Leland, who told them he ran a research lab at the site. He invited Rugen, who in turn invited the other squad leaders, to see the lab. Only Dobbler and Claire joined Rugen for the tour.

Leland led the three observers down a long corridor toward his lab. Looking over his shoulder he said, "We've learned quite a bit from the specimens the men have been carting back."

"When you say specimens, you mean dead gmorks?" asked Claire.

"Is that what you call them? asked Leland. "Gmorks?"

"Gordon told me that's what they were called," clarified Rugen.

"I've heard people call them a lot of different things." He looked at Claire. "To answer your question, most were dead when they got here, yes. We had one live one."

"Wow. How'd you capture a living one without anyone getting hurt?" asked Dobbler.

"I didn't say no one got hurt."

They rounded the corner and followed Leland into the lab. It was a large room with various metal tables, shelves of glass jars full of green-tinged liquid and hunks of flesh, labeled pictures on the walls depicting gmork anatomy, and dozens of surgical tools scattered about. Leland gestured to the empty tables and said, "As you can see we have no research subjects currently."

"So what can you tell us about them?" asked Rugen as he scanned the room.

"By performing necropsies we know a lot about their anatomy, but the physiology is a little...mysterious. We'll get to that later." He went to his desk and picked up a rectangular strip of dark gray leather the length and width of a sandal and handed it to Rugen, who inspected it and then passed it along. It was thick, dense, and stiff. Leland said, "Their hide is the toughest I've ever encountered. I've dulled many instruments trying to cut through it."

He waited until Dobbler was finished with the strip and said, "Beneath their skin is a thick layer of muscle, strengthening its integrity, and beneath that is what I like to describe as more muscle and then more muscle."

He invited them to sit at a wooden table near his desk and brought over a stack of papers of different sizes and colors. As he leafed through them, Rugen, Claire, and Dobbler saw many high-quality charcoal drawings interspersed with blocks of text.

He stopped on a page with a drawing of the hand and forearm of a gmork. The skin had a stony, textured appearance with overlapping triangular scales. The first two joints of each finger were proportional to the size of the hand, but the fingertips were extended and slightly curved into sharp claws, like the talons of an eagle.

"These are like wearing hardened steel gauntlets, except they don't slide on and off," said Leland. "They're fully functional, meaning all five fingers can move independently." He added as an aside, "Although I don't know what for. Have you ever seen the beasts moving one finger individually from the others?"

The three of them shook their heads until Leland corrected himself. "Actually I've seen one grab the sword right out of a soldier's hand by the blade. I don't know if that counts, though, because it's not like they turn the sword around and start to swing it. They don't seem to have the intellectual capacity for the use of tools."

Everyone stared at the drawing as Leland said, with a dreamy lilt to this voice, "If only we could design gauntlets as functional and dangerous as these and equip our soldiers with them."

"It'd be even better if the soldiers could grow them themselves," replied Claire.

Leland smiled at her and flipped to a drawing of the open mouth of a gmork. "They have twenty-four cone-shaped teeth. They get smaller as they go back, but they're all that same shape. The front four along the top are about the size of the last joint of my pinky finger," he said, wiggling that same finger. "Their throats are narrower than you'd expect for as wide as their mouths are."

Leland turned more pages until he came to a close-up of a gmork's horn. "Just like their gauntlet-like arms, the horns are as hard and dense as stone." He mimed hefting one in his left hand.

"What about, um, reproduction?" asked Dobbler sheepishly. "How do they make little gmorks?"

"They don't have reproductive organs I've been able to find, so I don't think they have the ability to spawn on their own." Leland added, "And while we're discussing that general area, they don't urinate or defecate either."

Rugen, Claire, and Dobbler all looked at each other with raised eyebrows.

"We had a live one here for a while," started Leland. "The men showed up one day carrying it on a stretcher they had improvised in the field. They brought it into the lab, and when we removed the blankets, the beast began snarling and pulling on its bindings. I don't know how they trapped it, and I still don't know how we safely transferred it into the cage without it getting loose. But we did." He stared off, recalling the images in his mind. "The thing was vicious. Scared the hell out of me to be around it every day. Any time it saw us it would rattle the bars, gnash its teeth, and ram the side of the cage with his body or horns. It wouldn't settle down until we left the room."

Leland flipped the pages to a picture of the gmork in its cage. "After a day or two we tried to give it food and water, but all it did was kick or toss the bowls around, making a mess of the lab. Again and again we tried to feed it, but it never ate. We kept it caged for several weeks, and these behaviors remained the same—quiet when no one was in the room, seething and snarling when it saw us. It never got used to us being around it."

"So how do you think they survive?" asked Claire. "I mean, if they don't eat or drink?"

Leland ruffled through a few more pages and settled on a drawing of a gmork lying on a table with its chest and abdomen open in dissection. "They have all the organs we have, well, mostly, but they're small compared to the body size." He pointed to the structures as he explained. "Lungs, heart, stomach...it's like everything is in miniature. The heart does pump blood, and if you manage to stab it or cut a major vessel, the creature bleeds to death. But with all that muscle, the toughened skin, and the organs being surprisingly small, it's not easy to get in there to puncture something important while it's attacking you."

He looked at Claire and said, "Regarding your question about how they survive, I did my first necropsy with that question in mind and was even more baffled when I finished. There has to be powerful magic poured into them. They survive partly by natural processes and partly supernatural."

"You mean a permanent magical enchantment?" asked Claire. "Like in Alex's battle armor or JJ's shield?"

"You'll have to show me those," answered Leland, eyebrows raised, "but I suppose it's the same idea. It was just a theory for a long time, but then we proved it with the living one we had caged."

"Proved it?" remarked Dobbler. "How?"

"We brought in a cleric to perform an aughra drain."

"What's an aughra drain?" interrupted Rugen.

Leland held out his hand to Dobbler and nodded, offering him the opportunity to explain.

"It's a spell that sequesters all of the aughra out of the vicinity of the caster," he responded. "The point of it is to use up all available magical energy, thereby rendering enemy sorcerers and clerics powerless." Dobbler turned back to Leland. "So what happened?"

"The creature started getting woozy and slowing down. After a few minutes, it collapsed in a heap. Once we were satisfied, the cleric stopped the spell. Gradually it woke up, stumbled to its feet, and in no time was back to its old grumpy self."

"This spell sounds like a good way to handle them in the field," said Claire.

"We can discuss it with Serra to be sure, but I don't think so," said Dobbler. "What I know about aughra drains is they only work over a small area. And if they affect the gmork as slowly as Leland says, it would have plenty of time to kill the cleric trying to cast the spell as it gradually falls unconscious."

They were quiet until Dobbler added, "Also an aughra drain prevents the casting of any other spell in that area. As you can imagine, sorcerers and clerics don't like eliminating their own ability to cast spells, even temporarily. Magic is really our only value in a fight."

"So what happened to the gmork?" asked Rugen. "The one you had caged?"

"After it had been with us a few weeks, we all sat down and talked about what to do with it. The decision was made to terminate. We figured we'd learned everything we could from keeping it alive, and we worried that eventually it could break out of the cage and kill one of us. Also, after a while you couldn't help but feel sorry for the thing, not enough to want to set it free, but..." Leland gazed at the drawings as he recalled the experience.

"You might be the only person in Hyboria to have sympathy for them," said Claire.

"These creatures are an abomination of nature," Leland clarified. "God can't claim responsibility for them. They have no souls, no thought, no consciousness. All they are is meat, claws, teeth, and fury. But even so, I believe a person who doesn't feel sympathy as he watches the suffering of another creature has lost his humanity, even if that creature is something as detestable as these are." He lowered his gaze and whispered, "I hate the guy who made them." He looked up and said, "If I were in charge of the Lundgren Army, I'd send every available soldier into the northern wilderness, just like our ancestors did all those years ago, and wipe out this evil once and for all."

Rugen, Claire, and Dobbler nodded agreement and then Rugen asked, "What have you learned about the other type? We call them ursinoxes."

"The giant bears?" Leland shook his head. "We've never caught one, living or dead. All I know about them is what surviving witnesses have said, and there aren't many of those."

"I saw one," Rugen admitted.

Leland's eyes got wide. "You saw one?"

"Yeah, just outside of Ravenwood, before I met the rest of these guys."

Dobbler and Claire regarded him, sadly.

"It killed my friends and left scars on my back."

"I'm sorry to hear that," said the scientist, staring at Rugen intently. "Listen, I hate to make you rehash bad memories, but I'd really like to learn all I can about these creatures. Do you mind telling me what you saw?"

CHAPTER 6

Rugen, Claire, and Dobbler related what they learned from Leland to the other members of Gordon's Army as they walked toward B-7. The RHS soldiers welcomed any information that led to improvements in the efficiency of killing gmorks. It was a topic that could bridge any silence or distract from any disagreement.

The usual routine of eating, training, sleeping, and morale-boosting sessions of Mogwai continued without any significant variance through the next three barracks-building segments.

The engineers who long ago constructed Graan Boulevard followed the topography of the mountain as much as they were able. In some places where the slope was too steep, they employed powerful sorcerers to help them blast gaps through the rock, leaving corridors with sheer cliffs on either side. Deep valleys were spanned with elegantly constructed bridges wide and robust enough to allow passage of large amounts of foot traffic.

The soldiers left B-9 and marched through the morning, climbing swelling inclines and descending into shallow depressions. Frequently they noticed having to pop their ears because of the ever-changing altitude. The prevailing elevation continued to increase as they distanced themselves from Lundgren, and at times when Graan Boulevard would rise, they'd find a lookout point and stop to appreciate the view. The sight of the beautiful vistas inspired quiet personal reflection in the travelers.

At one particularly expansive view, Rugen thought about how far he'd come since Gordon, JJ, and the others showed up on his doorstep. That afternoon in

Mourain represented a major crossroads in his life, and with all that happened since, it felt a lot longer than two months that had passed. It was amazing to him how the distractions of the journey made the last several miserable years since his mother and sister died fade from the forefront of his mind.

The thoughts that remained were of his father. It was only natural for a son to seek independence from his parents, but sneaking out of town before sunrise certainly wasn't how he had envisioned his coming of age. Flashes of how Hammond must have reacted when he'd found his bedroom empty made Rugen cringe. He tried justifying his decision by telling himself that his actions were the best thing for both of them.

All of the quiet introspection was shattered by the sound of an arrow splitting the air followed by a loud gong as it struck one of the grunts in the shield strapped across his back.

Everyone froze, and the grunt whose shield had been hit lurched forward and fell to the ground, less from the momentum of the arrow than from the instinct of self-preservation. The three soldiers around him reflexively ducked, but then sprang quickly into combat stance. Weapons and shields were drawn as everyone searched the landscape for where the arrow had originated. In a flash another arrow flew, and as heads turned toward its source, a third one split the air. Both of those clanged off shields too.

All three arrows had come from different directions, making Alex call out, "We're surrounded!" The soldiers crouched as several more flew over their heads.

"Show yourselves!" yelled Rugen, still crouching. He thought about the possibilities of who might be responsible for the assault. Duke Alonzo had done everything in his power to accommodate Gordon's Army, and it made no sense for that to be an elaborate setup and double-cross. Gmorks didn't know how to use weapons, as discussed with Leland. The only other thing he could think of was somehow Gruhl found out they were coming and dispatched a legion of archers to intercept them.

After a few moments of quiet, a heavily-accented response to Rugen's command came from the unseen assailants hiding among the trees, shrubs, and stony outcroppings, "Put away your weapons or next time our arrows won't miss."

The soldiers looked at each other, feeling vulnerable and exposed. Claire plucked one of the arrows off the ground and inspected its rounded tip. Her first thought was that the arrowhead became blunted when it struck the shield, but looking at it closer, she decided it must have been designed to be non-lethal. She held it out, showing the bell-shaped tip to her neighbors, which prompted others to gather the fallen arrows around them. All of them looked the same.

Rugen shouted, "What's the meaning of this?"

"Do we have your attention?" It was the same voice but had moved from where it had come earlier.

"You do!" yelled Rugen. "Now show yourselves!" He whispered to Serra and Dobbler, who were crouching next to him, "Can you do something to protect us if they start firing real arrows?"

"Already on it," answered Serra. Dobbler nodded in agreement.

Rugen gestured for everyone to stand. They did, slowly, into combat stances with weapons at the ready.

The owner of the voice had relocated again. "We'll come out when you put away your weapons."

"And if we don't?!" spat JJ.

Immediately an arrow zipped in and struck the back of JJ's gauntlet. The strike jerked his arm into the air and he reflexively cursed. All eyes scanned the area for an archer, but none was seen. JJ bent down and grabbed the arrow. It was blunt like all the others.

"Okay!" Rugen screamed. He lowered his voice, addressing his companions, "I think if these people wanted to hurt us, they'd be firing sharpened arrows and not aiming at our shields." He lifted his massive sword over his shoulder and gently slid it into the holster on his back.

The soldiers followed his lead and sheathed their own weapons, but those who had shields kept them in position to defend. Rugen waited for everyone to comply and then called out, "All right, we did what you…"

He stopped prematurely when he saw a man walking up the road. He had pale skin, was dressed in natural colors that blended with the landscape, and was wearing a longbow over his shoulder. His demeanor was that of somebody out for a leisurely stroll.

As the intruder got closer, Rugen noted how shockingly small and slight he was. Rugen was used to being a head taller than everyone around him, but felt like he was almost twice the height of the approaching archer.

His clothes were made of leather and furs from various animals. They were embellished with simple patterns of beadwork. He stopped walking a little ways from the soldiers and said with a thick accent, "Please understand, my companions' bows are still trained on you, but they will not fire unless you give them reason."

A din of contempt swelled through Gordon's Army until Rugen gestured for everyone to settle down. He turned to the stranger and said, "We won't give your men a reason to fire."

The small pale man smiled warmly and said, "Two of you are Ravens. I assume our unspoken no-harm agreement stands outside of the borders of Elsinore?"

Everyone was quiet and looked at each other, confused.

The archer narrowed his eyebrows briefly and then lit up, saying, "Ah, I forgot. You know our forest as Jamescorte."

There were several factors working against someone understanding what the man was talking about. First, only the Iones referred to the people of Ravenwood as Ravens. Second, an agreement between the two groups was a completely fictional construct made up by and known to the Iones only. Third, the man had pronounced the name with his Ione accent, "rah-FEENS." Even to long-term residents of Ravenwood this was a completely foreign pronunciation.

"You said Jamescorte," offered Serra, nodding. "That's where my school is; in the town of Ravenwood. Are you talking about me and Dobbler?"

Dobbler looked at her, making the facial expression equivalent of a shoulder shrug, and said, "We aren't aware of any unspoken agreement."

"Forgive me for presuming," said the archer, "I will clarify. My men and I are Iones. We live in the forest of Elsinore, what you call Jamescorte."

"Wait, you live in the woods surrounding Ravenwood?" interrupted Dobbler. "No one lives there."

"We do. The Iones. We've always lived there." He looked at Serra and Dobbler. "The unspoken agreement between our people is to not cause each other harm. My name is Blain. There has been a recent influx of monsters in our forest. My men and I left our land to investigate what they are and how to get rid of them. It seems you're doing the same thing?"

"We are," answered Rugen. "How did you know?"

"We've been watching you."

"Watching us?" asked JJ incredulously.

"We happened upon your group and have been following you ever since."

"Why us?" Alex chimed in.

"To be honest, we watched a lot of groups of Da..." Blain stopped himself before repeating the pejorative name the Iones used for Hyborians. "You were the only group of soldiers consistently heading north. We suspect you think that is where the...what do you call them in your language?"

"Gmorks," answered Rugen. His emotions were a mixture of embarrassment for being tracked without his knowledge, anger at the trackers for doing so, and confusion about the whole situation.

"Ah. We call them sunamors. Are they coming from the north?"

"Yes, but listen, can you order your men to stand down? I don't like the idea of arrows aimed at us."

Blain nodded and gestured to the left and right, and then said to Rugen, "Done. I assume you're the leader of this group?"

"I am," replied Rugen as he started approaching Blain. He kept his eyes focused forward. It would be a sign of weakness and mistrust to allow his gaze to be diverted to the foliage in search of the glint of an arrowhead. Serra quietly recited the language of Pallous as Rugen walked, enchanting him with further protection.

The tension that had built up in Rugen's mind during the approach seemed to collapse the moment he reached Blain and shook his outstretched hand. Their height differential was comical. He'd never been around an adult so small. It gave him a brief feeling of vertigo.

With the handshake completed, Blain made another gesture and five Ione archers leisurely exited their scattered hiding places and filled in behind Blain, saying nothing and showing no expression.

"You've been spying on us." Rugen swallowed and continued, "And now you met us. What can we do for you?"

"We'd like to travel with you and be your eyes."

"Be our eyes?" asked JJ.

"We followed you for a long time, and you didn't know we were there. Others might do the same and you'd never know it."

"So you're offering to join us," said Rugen, attempting to clarify.

"No," Blain said, shaking his head. "Sadly, we can't join you. It's against the nature of the Ione people to align with Da...the people of Hyboria. What we're offering is to be your eyes and ask that you be our arms. Together we'll be more prepared to take on the sunam...gmorks."

"And how do we know we can trust you?" asked Claire.

"You ambushed us," added Serra.

"We ambushed you because you're larger, in physical size and in number," replied Blain. "Trusting your kind is unprecedented for Iones. Using stealth is our way. We have the same goal but different abilities. You need us, and we need you. Isn't that enough for trust?"

"All right," said Rugen. "I agree to your terms, but we have to function as a single unit. By that I mean we need to be able to communicate with each other."

"That's fine for me, but my men don't speak Hybor."

"What do they speak?" asked JJ.

"Our language—Ione."

"How is it that you speak and understand Hybor?" asked Serra.

"It's a long story. But once I lived among your people. I learned Hybor to survive."

"It's decided then. Welcome to Gordon's Army," said Rugen.

Blain bowed his head.

"Dobbler, how many does this make us?"

"Well…" The sorcerer thought for a moment. "There's thirty-three of us." He gestured to Blain and his men, "And now thirty-nine."

Blain turned and waved in three more archers who were down the road behind him. He turned back to Rugen and stared blankly.

"So you trusted us enough to show most of your group but not enough for us to see the rest of you?" asked Serra.

"Yes," responded Blain, without any hint of shame. "The ability to stay discrete is what sets our people apart, and is exactly why you need us."

"So nine then," said Rugen, to which Blain nodded. "Gordon would be so proud of his army. Forty-two strong!"

Chapter 7

The newly bolstered Gordon's Army traversed the distance through the next ten Lundgren Army barracks segments with renewed vigor. Integrating the Ione archers into the larger group didn't happen smoothly, especially for the eight who didn't speak or understand a word of Hybor. That contingent conversed incessantly among themselves in their own language, and the lack of being able to communicate with the rest of the soldiers kept them functionally segregated, just as their leader Blain had anticipated. He knew far too well how a lack of common language could make a person feel like an outcast.

The other hurdle for them was that they weren't accustomed to being indoors. Their body language showed a lot of trepidation as they approached B-10, and it took a long pep talk by Blain to get them to agree to go inside. They eventually did, but categorically refused to go upstairs to use the bathroom or the beds. They reluctantly sat for dinner, all together at the same table, and took their time inspecting the food that was presented to them. They were accustomed to gathering or killing their own food. It was a new experience being served prepared, seasoned, and cooked meals. Forks and knives were a battle no one was willing to fight.

This initial struggle gradually subsided with each subsequent barracks experience. The first breakthrough was getting them to climb the stairs. The second was when they slept in the beds. Eventually a particularly persuasive barracks director got them to use the showers and put on nightclothes after dinner.

Driven by necessity, a working language quickly developed between the soldiers and archers—a mixture of gestures, nonverbal communication, facial expressions, and pointing punctuated by a smattering of Ione and Hybor words. This system wouldn't allow them to share their innermost thoughts with each other, but it did give them a basic understanding of what each side was trying to convey.

It takes only a few times of sitting at a meal with someone before you start building a kinship. Gradually the Iones went from huddling at their own table to mixing in with the others at dinner. Old stories were told and bonds were built, but there was always an unspoken difference between the Iones and Hyborians.

The thing that perhaps had the greatest effect on bringing the groups together was the card game Gordon's Army had become infatuated with during their journey along Graan Boulevard. The Iones had never experienced anything like Mogwai. They didn't have playing cards or anything analogous in Elsinore, but they took to it fast and quickly became competitive.

Finally, after nearly a month of travel, a journey during which they traversed hundreds of miles, Gordon's Army arrived at B-20, the final barracks building before the Red Gate. There they were met by the last in a long line of overly accommodating barracks masters, Sergeant Oxberger. He not only oversaw the day-to-day operations of the final boulevard checkpoint, but also was responsible for the maintenance and security of the gate to the north.

Oxberger went by "Ox" despite his diminutive stature. One night during their weeklong stay in B-20, over many glasses of ale, JJ asked the sergeant about his nickname. Ox admitted that all of the men, and some of the women, in his family were referred to by a derivation of the same moniker. Growing up he was always known as "Oxby," a name he accepted with pride until his beard started sprouting gray hairs. When that happened, he dropped the second syllable and went with the nickname that was his birthright.

Considering he had been marooned for many years at such a distant outpost as B-20, Ox loved talking to visitors and telling lengthy stories. There were ancillary staff at B-20, of course, but they rotated frequently, possibly more frequently than at the other barracks buildings.

He talked about his home life before joining the service, his days as a student at RHS, and many other things. The most memorable story he relayed was about the historical events leading up to the construction of the Red Gate. The Marion

War was a topic taught in all history classrooms in Hyboria, but Ox's version had many details never discussed in school.

"Lundgren was founded a little less than two centuries ago," started the sergeant. "It was in the same location it is now, but looked a lot different than what you've seen. It was a village, not a city. Cities didn't exist at the time, but Lundgren had far and away the most people in Hyboria. There were no canals, no stone streets, no buildings, and no Riser Helm School. The plot of land wasn't nearly as flat or as large. Over the decades the inhabitants smoothed it out and widened with soil recovered from the canal trenches and by cutting the toes off the foothills."

"There was no Lundgren Army. People from all over Hyboria, north and south, could come and go as they please and do whatever they wish without government intervention or police supervision. They traded goods and services without taxes or any kind of monetary system."

"Did they use the same road that just took us an entire month to walk?" asked Dobbler.

"No, son," answered Ox. "There *was* no Graan Boulevard. The only way people could get in and out of Lundgren was through mountain passes, same from the north as from the south."

JJ shook his head at Dobbler and chuckled quietly, murmuring under his breath.

"As you can imagine, population growth isn't always a good thing. When people immigrate from all over, they bring different priorities, values, and cultures. Sometimes that's great, but other times it's a source of social strife. There was a lot of lawlessness—stealing, fighting, murder—and other unsavory activities. Eventually, some of the older inhabitants established a rudimentary government, which paved the way for Lundgren to continue to grow into the city it is today." Ox leaned back in his chair. "Everything I mentioned earlier—expanding the site, smoothing out the topography, digging the canals, and whatever else you see got its start after government was established. But as with any group attempting to lead, debates can turn ugly. The details don't matter, really. So-and-so doesn't like what this guy's saying. 'I won't vote for your law unless you vote for mine.' Then there's the name-calling, mudslinging, undermining, and corruption." He waved his hand dismissively. "Typical political nonsense. Rather than think for themselves, the ones in charge aligned with the ideology of whoever was the loudest or most popular. Eventually the party lines morphed into north versus south."

"The northerners had a smaller, less educated and less organized population. They were thought of as a lower class by the southerners, and were treated as such. The government preached equality, but that's not how they practiced. A growing undercurrent of hate festered between northerners and southerners for years, until one day a couple of northern thugs murdered a southern-born leader right outside the administrative building in the center of Lundgren. I think there's still a memorial statue of him where it happened."

"The murderers fled over the mountains like cowards, leaving the man's body on the center plaza, leaking blood into the grass. Southern-born leaders held an emergency meeting and requested an investigation. Really it was a witch hunt. They rounded up every northern person they could find, innocent or not, and whipped, beat, and tortured them."

"Retaliation breeds retaliation, so a northern militia descended into Lundgren. Riots broke out in the street. There was so much violence; they say the canals ran red. In the end the south, with more people, better resources, and more training, chased the militia out of town. A call went out to every able-bodied southerner to invade the north as one large force. It was a massacre. Men were killed in every imaginable way. Women and children too. The lives of young women were spared for, well… I'm sure you can imagine." Ox made eye contact with Claire and Serra.

"The invaders burned their homes, salted their crop fields, and, by the end, obliterated the entire northern culture. All these long decades later it hasn't recovered as far as we can tell. I'm told settlements are scattered here and there, but I've been at this gate for a long time and we've never had anyone come a-knocking."

"And then what happened?" asked Serra. She was clearly enthralled by Ox's story, especially having heard a much less interesting version of it at Wallace.

"What happened was the southern invaders returned to Lundgren to celebrate. Then they explored the mountain range, blocking off every pass with man-made barriers. Well, every pass they could find. It's a long range. I'm sure there's more of them out there. There has to be with all these creatures I keep hearing about on Graan Boulevard."

"Have you seen one up this far?" asked Alex.

"No, there mustn't be any way through the mountains around here."

After nearly a month of anticipation, they couldn't tolerate not seeing the Red Gate any longer. The morning after their arrival at B-20, Gordon's Army traversed the half-mile out to where the looming and gargantuan gate stood. The structure consisted of two massive doors controlled by a pulley system. Ox informed them that regular maintenance was done on the gears, chains, and levers, but by standing orders of the office of the Duke of Lundgren, the gate was never to be opened. He admitted he'd never seen what was on the other side, except from the limited view visible through the two peephole lenses. After more than a decade working on the southern side, he was looking forward to laying his eyes upon the north.

Gordon's Army stayed at B-20 for the next several days—training, planning, and prepping supplies for the long trek through the wilderness ahead. Unlike the other barracks buildings, there weren't any Lundgren Army soldiers scheduled to come take their place at B-20, so there was no rush to clear the space. Ox said every few days a supply cart would arrive, but otherwise his barracks didn't have much in the way of visitors.

The extended relaxation at B-20 could not have been more welcomed. It was a break from the monotony of walking, a calm before the coming storm, and a terminus to what seemed like an endless line. Ox's sense of peace and solitude was contagious, and left some of the members of Gordon's Army with a longing to stay as they awoke on their final day in camp. Before leaving B-20 they stocked up on supplies: water, dried meats, fresh vegetables, biscuits, and spices. It wasn't meant to be enough to maintain them for what they anticipated to be a week in the wilderness, but their team consisted of twenty-nine people who had gone through extensive survival training at RHS, nine of the best primitive-living experts on the continent, and two people who could perform magic. The only ones who didn't have formal survival training were Rugen and JJ, and they'd had a crash course over the prior two months. Food supplies weren't anticipated to be a problem. As long as they could locate natural springs, their basic nutritional needs would be met.

Rugen led the way along with Ox and two of his porters. The leader of Gordon's Army had a sour feeling in his stomach; one he hadn't experienced since the ursinox attack outside of Ravenwood. A lot of troubling situations had happened since then, most recently being the introduction to the Iones, but in those scenarios they were thrown into peril and forced to react on instinct. Packing for the northern leg of their journey and marching toward the Red Gate caused an overwhelming sense of nervous anticipation.

Approaching the monstrosity was reminiscent of the first time they saw Riser Helm School up close and marveled at its size. Heavy hinges were bolted into the crossbars that spanned the vertical slots of the immense doors, holding fast to the sheer rock cliffs on either side. The gate was, at its name implied, a deep crimson color reminiscent of crushed pomegranates. Ox told them it was painted every year, and that a fresh coat had been added over the summer. When asked why the paint was reapplied so frequently if few people actually ever saw it, his response was, "What else are we going to do with the time up here?" Rugen wondered whose job it was to reach the top of the wall and how they managed to get there, but before he had a chance to ask, Ox called out in a booming voice, "The time has come for you to start the final leg of your quest. If I were a younger man and had free will to decide on my own, I'd much like to join you. But my place is here. I'll be here waiting for your victorious return."

"We can't thank you enough for all the hospitality," responded Rugen. "You... well, the whole Lundgren Army, treated us like they would their own. Better, I bet, and for that we'll be forever grateful."

The two men shook hands and then Ox nodded to his porters, who had taken their place at the flywheel that worked the gate mechanism. Given the countless times they inspected the functionality of the levers, gears, and pulleys without them being engaged, the prospect of articulating everything and moving the main control wheel was exhilarating.

The porters grasped the wheel and pulled. The resistance in the gears was apparent on their faces and in their guttural moans. No matter how hard they strained, the wheel didn't budge. They let go and looked at each other, shaking the strength back into their arm muscles and rubbing their sore hands. They counted down from three and tried again. This time there was a crunching sound followed by a high-pitched whine as the momentum of their pull was transferred to the gears that controlled the gate itself. They struggled with the heft of it, faces turning red and breath being held as they put all of their weight behind the effort. Suddenly a loud crack sounded as sunlight burst through the split between the two gate doors, making the army reflexively step back.

There was a rumbling grinding roar mixed with a metallic squeal and a repetitive clanging from the gear system as the doors slowly parted, rounding out the cacophony of sound.

The northern territory came into view. Rugen was expecting to see a continuation of perfectly-groomed Graan Boulevard, which in hindsight wasn't unreasonable. The reality was underwhelming—a dilapidated gravel road overgrown with grass and other plants. The best part about the view was the absence of gmorks waiting to rush them. There wasn't a living soul behind the gate aside from some scampering squirrels and a few chirping birds.

"Good luck in your journey through the north," said Ox, with some sadness in his voice. "We'll post lookouts here for when you're ready to return." He proceeded to shake the hand of every member of Gordon's Army as they stepped into the wild territory beyond.

Chapter 8

On the roof of a fortified building known as The Emporium, set into a mountainside in the far north, an old man stood next to an open bird loft. His name was Torrance, and he had been breeding and training the crows who resided there for many years on the orders of Brian Gruhl, whom he referred to as *the commander*. The crows were capable of navigating to and from various locations to transport written messages, but the main reason for their existence and employ was one singular task; that being the locating of a particular bleached white bone.

Torrance noticed a crow had appeared in the distance; starting as a black dot on the blue horizon. He watched as it glided toward the building and landed on a parapet near him. The bird cawed as it made the gentle and short flight into the open loft. Just before it landed inside, a high-pitched rattling *tink, tink, tink* sounded from the stone floor beneath Torrance's feet. It was a sound the bird keeper had been waiting to hear for longer than he could remember, but oddly he almost missed discerning it from the wash of other noises around him. Although the brief delay in his reaction accounted for what amounted to an insignificant measure of time, he later kicked himself for allowing it. Torrance often found he had more anxiety when thinking about mishaps that could have happened than he did about ones that actually did.

He stopped mixing bird feed as he replayed the gentle tone in his head, trying to place its meaning. When he realized its significance of the sound, his head reflexively jerked to attention. Resting at the base of the loft structure was the small, cylindrical, pure white femur of a small cat. The bone stood out among the grime and black feather dander, almost as if it were calling to him. He picked it up and turned it around a few times in his fingers, examining it closely for the tell-tale carved inscription along the side. The moment he saw what he was looking for, the memories of a decade of patiently working with the birds fluttered through his mind. He expected that time would soon come to an end.

He didn't praise the crow like he normally might. Not that it made much difference to the bird, but neglect of love and kindness was out of character for Torrance. He adored his crows more than he did any living person and spent more time with them than anyone else. Instead, he stood gawking at the inscription, blinking to make sure he was seeing what he was seeing, and then pocketed the bone so he could hurry down the wooden steps to report to the commander.

Brian Gruhl was sitting in his basement lab hunched over the corpse of a giant centipede. The short-cropped tight blond curls of his youth had grown into an unkempt gray-streaked poof. He was inspecting the jaws of the centipede with a magnifying lens and metal probe.

Torrance had a love of all animals, but refused to go anywhere near *those bugs or anything else Mr. Gruhl was tinkering with.* It was a rare event for him to even set foot in the basement, much less the lab, and as a result Brian didn't immediately recognize him out of the context of his rooftop loft.

The bird keeper cleared his throat, prompting the commander to look up from his specimen and aim his aughra-powered headlamp in his direction.

"What do you want?" grumbled Gruhl.

"Sorry, sir. I wouldn't bother you without important news." Torrance was standing in the lab doorway looking uncomfortable and nervous.

"News?"

The old man reached into his pocket and removed the bone, saying, "The gate to the south has been opened."

"What?" barked Brian as he peered at the small white object in Torrance's hand. "What are you holding there?"

Torrance shifted his weight to the other foot. "If I may explain, sir." His eyes shifted to an empty table and chairs in the corner. He felt like he'd be more relaxed sitting there away from the dead thing lying in front of the commander, but he was afraid to verbalize the thought.

Brian recognized and relished Torrance's discomfort. He answered, "Explain yourself," as he put the magnifying lens to his eye and continued poking the centipede with the probe.

"Um, thank you, sir." Torrance glanced at what Brian was doing, swallowed hard, and started his report. "You asked me to keep watch on the gate to Graan Boulevard without letting anyone know..." He trailed off as Brian put down his lens and probe and picked up a scalpel and forceps.

"Go on." Brian grasped one of the legs and flopped the dead centipede over with a splat.

"The idea I came up with was this bone," he stated as he held the white cylinder. "I housed it in a wooden tube, which I hung between the gate doors in such a way that as they were opened, the tube would break, allowing the bone to fall to the ground where it could be retrieved by one of my crows." As he said this, he couldn't help but feel a brief flash of pride.

"Industrious," said Brian without emotion. He didn't even look up at Torrance. He was trying to make it seem like he couldn't care less about what the older man was saying, even though he did. He held the head of the centipede with his forceps and carefully and methodically sliced through the neck with the scalpel. Usually, when he wasn't trying to put on a show, he would haphazardly whack the heads off of his specimens. He thought it was fun and made a game of it, but he knew this slow deliberate effort was torturing the sensitive-minded bird keeper.

"Well, sir, you see..." He swallowed. "The gate was overgrown with plants, vines, and other natural material. I figured no one would notice a flimsy wooden tube braced across the seal."

"Spit it out, Terrance! I'm a busy man."

"Yes, sir." Torrance cringed when he heard the mispronunciation of his name but made no attempt at correction. "I don't think the Lundgren Army had a way of inspecting our side of the gate. If they did, they would have cleared the debris long ago. I checked on it many times over the years, and my tube was always in place where I'd left it."

Brian sighed dramatically. "You're babbling. Get to the point."

"Forgive me, sir. I designed the tube so when the doors was opened, it would split in two. One end was attached to a string designed to swing free, allowing the bone to slide out and gently fall into the dirt."

Brian set his instruments down in a huff and looked up at Torrance with a scowl. "I understand that. You're repeating yourself. Tell me how it was retrieved."

"I have identical copies of the bone. I use them to train my crows so they get familiar with searching for and handling them. I bring the crows to the gate so they get a mental image of where it is and how to get there and back. I feed them there so they develop a positive connection to the place."

"Am I to understand you only feed them while you have them there? Are you starving these poor animals?" Brian quickly glanced up, feigning contempt, then returned to his work of removing the carapace from the head of the centipede.

"No, sir. We only journey to the gate every few months. It's a long way from here. At home I feed them dry grains, seeds, bread. At the site I feed them treats: fruit, snails, worms, bits of meat. They can have as much as they want while I'm there with them. Crows are smart. It doesn't take them long to make a deep visceral connection to the gate."

Brian dropped his tools and leaned back in the chair. "If that's true, why would they ever come back here?"

"Well," Torrance wasn't sure how to answer this. In truth he never really thought much about it. They just always came back. He offered, "This is their home, sir."

"That bone in your hand," breathed Brian, "How do you know it's the real thing and not one of your…" he waved his hand dismissively, "training devices?"

"Because…" He held the bone out in front of him, trying to display the inscription in his shaking hand. "This is the only one that says 'GB Gate.'" He paused for a moment and then clarified, "Graan Boulevard Gate."

After dismissing Torrance back to his rooftop quarters, Brian descended the stairs to the sub-basement. It was at this level, deep under the mountain, where the sorcerer Deckard worked.

At one time, Deckard was a respected Mitchell Wyatt School of Sorcery professor. Now he was the Director of Creature Development at The Emporium, a self-imposed title he'd never voice in front of Brian, who only recognized two layers of hierarchy—himself and everyone else.

The details of his dismissal from Wyatt were sketchy, but had to do with research into the transmutation of animals, a practice outlawed long ago by elders who had set guidelines for the use of magic. When confronted about his actions by administration, he refused to acquiesce. Instead, he felt he had no option but to lash out, resulting in several injuries and damage to school grounds. To avoid having his ability to practice magic forever blocked, he fled Ravenwood and was never heard from again. His credentials at the school were revoked in absentia.

"Deckard?" called Brian.

Deckard was sitting at a large desk cluttered with glass vials containing various colored liquids. He was taking notes on his observations of several test tubes full of bubbling liquid. Over his shoulder he responded a half-hearted, "Yeah?"

"The gate to the south has been opened."

Deckard, realizing it was Brian behind him, quickly turned around in his chair, and said, "The gate?" He set down his pencil and stood. "How...how do you know?"

"Torrance just told me."

"Who's Torrance?"

"The old man. The one who tends to the birds on the roof."

"Right," he said as his face registered vague recognition. "So what does it mean?"

"Well, it could mean nothing. Maybe Torrance has grown senile and doesn't know what he's talking about. Maybe the complex warning system he installed at the gate failed." Brian paused for effect and then said, "Or maybe there's a southern army on its way here right now bent on crushing us."

Deckard's mind raced as he said nothing.

"So I came to ask you," said Brian with artificial nonchalance, "how many creatures do we have ready to deploy?"

Deckard swallowed. "Has it come to that?"

Brian nudged a ball of lint on the floor with his foot. "We don't know anything for sure until I can get some spies in the field, but we have to assume the worst."

"We're at capacity; about two hundred of them awaiting activation."

"And the big ones?"

"Two."

Brian laughed to himself. "If only those numbers were reversed."

"Well, as you know, sir, the production of viable ursinoxes is difficult," said Deckard. "It requires us to safely trap juvenile bears. Baby bears that haven't been weaned from their mothers are no good because they end up becoming so tame they serve us no purpose. We haven't been able to successfully convert mature bears either. They lose physical and mental malleability once they become adults, and nothing I've tried has any impact on that."

The Commander silently processed this for a moment before Deckard added, "Not to mention the fact we're talking about trapping a large, man-eating, vicious animal. Bears of any age don't come along easily. And mama bears don't offer their cubs without a fight."

Brian yawned as he nodded, not caring about the mother bears, their cubs, or the men he asked to catch them. "Can you take me to creature storage?"

"Sure," Deckard responded as he stood up and made his way toward the door where Brian was standing. He stopped; learning long ago that letting Brian walk behind you is never a good idea. Doing so puts a person at risk of (literally) being stabbed in the back, something Deckard had seen firsthand during his time serving under him. He held out a hand toward the door to the hallway and said, "After you."

The two men walked to a stairwell and climbed several flights before coming to a blank wall. Deckard removed a set of keys from around his neck and placed one into a small, almost imperceptible hole at hip height. He turned the key to the right, which caused an explosion of bright green light. All of the sudden a door stood where there was nothing before. Only Deckard was able to clearly see it because he'd closed his eyes in anticipation of the flash. The sorcerer hadn't warned Brian about it, so his retinas were still recovering as Deckard twisted the knob and opened the door. Beyond was a balcony overlooking a large hall, where rows of gmorks lay dormant on low tables. In the dim light, the end of the room could not be seen so it was impossible to judge the number of gmorks present.

"I have to admit I've been so busy with my own endeavors that I've lost track of how you've made this production run as smoothly as it does," said Brian.

Deckard wasn't used to complimentary words from the leader of the Emporium, and could never be sure about their validity, so instead of chancing a response, he cast a spell, making an illuminating beam emanate from his right index finger. He shone it along the wall until it landed on a tile, which reflected back in a sheen. He said, "There are several attractors along the walls. They draw aughra from the surface into this room, which keeps the creatures alive."

Brian followed the movement of Deckard's light beam as he slid it from tile to tile.

"Each time we bring a newly-created gmork down here, we wake the oldest one and release it to the wild," explained Deckard.

"Your work may just save us if Torrance's bird is correct. Good job."

Deckard felt it was in his best interest not to repeatedly ignore praise from Brian. "Thank you sir, but you deserve the credit." He extinguished the beam and said, "So shall I start waking them?"

"How long does it take for them to be ready to fight?"

"About a half hour."

"Oh, good. In that case, do nothing until I hear back from the scouts. Although if there's any way to increase production, by all means do it."

"I will."

As Brian turned to walk back upstairs, he whispered, "And so it begins."

CHAPTER 9

Two days had passed since Gordon's Army became the first people to breach the threshold of the Red Gate since its construction. Two days spent in the brisk, bleak, and windswept land of the north. The comforts of Graan Boulevard and the Lundgren Army were well behind them now, a fact that they were constantly reminded of by how less accommodating the northern wilderness was. Getting used to the rapidly chilling air and morning frost was definitely going to take some time, but they had no choice but to make the best of it.

At times their surroundings seemed dreary and lifeless, especially with the piles of desiccated vegetation strewn about. Hunting was going poorly as well. With all of the stories about how few people were left in the north after the war, Rugen imagined swarms of large game animals thriving unchecked. Each time the soldiers would approach a hill or come around a bend, they hoped a plump deer or elk would be standing there just waiting to be picked off, butchered, and roasted over a fire, but that had not been the case.

Autumn is arguably the most beautiful time of the year. The bright greens of summer shift to brilliant oranges, reds, and yellows, painting the landscape into a masterpiece that would stir the soul of even the most apathetic onlooker. As it progresses, however, the temperatures drop and the kaleidoscope of color fades. What gets left behind are the craggy skeletons of trees draped with shivering tufts of brown dead leaves.

The gradually cooling weather combined with high elevation and latitude made gathering food an ordeal. The most prevalent edible flora were bearberries, small red fruits that looked like unripe blueberries. Their mundane-sounding name was matched by the unsatisfying, mealy, and tasteless experience of eating one. Supposedly their leaves acted as a diuretic, which was something the thirsty travelers had no wish to learn firsthand. Several varieties of apples were found and collected, but eating them raw wasn't any more pleasurable than the bearberries, as they were small, hard, and sour. Cooking them over a fire made them slightly sweeter, but if they were cooked seemingly only a moment too long, they became unpalatably bitter.

Not everything they gathered was unpleasant. The two most notable blessings the north bestowed were chanterelles and persimmons. The golden mushrooms could be found crowding the bases of trees. They were fleshy and aromatic, and their bright colors were easy to spot among the otherwise drab landscape. Cooking them alongside meat brought out their nutty, earthy flavor. There was nothing quite like the taste of a chanterelle roasted in animal fat and wild herbs.

Persimmon trees were themselves a juxtaposition. Their stark branches looked completely barren of life and yet harbored an explosion of bright yellow-orange fruits. A team of foragers would pick a tree bare, sending smaller climbers into the high branches to collect as many as they could reach. No cooking was required. They were eaten right on the spot with the excess tucked away for later.

As pleasurable as the fruit and fungus finds were, concentrated protein was harder to come by. A few rodents or other small game wasn't nearly enough to sustain the nutritional needs of forty-two weary soldiers. They were exhausting the preserved meats they'd packed at B-20 faster than what was sustainable.

Finding adequate amounts of fresh water was another burden. With the scarcity of a resident human population, they could be fairly sure any moving water was generally safe to drink. The army scientist Leland taught them that the gmorks didn't drink or excrete water, so unless Gruhl himself intentionally fouled the rivers and streams as a form of defense, Gordon's Army could have confidence that the water was safely potable. Natural springs flowing from the caves deep beneath the surface was synonymous with cleanliness, so the travelers spent a significant portion of the day keeping an lookout for them. It was a frustrating task even for well-trained survivalists.

The constant headache about where to find adequate supplies of food and water would not have loomed as large if they knew exactly where they were going and how long it would take to get there. Many on the team had experience using the sun and stars to find their way, and during conversations with soldiers at the various Graan Boulevard barracks, they'd collected opinions about landmarks and which direction to follow. However, none of the people with whom they spoke had any first-hand knowledge of the north, and most of the landmarks they referenced in their stories no longer existed or never existed at all. The army started off by following what they assumed was a direct line to Gruhl's hideout, but they were quickly thrown off course looking for game trails, clean water, and foraging sites.

On the morning of the third day, Rugen pointed out they were getting nowhere and should split the army into its predetermined squads to better scout the area. The five squads agreed to reconvene before sunset at what was designated as temporary home base. Some of the leaders had trepidation about leaving the safety of numbers, but not the RHS grunts and sub-elites. Most of them had secret fantasies of fighting one-on-one with a gmork and slaying it. None of them had ever seen one in the flesh and looked forward to the opportunity to be a hero.

The Iones had no apprehension about separating from the Damones. They were accustomed to being with their own kind and relished the chance to get away. While the rest of Gordon's Army gathered information about where they were in relation to the Red Gate and tried to make sense of the reported landmarks, the Iones went on long-range scouting missions in groups of three.

By the end of the day, all squads returned to base and compiled the information they'd gathered to construct a crude map. They also managed to get ahead on their fresh food supply while exploring and returned to find some of their traps had successfully sprung. It was much easier to gather food when there wasn't the additional distraction of trying to figure out how to find Brian Gruhl.

None of the Iones returned to camp that night, as was expected. They'd planned to range out farther than a day's walk would take them and weren't due back for at least a few days.

Two more nights passed with no Iones. In that time the squads ventured out again and again, further refining their map. The squad led by Claire found a much better site for a home base. It had a good view of the surrounding area, close access to fresh water, and an oasis of collectible food, but they were hesitant to relocate without somehow getting a message to the missing Iones.

During this time the local resources started exhausting, and there was a lot of dissension in the group over whether to stay where they were or leave before the missing Iones returned. Some wondered if the Iones had been killed, and if so waiting around for them was a waste of time. The other argument, started by a sub-elite named Duncan, was "if the Iones were such great trackers they oughta be able to find us no matter where we went." Some people's opinions were that the Iones were lost and needed rescuing. This was abandoned when it was realized no one knew in which direction they'd struck out.

It wasn't until the middle of the sixth day, by which time the team was frustrated at not being able to continue their mission, that the first Ione group returned. Unfortunately, Blain wasn't in this trio, so if they had any information to share, it would remain mostly a mystery to the Hybor-speakers. It was nice to have three fewer people to worry about, though, and the Iones had returned with a freshly killed deer.

By the next evening Blain's group returned with the news that they had identified the remnants of a road, which they had followed for some distance. The first three that had returned confirmed that they'd found the same road, although a different stretch of it, and all of the collected information was added to the map the team had been compiling.

More agonizing days passed with the final three team members missing. The army had been waiting for so long, one of the grunts nicknamed the location "Camp Lost Ione", a name that instantly stuck. All the while Rugen was kicking himself for not demanding they come back within an agreed-upon deadline. In actuality, the Iones lived on their own conception of time and probably wouldn't have been able to honor such an agreement.

The final three Iones returned as the team was eating breakfast the morning of the twelfth day. They walked into camp with smiles, large ones by Ione standards. The leader of that trio, Poncho, greeted Blain in the traditional backhand slide handshake common among Ione warriors. They conferred with each other in their language as Poncho held up what appeared to be a leather pouch. The two of them walked to where the squad leaders were standing.

"What's that?" asked JJ.

It wasn't a pouch. Instead, it was a leg belt and dagger wrapped around a pocket-sized, leather-bound book. Blain handed everything to Rugen and said, "My men caught and killed a spy. These were his effects."

"A spy?" remarked Dobbler as he looked at the book in Rugen's hand.

"How did they know he was a spy and not just some random northerner?" asked Claire.

"They followed him for two days. He was watching your groups and taking notes." He nodded at Poncho. "They said he was an excellent scout, but..."

"We were better." finished Poncho in his heavily-accented version of the Hybor language.

Blain patted Poncho's shoulder in a show of approval.

Rugen handed the book to Dobbler, who seemed very interested in it, and asked, "Where's the body?"

"Buried," responded Blain. "He won't be found."

"Why follow him for two days?" asked Alex. "Seems like a risk. Why not confront him immediately after identifying him as a spy?"

Blain posed the question to Poncho, who responded in Ione.

"They wanted to make sure he was alone," translated Blain, "and they were hoping he'd lead them to other scouts or soldiers."

"And?" asked Rugen.

"They didn't see him interact with anyone."

"So maybe Gruhl still doesn't know about us," said Claire. "Maybe that was just a routine patrol."

"I don't think so," said Dobbler, as he was reading some of the pages of the book.

"Why? What's the book say?" asked JJ.

Dobbler looked up. "All about us—how many, what we look like, who the leaders are, what weapons we carry, where we are, dates, everything."

"Where we are?" asked Serra.

"In relation to Landmarks. The same we've been seeing the past week. But that's not the reason I think Gruhl knows about us."

Rugen raised his eyebrows at Dobbler, who turned to the front of the book and pointed out the edges of torn-out pages. "Some of the pages are missing. He could've ripped them out and sent them back to his superiors."

"Or he could've ripped them out and trashed them on the ground," retorted JJ.

"No," said Alex, "he wouldn't risk them being found. I think the only safe assumption is that Gruhl knows about us."

"How would the spy get the pages back to him?" asked Serra.

"Maybe there's a network of spies," responded Alex. "Someone could have run the pages back before the Iones caught this guy's trail and left him here to gather more information."

"Or maybe he drops them in a hiding spot. Someone comes by and grabs them later," added Claire. "That way he wouldn't have to wait around for a runner."

"This is enemy territory," said Rugen coldly. "I'm sure they have lots of means we know nothing about."

CHAPTER 10

The execution of Brian Gruhl's former mentor-turned-partner Marvin Stiles all those years ago had served several purposes. First and foremost, it established Brian as the unquestioned leader of the operation. Brian had chased out, discredited, or murdered all of the original mining company personnel during the first few years of occupation, and Marvin was the last link to the past. Second, for as much as Brian grew to hate Marvin, he had to admit the man had a talent in convincing others to do things they otherwise wouldn't, and thus his absence reduced the likelihood of a rebellion against Brian. The final purpose of the execution was purely logistical. The method of Marvin's death served as proof not only of the utility of the giant centipedes as a torture device, but, by extrapolation, of the entire creature development program.

Ever since that grotesque but triumphant day, Brian secretly longed for people to refer to him as "Emperor." He considered it prosaic to self-apply that title, so instead he named the compound "The Emporium," hoping that as the legend of his work grew, alliteration alone would encourage other people to start referring to him as such. Of course if that came to pass he would at first scoff at the suggested notion, and then after feigned consideration he'd gradually and reluctantly accept it. Unfortunately none of the staff came up with it, likely because they knew referring to Brian by anything without a prior directive from him was a terrible idea. Someone was brave enough to refer to him as "commander," which caught on and in Brian's eyes was an adequate approximation.

Regarding the topic of names, neither Brian nor Deckard conceived of the popularly known monikers for the creatures they created. *Gmork* and *ursinox* originated in Lundgren, and had worked their way back to The Emporium via a trade network that utilized hidden passes through the Ovid Graan mountains. Brian was so excited for any recognition by the public at large that he gladly accepted them. Prior to that, the creatures were known only by a mouthful of letters and numbers representing their iteration and date of production.

These were the best years of Brian's life. He was out from under his father's thumb, his brother's shadow, and his mother's neglect. He'd learned everything he wanted to learn from Marvin and now was free from him as well. He had run a successful business for long enough to bank a lifetime of self-sufficiency, and most recently had found a way get back at the world for the way he was treated when he was young.

All of his mirthful bravado was called into question the day Torrance interrupted his work to inform him that the Graan Boulevard gate had been opened. It was fully extinguished several days later when the approach of a southern army was confirmed in the notes his spy sent back. The spy, Ridley, had slid the rolled up pages into a tiny bone-colored cylinder and left them along the road at the designated messenger-crow pickup point.

He was rereading the crinkled notebook pages as Deckard entered his office.

"You called for me, sir?"

Brian didn't bother looking up. "Forty-two soldiers are on their way here," he droned, as if this sort of thing happened every day.

Deckard nervously folded his arms and choked, "Wh...where are they now?"

Brian's half-closed eyes met Deckard's. "Southeast of here, not far from the mountain pass."

The two men were silent for a moment while Deckard regained his composure, "You mean the Graan Boulevard gate?"

"Yes. Apparently they've been struggling to find their way around our..." Brian searched for a smart-sounding term, "geographic diversions. We've done a good job covering up the roads around the gate."

"How much time does that give us to prepare?"

"I don't know. At least a week. I'm expecting Torrance's crow battalion to be quite busy over the next few days retrieving updates from Ridley."

"Just give me the word on when to awaken the creatures."

"We need to be patient. Releasing them too early would be a waste. Gmorks have a tendency to scatter. We don't want our guests to have the benefit of fighting only one or two at a time, said Brian. "Waiting until their main force is close and then releasing a large number of them is a better strategy for a quick annihilation."

Deckard nodded in agreement, and with annoyance in his voice asked, "Is it the Lundgren Army?"

"Ridley's note didn't specify, but it said they have archers, swordsmen, a couple of wizards."

"You mean sorcerers?" Like all purveyors of the magic arts, Deckard hated his kind being referred to as wizards, magicians, warlocks, or the rest.

"I assume so." Brian knew this distinction was important to Deckard but to him the words were interchangeable. "This was an inevitability. We have our own army lying in wait."

"So it's our two hundred versus their forty-two," said Deckard with gravity in his voice. "I like those odds."

"And don't underestimate the significance of the fact that they're coming here to us. Our home ground," Brian added as he pointed to the floor dramatically. "We know subtleties about the layout they'll never know. And with Ridley's continuing stream of notes, by the time they arrive we'll know more about them than they do themselves."

Gordon's Army, once again whole, collected their things and made their way to the gravel roadway the scouts had found. They were sure Gruhl was now aware they were heading his way, they didn't feel it was necessary to cover up evidence of where they'd been to this point, but would try to be more careful and discrete going forward.

The group guessed that the road was likely much more robust before the war, but the fact that it hadn't been totally reclaimed by nature suggested that someone had been at least partially caring for it over the years. It ran almost due west. By projecting on the map they'd compiled, the team assumed the eastern end had once abutted The Red Gate. That section had long since grown over, which was why they hadn't seen anything as they were leaving B-20. They hoped by following the road to the west they'd land in Gruhl's lap but imagined it wouldn't be so simple.

After one day of westerly travel, they'd walked beyond the borders of their map. They made camp, primed animal traps, searched for water, and then Serra set up an exclusion field.

Rugen awoke the next morning to see the Iones standing together facing the rest of the group, packed and ready to go.

"My men and I are going on ahead," said Blain without fanfare.

"I don't think that's a good idea," responded Rugen, as he rubbed the sleep out of his eyes. "We're stronger if we stay together."

"And the last time you left we felt completely helpless waiting for you," added Serra.

"This will be different," answered Blain. "You thought you needed to stay in one area waiting for us. Now you realize we would've easily found you wherever you went. Just keep following the road and we'll double back to meet you."

"So you'll be just ahead of us on the road?" questioned Dobbler. "What's the point in that?"

"We'll scout far ahead, on the road and off. We can move quickly and silently without having to wait for the rest of you," responded Blain. "We'll make sure you don't wander into a trap."

"What if you wander into a trap?" asked Alex. "You'll have no backup."

"Don't underestimate us." Blain looked at Alex with a severe expression. "If we don't want to be seen, we won't be seen." He looked at Rugen. "We made an agreement to be your eyes—nothing more and nothing less. That's what we offer for this mission, and standing here debating it is just wasting time we could be using to fulfill our side of the arrangement."

Brian Gruhl sat in his upstairs office poring over several maps of the region with his hand planted on his forehead. He had been mindlessly running his fingers through his hair, and as a result it was misarranged into a wild plume.

Deckard lightly knocked on the doorframe as he entered.

Brian sighed heavily in frustration, sat back, and breathed, "Yes?"

"Any news from our spy?"

"No," responded Brian.

"How many days has it been since you've heard from him?"

"Four."

"You mean that first report was the only one?"

"Yes," answered Brian as he looked down at his maps and, devoid of emotion, said, "I think the only assumption is that he's dead."

"This army might be a bigger problem than we think," said Deckard as non-confrontationally as he could. He added, "Ridley was our best spy. He could blend in anywhere, be invisible."

"Not invisible enough as it turns out." Brian sat back from his maps and peaked his fingers in front of him, with the tips of his index fingers touching his chin. He didn't think Deckard was owed any more explanation, but just to keep him quiet he said, "Ridley made for a good spy, but he could overreach sometimes. He may have slipped up and they caught a lucky break." He turned his chair and looked out his open window.

"Now what, sir?"

"Not to worry. I've already dispatched two more scouts."

Deckard laughed to himself, then asked, "How can I help?"

"It's time to order the men to stop what they're doing and start preparing for an invasion."

"I will. And I have some final preparations with the gmorks." Deckard took a step back, but then stopped himself and asked, "Will there be anything else?"

Brian attempted a reassuring smile and replied, "Listen, don't worry. I have several tricks up my sleeve. I didn't make it this far in life without having backup plans."

CHAPTER 11

After several days of westward travel, Gordon's Army reconnected with the Iones who had scouted ahead. Rugen made a welcoming motion with his arms and boomed, "Blain, my friend, so good to see you and your men." He nodded to the other eight Iones.

"We made it," responded Blain, as he put out his hand to shake Rugen's. "We saw Gruhl's building."

"Are you sure?" asked Rugen.

"Well, no one came out to offer us drinks, but we're pretty sure it was the place."

"Good one, Blain," laughed JJ. "I'm starting to rub off on you."

"What was it like?" asked Dobbler.

"It has a high wall in front and seems pretty impenetrable. The rest of the structure is inside the mountain. Gruhl has made himself a great spot to wage war from."

"Any good news?" asked Alex.

"Yes. We found where my people will be stationed during the battle; assuming a battle will be necessary. There's a hill off to the side that overlooks the large clearing in front of the building. From there we can observe everything going on and provide coverage."

"Don't you think Gruhl will have his own archers there?" asked JJ.

"Of course, which is why we'll bring a squad with us to siege the hill and take it for ourselves," answered Blain. "We can discuss the details later."

"Outstanding," said Rugen, smiling.

"There's something else." He reached into his bag and removed a pocket-sized notebook similar to the one that belonged to the spy they had eliminated the week prior. "The owner of this met his end while we were looking for the fortress."

"Any evidence of torn-out pages?" asked Dobbler.

Blain shook his head as he handed over the notebook. "I figured you'd want to see for yourself."

Dobbler noticed a spot of dried blood on it as he took it from Blain.

"On our way back, we found a man standing in the open waving a white handkerchief."

JJ chuckled. "A white handkerchief?"

"He kept scanning up and down the road. He didn't expect we'd be hiding in the brush. Poncho flew an arrow over his head and he starting hollering, 'I surrender! I surrender!'" Blain quoted the man in a sarcastic tone.

The men started laughing. Poncho joined in mocking the man. He danced in a circle, waved his arms, and teased in heavily-accented Hybor, "I surrender! I surrender!" This prompted another wave of laughter.

Serra glared at Rugen, who caught his breath and said, "So then what?"

"After making sure it was safe, I confronted him. He said he was sent by Gruhl to request a meeting with our leaders."

"A meeting?" repeated Alex.

"Yes. He said no more than two of us. Tomorrow. When the sun is at its highest. Outside his fortress."

"You think it's a trap?" said Claire. "I'm sure they have their own archers. They kill our leaders to send the rest of us into disarray?"

"Possibly," said Rugen, "but I'll bring Serra with me." He looked at the cleric. "You have spells to deflect from arrows, right?"

"Yeah," she reflexively responded, and then the realization hit her. "Wait, we're going? You and me? To meet Brian Gruhl?"

Rugen nodded.

She continued, "Is that a good idea?"

"Me too," said JJ. "You aren't leaving me out of this."

"He said two leaders, JJ," said Dobbler. "Not three."

"I realize that," replied JJ, "but we can't bow to everything he says. If we don't offer a little rebellion, he'll think we're weak."

"Fine," said Rugen. "Tomorrow the three of us will negotiate with the man who's responsible for this whole mess."

Gordon's Army spent the rest of the day making their way along the road to Gruhl's fortress. They had wandered for two weeks in the north without much direction, but now that they were officially invited to their planned destination, their emotions were a mix of confidence and foreboding.

They all needed a good night's rest, and there was nothing more welcome than the exclusion field Serra cast that night. The prevailing opinion was without her magical contributions they would've been an army of insomniacs.

The next morning, after much deliberation about how to handle the meeting, Rugen, Serra, and JJ marched the distance to the predetermined spot, an open field outside of the fortress. It seemed to be the perfect place to stage a battle. They got there long before noon to allow time to get the lay of the land.

The trio had decided that the prescribed tone of the meeting should be diplomatic. This consensus was reluctantly agreed to by JJ, whose suggestion was to kill whoever showed up and deal with the consequences later.

The Iones trailed behind, staying out of sight. JJ's presence was provocation enough, and they didn't want it known that they also harbored a secret squad of archers for this meeting. Serra offered to cast an invisibility spell on the Iones, but they vehemently refused to be the subjects of "Raven magic."

There was no visible activity at the fortress throughout the morning. When the sun was at its highest point, Rugen, Serra, and JJ came out of hiding. Shortly thereafter, the main gate of the fortress opened and out walked two men.

Both had graying hair. Neither one of them had a soldier's build. The best word to describe them was *average.* One was slightly taller and lankier than the other, but nothing would distinguish either of them from a crowd of randomly selected people. The taller one was wearing a traditional but faded sorcerer's robe and the other was in casual clothing. Neither appeared to be armed.

The five diplomats met at the center of the open field and introduced themselves, opting to shake hands as if it were a pleasant business meeting. The shorter one turned out to be Brian Gruhl. Rugen, Serra, and JJ were expecting some elaborate costume or symbol of regality but instead were wildly underwhelmed by his appearance. The taller one in the sorcerer's robe was introduced as Deckard.

"You completed a long journey to meet us today," Gruhl started. "I wonder if you bring civility, or are you just savages looking to mindlessly kill?"

Rugen was initially startled by the forwardness, but once he reminded himself with whom he was dealing, he responded with a line he had prepared in advance: "No more lives need to be lost. We'd like to discuss a truce."

"A truce presumes a disagreement. I don't see how I've wronged any of you."

"You created monsters that killed thousands of people and made life miserable where we're from," Rugen calmly responded, "and I'm sure it's the same in the north."

"I didn't realize Lundgren's army spoke for the north," snorted Gruhl.

"We don't, but then again I assume no one does, especially when it comes to the creatures you've unleashed."

"So what would you like from me?"

Rugen took a deep breath. "We want you to stop making the creatures and to terminate any you have."

"Oh is that all?" mocked Gruhl, "and what do you offer in return?"

"In return we'll pack up our army and leave for Lundgren."

"Just like that? You collect your army and go back to where you came from, and all we have to do is destroy decades of our work?"

"Well…" Rugen looked at Serra and JJ. "There's one other thing."

Gruhl stood in silence for a moment and then gestured for him to continue.

Rugen looked into Gruhl's eyes. "When we leave, you come with us to Lundgren to answer for your crimes."

Gruhl put a hand to his chest in mock-horror. "My cr… my crimes?! Which crimes are those?"

Rugen was momentarily confused, until he realized Gruhl was being patronizing. He replied, "As I said, you made creatures that killed countless people."

"Not to mention murdering your family in cold blood," added JJ.

Gruhl flashed the redhead a fiery look. "None of this is any of your concern. You weren't invited to this meeting." He gestured to Rugen and Serra. "I asked for two. I assumed the highest ranking officer and a magical protector." He looked at JJ. "You are neither of those. So I don't recognize you being here."

Rugen signaled JJ to stand down.

"An army of children," continued Gruhl. "Lundgren has the audacity to speak its mind through the mouths of grammar school rejects. Go home and tell Duke Alonso if he wants to make such demands on me he needs to back it up with the real Lundgren Army."

"How about I show you what this reject can do right here and now?" JJ snarled. He grasped the hilt of the sword in its sheath.

Deckard stepped forward between JJ and Brian and said, "Gentlemen! Please! This is a diplomatic meeting!"

Rugen put his hand on JJ and calmly said, "I agree. We came here to discuss a truce and prevent death."

Gruhl flashed a wide grin for a moment and then spat, "To prevent death? You forget you've already killed two of my men? I guess we're not counting them?" He paused, but before Rugen could respond, he shook his head and said, "No, no, you're right. We've been treacherous, and that's on me. I need to answer for my crimes." He put his hand to his chin, pretending to mull it over for a moment, and then said, "We'll stop making our creatures. We'll terminate the ones we already have. And I'll come with you to Lundgren to face judgment." He stared at Rugen for a few beats and then added, "On one condition."

Rugen swallowed, dreading the next words out of Gruhl's mouth. Met with silence, Rugen prompted, "And that is?"

"If I'm going to pay for my crimes, you should pay for yours. You killed two of our men." He turned to Deckard, who dropped his head. "Two of my best men," he added. "I believe an eye for an eye is in order. Tomorrow morning, meet me back here with two volunteers. Bring them to me, and we'll put them to death." He paused for a moment and then continued, "Painlessly, of course. We don't want to be responsible for any undo suffering. God knows there's been enough. Do that and all of your demands will be met."

Rugen closed his eyes for a long blink and quietly said, "You really are as deranged as people say. We'll meet you on this battlefield tomorrow morning, me and my entire army."

With a ring in his voice, Gruhl sang, "See you then!" And without another word he and Deckard turned and strolled back to the fortress, laughing to each other.

CHAPTER 12

Deflated and disturbed, Rugen, Serra, and JJ trudged back to the campsite. The rest of the day was full of discussions about strategy and reflections on how far they'd come. The Ione scouts continued to watch the fortress in an attempt to glean intelligence, but despite staying on the hill until sunset, they had nothing significant to report.

That night the army sat on logs and boulders trying to stay warm near Dobbler's indagio campfire spells. With how cold it was becoming, everyone celebrated his efforts and joked that the top priority was to make sure he survived the assault. The sorcerer sat with Serra near their own fire, drinking spruce tea, eating dried snacks, and feeling full of himself.

Serra took a sip and asked Dobbler, "So what's your strategy tomorrow?"

"I plan on being in the thick of it, battling gmorks with magic. I'm kind of excited, actually."

"You can't be serious," said Serra with eyebrows narrowed.

"This is a long time coming. I've never had the chance to flex my powers in a real battle. I've never seen what I can do with no restraints."

"Don't be so cavalier. You don't know what it's going to be like on that battlefield. None of us do. I've never heard of people fighting more than a handful of gmorks, and a lot of those battles didn't end well. How can we possibly expect to kill a legion of them?"

Dobbler smiled into his tea and said, "We'll have swords on the ground wielded by men enhanced by your magic. We'll have arrows in the air flown by Iones who have experience killing gmorks. And we'll have the full power of Obsidian wreaking havoc."

"And the ursinoxes?" questioned Serra.

"That's where you come in with the aughra drain."

"I'm amazed by your level of confidence. You make it all sound so easy," said Serra. "How can you be sure the spell will work? No one's ever tested it on an ursinox."

"Maybe I am being overconfident, but it's better than going in already defeated."

"I need you safe, Lane," said Serra, nudging closer to him. "I have plans for you after this."

Dobbler gazed deeply into her heather gray eyes, which were flickering orange by the firelight, and whispered, "And I you."

Serra set down her cup and put her hands into his, quietly saying, "Promise me you'll stay near the back. Wreak your havoc from a distance."

JJ flopped down next to them in a huff and quipped, "If you hang back you'll miss all the fun."

Serra and Dobbler quickly slid back to their own spaces and Serra scolded, "JJ, this is none of your business."

JJ took a bite of dried meat and laughed.

"He's right," said Dobbler calmly. "Annoying, but right. I didn't join this journey to not play my part. You asked me to come along to be the sorcerer, and I'm all in. I can't be effective if I'm far away from the action. Imagine our guys are tangled with a bunch of gmorks in a big mess of bodies all moving around each other. How can I fixate on a target with fire or lightning unless I'm right there in the thick of it?"

Serra made a face and looked away. "I don't like it," she said quietly.

"What about you?" asked Dobbler. "What if I told you to hang back?"

"You know I can't. Our warriors need me to protect them and heal their injuries."

"Just so you know I'm not going to need any of your protection or healing," interjected JJ. "I'll be fine."

Curtis, the grunt who had sparred with Claire outside of B-1, joined them, and meekly said, "Excuse me, Dobbler?"

Dobbler acknowledged him with a nod.

"I was thinking. I've always wanted to fight with a flaming sword."

Some of the other grunts lifted their heads, eavesdropping.

"When we engage with the gmorks, can you cast a spell to light my sword on fire?"

"Um..." responded Dobbler.

"Have you ever worked in a blacksmith shop?" asked JJ, interrupting.

"What?"

"A blacksmith shop. You know what a blacksmith is, right?"

"Yes," said Curtis, dreading pending embarrassment.

"Do you know how blacksmiths are able to handle molten hot swords?" He paused for a moment before answering his own question. "Fire-resistant gloves, metal tongs, face masks...all things you don't have out here." He widened his eyes at Curtis and continued, "How do you plan on fighting with a flaming sword without setting yourself on fire? Not to mention the first hard thing you hit, like a gmork's stone hands or horns, would dull the edge or bend the tip."

Curtis flushed as the other grunts laughed in the background. He quietly retorted, "I didn't mean it had to be *that* hot, like forging hot."

"Oh, so you just want a little flame; just enough to look impressive...until you swing the sword." He mimed holding a sword to his lips and blowing it out like a candle. "Even if the fire didn't go out immediately, the heat wouldn't do any more damage than the blade itself." He glanced at Dobbler and Serra, and then asked, "And who are you trying to impress anyway? You think the mindless hunks of meat we're fighting care what you're swinging at them? Why don't you just paint some flames along the blade? That would be just as effective."

The other grunts roared with laughter.

"Or give it a scary name." He stood and unsheathed his own sword, brandishing it in the direction of Curtis. "Mine is called *Distributor of Pain*," he said with a menacing grin.

Curtis backed away looking frightened, making JJ step forward and loom over him, the edge of his blade gleaming in the firelight.

The crowd got quiet and looked tense until Rugen yelled, "JJ! Put that thing away and sit down!"

Rest did not come easy that night. The minds of the soldiers were too frantic with anticipation to have anything but a broken, fitful sleep. When they awoke, any potential hangover effects were quickly overwhelmed by excitement and apprehension for the day ahead. Everyone made their best effort to keep their normal routine, but staying focused was difficult. When they had prepared as much as they could, Alex called them to attention.

It had been decided by the other squad leaders that he would be the one speaking to the army, not only because of his leadership qualities, but also because of his status as a Riser Helm graduate who had experience fighting and killing gmorks. Alex longed for the opportunity to give the pre-battle pep talk. It was an honor he'd dreamed about since his days as a student.

He stood in front of the RHS graduates wearing his Naga armor, all except the mask. He projected his voice, saying, "Today you will be presented with immortality. Grasp it by its ugly horns and drive it into the dirt!"

Alex was expecting a rousing cheer in response, but received little more than a half-hearted murmur. He continued, "We are one team. If the man next to you goes down, he's your responsibility. Get between him and the gmorks and call for our cleric." He gestured to Serra. "The worst thing you can do is leave him unprotected. The monsters would leap at a chance to swarm a soldier on the ground. Serra will heal his wounds and have him back on his feet and ready to fight in no time."

Serra nodded to the crowd, some of whom were staring off into the distance, obviously not giving Alex their full attention.

"The creatures are dumb and slow. But they're incredibly strong and have an almost impregnable defense. We're assuming there'll be scores of them. Our best shot is Claire's strategy." Alex put his arm on his sister's shoulder. "Hit and move. Hit and move. Don't stand toe-to-toe with one gmork and let two others flank you. If you knock one down, move on to the next. If you're free and see one on the ground, kill it quickly, but keep an eye on the others around you. Before you know it, another one will be breathing down your neck. Keep moving or die."

JJ clapped a few times in support of his friend and exclaimed, "That's right!"

"While we're expecting a lot of gmorks, there won't be an infinite amount. If you stay in the fight and follow the strategy, their numbers will eventually dwindle, and that's when we siege the fortress and capture Brian Gruhl."

There were more positive responses as the crowd started to focus in.

"Men, this is the day you've been waiting for ever since you sparred with your friends in the parks of Lundgren. This is the day you've been waiting for since your first lecture at Riser Helm. All of those hours of learning, training, sparring—today is what you sweated and bled for. This is the day you are officially soldiers in the Lundgren Army." Alex was getting louder as he spoke. "There's trouble in the north, just like years ago when our ancestors invaded this territory and freed the world from evil. Men, the world needs us to free her from evil again! This is the day to answer the call!"

A cry went up. A cry that was heard in Gruhl's fortress. A cry to be heard in the thoughts and prayers all over Hyboria.

CHAPTER 13

Around of handshakes and back slaps punctuated Alex's speech. Afterward, JJ and the six members of his squad left camp to connect with the Iones at the hill they were planning to seize. They didn't know how many of Gruhl's soldiers to expect when they got there, but assumed the presence would be significant, as the hill was of crucial strategic importance.

The sun was still working its way over the horizon, and the morning air was chilly enough for frost to glisten on the blades of grass and low-lying vegetation. About halfway to the hill, the Iones suddenly appeared all around JJ's squad without warning, which at first was alarming, but quickly gave JJ a sense of comfort that people who were blessed with such stealth were on his side.

Blain reported that the hill was crawling with enemy archers, and that there was a disagreement among the Iones as to the best way to approach without being seen.

"Forget that. We rush in and cut them down," said JJ. "They won't know what hit them until it's too late."

JJ's men excitedly voiced their agreement. They were craving a fight after the long weeks of wandering through the mountains and northern wilderness.

"No," said Blain. "We move without sound and we surround them. There are only forty-two of us against who knows what odds. We need to minimize our casualties. Besides, how fast can you rush up a hill covered in bushes and vines?"

JJ smiled at how animated Blain had become. It occurred to him that this was probably his own influence. He was happy to defer to him. "You lead the way."

The two groups split in half and fanned out along the perimeter of the hill. JJ,

Blain, and a mixture of Iones and grunts crept to the right while the two sub-elite soldiers, Emilio and Duncan, led the other men to the left. They positioned themselves around the base of the hill and silently ascended as one unit, synchronized by the Iones communicating via shuesa.

When they reached the top, they did their best to obscure themselves behind trees. Gruhl's archers were milling about, talking to each other and inspecting the bows they were holding, oblivious to the threat closing in on them. JJ looked at Blain, questioning with his eyes what the next move was. When he looked back he saw one of the enemy archers staring right at him, eyes wide and mouth drooped slightly open. Seeing that they'd been spotted, JJ pulled his sword and rushed at the man.

Rather than raise the bow he was holding, the archer dropped it and put his hands out in front of him. He yelled, "Stop!" prompting the rest of Gruhl's men to discard their weapons and show their empty hands.

Blain and the two squads exited their hiding spots and quickly surrounded the unit, cutting off all exits.

"Please don't kill us!" cried the man. "We surrender!"

Blain looked at JJ and asked, "Do you think this a trick?"

"No trick," said the man, with his hands still in front of him. "We aren't soldiers like you. We're miners and lab assistants."

"I'm a chef!" yelled one being held at sword-point by Duncan.

The first man continued, "We have no combat training. The first time I held a bow was just the other day."

"So why are you out here?" asked Blain.

"The commander told us to grab bows and get to the hill," said the chef. "We do what he says. But when we got here, we talked it over and decided our best chance would be to surrender."

"Surrendering is your best chance?" asked JJ, eyebrows raised. "Even if you're right and we don't kill you, you expect Gruhl will let you live?"

"You have a point," he agreed. "We can't return to Gruhl. If you let us go we promise we'll head south and never come back."

"We let you go and you flank our army," said Blain. "Is that the plan?"

Gruhl's men frantically shook their heads.

"Look, we came here to fight a battle," explained JJ. "An unfortunate but nonetheless important part of that is killing the enemy." He raised his sword. "So who's first?"

The man closest to JJ stepped back. "Please," he begged, "don't hurt us. We surrender. We just want to live our lives in peace."

"You made creatures that killed people all over Hyboria," said JJ.

"We're just servants," said the man, looking at JJ with pleading eyes. "The small part we played in producing those monsters was under a constant threat of death."

"Okay," started Blain. "I suppose it'd be cruel to kill you after you've surrendered, but we can't exactly set you free either."

JJ ordered the two squads to search the men as he and Blain talked.

Once they were finished, JJ said, "Okay, we'll take you as prisoners back to our camp. Our leader will decide what to do with you."

Blain shook JJ's hand and said, "Tell Rugen we own the hill. We'll do all we can to cover you."

JJ and his squad marched Brian Gruhl's eleven would-be archers into camp. The prisoners were walking single file with their hands together folded in front of them. Each was doing his best to appear calm.

Rugen saw the parade and asked, "What's this?"

"Prisoners from the hill," answered JJ nonchalantly.

Rugen looked stunned. "Well that was fast. Why did you bring them here?"

"They surrendered willingly, saying they joined Gruhl as servants, not soldiers," answered JJ, as his squad directed the prisoners to form a line in front of Rugen.

"This one here says he's a chef!" said Duncan, pointing at one of the men. Everyone looked at the chef, who half-nodded, half-shrugged his shoulders.

Rugen thought for a moment and said, "This could be a trick. They gave themselves up willingly? After you guys fought and killed a few of them I assume?"

"We didn't kill anyone. They surrendered as soon as they saw us."

"Were they armed?" asked Rugen.

"With bows, yes," answered JJ. "And we found a few small knives when we searched them. They don't seem to be a danger to us."

"I hadn't planned on us taking prisoners today. What are you thinking we do with them?"

"I dunno," shrugged JJ. "Tie them to trees I guess."

"What about magic?" suggested Serra. "Any of you a sorcerer or cleric?"

All of the men gave tentative but negative responses.

"Well, just to be safe…" said Serra. She walked up to the first man and touched his forehead, saying "Hrousy emfoi."

He winced as she said it, but didn't try to resist.

Serra went down the row and repeated the spell and forehead touch to each man in turn. "That will block any magical ability they might have. They won't cast anything now."

"So we just tie them up and leave them here?" asked Rugen.

Everyone looked at each other, unable to come up with any better plan. "Seems like our only option," replied Alex.

"Wait a second, what if one of the gmorks gets past us and wanders over here?" asked Claire. "These poor souls would be helpless to defend themselves if they are tied up."

"And?" asked JJ.

The prisoners remained expressionless.

"And?" mocked Claire. "Leaving them defenseless with the monsters coming is no better than killing them ourselves."

"If their own creations kill them, so be it," said JJ, looking right at the prisoners. "I can live with that."

"That sounds like something Gruhl would do," said Claire. "We're better than he is."

"I can put them in an exclusion field," suggested Serra. "We'll tie them up and they'll stay there, invisible to the rest of the world. I'll retrieve them after the battle."

"Right," agreed Rugen. "How much rope do we have?"

"Sorcerers don't need rope," said Dobbler.

After securing the prisoners, Gordon's Army made its way to the large clearing at the base of Gruhl's fortress. The front of the building was an imposing stone wall set into the mountain, jutting out ten feet from the rocky face. It appeared that the fortress was carved out of the mountain itself, which it essentially was. Small, rectangular windows peppered the facade above a massively thick entrance gate made of reinforced wood. The arched gate was five times the size of a standard door.

Rugen and the other soldiers arranged themselves in a line at the opposite end of the clearing, organized by squad. They stood tall, comforted by the knowledge that nine Ione archers were on the high ground providing aerial support. They waited for a long while, but there was no visible activity in or around the fortress. They'd been expecting to be greeted by a legion of gmorks and armed soldiers but instead were met with silence.

Eventually Rugen could no longer stand the wait. He screamed Gruhl's name as loud as his voice could go.

A calm and innocent sounding "Yes?" called back from the other side of the wall. It was as if Gruhl were surprised by unexpected and friendly visitors.

Rugen looked around at the other squad leaders with a befuddled expression. He wasn't quite sure what to say next. He yelled, "I'll remind you of the offer I made yesterday. If you give yourself up and willingly come to Lundgren, there will be no reason to harm anyone."

"Did you bring your sacrificial volunteers?" asked Gruhl, almost sweetly.

"You know I can't do that," responded Rugen. The wind was quiet enough that two men could hear each other almost like they were using the shuesa.

"Then turn around now and head home," responded Gruhl. "Remember, you are the aggressors here. This is our land and you are the ones harassing us."

Inside the building, Brian quietly said to Deckard, "Make sure our archers are ready to fire, and release the gmorks on my signal."

"And if the army grants your request to leave?" asked Deckard.

"Release them anyway. The gmorks are already awake and we can't have them tearing things up in here."

"Yes, sir," said Deckard. "You wanted only fifty gmorks, no ursinoxes, right?"

"Fifty ought to be more than enough to annihilate this group of children.

We'll need to keep the ursinoxes and the rest of the gmorks in reserve for when reinforcements come."

As the invading army gathered at the far end of the battlefield, a shaky arrowhead tentatively poked its way between two parapets on the roof of the fortress. The man holding the nocked arrow took his time scanning the field for the best possible target. His eyes were drawn to one soldier standing in the middle of the line who measured a head taller than everyone else. He presumed this to be the leader. But even if that weren't the case, the archer reasoned that shooting a brawny soldier armed with an enormous broadsword would certainly help swing the odds in his side's favor.

The archer leaned forward and aimed his arrow so that it would fly down and strike the soldier dead center in his chest. Gently but smoothly he pulled the bowstring, thinking about how much making the shot would please the commander. His heartbeat quickened with anticipation, knowing that shortly after releasing his arrow, chaos would ensue among the ranks of the invading army. He blinked his eyes, pressing them closed for a moment, took a calming breath, and visualized the arrow hitting its intended target.

Just as he was poised to release the bowstring, his head jerked violently to the side. His body followed, slamming against the parapet, and his nocked arrow harmlessly looped into the woods. He fell onto the stone roof, landing among white streaks of crow droppings.

The fallen archer immediately realized that he couldn't move his body at all, but he felt no pain, just a fullness in the area below his jawline. He couldn't lift his arm to inspect what was causing it. He then noticed he wasn't breathing. He tried to force a deep inhale, but no air came into his lungs. The realization that he would slowly suffocate to death if he couldn't take in a breath caused a feeling of panic.

Seconds later, a few of the other archers stationed on the roof rushed to the man, calling his name. When they got to him they looked down with horror on their faces. He wondered if they knew he couldn't breathe, and if so how they could have figured it out so quickly. He was curious to ask but was unable to speak.

The gawking onlookers frantically chattered with each other. Their words sounded distant and garbled, as if he were hearing their voices from underwater. As he watched them, trying to understand what they were saying, their faces gradually faded until he could no longer discern any identifying features. Their heads became blurry and darkly silhouetted against the blue background of the sky above.

The sky. It caught the man's attention. When he focused on it, he felt the panic leave his mind. It was a glorious deep blue color, highlighted by light fluffy clouds carelessly floating by. There was no sound now, no odor on the breeze, just that beautiful sky. What a lovely day it was.

CHAPTER 14

The heavy wooden gate enclosing the entrance to Gruhl's fortress creaked open, revealing a dark passageway beyond. A gmork appeared in the void and stood, squinting in the sunlight, its muscular shoulders rising and falling as it breathed. Several others joined it, and their beady, lifeless eyes scanned the row of soldiers on the far opposite edge of the battlefield. Their mouths were abnormally wide by comparison to the rest of their head. Although the soldiers knew it was unlikely that the beasts were capable of human emotion, the curve of their mouths suggested toothy grins.

They edged forward as a group but were halted by a barrage of arrows pelting them in the arms, necks, and sides. One arrow bounced harmlessly off of a horn and landed on the grass. It might have lodged itself in an eye had that gmork not turned its head at the very last moment. None of the beasts were felled by the assault, but they were definitely distressed. The progression of gmorks still in the tunnel was impeded by the obstruction caused by their skewered vanguard. Dexterity was not a strong suit of the gmorks, and watching them unsuccessfully groping for the arrows sticking out of them gave the soldiers a modicum of humor.

The soldiers' laughing was cut short by a sudden bright flash. It started as a point of light in the vicinity of the gate; then rapidly expanded to fill their entire field of vision. A sphere of haze followed after the flash blinked out. It looked like a cloud of buzzing white bees sweeping at lightning speed in all directions. It was made more visible by how the tall grass swayed as it whooshed past. It moved so fast there was no chance for anyone to get out of the way or even brace for its impact.

When the wavefront struck, it felt like a kick to the chest. On its heels was a thunderous blast that sounded as if the sky had been violently and irrevocably fractured. At the gate several gmorks flew through the air in slow-motion in the midst of a swelling cloud of dust. As their bodies crashed down, the cracking sound echoed back, having ricocheted off the landscape. It was as if a second explosion had occurred in the distance.

All activity stopped in the aftermath of the blast. Rugen felt lightheaded and nauseous. He noticed that others seemed to be feeling the same way or worse. Many of them were holding their heads or chests, and some of them had taken a knee or were doubled over. No one was talking, and all of them had expressions of unease or discomfort.

"Is everyone all right?" coughed Rugen. He felt tingling in his fingers and flutters in his chest.

Nobody verbalized an answer. Most of them were blinking their eyes and wriggling their jaws, trying to clear their vision and hearing. Some of them waved his question away.

"What was that?!" demanded JJ.

"Me," mumbled Dobbler quietly with his hand to his forehead.

"What do you mean, you?" groaned Claire.

"I didn't realize it would do… that."

"You never tried it before?!" growled JJ. "I thought you were supposed to be some kind of super-wizard with perfect training!"

"I practiced it on a small scale but had no idea how powerful the full spell was."

"Now that you know," sputtered Alex, "Can you never do it again? At least not anywhere near where I'm standing?"

By this time most people were back upright but had their hands on their hips.

"Yeah, Dobbler," scolded Claire. "Maybe a little warning next time?"

"Don't worry," the sorcerer answered. "I think I used up all the aughra in the area with that. There won't be any more spells for a while."

"The gmorks don't seem too pleased with you either," ribbed JJ. He gestured to the fortress wall, where the broken bodies of several gmorks had been flung.

A cloud of dust floated around the entrance to Gruhl's fortress but it was clear the explosion had obliterated the gate.

"Yeah, I think you took out at least four or five of them," said Claire.

"That's just the ones we saw," added Alex. "Who knows how many you killed in the tunnel."

Dobbler looked at Serra with a half-smile, hoping for her approval. She frowned back and slowly shook her head, deflating him further.

Overhead a few arrows flew from the Ione's hill toward the fortress as a small group of gmorks exited the opening. They were pelted just like their brethren before them.

Rugen pulled his sword from its scabbard over his shoulder. He looked to his left and right and yelled, "Well then, are we ready to slay these beasts or what?"

The others responded with enthusiastic nods, which prompted Rugen to lift the giant weapon over his head and roar a battle cry.

Everyone else responded with cries of their own and followed Rugen as he ran. The sound encouraged a handful of Gruhl's arrows to take flight from the top of the wall. They lurched through the air, landing pathetically in the dirt after a short, doddering journey.

A seemingly endless stream of gmorks spilled out of the tunnel, spurred on by the activity in front of them. The arrows poking out of the flesh of the first few bounced as the beasts ran but didn't seem to impede them. The distance between the Ione's hill and the gmorks was just too great for the arrows to pierce deeply enough to do any real damage.

JJ, who was as fast as he was courageous, ran with abandon and quickly surpassed everyone. He turned his head slightly to look at his fellow soldiers and screamed, "Let's go!"

The two groups crashed together and combat commenced.

The explosion at the gate had stunned the workers inside The Emporium into silence, but after the shock of it wore off, chaos reigned. People were running in all directions. Gruhl and Deckard were in separate parts of the fortress barking out orders in an attempt to get them to focus on their duties rather than run around aimlessly. Eventually the two men found each other in a hallway.

"What's the report?" snapped Brian.

Deckard was out of breath from running. He held out his finger, asking for time to collect himself. After a moment he responded, "Three of ours were shot with arrows."

"Shot dead?"

"Yeah. One on the roof took an arrow in the neck." Deckard pointed to a spot under the angle of his jawbone. "The other two were at windows."

"Where are the arrows coming from?" spat Brian.

"The overlook."

"I sent archers there!"

"Well, either they've decided to betray their own side and shoot at us, or the hill was taken over by the Lundgren Army."

"Believe me," started Brian, "Those aren't our men doing the shooting. Accurately hitting someone on the roof or through a window takes a lot more ability than those imbeciles have."

"So then our archers on the hill are dead," Deckard stated coolly. "They're dead, the front gate is destroyed, and we can't go anywhere near the windows at the risk of being impaled by arrows. Is it time to awaken the rest of the creatures?"

"Not yet," answered Brian. "We're just getting started. Have some faith. Our gmorks are fighting the invading army as we speak. The fact that we can't safely peer out the window to assess how it's going is a minor annoyance."

"So you're comfortable relying on faith?"

"I am," muttered Brian, "But if you really need to know for sure, go ahead and get more spotters at the windows." Then he added, "Choose young people. They have better eyes, better reflexes... and they're more expendable."

CHAPTER 15

"Serra!" yelled a frantic voice from the midst of the melee.

The gray-eyed, auburn-haired cleric was kneeling in the dirt over a soldier who had been wounded by a gmork. She briefly glanced up from her efforts to see a wall of frenetic movement partially obscured by a cloud of dust. As she did, noises of battle flooded her ears—swords clanging against the stony skin of the gmorks' hands and arms, claws screeching across shields, yelps, grunts, and yawps. She was able to block out the sounds while concentrating on healing but they flooded back in when her name was called.

The wounded man she was attending to—his name was Brett—was unconscious on his back. Serra had already mended the multiple bleeding cuts and abrasions across the exposed portions of his skin. She was wondering how much damage was still underneath, what she could do to fix it, and how best to wake him without causing further harm.

She gently shook him and called his name several times but got no response. She frowned and turned her attention back to the fray. The action was dizzying. She squinted in the direction from where the latest call had come but didn't see anything amiss. Her focus then drifted to Dobbler, who was easy to spot because of the little explosions he was causing.

"Serra?" This time it was Faison, the grunt whose job it was to be Serra's assistant and bodyguard while she tended to the wounded. When Rugen had split the army into squads, he allocated three grunts to follow and protect Serra and Dobbler. If they had been able to fight side-by-side, this allocation would have worked out fine, but from the first moments of the battle it was clear that staying together would be impossible. For Dobbler to target gmorks while preventing collateral damage, he needed close proximity to the fighting. Serra, conversely, needed to be as far from harm as she could to safely care for the wounded. So they split up. She kept one guard with her, Faison, and the other two went with Dobbler.

The decision of who was to go with whom was made when Serra asked if any of them had medical experience and Faison half-raised his hand. It wasn't that they'd be doing much conventional field medicine, but someone with that sort of training could maybe aid with her diagnosis, and it seemed as good a way to split them up as any.

Faison had no more access to such training than the other two RHS graduates, but he singled himself out at that moment because over the prior month he had watched the cleric with curiosity and developed a respect for her and what she did.

When Serra and Faison were called to a wounded soldier, his body was invariably lying just a few feet away from the skirmish. Serra needed to move the injured man away from the distraction of the noise, rapid movements, and constant fear of assault in order to properly treat him.

They accomplished this with a mixture of magic and muscle. Once they got to their patient, Serra would cast a levitation spell and Faison would grab a hold of whatever he could to drag him out of the fray. Serra would then pick up any equipment left behind. It was a tension-filled process, but after a half-dozen fallen soldiers, they had the procedure pretty much figured out.

Casting spells required a lot of concentration, and regardless of the protective presence of Faison, the thought of claws raking across Serra's back was always somewhere in her mind. While it would have been safer for her to do all of the healing work within the protection of an exclusion field, Serra didn't want to separate herself from what was going on around her. She needed to stay aware of gmorks approaching and soldiers calling out.

"Serra..." Faison calmly said, "someone's calling for us." He found using a gentle tone to be the best way to get her attention while she was focused on healing. Startling her interfered with her magic.

She nodded and looked at her current patient Brett. He was still having some difficulty breathing, and she wondered how much internal damage the gmork had done when it swiped him. She gently put her hands on his chest and cast another collection of spells.

Faison squinted in the direction from where the latest call had come and saw a form lying in the dirt. He was anxious for Serra to finish so they could go help that person. Seeing someone bloodied and helpless was terribly upsetting, especially when it was a classmate and friend Faison had known since the age of twelve.

"Brett?" whispered Serra.

He didn't respond.

"C'mon, Brett!" she begged, "aerja ulrab!"

The wounded man opened his eyes, moved his hands to his chest, and winced. He looked confused as he tried to focus on the woman kneeling over him.

Serra put her hand on his shoulder and whispered, "You're okay now."

He coughed a few times and then propped himself up on his elbows. In a raspy voice he asked what had happened to him.

"Rest for a few minutes. After that you'll be good as new." Serra knew the reality was he needed a few days of rest rather than a few minutes, but that wasn't possible. She stood, joining Faison, and whispered, "Let's go help the next one."

"You saved my life," called Brett, his voice raspy. "How can I thank you?"

Serra smiled. "By rejoining the fight. But for now I'll put a small exclusion field around you. Stay as long as you want, but remember we need you. Just walk out whenever you're ready."

Serra enveloped him in the protection field, and she and Faison ran off.

As they were making their way to the next injured man, she spotted Alex and Claire fighting side-by-side. Just as Alex had suggested in his pre-battle speech, they were following Claire's strategy. Each of them was engaged with multiple targets, doing their best to stay out of claw's reach.

Claire's staff moved in a blur. She would rattle off three strikes in the time it took for the gmorks to swing once. By the time it did, she had completely disappeared from its view.

Alex was nearly as fast as his sister. He adeptly used the Naga blades to leave multiple slices in the hides of the gmorks around him. Most of his attacks were on their upper arms and backs, gradually incapacitating them so that one of the grunts or sub-elites could make an easy kill.

Rugen had a different strategy. He engaged with only one gmork at a time, using the leverage of his enormous longsword to overpower it. This method put pressure on the rest of his squad to prevent the other monsters in his vicinity from distracting him, but Rugen's success rate spoke for itself, as measured by the detritus of dismembered gmorks in his wake.

The gauntlet JJ had taken from Igayim's ruined castle had two magic abilities. One was to deflect any fast-moving and thus dangerous objects flying at him. The other was to amplify the thrust of his left arm as he shoved. This allowed him to knock the gmorks off balance, weakening their defenses.

A constant antagonizing and distracting presence for the creatures was the barrage of arrows coming from the Iones at the top of the lookout hill. The arrows themselves didn't incapacitate them, but they split their attention away from the soldiers on the ground. The Iones were also periodically finding targets in the windows and on the roof of the fortress. Arrow stock wasn't a problem. In addition to their homemade supply and the large cache gifted to them at B-20 were the ones they'd confiscated from Gruhl's would-be archers.

The one person Serra was most interested in checking on, and the easiest to see from afar, was Dobbler. He was on the front line with the rest of the fighting force using smaller, more targeted spells than his opening salvo.

"Serra!" called a voice just ahead of them. It was Emilio, one of JJ's sub-elites. He held off the gmork he was fighting and briefly gestured to the ground behind him with his sword.

Serra saw a soldier lying there. He was all but unrecognizable with the amount of blood and dirt covering his face. Serra kneeled next to him and quickly noticed he was barely breathing. She looked at Faison and stammered, "Can you...can you tell who this is?"

"I think it's Duncan," answered Faison.

"Duncan," whispered Serra. She was attempting to draw a connection between the vibrant young man she'd come to know over the past month and the dying bloody mess in front of her.

Faison was staring, frozen, until Serra yelled, "Let's get him out of here!"

They followed their usual routine to bring Duncan to a safer area. She inspected him as best she could and started casting healing spells. He was gashed across his face and neck, and it was clear he'd lost a lot of blood. She mended his wounds and then wiped his face with the already well-used rag she'd brought.

His breathing continued to slow. Serra checked him again and cast more spells; frantically yelling, "Eofa sylmea!" and, "olmba raehoum!" There was no response. She looked at Faison, who was looking around, wide-eyed. He had no helpful response.

Serra gently touched the sides of Duncan's face and cried, "Aerja ulrab!" She could feel a lump forming in her throat.

Duncan gasped for breath. His eyes opened lazily and then closed again.

"Wake up." Serra begged. "Aerja ulrab, Duncan, wake up."

He opened his eyes again. He said, "Where am I?"

"You were hurt, but don't worry. I've got you. Save your strength."

"Serra?"

"Yes, it's Serra. Save your strength." She looked him over, blinking back tears as she searched her mind for something else she could do to help.

"Serra..." started Duncan. "I never..." His lips and tongue were dry as he opened his mouth to speak. "I never got to kill a gmork."

She looked at Faison, who made no movement. She looked back at Duncan and grasped his hand. "You will," she reassured him. "Just rest for a minute. The spells will work." Serra leaned into him and repeated, "Just give them a minute."

His voice was barely a whisper. "I never got to kill one of them, Serra. That's all I wanted to do." He coughed lightly.

"Just rest a little. It'll be okay."

He looked at Serra's face and wheezed, "Tell my father I'm sorry..." He coughed, then continued, "Tell my father I'm sorry I never killed one of them." His eyes closed, and his breathing fell silent.

"Duncan!" yelled Serra. She started casting spells again until Faison put his hand on her shoulder.

"He's gone, Serra."

"No he's not!" she screamed. "I can fix this!" She laid her palms on his chest plate and squeezed her eyes shut.

"Serra," Faison gently said, "we have to go now."

She stopped what she was doing and stared at Duncan's lifeless body for a long moment. Gradually the sounds of battle worked their way back into her ears.

"He was a good man, but we have more to do."

"I know," she said. She wiped her face with the back of her hand and stood. "I know."

Faison nodded and the two of them made their way to the source of the next distress call. A man was on the ground, sitting upright, his hand covering his upper left arm.

"That's Deke," said Faison as they walked toward him. "He's on Alex's squad."

She nodded and called out, "Deke, what happened?"

"I'm okay," he responded. "One of them pushed me and I lost my balance. The next thing I knew another guy's sword swung back and hit my arm. It was an accident."

There was a deep oozing gash, and the front of his armor was soaked in blood. He couldn't bend his elbow. Serra bent down and touched the wound, chanting her healing spells. It quickly mended from the inside out. She asked, "Why doesn't your chain mail have sleeves?"

"I don't like the sleeves. They're too restricting," responded Deke, allowing Serra to guide him to a lying position.

Serra looked up at Faison. "I'm going to put the two of us in an exclusion field. Stay outside in case someone yells for me." Faison agreed and Serra cast the spell.

Deke looked pale and tired. His eyes were half shut. Serra asked, "Does it hurt anywhere else?"

"No," he quietly responded, "But I can't move my arm." His eyes shut for a few seconds and then partially opened again. "Can you make it so I can move my arm?"

"I'm working on it. Just relax." The cleric continued chanting the words of Pallous.

"Serra?" He drifted away for a moment, and then regained attention, "Am I going to die?"

She watched him intently, wondering how best to respond. She was trying not to think about how much blood he already lost.

"Please... Serra. I don't want to die." Deke's eyes closed again. His breathing became fast and shallow. He whispered, "Serra..."

A sickly feeling of dread rose from the pit of her stomach. She was physically and emotionally exhausted by all of the suffering surrounding her. The interior walls of the exclusion field acted like a mirror; a parabolic lens reflecting all of the misery and sorrow she had experienced throughout the day of fighting; concentrating it at a single point in the center of her heart.

She grasped Deke's good hand. It was cold and white. She gathered herself from her emotions and said, "It's okay, Deke, just rest now."

"Please..." he whispered one last time before he stopped breathing altogether.

CHAPTER 16

Brian Gruhl stood in his upstairs office studying a yellowed square of paper depicting a schematic of The Emporium's mine system. This map was different that the one used by the lead foreman because on it were tunnels known to no one but Gruhl himself; tunnels that had been abandoned for many years, designed and built by workers long since relieved of their duties. Since its creation, the map was hidden in the false bottom of a locked drawer near the floor of his office closet.

A dozen loose keys were stored with the map. They were all equal in size and shape but had different symbols on them. It was a frustrating process looping them one-by-one onto their key ring, especially with the battle outside splitting his attention. Brian had stored the keys off the ring to make stealing them that much more annoying for any would-be thief.

Opposite the closet and beyond the desk was a window overlooking the fighting armies. He was mildly curious to see how the battle was progressing, but was reluctant to go anywhere near the window for fear of getting struck by one of the arrows that periodically whizzed by. He gripped the map in both hands, watching and listening until he could no longer suppress his curiosity.

Setting the map on his desk, he slowly approached the window. Each tentative step increased the temptation to go a little farther, which he did, until the edge of the battlefield came into view. There he paused, remembering the archers, and gently sidled along the wall with his back pressed against it. He waited as he got a grip on his nerves, appreciating the protection afforded by the thick stone.

He edged forward, breathing deeply, and slowly twisted his neck until he could see dust being kicked up from the fray. He only allowed himself a moment's glance before jerking his head back to the safety of the wall. He took another deep breath and slowly let it out while summoning the courage to look again.

As he surveyed the field, he was shocked by how few soldiers he saw. It was hard to get an accurate count with all of them moving around, but his best estimate of the remaining force was about half of the number the spy Ridley had reported. He was baffled as to where the others might have gone. Strategically, it didn't make sense to have that many people stationed on the overlook. Any army would need all the able-bodied infantry it could get when pitted against fifty gmorks, especially when arrows were known to be non-lethal from a distance.

Even more puzzling was while there were many dead gmorks on the ground, he didn't see even one human casualty. It was possible that the dead and injured had been carried back to camp, but that seemed like a complete waste of resources and manpower. Then a frightening thought struck him. He feared The Emporium had already been infiltrated through the destroyed front gate, but again why would they leave such a small unit behind to fight the gmorks? And where were the dead soldiers?

He stood blankly staring until he saw something even stranger. A man appear out of nowhere, far away from the front line. Where once there was empty space, he spontaneously materialized. Then he stretched, checked his sword and shield, before starting toward the skirmish. Brian furrowed his brow as he tried to process what was going on. The only explanation he could fathom was that the army clerics had made a portal to Lundgren, and they were sending wounded soldiers home and replacing them with fresh recruits. It occurred to him that they would have to be terribly powerful clerics to pull off such a spell. That had to be the reason they were having success against the gmorks. He wondered how long it would be before an entire legion passed through that portal.

He leaned closer to the window, eyes wide, mumbling his disbelief, until his thoughts were violently interrupted by an arrow whistling over his shoulder and into the office, missing him by mere inches. He jumped back reflexively as it struck the wall behind him and clattered to the floor.

He dropped to his hands and knees and scurried away from the window. Once clearing the door, he stood half-stooped and loped into the hallway as quickly as he could. He made it to the stairwell and bounded down, yelling for

Deckard. When he reached the bottom he doubled over, giving himself time to catch his breath.

Chaos ruled the scene. People hurried in every direction, and no one Brian asked knew where Deckard was. He called out several times as he frantically checked various rooms.

Finally Deckard appeared, startling him by saying, "I heard you're looking for me?"

"Wake the creatures," the commander ordered.

Deckard's eyes got large. "Sir?"

"Wake them. Now!"

"All of them?"

"The more you question my orders the sooner *that army*," he seethed, pointing at the front wall, "is going to breach this fortress and obliterate us. Yes, wake all of them."

"Yes, sir." As Brian turned to leave, Deckard added, "You mentioned earlier you had a backup plan?"

Gruhl paused for a few seconds before responding, "I do."

"Anything I need to know about?"

"Your only job right now is to wake those creatures and get them outside," he spat, glaring at Deckard. "All other plans are my concern." Before Deckard could respond, Brian stormed off.

Deckard fumed as he trudged down the stairs. He was weary from the years of feeling marginalized. Fleeting thoughts of rebellion ran through his mind. His first consideration was to not wake any of the creatures, as that was in clear defiance of what was demanded of him. He realized this could mean death, either by the invading army or by Brian's reprisal, but following orders and releasing all of the creatures could also mean death by leaving The Emporium defenseless against reinforcements.

He decided the most strategic plan would be to release a portion of them—say fifty more gmorks along with an ursinox—they would easily wipe out the invading army. Doing so while keeping double that in reserve could make Deckard the hero.

He wondered what had happened that changed Brian's mind about the amount of gmorks to wake up. Until the confrontation in the hall, the plan was to keep as many creatures in reserve as possible. From the intelligence Deckard received, the gmorks were fairing very well and The Emporium staff would easily extinguish what was left of the invading army. What had compelled Brian to make such a drastic change?

He arrived at the cavernous room where the creatures were stored. The process of arousing them was nothing more than reciting a few spells. It was the time delay that was frustrating. Generally they needed about thirty minutes before they were alert and ready to fight. He didn't have a lot of experience with releasing ursinoxes, but the few he had seemed to be ready more quickly than the gmorks he'd awoken over the years. Because the ursinox was the far most lethal of their creations, Deckard decided to start the process with it before doing anything with the gmorks.

Brian Gruhl had two offices in The Emporium. His main workplace was on the top floor, where he'd retrieved the keys. After ordering Deckard to wake the army, he jogged downstairs to his laboratory office. Once inside, he opened a cabinet to find a fully stocked backpack. He grabbed it, threw it over his shoulder, and then pulled a sword and scabbard from the wall-mount above his desk.

He left the lab and headed toward the mine, along the way reassuring the frantic people he passed that they needn't worry because reinforcements were just minutes away. He knew that statement to be completely false, but thought it was a nice thing to do to make them feel better before they were slaughtered by the Lundgren Army.

At the mouth of the mine, he removed a portable torch from its holder. The torch was fueled by aughra, which was drawn into the tunnels by a series of amulets set into the walls. It remained constantly lit but gave off no heat or smoke; just like an indagio spell.

He walked the main corridor, a tunnel almost exactly perpendicular to the mountain face. It continued until it split into left and right branches. Brian followed the leftward path, which was the older section of the mine. The miners had long since stopped tunneling in this direction. As Brian proceeded he kept one eye over his shoulder and the other watching the left wall, eventually stopping when he noted a subtle change in the texture of the rock—something that would likely go unnoticed by a person not specifically looking for it.

He lowered himself to the floor and felt around the base of the wall. Not finding what he was looking for, he set down the torch, sword, and backpack and used both hands to scan every contour. Eventually he detected a small hole. Keeping his finger in the space, he twisted his body to reach into his pocket and fumbled with the stack of keys. As soon as he touched them, it occurred to him that he'd left the map sitting on his desk.

He slapped the rock floor and cursed loudly, furious at himself for the oversight. There was a legend on the map that would have helped identify which of the keys fit the lock. Instead he had to try each one in turn. He ran through the entire collection, and none of them made the lock budge. He had a momentary panic as he wondered if he had left a key back in the drawer in his office, but calmed down by telling himself the lock was probably stuck simply because of the years of non-use. He started at the beginning, trying each key a second time, focusing on gently rocking each one back and forth inside the lock. After a few cycles, the key he was using flipped to the side and a drawer about two inches high and as long as his forearm slid open on rails.

He reached into the drawer and pulled out a small wooden wagon wheel. The very center of the hub had an irregularly shaped cutout. He set the wheel on the ground and checked both directions of the tunnel for anyone approaching. Seeing and hearing nothing, he continued on with what he was doing. Using the edge of the drawer as a guideline, he slid his hand up the wall to locate the second keyhole.

This lock needed a different key than the one he'd already used, which was a security feature Brian wished he hadn't designed into the system. After more trial, error, and loud cursing he found its match. As the key turned, a post sprung out of the wall with a loud thump and a puff of dust. It had the same odd shape as the cutout in the center of the wheel. It took some finagling, but eventually he was able to seat the hub on the post. Once it was flush, he slowly turned the wheel to the left, which caused a series of mechanisms to move inside the wall. After completing two full revolutions, a large door popped open.

Brian collected his bag, sword, torch, and the wagon wheel before passing through the door. He pulled the door flush and placed the wheel on the hub post on this opposite side. He spun it, sealing the door.

He held out the torch but couldn't see down the tunnel more than a few feet. It all looked the same; stone walls surrounding a black void. To his knowledge no one had entered this hallway in more than two decades; those being the men who'd carved it.

He trudged through the lengthy, winding pathways. As he walked along, the source of his anxiety shifted to the torch he was carrying. He wondered if the magic that kept it illuminated would eventually run out with him being so deep in the mountain. Without light, the journey might be impossibly treacherous because of the risk of hitting his head on some low-hanging part of the ceiling or twisting an ankle on a loose stone. He regretted not having aughra attractors installed along the walls in this area.

Every so often he came upon a door that required the same unlocking routine as the first one. There were four over the course of the several miles of tunnel, each requiring a different pair of keys and a wheel with a unique cutout. Whenever he successfully passed through a door, his confidence grew. There was only the one set of keys, which he kept with him as he progressed, and one set of wheels, which he discarded on his side of the locked door.

After what felt like hours, he finally came to a door that opened to the light of day. Clean cool air rushed into the cave in which the door stood. The air was an indulgence after the staleness of the tunnel. Although during his escape he had been breathing comfortably, the difference in the quality of the open air made him momentarily wonder if he'd narrowly cheated suffocation.

He closed and locked this final door, which gave him a great sense of relief. As he walked outside, he looked up at the clear blue sky and took a deep breath. He stared at the ring of keys in his hand for a few minutes, shaking his head and swearing. Then he disassembled the ring and flung each key as it came off. He threw them with purpose, as far and as hard as he could into the trees, scattering each one in a different direction. He imagined the keys were daggers, and the trees were Lundgren Army soldiers, and each time his arm whipped forward a soldier shattered like glass.

His comfortable life at the Emporium had come to an end, and there was nothing he could do now but save himself. This enraged him. His mind was already racing with thoughts of revenge, but he was glad to be alive.

He sat on a boulder and pulled an apple from his bag. The apple was from his own orchard, one of the last pieces of fruit his men were able to collect before the invading army showed up. Those same men were either dead now or would soon be, and everything for which he once lived was about to be completely destroyed.

As he ate he scanned the landscape and was struck by the silence surrounding him. The only sound aside from the apple crunching in his mouth was the wind rustling the autumn leaves. The screams of battle, chaos, and death were way too far away to be heard. He tossed the apple core on the ground and sat, staring at nothing. Eventually he told himself he'd need to get moving if he wanted to find shelter before the sun went down. He stood, hoisted his bag over his shoulder, donned his sword belt, and started the long walk south.

CHAPTER 17

A triumphant cheer exploded from the beaten, bloodied, but otherwise standing soldiers of Gordon's Army as they loomed over the bodies of fifty fallen gmorks.

"That's the last one!" yelled Rugen as he pulled his sword from the back of a slumping gmork. "But this isn't over yet. We need to find Gruhl."

The uninjured members of the army gathered together for Dobbler to do a full head count. Until the moment Rugen had stabbed the heart of the last infernal beast, there was too much going on for anyone know how many soldiers needed healing and how many were beyond assistance.

The breaching force would be nineteen, including JJ, Alex, and Claire. Twelve soldiers were either being tended to by Serra and Faison, recovering in exclusion fields, or deceased. The nine Iones would remain on the hill in case aerial coverage was needed.

"We'll follow you anywhere," said JJ as he regarded his filth-covered brethren, who were wide-eyed, breathing hard, and nodding in agreement.

Rugen thanked him and then called out, "Serra, we're going to bring out Gruhl."

Serra was in the distance kneeling over the body of a wounded soldier, and didn't give any indication that she heard him, so Faison signaled on her behalf.

"Okay, everybody ready?" asked Rugen. He was answered by eager nods. "If anyone attacks, dispatch them. They don't seem to have any military training, so we should have the advantage. My bet is they'll surrender at the sight of us."

"I'm going to find the sorcerer," said Dobbler.

"And Gruhl is mine," JJ added, playfully eying Rugen.

Rugen frowned, then looked up at the Ione's hill and yelled, "Archers, you covering us?"

An arrow flew from the hill up and over the facade of the building, landing out of sight on the roof.

"That's a yes," said JJ, smiling. Everything about their current situation pleased his warrior nature.

Rugen raised his sword and bellowed a war cry, which was echoed by the rest of the infiltrating force as they ran toward the open gate, weapons drawn.

Deckard had finished the necessary spells to wake the fifty gmorks and the ursinox. Rather than wait for the magic to set in, he decided to find Brian to give his report and receive the next set of orders. He left the room's large metal door open so the creatures could amble out to the battlefield when they were ready. He searched in the various labs and other work areas, guessing that's where the commander would be busy instituting the next phase of his plan to defend The Emporium. Not finding him, he headed upstairs.

Brian wasn't in his main office, either, but while there Deckard found a conspicuous piece of paper lying on the desk. He picked it up, assuming it was a note left for him. Instead, it was a crudely drawn map of what appeared to be the older section of the mine with symbols marked at various points.

He worked on deciphering the map until he heard a cheer rising from the battlefield. It could only mean one thing—the invading army had defeated the gmorks and was getting ready to breach the building. He quickly folded the paper and pocketed it before running out of the office.

JJ led the infiltrating party into the building and was met by a visibly frightened guard. From the man's posture, JJ got the impression he was holding a sword for the very first time in his life. The flame-haired warrior was quite the opposite—adept at swordplay and brimming with confidence. He smiled at the guard and said, "Knock, knock."

The guard ran toward them with his sword waving above his head in the best approximation of a pre-swing position he could muster. JJ lifted his gauntlet and easily deflected the downswing. The next thing the guard knew he was pinned against the wall with a blade at his neck.

"You really want to do this?" asked JJ, calmly.

The guard stood perfectly still and allowed his weapon to clatter to the ground. JJ turned his attention to the other foyer guards and said, "Anyone else want to be the hero?"

Each of them dropped whatever they were carrying and raised their hands over their heads in surrender. Without taking his eyes off them, JJ said, "Emilio, you're in charge of the prisoners. Make sure they stay out of the way."

"Nicely done, JJ," said Rugen. "Now let's go find Gruhl."

JJ nodded and then addressed the prisoners again, asking, "Where do we find Brian Gruhl?"

All of them shrugged or shook their heads.

Rugen put his hand on JJ's arm and said, "It can't be that big of a place."

Half of the soldiers stayed behind to supervise the prisoners as Rugen, JJ, Alex, Claire, Dobbler, and a few others searched the halls and rooms of Gruhl's fortress. Along the way they came across and disarmed several more of his men. None of them put up any resistance. They were gathered into small groups and marched to the dining hall, which had been converted into a temporary holding area. Emilio found rope, and one by one they acquiesced to him binding their hands and feet. He didn't suspect they'd try anything, but he wasn't taking any chances.

Rugen and the other leaders continued searching the first floor of the fortress. There were many more rooms than they expected by look of it from the outside. While exiting one of the rooms they met eyes with a robed figure running down the hall. Rugen pointed and yelled, "That's the sorcerer!"

"He's mine," growled Dobbler as he sprinted away, giving chase.

Deckard ducked into a stairway and started making his way toward the mine, figuring that was his only option for refuge. He ran through the main lab, but before he got to the exit, a fireball zipped over his shoulder and exploded on the wall in front of him. He turned to see the Lundgren Army sorcerer casually approaching from the other side of the room.

"You're a sorcerer," stammered Deckard. "What's your name?" He was attempting to stall while looking around for something that could give him an advantage. He was the lab manager, after all, and rusty in all things magical, so a strategy of fair play was unlikely to end well for him. The man he was facing was clearly younger and more practiced in battle, and the concept of magic duels hadn't crossed his mind since his days at Wyatt, which was a lifetime ago.

"Never mind my name!" Bright blue sparks shot out of Dobbler's fingers, tracing an arc on the wall around Deckard's cringing body. After the crackling subsided, he barked, "Where's Brian Gruhl?!" Behind Deckard was a jagged line of burn marks where the electricity had licked the wood.

"There!" screamed Deckard, pointing, "behind you!"

Dobbler whipped around, preparing to defend himself, but saw no one. When he heard the older man run off he realized he'd been duped. Dobbler sighed angrily, frustrated at himself for being so gullible, and made chase again.

It didn't take long for him to catch up, and when he did he used his magic to slide a chair into Deckard's path. The older man crashed into it and sprawled to the floor. There he remained, face down and not moving, as Dobbler cautiously approached.

Dobbler wondered if he was unconscious, and got his answer when Deckard suddenly flipped over and yelled, "Ixpao!" The spell knocked the younger sorcerer backward and off balance.

Deckard used the diversion to awkwardly climb to his feet and start hobbling off, but he only took several pained steps before Dobbler recovered enough to cast a focused pressure beam targeted at the center of his back. It threw his body forward, cracking three of his ribs as it struck. He didn't have the time to lift his forearm to block the doorframe, and as a result his eye socket was crushed as his face collided with the dense wood.

He tumbled to the floor, landing in a heap.

Dobbler stood there, fuming, as the older sorcerer lay completely still. He had heard the sickening crack that Deckard's head made when it struck the door frame, but didn't want to take any chances with him springing back to life again. "Stay on the ground!" he scolded. "Where's Brian Gruhl?!"

Deckard stayed where he was, unmoving.

Dobbler took several tentative steps and spat, "If you cast any more spells, I will kill you."

"I think," croaked Deckard, "you've already done that, boy."

"Where's Brian Gruhl?" he repeated.

Deckard slowly lifted his head toward Dobbler. Blood was filling his broken eye socket and dripping to the floor. He whispered, "I don't know."

"Yes you do! Tell me!"

"My guess is he ran away, through the mines," coughed Deckard. "I found this old map in his office." Deckard produced the map and held it out to Dobbler with a shaky right hand. "He left us. He realized we were doomed and he left us."

"You're lying! Tell me where he is."

"I'm not," retched Deckard. "I'm sure he ran…" He coughed. "To save his own skin." His breathing was beginning to sound labored.

Dobbler looked at the map he'd received from the dying sorcerer. "Tell me how we find him."

"You probably won't. Knowing him, he's been planning his escape for years." Deckard coughed again, spraying blood on the floor. "Self-preservation has always been," he sputtered, "his top priority."

Dobbler watched in silence, feeling a mixture of guilt and pity for the older man. He hadn't meant for the spell to cause so much damage.

"I've been…" wheezed Deckard. "I've been a terrible person for most of my life. Nothing I've done has been for any good." He met Dobbler's gaze with his one working eye. "I'm dying… and I don't blame you for that." He coughed up more blood.

Dobbler stepped back to get out of range of the blood as it sprayed.

"Listen to me," the older man continued, "more gmorks are waking up now. More gmorks and an ursinox."

Dobbler blinked slowly. "How many more?"

"You still have time. You need to get to where they are. I left the door open." He winced as he swallowed. "Go to the storage room. Close the door. Lock it. Block it. Do whatever you can to keep them in there." His voice was raspy now. "I want... I need… to do something good before I die." He pointed in the direction from where they'd come. "Go! Lock them in and save your army."

Dobbler stepped back a little, unsure if he was doing the right thing.

"Go! Before it's too late." He coughed again. A mass of blood lolled from his mouth. He started gasping and choking.

Dobbler turned to run; unsure where he was heading but driven by a dying man's warnings. He followed the hallway for some distance until up ahead he saw an enormous silhouette coming from the right. He stopped as artfully as he was able and ducked against the wall. Even though he had never seen an ursinox, he knew this was one.

By some miracle the thing didn't turn its head to look where Dobbler was cowering. Instead it continued on its path, disappearing out of sight to the left. Dobbler was afraid to move a muscle. He stayed where he was, breathing heavily and hoping the beast didn't realize what it had missed.

He kept still until he felt safe enough, and then tentatively tiptoed to the end of the hall to have a look. Seeing no sign of the ursinox, he continued his search for the storage room. He imagined a legion of gmorks waiting for him behind every turn.

Eventually he came to an open door with a darkened room beyond. It was full of dozens of slabs, some empty but most occupied by a large sleeping form. He didn't spend any time studying the gmorks, knowing many of them would be waking soon. He scampered out of the room and got to work on barring the door.

It closed and latched easily enough, but there was no obvious lock he could see. He doubted the gmorks could work the handle on the other side, but in case they could, he would need to find a more permanent closure. He quickly scanned the area, his worry increasing by the second. There were no obvious means to bar the door, so he'd have to try magic.

Lightning or freezing was of no use. He considered using intense flame to melt and fuse the metal around the opening but didn't have a way of shielding himself from the reflected heat, and it occurred to him that anything interfering with the structural integrity of the only door between his friends and a slew of demons was a bad idea. He looked at the stone floor and had an epiphany. He smiled and yelled, "Oktua tukoo!"

With a rumbling growl, the floor rose in front of the door. By the time it stopped moving there was an eight-inch-high mound of solid rock preventing it from opening.

Satisfied, he turned around and cautiously traversed the same hallway the ursinox had used, hoping to find Rugen and the others to inform them of Gruhl's escape. When he was confident the beast had left the building, he ran through the empty halls of the fortress, getting lost several times in the process. Finally he bumped into Rugen and JJ, at which point he was out of breath and had to put his hands on his knees to collect himself.

"Dobbler!" exclaimed Rugen, relieved. "Did you see Gruhl? We can't find him anywhere."

Dobbler shook his head and frowned.

"What happened with the sorcerer?" asked JJ.

"He's dead," said Dobbler flatly. Then he looked away, suddenly embarrassed by his actions.

"Oh," said Rugen, detecting the discomfort on his face.

"He told me Gruhl ran away," Dobbler said, collecting himself, "through the mines."

"Well let's go down there and bring him back!" shouted JJ excitedly.

"I don't think that'll work, but regardless, we have a bigger problem. Did you see the ursinox?"

"The what?" asked Rugen.

"There was a second wave of gmorks and an ursinox. I blocked the gmorks from escaping but not before the ursinox got out. If you didn't see it in the building, that means it went outside."

"Outside?" exclaimed Rugen, half-whispering.

Dobbler nodded. "Serra's outside."

"How long ago did you see it?"

"I don't know. Ten minutes?"

"We need to split up," suggested JJ. "Gather everyone to meet at the front gate."

"C'mon, breathe!" Serra yelled to the unconscious soldier lying in front of her.

"Serra, he's gone," Faison quietly said.

If this man, Quinn was his name, was indeed dead, it would make five soldiers Serra hadn't been able to rescue. She had healed three times as many, but in her mind the combined magnitude of that success was far outweighed by the ones she couldn't help.

"No! I just need to try harder."

"Serra," begged Faison, "let him go. There are others who need you."

Serra continued to work on Quinn's body, ignoring Faison. As she did she couldn't help but think about two parents who would never see their son again, untold children and grandchildren who would never have the opportunity to be born, and the potential of a lifetime spent in peace forever extinguished. She didn't want to give up, no matter what Faison said.

"Um... Serra?"

"What!" she spat. She whipped her head up to look at him standing above her. "Can't you see I'm..."

Her rebuke was cut short. Faison wasn't facing her as she expected. He was staring in the other direction with fear in his eyes. Serra followed his gaze to the destroyed fortress gate. Standing at the precipice was the largest animal she had ever seen. It looked like a bear, but much, much bigger. It scanned the battlefield, sniffing in the direction of the handful of soldiers recovering on the ground. A long black tongue extended from its mouth, licking furry lips.

"That's an ursinox," said Serra, stating the obvious. She slowly lifted herself to her feet, not taking her eyes off of the beast.

The ursinox broke into a gallop toward an injured soldier, who was frozen in place, too frightened to flee.

"No!" shrieked Serra, which got the creature's attention long enough for its intended target to scramble away on his hands and knees. "That's right, I'm over here," she taunted.

"What are you doing?" asked Faison incredulously.

The ursinox started moving toward her.

"We're supposed to heal and protect," responded Serra. "Are you with me?"

Faison kept his eyes on the ursinox, imploring, "What do you expect to do when it gets here?"

"Just keep it occupied long enough for me to put it to sleep."

"That's a brevell," said Poncho, staring at the mountain of muscle and brown fur that suddenly appeared in the busted fortress gate. All of the descriptions of the creature paled in comparison to seeing one in the flesh.

"What do we do?" asked Dillon.

"When's the last time any of you saw Gruhl's men in the windows or on the roof?" asked Blain after a short pause.

"Not for a long time, certainly not since the Damones went in," replied Poncho. The archers nodded agreement.

Blain watched as the creature sniffed the air, and said. "Well then, there's no more we can do from up here."

"Are you suggesting we go down there and fight a brevell up close?" asked Dillon.

"It's either that or stand here and watch it kill the Damones one by one," said Poncho.

The brevell broke into a gallop toward a wounded man on the ground but stopped when the cleric screamed at it.

"I guess we do what she's doing," started Mac, "split its attention however we can."

"Maybe because it's newly born it will be weaker and easier to confuse," suggested Jesse.

"Well, let's help confuse it while the cleric uses her Raven magic," said Poncho.

Blain thought for a moment, assessing the few options he could think of, and said. "Okay, it's the best plan we have. Everybody ready?"

"Learn the sounds, learn the smells, learn the marks of our forest dwells," whispered Phil quietly. He was reciting an old Ione prayer, one that mothers recited to their children, assuring them they will always be protected. He glanced at the others staring back at him, feeling embarrassed.

Dutch closed his eyes and continued the prayer, "Paths we take, paths gone by, some paths lead to the open sky." He had his head bowed, so the other Iones did the same.

Phil took over again, reciting, "Trust no one your mind can't hear, travel not away from near."

Others joined him, chanting, "Tread you light, your heartbeat thrums, in the dark of night when the stranger comes."

All the Iones chimed in, chorusing, "Don't call out, keep words confined, or else reveal my form behind."

They got louder as they spoke, culminating in a crescendo. "Brave soul yours have no despair, eternal quiet my trap ensnares!"

When the cheers died down, Blain said, "Gentlemen, it's been a real pleasure working with all of you."

"Same here, sauti," said Poncho, shaking Blain's hand in the standard way of Ione warriors. He smiled at his friend and added, "You could join my squata any time."

"I'd be honored," responded Blain. He looked at the rest of the Iones and called out, "Now, let's go down there and end this!"

The group broke into a run, slipping between trees and hurdling obstacles down the hill and onto the battlefield.

The aughra drain spell was designed to sequester all spell-casting fuel from the area, diminishing the power of a stronger magician in a duel. In the case of using the spell against an ursinox, the hope was, as the scientist Leland implied, the beast needed magic to survive, and the absence of vital fuel would weaken it to the point of sedation. Even though the effects of the spell on the environment are thorough and rapid, Serra wasn't expecting the ursinox to respond in kind. In the story Leland told about having tested it on the caged gmork, it took several minutes before the wretched thing lost consciousness, so Serra knew she'd have to be patient. He also said no one had ever tried it on an ursinox, so there was a chance the spell would be completely ineffective.

Faison dutifully stayed at Serra's side, even though he had no idea what he could possibly do to help the situation. Most of the soldiers Serra had healed were upright and available, but some of them were still resting in their exclusion fields, completely oblivious to what was happening outside. The ones who had come into the open were slow and weak but were doing their best to help split the attention of the ursinox by yelling at it and jogging in all directions.

The ursinox bounded as it moved. It had an almost playful gait, which was an odd thing for such an otherwise abominable creature. It didn't bellow or growl.

Instead with each gallop it made a panting grunt. It seemed to be having fun playing chase.

It increased its speed as it neared Serra and Faison, who responded by running as fast as possible out of the way. Four arrows zipped through the air, hitting the ursinox in the shoulder and side. It stopped moving and looked in the direction from which the arrows came.

The strategy Serra had stumbled upon fit the Iones well. They were fast, small, and nimble as they encircled the creature. They could distract with their numbers, their movement, and their arrows. As a result of their presence, the semi-mobile recovering soldiers were able to leave the area and find safety.

The chase carried on for what felt like forever. The ursinox would lope after a target, get peppered with arrows, and then change direction to chase the archers who'd shot it. The Iones quickly learned that shooting from one side was a better strategy than from all around. Whatever side they shot from drove it in that direction, and when shot from multiple sides, the ursinox would turn less predictably.

The ursinox wasn't slowing down. If anything it was getting more desperate and frenetic by being surrounded by prey it wasn't able to catch. Serra's strategy was working fine until the moment it shifted directions unexpectedly and found itself within lunging distance of her and Faison. It was about to grab Serra until Faison jumped into its path, shielding her.

It caught him by the hip and wrenched him off the ground. He waved his arms and free leg, crying for help, but there was nothing anyone could do. The Iones tried loosing all the arrows they had nocked, but now that the creature had what it wanted, it couldn't be distracted. It bit down, crunching the bones of Faison's hip and pelvis. The wail he let out chilled Serra to her core, but she was helpless to do anything to ease his pain. The aughra drain spell had already sapped the area of any magical fuel she could have otherwise used.

The ursinox violently shook Faison a few times and then slammed his body onto the hard ground, ending his suffering. His body lay still as the creature placed one enormous paw on his chest and ripped an arm from its socket with its mouth.

Serra fought the urge to retch. Rugen had told her about this deplorable aspect of the ursinox's behavior, but seeing it with her own eyes was far worse than anything she could've summoned in her mind.

She and Faison had known each other for only a handful of weeks, but during that time, and especially over the course of this traumatic day, she had developed an affinity for him. She harnessed her emotion, not letting it blur her focus. She knew losing concentration now would let the ursinox win, nullifying Faison's sacrifice and endangering more of her friends.

As she held focus on the aughra drain, she found herself praying to Pallous for help, which is something she'd never done in earnest before. Maybe he would hear her and intensify the spell somehow. The death of Faison was a senseless loss, as were all of the deaths directly or indirectly caused by Brian Gruhl and his actions, and she didn't know how much more she could tolerate.

A form wandered from the open fortress gate. Serra quickly saw that it was Curtis, the RHS grunt who had belittled Claire's abilities when they first met and was later ridiculed by JJ when he asked Dobbler to engulf his sword in flames. He saw Serra absent her bodyguard and without a second thought rushed to protect her.

The ursinox had been desecrating Faison's body for several gruesome minutes, during which everyone who had been trying to distract it got a chance to relax. Serra maintained her pressure on the aughra drain spell while keeping an eye on the hairy beast, waiting for it to start the chase again. Faison's death, as horrible as it was, would save the lives of others, as long as Serra's effort was effective.

Serra nodded as Curtis approached. He looked at the scene around them and asked, "How can I help?"

"Just keep it off of me," she quickly responded. The last thing she wanted was to allow aughra to flow back into the area, so she refocused on the spell and prayer.

Faced with the mammoth, foul-smelling creature up close, Curtis wasn't sure what to do, but he knew to stay between it and Serra. When it finished with Faison's body it looked right at him and licked the gore off its lips.

The Iones reinitiated the plan of splitting its attention: making noise, running away, shooting arrows. Their evasive ability and speed were impressive. They moved as one, coordinating using not only their instincts but also their special method of communication, shuesa.

By comparison to how the Iones ducked and dodged, the ursinox looked almost sluggish. As Serra watched a little longer she wondered if after all of this time the thing was finally slowing down. She shook off the thought and renewed her resolve.

Faces appeared in the windows of the fortress; faces of Gordon's Army peering at the scene below. Their disappearance was followed by soldiers pouring out of the open gate.

The ursinox's movements were no longer quick or agile, and it started tripping over its own feet while trying to keep up with the Iones. In a huff it spun around and lunged again at Serra, but this time was slowed enough that her bodyguard could effectively intervene.

In one fluid motion, Curtis stepped out of the way of the snapping jaws and hammered his sword down onto its snout with all of his might. Between the force of the blow and the weakening from the spell, it slumped to the ground and expelled a long, foul-smelling wheeze.

Curtis was as shocked as anyone at what he'd done. He stared blankly at the mountain of bristling fur lying next to him. He took a guess at where the important structures were located under the mass of flesh and, mostly on instinct, plunged his sword up to the hilt in soft tissue. He looked at the other soldiers, who had now gathered around the fallen foe, with wild eyes.

Without a word, or even any further thought, they thrust their swords, repeatedly stabbing the ursinox until it was dead.

Serra wearily gazed at what was left of Gordon's Army gathered around the colossal heap. Everyone looked exhausted but relieved. The mental toll was as evident as the physical one. She quietly asked, "Did you get Gruhl?"

"We couldn't find him," answered Rugen.

"What do you mean?"

"Apparently he escaped through the mines," said Dobbler.

"Oh," said Serra, looking at the ground. "So, are we going to follow him?"

"We were about to until we heard about the ursinox so we came out here," explained Rugen.

"We came all this way for Gruhl," said JJ. "We can't stop now. Let's search the mine. He can't be that hard to find."

Epilogue

Shortly after the battle, Gordon's Army dispersed itself into every twist and turn of the mine's many corridors, searching for Gruhl's escape route until they were exhausted. They were back at it the next morning, retracing their steps and feeling along the walls until their hands were raw. The map that Dobbler had taken from Deckard was of no use, as there was nothing on it that described where the entrance to the secret tunnel was located. Gruhl had covered his tracks far too well.

Eventually they gave up. Winter was descending in the far north, and there were many more pressing preparations to undertake. They decided the cold would make the long trek back to Lundgren too treacherous. Staying in the compound until spring was the much safer option, so they renamed it Gordon's Fortress, which made it much homier.

There were many fallen soldiers to be buried before the ground became too frozen to dig. Ceremonies were held for all of them—Rugen's and Gruhl's men alike. The respect shown by the triumphant army to their deceased opponents helped foster a relationship between the two groups.

The next step was to terminate the remaining gmorks and the sleeping ursinox. Dealing with the awake and snarling creatures was a harrowing task that required a month of planning and construction. Unfortunately, being left without food, water, or the light of day for great lengths of time had no effect on the gmorks. It didn't even slow them down. Even more unfortunate was that the beasts had no interest in killing each other. The soldiers designed a process that allowed only one (or sometimes two) out of the building at a time. Once outside, they were shepherded into a buried cage through a trapdoor, where Serra was waiting to put them to sleep with her aughra drain spell. Once that was done, soldiers could safely snuff them out. The cage was then removed and the hole was filled in with dirt to bury the body. Then a new plot was dug and the process repeated.

The ones the sorcerer Deckard hadn't yet awoken presented their own problem. There was no risk of them harming anyone while in suspended animation, but disposing of them meant carrying their bodies through the building to another burial ground. It was backbreaking work; not to mention the fact that there were twice as many sleeping ones. A suggestion was made for Dobbler to figure out the awakening spells so they could traverse the distance under their own power, but Serra said she was finished with the monotonous and grisly process of overseeing their deaths. Also, after housing fifty flailing creatures, the trapdoor and cage were in disrepair.

Processing the gmorks took the entire winter and spring and continued into the summer. There really was no reason to rush, and there were other things to be done, such as the disassembly and repurposing of Gruhl's various laboratories. Once that was complete, the man himself wouldn't have been able to recognize what had become of the space.

All of Gruhl's men, including the first group taken from the overlook, stayed at the fortress to help with the transition. At the end of the winter they were given the option to either remain indefinitely or leave on their own recognizance. Most of them stayed, except for the chef, whose name was Rolf. In the spring, he followed Rugen, JJ, Serra, Dobbler, and some of the others back to Lundgren where he worked as the executive chef and manager of a spectacular and popular restaurant called JJ's Gruel. Once it got up and running there was usually no less than a two-month wait to get a table.

When the others left, Alex and Claire stayed behind to supervise the fortress, making it their base of operations. To this day the largest and most beautiful gemstones continue to be harvested from the mines, and the operation is the largest employer in the Hyborian north.

The long since passed afternoon when Rugen's original group arrived as prisoners in Duke Alonso's office had not only led to the dismantling of Gruhl's headquarters, but also to changes all across Hyboria. Duke Alonso and Lord Volguus had already known Brian Gruhl was ultimately Lundgren's problem. Serra reminding them of that was a source of guilt, embarrassment, but most importantly, motivation. Lundgren's leaders decided to do more than provide men, provisions, and hospitality for Gordon's Army. They took the additional steps of gathering up and dispatching every non-essential Lundgren Army soldier and ordered them to spread across the south to eliminate gmorks and reconnect the dozens of little towns and villages that peppered the region.

Within the Lundgren Army, Curtis was known as the first person ever to kill an ursinox. While everyone present that day understood bringing the infernal beast down was a team effort, they weren't afraid to entertain the slight possibility that it was indeed *his* sword, and not the multitude of others, which was ultimately responsible for its demise. None of Rugen's men did anything to stifle the growth of his legend.

The Lundgren Army promoted Curtis to the rank of Captain, and currently he leads his own band of soldiers and diplomats through the northern half of Hyboria. Their charge is to exterminate gmorks, negotiate a peace with any inhabitants they find, and continue the search for Brian Gruhl.

The ex-commander, unfortunately, still hasn't been found. Most people believe he succumbed to the harsh northern winter or was killed by one of his own creations. The latter being the favorite theory among those who know the story. The possibility remains that he's hiding in plain sight, likely under a different name, using his over-developed charm and manipulation skills to survive.

Serra and Dobbler eventually went back to Ravenwood, where they were honored for their role in defeating Gruhl and his creature army. Serra was officially recognized as a Wallace graduate, and they both signed on as professors at their respective schools.

It took a lot of convincing, but over time and due in part to attrition of some of the old guard, the curricula and method of teaching at the two schools were retooled to focus on the study of learning the languages of Pallous and Obsidian. Copies of the gods' original manuscripts were handed out to every student and teacher as reference sources, and the originals were prominently displayed in the school lobbies under protective magical barriers for all to appreciate.

Several years later, Lane Dobbler and Serra Frye were married in a lovely ceremony in the center plaza of Ravenwood. The wedding colors were white and black, as is traditional with Wallace and Wyatt graduates (who often marry). It was the first Ravenwood event in many decades that had a large contingent of attendees who were neither magical nor school-affiliated. The members of the original

Gordon's Army in attendance jokingly referred to themselves as Damones and the happy couple as Ravens.

Those terms of endearment were in reference to the one subset of Gordon's Army who did not attend the wedding. The Iones left shortly after Gruhl's fortress had been commandeered. They wanted no credit for their part in the battle; no statues, plaques, medals, or even mention of their names, neither collectively nor individually. They asked that the only gratuity awarded them be complete and enduring privacy, including a promise of no visitors to Elsinore Forest.

The other members of Gordon's Army begrudgingly agreed to respect those wishes, but said that the memories of who the Iones were and what they did would live on in their hearts and minds forever. The soldiers punctuated what was to be the end of their relationship by taking part in the backslide handshake traditional of Ione warriors. Tears were shed as the forest people, without whom the battle would not have been won, trekked off into the mountains, planning to never again enter the domain of the Damones.

Along Graan Boulevard and inside the city of Lundgren, accolades were showered on Rugen. He stayed in the city for banquets, speeches, and personal appearances, but eventually he made his way back to Mourain. It took a long time to get there, not only because of the distance, but also the emotions involved.

News of his deeds preceded him, a fact for which he was glad because it eased the burden of his coming face-to-face with his father. His walking into town and handing out bags of Lundgrenian coins from the haul at Castle Igayim to the people of Mourain also smoothed things over somewhat. With the restored trade network, the coins would for sure come in handy.

Hammond Sloane was elated to see his son. The shock and anger of his disappearance had long since simmered down, and because he had assumed Rugen died in the wilderness, seeing him again was more like a resurrection than a return, and thus was welcomed with open arms.

JJ took a portion of his Igayim money and used it to open the aforementioned restaurant with Chef Rolf. Their partnership deal went like this: Rolf did all the work and JJ reaped most of the profits. Actually, the chef was very pleased with the deal. There was enough money to go around and JJ was rarely there aside from the occasional promotional appearance; so Rolf could run things however he wanted. JJ's notoriety was what brought the customers in, and Rolf's cooking was what brought them back.

JJ took his restaurant profits and invested them into several other Lundgren hotspots, which made him a popular fixture at the Bank of Lundgren as well. He found Lundgren to be a place where he could finally live the life he always wanted: that of a famous, handsome, and rich bachelor without a care in the world. He vowed never to pick up a sword again, and for many years he didn't have to. But that's another story...

www.ingramcontent.com/pod-product-compliance
Lightning Source LLC
Chambersburg PA
CBHW051947150726
47999CB00004B/1286